PRA

'Captivating, vivid writing. Descriptions seem to leap off the
pages and permeate deep into your senses, and a truly
electrifying pace. Quinn is a brilliant new talent!'
— Peter James, international bestselling author

'A fast and dangerous ride through Restoration London where
plague stalks every street and death is hidden behind the iron-
beaked mask of a plague doctor. Sharp, atmospheric
and sumptuous.'
— Simon Toyne, author of *Sanctus*

THE THIEF TAKER

C.S. QUINN

THE THIEF TAKER

A key, a killer, a secret . . . .

THOMAS & MERCER

Text copyright © 2014 C.S. Quinn
All rights reserved.

Published by Thomas & Mercer, Seattle

www.apub.com

Amazon, the Amazon logo, and Thomas & Mercer are trademarks of Amazon.com, Inc., or its affiliates.

ISBN-13: 9781477824931
ISBN-10: 1477824936

Cover design by bürosüd° München, www.buerosued.de

Library of Congress Control Number: 2014936220

Printed in the United States of America

To
Professor Vivien Jones and Dr Robert Jones.
Thanks for all the history.

London, 1665

In the year of the Black Death London is a city of half-timbered houses and dark towers. In the narrow backstreets, astrologists predict the future, and alchemists conjure wonders. Traitors' heads line London Bridge, where witches sell potions, and gamesters turn cards. The river flowing beneath lands a daily cargo of smuggler gangs and pirates.

England has a new King, a monarch of the blood. But since his arrival, plague sweeps into the city like a deadly judgement. And already, there is talk amongst Londoners that blood has become dangerous currency.

Prologue

No one said it out loud. But there had been signs. Tokens. On her body.

At one time the family had considered themselves fortunate. Their half-timbered house set them proudly apart from the tenement-dwellers who were crammed three generations to a single room. Now they sat blank and scared in the dwindling twilight.

A fire had been lit to clean the air, making the summer heat stifling. Cleansing spices wound a sickly smoke into the shadowy room. The cauldron holding yesterday's pottage sat desolate on the dirt floor.

Anna-Maria, the second-eldest daughter, sat on a three-legged stool with her sisters arranged at her feet. She was sewing, but the needle kept slipping from her sweat-slicked fingers.

There was a heavy knock at the door. Anna-Maria laid down her work on the worn wooden table and made to rise. But her younger sister was already on her feet, gait little more assured than a toddle. The tiny hand lifted the latch and with difficulty drew back the heavy door. Her mouth dropped open in terror.

The monster was shrouded from head to toe in heavy oilcloth. An iron mask covered his features, jutting forward into a foot-long beak. Two eye-holes had been reduced to blank black spaces by a pair of thick crystal goggles – a grotesque bird peering curiously into the house.

She took a step back and collided with the reassuring warmth of her father.

'It is only the plague doctor,' he said, as a thin wail of horror began to emit from the child. 'Come,' he beckoned the guest, looking uneasily at the unseeing figure which appeared to have cocked its head to one side so as to better hear the girl's wail.

'I am sorry for the warmth of the house,' he added.

'The girl is of twenty-two years?' A guttural voice came from somewhere within the dark shape. Now that the doctor had been ushered by the hearthside his eye coverings glinted in the firelight.

'She . . . she is twenty-two,' agreed the father.

'And strong?'

'She is . . . was a healthy girl,' said the father, his face tightening at the thought of his daughter helpless with the sickness.

The doctor opened the dark oilcloth and drew out a large pouch. Then he unrolled a length of leather. Strapped pitilessly inside, its eyes bulging in pain, was a live toad. Anna-Maria's face twisted in sympathy, but her father took her hand. 'It is a necessary remedy,' he said. 'The creature will not suffer.'

The doctor's black cloth gloves grasped the toad firmly, causing it to writhe and croak in his grip. The tapered fingers of the gloves looked like talons, thought Anna-Maria. Not like a human person at all. She had a sudden image of a deformed fiend hunched inside the dark canvas coat.

'Keep it alive,' explained the doctor, handing the toad to the father. 'It will purify the air and save the young ones from harm.'

The man gulped, nodded and handed the toad to Anna-Maria who recoiled from the slimy skin. She moved to the collection of clay crockery and wooden utensils arranged around the wooden fireplace and dropped the wriggling animal into a long jug.

'The daughter is upstairs?' The doctor was pointing to the ladder.

'I will take you to her.'

The doctor put up a warning hand.

'If the tokens are already upon her then breathing her air is deadly. I shall treat the girl alone.'

The father looked to his other children and nodded. 'Do whatever you can to save her,' he said. 'No matter the price I will find it.'

The mask waved slowly in agreement. And then the heavy figure began a lumbering ascent to the second floor.

───────

It was over an hour later that he moved heavily back down the ladder, the oversized beak swaying with his step.

'I have done what I can and she is resting now.'

'She is . . . will she be well?'

The gloved hands folded themselves in a steeple gesture. 'If she lasts this night then all may be well. But none must disturb her.'

He moved towards the low wooden door, his oilcloth shroud sweeping behind him. There was a line of blood on the hem, Anna-Maria noticed. He must have bled Eva to bring down her fever. She shuddered at the thought of the medical knives beneath the cloak. Her father closed the door gently behind the doctor.

The littlest girl took up a piece of cloth, her childish fingers fumbling with the simple needlework.

As the fire settled to a red smoulder, the atmosphere thickened with the smoke. On the mantle, the toad scrabbled pitifully in its warm confines. The heavy walls seemed to be closing in.

Several hours rolled away, and the small girl held up the finished fabric for inspection. Her father gave it a distracted half glance.

'It is a fine stuff and will fetch a pretty penny,' he said. But as he looked the white cloth took on a sudden red stain, which bloomed like a poppy amongst the other stitched flowers. Then another blossomed, and another. Something red was dripping from the ceiling. From the room in which Eva lay.

Anna-Maria looked up in alarm. But before she could find her voice her father had run past her and scaled the ladder. From the ground floor they heard his cries.

Anna-Maria was the first to reach him. Her father tried to push her away, but she had already seen it.

She gasped out a sob. The blood-soaked room blurred.

Through her tears the terrible remains began to shift and distort. There was a shape on the red-raised skin of the corpse. It was a crown. Above a loop of three knots. And two words.

'He Returns.'

Chapter One

'Are you the Thief Taker?' The man's voice was parched and a good deal too urgent.

The Bucket of Blood alehouse was lively with afternoon trade, and to Charlie's practised ear the whispered voice spelled trouble. His fingers sought out the key around his neck, tracing the shape at its head – a crown above three loops of knots.

As a boy, Charlie had been found clutching the key. He regarded it as a lucky charm of sorts.

'I have not taken a case for months,' replied Charlie. 'Plague times are not good for thief takers.'

The man's face registered confusion. He wore clumsily-stitched trousers held up by a string belt – the uniform of London's multitude of struggling commoners. And Charlie assumed he was in search of a lost wife or daughter.

'I haven't the heart, to take on all the missing person's cases,' Charlie clarified. 'Hundreds have vanished into plague graves. Often they cannot be found.'

'I don't seek you to find a relative. Nor catch a thief,' answered the man. He took a step closer, turning his head this way and that, assuring himself they weren't overheard.

In the high babble of the alehouse, this was unlikely. The only table was crowded round, and the more dedicated drinkers had made a jostling huddle next to the Bucket of Blood's single barrel.

A set of card players were sat on their haunches in the far corner, where the diamond-pane window illuminated their game in dusty shafts of sunlight. And between the laughing adults squeezed skinny barefoot boys, selling Hyde Park hazelnuts by the handful.

A jar of plague water was the only sign that disease was growing in parts of the City. Here in Covent Garden the summer heat had mingled with the march of death, to bring a strangely carnival atmosphere.

Charlie's head still rang with the bruised ache of last night's drinking, and the noisy regulars were louder than he would have liked.

The man's voice was low. 'I heard that you have certificates.'

Charlie's frown lifted. In lieu of thief-taking, the plague certificates were proving a popular sale. Something which should probably disturb him more than it did. Since plague had tightened its grip, rich Londoners had insisted that only those with Health Certificates were allowed in the wealthy streets in the west. And forged copies were a valuable commodity.

His hand slipped nonchalantly inside his coat. The naval-style garment fitted close at the torso with a line of tiny buttons, flaring over his skinny thighs and looping in large cuffs at his finely-muscled forearms. Though it lacked the gold stitching of a naval officer's uniform, it did everything a fashionable top-layer should and was only just beginning to fray at the edges, after years of daily wear.

The thick brown fabric housed Charlie's money, weaponry, eating apparatus, snacks and various found objects, with admirable discretion. And the long coat also did a passable job of hiding his grubby linen shirt and cheap woollen hose, which hung in many-mended seams to his knees.

Charlie's bare feet he could do nothing to disguise. After a lifetime of feeling the London mud beneath his toes, he couldn't get along with shoes.

The man watched, hypnotised, as Charlie's hand turned with a pick-pocket's assurance and produced a roll of certificates from the dark depths of his coat.

'Two shillings,' said Charlie, his lips barely moving.

The man swallowed. His eyes swept the uppermost certificate.

'This will assure them at Westminster I do not have plague?' he asked. His voice was trembling. Charlie gave the slightest of nods.

'It will carry you anywhere in the City,' he said. 'These copies bear the City seal. They are the best you will find.'

'What of beyond the City?' pressed the man. 'We hear it now, that some towns are not letting Londoners travel out, without a certificate.'

Charlie nodded again. He unrolled the paper a fraction.

'See you there?' Charlie gestured with his little finger to a little circle of dark-red wax. 'That is the official stamp. Made at City Hall.'

The man nodded. 'They told me you know people. High-up people.'

Charlie held back a grin. 'Let's just say, I know a girl in Guildhall.'

The man was chewing his lip now, and Charlie's heart sank, waiting for the inevitable.

'I do not have two shillings,' the man admitted.

The roll of paper vanished.

'My daughter,' said the man, his voice choking. 'My daughter works in Westminster. She is a servant in a fine house. There is plague there. I must see her before . . . .'

His voice tightened, and trailed off. 'Please,' he managed.

Charlie sighed. His rent was due a week ago, and two shillings would only cover half of it. This was his last certificate, and he'd been hoping its sale would buy more time from his landlord.

'How much do you have?' he asked.

'Tuppence.'

Charlie shook his head in exasperation. 'Londoners are queued ten thick, along four streets to get these certificates. And you think to buy one, for less than the cost of a mutton chop?'

The man looked at the dusty floorboards and then back up again, pleadingly.

Charlie rubbed his forehead, wishing his thief-taking work hadn't become so problematic. A single case could have paid off his rent threefold.

'You live in Billingsgate?' Charlie asked, after a moment's pause.

'How did you know that?'

'Your trousers are made of wharf sacking, and your finger has a fish-gutting callous.'

The man's eyes widened, and Charlie mentally admonished himself. He still sometimes forgot that his talent for observing details unnerved people.

'Take a good look at my face,' said Charlie. 'I want you to remember it.'

The man nodded uncertainly, staring back.

Charlie's youthful face and round brown eyes gave him an air of innocence which though not strictly accurate, inspired trust. Now in his late twenties, the golden curls of his childhood had settled to a less angelic dark blonde. And a bucking horse had added a sliver of pearly scar on his lip and a slight kink to his nose.

The overall effect was of the kind of man who, when he wasn't selling things illegally, wrote the odd poem. It was a look which came in handy in the delicate web of favours and debts, which was the second currency of poorer Londoners.

'Remember it well,' said Charlie. 'I will count this as a favour owed.'

The certificate magically reappeared and insinuated itself into the man's unresisting hand. He clutched it immediately, but his face showed he didn't yet believe his good fortune.

'There might come a time, when I need information from Billingsgate,' continued Charlie. 'If that time comes, I will trust you to tell me true.'

Suddenly comprehending, the man began nodding furiously. He beamed in wide gratitude.

'Even if it is your friend I ask of,' cautioned Charlie. 'You will tell me honestly?'

'You have my promise.' The man's words were garbled in his unexpected relief.

He fumbled with his hanging pocket and clumsily pressed two battered pennies into Charlie's hand.

'Thank you, thank you,' he stammered. 'You are an angel, truly. My daughter . . . I thank you, with all my heart.'

'Do not tell anyone you got it from me for that price.'

The man shook his head violently. 'I will take it to the grave.'

Charlie gave him a tight nod and sidestepped neatly into the crowd.

'I will remember my debt to you,' the man called after him, as Charlie slid effortlessly through the muddle of drinkers. He still had the problem of his rent to solve, and he doubted this particular favour would ever be repaid. Charlie admired the man's family loyalty. But those soft-hearted enough to stay and nurse relatives, stood no chance at all.

There were rumours that turnpikes and barricades were soon to be set up, preventing any from leaving London, and Thames Street had already been sealed off as a ghetto of disease. Reports were drifting in that parts of the east were now almost abandoned.

As the summer heat closed the plague had begun flexing its muscles, snatching up district after district and shaking them free of life.

Chapter Two

The Bucket of Blood landlord took one look at Charlie's face and reached for his special barrel.

'The strong beer?'

Charlie nodded, waving his newly-earned two pennies at the landlord. The certificate had at least bought him enough to pay off some of his drink tab.

The landlord's long dark wig swayed, as he heaved a small barrel onto the battered bar.

'What of that spinster last night, Charlie?' he inquired conversationally. 'I'm told she stayed until the small hours, hoping for your favour.'

'The one with the squint?'

The landlord's brow furrowed, and he straightened his moth-eaten lace absentmindedly. Since the King's return, he dressed in tribute. A habit which had earned him the nickname Merrie, after the Merry Monarch.

'She is rich Charlie. Five goats and her own cauldron,' pressed Merrie. 'You would be set up for life.'

'I am not of a mind to marry for money.'

Merrie was shaking his head, and his wig shifted up to reveal a neat row of flea bites. 'So many fine girls who'd have you,' he said, 'and you always choose the difficult ones.'

'The difficult ones are more fun.'

The landlord gave the expansive shrug of a man who didn't care enough to question an obvious idiocy further. He'd been running the Bucket for long enough to choose his debates.

Charlie took three deep swigs of beer, emptying his cup, and refilled it for a second time. The ale was helping ease his hangover, but he still had the issue of his rent. His mind flicked over the problem.

'Where's Bitey?' he asked, thinking the old man might take his mind off things.

'Poor ole Bitey,' said the landlord, nodding over to a huddled shape at the back of the alehouse.

'He fell asleep on that table last night,' continued Merrie, 'A little after you left. When he awoke he found they had impounded his pig because of the plague. He feels the loss most heartily.'

Bitey's pig had become a regular fixture in the Bucket of Blood. He had kept it inside his cloak from a piglet, feeding it sips of beer. As a larger animal it had been allowed to lie under the table, where it snuffled happily as its owner scratched its back with a stick.

'Bitey woke a few hours ago asking for beer,' added Merrie.

Charlie picked up one of the battered wooden cups scattered around the bar. 'Chalk this one up to me,' he said, drawing another cup of strong ale.

He approached the morose Bitey with caution. The old man was named on account of his homemade wooden teeth. Bitey's oak dentures were hinged with a rusty wire and hopelessly ineffective.

When he smiled it was the grin of a man who had swallowed a length of timber.

Today his mouth was closed and downturned. Charlie tended a sympathetic pat on the shoulder, proffering the beer.

The old man's raddled hand closed gratefully on the handle, and he took a long draft.

'Only a few more weeks it would have been,' said Bitey, looking up at him through red eyes. 'I would 'a made a penny per leg and had a brawn soup for weeks from the head. There would have been three buckets of blood for black pudding besides . . . .' He sniffed loudly and pushed the wooden teeth further back into his mouth.

Bitey was a squat square of a man whose louse-ridden outer layers hinted at a dense core impenetrable to cold, discomfort, or possibly even sharp weaponry. His tattered coat had been waxed into stiff tendrils and he sported an ancient Cavalier hat, the smallest slice of face sandwiched between chaotic beard and filthy headgear.

'I'd already closed with a butcher at Smithfield,' Bitey added. 'He was to do the job for a side of ribs. An' then there was the chops and trotters . . . .' His voice drifted off in anguish.

'How did it happen?' asked Charlie.

'I only let him out to truffle around the muck on Covent Garden.' Bitey's face implored Charlie to take his part. 'I was not but a few streets away. When I came they told me the dog-catcher had been. Taking up all the strays from the streets on account of the plague. Says the piggy was a health problem, so they took him off and had him a'killed. But I tell you Charlie,' Bitey's expression darkened. 'He was a cleaner animal than many men that is in here.'

The old man took a long swig of beer. 'Things will turn against the King if this kind of business continues,' he said. 'Plague or no, you cannot take a man's pig and expect him to stay a lover of royalty.'

Charlie's eye slid over to where Merrie was pouring drinks. The landlord had been known to forcibly eject drinkers, for speaking ill of the monarchy.

'Our Merry Monarch has made a Palace full of whores,' added Bitey. 'And now plague has fallen on us, like a terrible judgement.'

'Royalty is no easy business,' suggested Charlie, noticing Merrie was headed in their direction.

'What is difficult to understand?' challenged Bitey. 'We had a bad King, and we cut off his head. Then we had Cromwell's Republic for a time. But we did not like the strict religion of it. So now we bring back the bad King's son from exile. But many think it unwise.'

'Not that I be one 'a them,' Bitey added quickly, noticing that the landlord was now upon them, his face thunderous.

'You forget the Civil War in between times,' said Merrie, who'd caught the last of the conversation. 'All the death and horror of it.'

'No one has forgotten,' said Bitey darkly. 'Least of all those who lost. And to what purpose His Majesty's fine parades and clothes? Now the streets are blocked from Covent Garden to the Tower.' Bitey shrugged expansively. 'And who is to repair the streets after the wagons have made ruts of the mud and broken the cobbles? The parishes can no longer afford it. All the money they have is gone on taking away plague bodies and wood for bonfires to clear the foul air.'

Charlie felt the familiar pang in his stomach twist tighter. Only a few weeks ago the dead bell counted out the departed twice a day. Now it rang so frequently they no longer noticed it.

When the plague had first been reported in May it had seemed far away. Imperceptibly it had crept closer, until June saw nameless corpses become locals and July made the locals into acquaintances. How soon before it was friends and relatives being rung out in the unending toll?

Bitey continued his tirade. 'The plague is now so high that there is no escaping it. The astrologers. They all say the same. This is God wrath. God's wrath on account of the King and his ways. And the sinful ways of Londoners. There was a blazing star this year and they all agree this is a very bad sign.'

'I mean to go to Wapping, first chance I get,' he continued, barely pausing for breath. 'Reckon I can hole up there right enough. You should look to get out of the city yourself.'

Charlie nodded, his mind elsewhere. He was used to such portents of doom from Bitey and his hand slipped towards the key at his neck again, warding away the illness.

'Still got your lucky charm, Charlie?' said Bitey, changing tack in a bid to keep his listener engaged. 'I bought me a similar thing myself,' and he drew out a balding rabbit foot with his old fingers. 'Lost a claw, but it still works right enough, so the gypsies tell me.'

'Did you not hear the story of how Charlie still has his key?' asked Merrie. 'Last month the gaming house on Peace Street burned down, and young Charlie here ran back into the flames to get that memento. We thought he had seen some person or money inside. For you know how he plays hero. How we laughed when he came out with nothing but a keepsake from his long-lost mother. A key that fits no lock.'

'Do you still think your key will find her, Charlie?' asked Bitey.

Charlie closed the key into his fingers defensively.

'No,' he admitted. 'It is sentiment, that is all. This key is all I had, when the nuns found me and my brother. I should not like to lose it.'

'Hi!' Merrie had spotted a hazelnut boy helping himself from the beer barrel. He sprinted across the bar, leaving Bitey and Charlie alone together.

The old man's eyes were settled on Charlie's closed fingers.

'Strange shape at the head of it,' he muttered. 'A crown over knots. I still think it must be something from before the Civil War. From the time of the old King.' Bitey's eyes misted.

'Who would have thought it Charlie?' he added. 'You the finest thief taker London has ever known. Yet you carry the only mystery you cannot solve.'

Charlie took a long sip of beer in answer. And Bitey, exhibiting rare tact, didn't pursue the topic.

A loud whistle piped up behind then and Charlie turned to see a rare sight in the Bucket of Blood. An attractive woman. As a den of bare-knuckle fighting the ale-house tended to repel rather than invite females who weren't on the make. 'Rough old boot' was one of the kinder descriptions.

He watched the girl approach the bartender. She was a good height. Tall enough to suggest she'd been well-fed growing up. Charlie was not a short man by any means, but he frequently maintained that were it not for a childhood of thin soup he would be tall as King Charles himself.

He let his eyes slide the length of her figure. From her posture he judged her to be no more than twenty-five. She wore a simple, yet well-made dress in green. Not rich but not poor either. Perhaps something approaching the Yeoman classes. And she'd made her own creative additions, banding white sleeves with black ribbon in a loose imitation of the aristocratic fashions.

His gaze moved downwards. The shoes matched the green of her dress and were embroidered with white flowers, turning to a delicate point with a little heel. It was footwear of cloth rather than silk, but even as a replica they were a costly item.

And despite a few mud-spots they were by far the cleanest shoes on the Bucket of Blood's dusty floorboards.

'Not employed in any of the hard trades either,' he said to no one in particular. In contrast to the laundresses and orange-sellers who frequented the Bucket there was a youthful symmetry to this girl's limbs. He could see where the creamy skin of her neck and back joined with the blonde hair.

This, he judged, was one of the most attractive things about her. She wore it falling free and curled in the courtly fashion, partly gathered in a knot at the crown of the head. It was a stylish choice considering most common women clung to their Puritan linen caps. Even more daringly the flowing locks had been rinsed in a berry wash to heighten the yellow colour.

'Charlie?' He turned to see the landlord had arrived at his side and had lowered his mouth to his ear.

'Do you know that girl Charlie?' The landlord inclined his head towards the tantalising newcomer.

Charlie shook his head slowly. 'Never seen her before. Why?'

'Because she is asking for you.'

Chapter Three

'Is she Dutch?' asked Charlie. This was the most likely explanation. Another unsolved mystery of Charlie's orphan past, was that he and his brother both spoke Dutch, though neither knew how or where they'd learned the language.

People occasionally sought Charlie out to translate, or bargain a case with a sail boat.

But the landlord shook his head.

'She is English, Charlie, and a right nice accent she has too. I'd say her family has some money.'

Charlie took a seat a safe distance from Bitey and watched transfixed as the girl made her way over. Now that she was facing him he could see she had fine-set features – handsome in their neatness, with a straight Roman nose and large blue eyes. Something about the arrangement suggested instant respectability. As if she were of a class which belied her simple clothes.

'Are you the Thief Taker?' The words were out before she'd got to the table. Charlie was glad his customer was studying the Health Certificate in another part of the tavern. He had a hunch a girl of this sort wouldn't look favourably on his current side operation.

'That I am,' he said, leaning back in his chair so that the front legs left the ground. Charlie had become well-known as a private thief taker, and his reputation meant victims often sought him out in the Bucket.

'What can I do for you my lovely? Have you a purse or a pocket taken?'

The girl narrowed her eyes. 'I want it known that it is not usual for me to come to a person of your kind.' She said. It was not clear what she meant by 'your kind' but Charlie rolled a little more upright.

'You could always call on the services of The Watch,' he said. 'If respectability is so important to you.' As a thief taker Charlie operated somewhat outside the law, solving theft cases for a fee.

'You know as well as I that The Watch cannot be expected to stop serious crimes,' said the girl. 'Not a man of them is under fifty years of age, and for a shilling a week they will not risk their old limbs beyond lighting the streets at night.'

'And so,' she concluded with an angry sigh. 'I have come seeking your services.' Suddenly all the annoyance seemed to rush out of her, and her face sagged for a moment in an exhausted, broken look.

'What is it I can do for you?' Charlie was intrigued now. Clearly she had lost something of great personal value. Perhaps some expensive keepsake from a sweetheart or husband.

'My sister,' she began, but her face reddened and her eyes filled before she could finish the sentence. She coughed, driving the emotions down by dint of willpower.

'My sister has been killed,' she concluded.

The front legs of Charlie's chair came back to the wooden floor with a thump, and his hand smacked onto the table to steady himself.

'You have me wrong, indeed,' he said. 'I track thieves and cutpurses mistress. For this crime you must see the magistrate.'

She shook her head violently.

'He does nothing. The magistrate attends only to removing himself and his family from the danger of the plague. Everyone fears for their own lives and looks to their own skin. There is . . . there is no law at all.'

She sat down heavily in the nearest unoccupied chair, looking straight past him. Then to Charlie's great alarm she began to sob in unselfconscious wracking gasps.

He looked about for a way to end the spectacle and for want of a better plan stood to urge her outside.

Moving beside her, Charlie put an uncertain arm around the girl's waist and nudged her gently away from the table. To his great relief she stood and allowed him to lead her out.

'Come on,' he muttered as they passed the motley assortment of staring drinkers. 'This place is not proper for your sort in any case. I will take you somewhere better.'

They stepped out onto the street. A large carriage rolled past, the gold leaf on its doors glinting in the sunlight. Charlie was momentarily distracted from the girl, who was now calming herself and rubbing away the tears.

He let his eyes follow the huge wheels, imagining, as he always did, what it would be like to sit inside on the plush seats, screened from view.

His hand drifted to his key. And he wondered, as he often did, what past he had come from, before the orphanage. Charlie and his brother had the scantest of memories before they were orphaned. Snatches involved a grand house, and a finely dressed lady, who hid herself away in a private room.

The girl was watching him now, and he looked away from the coach. His gaze settled on the tailor next door to the pub. He was hammering heavy planks over his shop windows.

'Sure the plague is not in this part of town?' asked Charlie.

'Not yet so far as I know,' said the tailor, wiping a line of sweat from his brow. 'But with this weather and the godlessness of Londoners, it will be. There will be an Armageddon of pestilence come August. I had it from a trusted astrologer and I will not wait to be among the dead.'

He put down the hammer to admire his handiwork. 'Yesterday I went to a plague district to collect a debt and decided in that moment I would stop no more in the City,' he added. 'Never in my life have I seen such horrors. All diseased and the very streets rot on their foundations.'

A cart stood ready and loaded with what appeared to be his life's possessions, and he turned away to secure them.

Charlie felt himself shudder despite the cloying heat of the day. If the shopkeepers were vacating it meant only one thing. The plague was spreading.

He crossed himself and turned back to the girl, who had now collected herself and was standing with a faraway look in her eyes.

In a sudden urge to impress her, he decided to get them both a hot roll.

'Wait here,' he said, 'I will be back in a moment.'

He took a quick sweep of the shops and headed towards a stall where he knew he could bargain for credit.

'Charlie Tuesday,' said the baker girl, eyeing him with a mix of flirtation and trepidation. 'Do not think you can spend your forged coins here.'

'I have something better,' said Charlie, dropping his voice. 'Hold out your hand.'

She looked uncertain for a moment and then squeezed her eyes tight shut.

Charlie brushed his fingers over hers. 'You can open them again now.'

She opened her eyes in confusion.

'Look at your hand.'

The baker girl's gaze dropped to her hand, not understanding. Then she squealed with delight. 'Charlie! You found it!'

She held out her fingers to admire a battered tin ring.

'Did I not say I would?'

She seized his head in her hands and kissed him quickly.

'Thank you Charlie. How did you get it back?'

'Thief-taker's hunch. I asked a few of the right people.'

His eyes slid to the basket of hot rolls. 'Can you spare a few of those?' he asked.

The baker girl beamed at him. 'How many do you want?'

Chapter Four

Charlie discovered two things about the mystery girl in quick succession. First that her name was Anna-Maria and second that she was of a decidedly better-fed upbringing than his own. It had been a flash of chivalry to cash in his only credit with the bakery. But as they sat outside she let the gift rest uneaten in her lap. Charlie watched it with hungry annoyance. He'd dispensed with his in two short bites. The rolls were a half-penny a piece, and he pushed down his outrage as she began to turn it absentmindedly in her hands, picking at it and letting the crumbs fall.

If it wasn't for the fact that Charlie hadn't paid for the food, he would have considered snatching it back.

The second clue to Anna-Maria's privileged upbringing was her reaction to his name. 'Charlie Tuesday?' she had retorted when they'd exchanged names. 'What kind of a name is that?'

The kind of people who Charlie associated with were well-versed with Foundling Hospital names, where surnames were allocated to children based on what day of the week they'd been abandoned outside. Not a single acquaintance had ever found his name strange.

Clearly, he thought, she had never before had reason to associate with those who had fallen so low on the City's charity as to be orphans.

'We were frightened they would shut up our house,' she was saying. 'We hoped Eva had some other illness and not the plague. But you know how strict the rules are if any illness is reported.'

Parliament had ruled that heavy red crosses be scrawled across the doors of plague houses. As a result fewer Londoners than ever were willing to report an outbreak.

Charlie nodded. 'I have moved to a different part of town,' he said. 'I had a penny bed in a lodging house on Drury Lane. Now I sleep on the floor of a butcher's shop for five times the price. The walls are horse-hair and mud, and they take in the summer heat so it is stifling. But it is better than risk being shut-up in a plague district.'

'That was wise.' Anna-Maria for once seemed approving. 'Father did not send for a plague doctor,' she added. 'We are a country family by origin, and though some might think us backward, we do not like the tricks of City physicians. Their leeches and toads and such seem strange to us. And besides, in their plague dress they look like monsters and we thought they would fright the younger children.'

Charlie summoned the image of a plague doctor to mind. In their dark capes, ghoulish masks and crystal eye-glasses they frightened adults as well as children. The long metal beaks were stuffed with camphor and vinegar to protect the wearer from the foul air, lending the doctors an acrid stench. And their treatments almost always involved blood-letting and lancing of plague buboils. Certainly he crossed over the road if he saw one.

Anna-Maria fiddled with the last few crumbs of bread roll in her hand.

'But my sister asked for a plague doctor when she took to her bed. So there was nothing to do but let him inside, and in truth I was relieved that we may know whether she had the plague or no.'

She paused to take a great shuddering breath. 'When we found her . . .' A dead tone crept into her voice. 'She was murdered, that is all. Most dreadfully.'

Charlie nodded in what he hoped was a respectful fashion, but he was wondering how he could best escape. Not only had he no intention of helping solve a mystery which was so vastly out of his usual jurisdiction, but the girl had self-confessedly had contact with a plague carrier. Following her to the jaws of death was not how he planned on spending the rest of his afternoon.

'I will pay you handsomely,' she said suddenly, sensing his desire to leave.

Charlie coughed in an embarrassed kind of way. 'It is not the cost of engagement which prevents me,' he explained in what he hoped was a gentle voice. 'This is not a crime I can help you with. I catch thieves Maria.'

'Anna-Maria.'

He ignored the correction. 'I do not find out those who have made murders. That is for the coroner and the magistrate. My talent is in tracking property. With no stolen item to trace my skills are limited.'

'I hear you are the best,' challenged Anna-Maria. 'Surely a murder is not so different from a theft?'

Charlie opened his hands in explanation. 'It is very different,' he said, wondering how best to explain the complex network of fencing and favours which comprised thief taking.

'And they say that you often let the thieves escape the gallows, once property is returned,' added Maria. 'So I know you have a soft heart.'

Her hand closed around her purse.

'I will pay you three guineas,' she added evenly.

Charlie was a better bargainer than to let the involuntary gasp slip out. But she had just offered to pay his rent for three months. The sum was considerably more than he had been paid even by his most noble of clients.

The impulse to accept sprung up, and he drove it back down with some effort.

'It would not be right or fair,' he said, realising he had probably brought this temptation on himself by admitting his recent rent increase was troubling him.

'Four guineas.'

'I . . . It is not the money. I do not find murderers where there is no property taken.' He folded out his hands helplessly.

'I will pay you a guinea just to come to the house and see the situation there,' said Anna-Maria. 'It is a fair price to risk your life in a plague place. I know that well enough. If you decide you can help I will pay you three more.'

Charlie swallowed. He had experienced similar feelings only a few times in his life, but always with the same inexorable conclusion. Something inside him was going to accept her offer, and when it did a knowing voice told him he would be drawn into a whole hornet's nest of trouble. It was like watching a ship slowly ground itself without having the slightest power to turn its course.

'Very well,' he heard himself say. 'Take me to the house then. But likely as not I will not be able to find this murderer for you.'

Anna-Maria nodded, but she didn't smile.

'And I am given permission to call you Maria,' he said, thinking he had nothing to lose. She waved her hand in dismissive acceptance, as if disgusted but too well bred to show it. Charlie had already decided he would take only one guinea from her and leave the residence as soon as possible. Her father must be well off, he thought suddenly, to have a whole house.

Families he knew considered themselves lucky to have a single room. But that was the way it was in London. Land was expensive and life was cheap.

Chapter Five

Charlie had thought that Maria would want to purchase some kind of protection against the plague before returning to her house. But a lethargy descended on her once they'd made an agreement. As though she'd held her grief at bay only long enough to secure his services and now despondency had swept back in.

She must have loved her sister, he thought, feeling a flash of pain at the thought of his own brother. They had been orphaned together but were not close. Charlie always felt his elder sibling Rowan resented his mysterious key.

Charlie managed to buy a little bunch of lavender from a street vendor to hold in front of his nose, though he would rather a vial of vinegar to sip on. His stomach had begun to twist in on itself at the idea of what he was doing, and he sent up yet another silent prayer that he might escape with his guinea and his life.

'What made you become a thief taker?' asked Maria, as they passed the squawking mayhem of Cockspur Street. Under King Charles cock-fighting was no longer banned and Londoners had returned to the sport in earnest.

'Mother Mitchell,' said Charlie unthinkingly, distracted by the sparring cockerels.

'I helped one of her girls retrieve a locket and she saw some profit in me,' he added, seeing Maria's confusion. 'Said she would put aristocratic clients my way for a cut. That was how I begun making money from finding out thieves.'

Maria sniffed disapprovingly.

'I did not find Mother Mitchell out for her girls,' said Charlie quickly. 'Indeed I should not have the coin even if I wished it. Her house is now so expensive the suitors need credit to take a glass of wine there.'

'Then how did you meet a woman of that kind?'

'I met her many years ago,' explained Charlie. 'When I was but a little foundling. She began to employ me in servant's work for a few pennies and then took me as an apprentice when I came of age.'

'Sure but the nuns who care for London's orphans are not so mindful with their charges,' said Maria, 'if they cannot protect them from the company of notorious harlots.'

Charlie laughed. 'They are careful enough. The nuns make visits to London's less fortunate women. To try and save them from syphilis or hard labour at Bridewell prison. Some of the boys wanted to see what a fallen woman looked like. We followed a nun on her missions. Hid and watched. That is when I first saw Mother Mitchell.'

Charlie smiled at the memory. Mother Mitchell had been the most terrifying and wonderful thing he had ever seen. A great gaudy butterfly spread imperiously across her doorstep. She'd not been so stout back then, but already lines had settled around her eyes and mouth. The enormous bosom jutted from beneath swathes of purple silk.

What business have you? she'd asked the nun. *To tell my girls they should work to death in some hard employment, rather than join me and prosper?*

'And then what happened?' asked Maria. 'She invited you in?'

'No, she caught hold of me. The other boys ran away. Then my shirt rode up and she saw some stolen ship's biscuits hidden in my waist band.'

'Ship biscuits? Surely you did not mean to eat them?' asked Maria, revealing once again her comfortable upbringing. Naval rations were inedible to well-fed landlubbers, but to hungry sailors and starving orphans they were as good a food as any.

'When Pudding Lane ovens are at their hottest the bakers do not guard their baking, and the windows are small enough for a child for slip through,' answered Charlie. 'My hand was well-blistered for it, but those half-cooked biscuits likely kept me from starving. Foundling soup is thin,' he added.

'So what then? This harlot would have reported you for stealing?'

Charlie shook his head. When she had seen the biscuits Mother Mitchell's hold had lessened slightly.

Oh ho! she'd said. *So the little foundling has learned to survive in the big City.*

She had looked at him with something like admiration as he writhed and struggled to get free from her grip.

Where is your tongue boy? I am not about to hand you to the constable. Why do you not eat the biscuits straightaway? The crown stamped on them shows your crime. It is foolish to carry them around.

He had told her he saved biscuits for his older brother and Mother Mitchell cocked her head, amused. She had asked why the elder could not feed himself and Charlie's youthful innocence had unwittingly returned the only honest answer.

'He has given up.'

Mother Mitchell's face gave the smallest flicker of emotion which had confused the younger Charlie. It had not occurred to him that there was anything untoward in the dynamic between him and his sibling. If he did not supply food Rowan would starve. It was how life was and that was that.

'So what did she want you for?' asked Maria, interrupting his thoughts.

'She said she had work for a bright boy.'

'And you went?'

'She offered me money.'

Mother Mitchell had looked thoughtful for a moment before producing a shining penny. It was more money than Charlie had known how to spend. *Come inside then boy. I do not wait on ceremony for foundlings.*

'What did she wish you to do?'

'She wanted to start up a fine sort of house. Where the highborn of men would come. But it was hard for her to get servants. This was during Cromwell's Republic and Puritan feelings ran high. Women risked being publicly whipped for being seen with her. She employed me to plant out cuttings for trees, such as grew outside the wealthiest houses.'

Look at this sapling, Mother Mitchell had said, handing him the slim branch. *You cut off all its roots and still it will find a way to grow. That is not so different from us now, is it boy?*

They stopped suddenly. A set of new guards had been posted on Shaftesbury Circus. Plague security was certainly stepping up, thought Charlie.

His fingers traced the forged certificates inside his coat, searching for the one with his name on it.

Maria stuck her certificate out close to the guard's face, as if daring him to find fault with it.

Charlie slipped out his own certificate and presented it with practised nonchalance, rubbing the back of his neck and looking down at the ground. His eyes slid to Maria's papers, noting the

27

practised neatness of her signature. By the number at the top, she'd been one of the first in London to get one.

'Why is there a new checkpoint here?' Maria demanded, as the guard studied their certificates. 'Isn't it enough we must queue to go along the Strand and into Westminster?'

The guard eyed her, as if deciding if she might be a trouble-maker. Charlie silently prayed that Maria's accusation would not submit his forgery to greater scrutiny.

'The rich folk on Warwick Lane have banded together,' said the guard eventually. 'They want to be sure no plague travels their way.'

'The fools should realise that plague travels everywhere,' fumed Maria. 'Inconveniencing innocent citizens will not halt it.'

The guard shrugged.

'It is the rich who make the laws,' he replied. 'There is to be another check on Cornhill by the end of tomorrow.'

Charlie mentally added the new checkpoint to his map of London. The city was closing up. Soon there would be few places it was possible to travel without a certificate.

The guard took in the official stamps of both certificates and waved them through.

'This way,' Charlie steered Maria away from Holbourne, pleased to have passed the guard.

'That way is longer,' protested Maria.

'There are some gaming houses near Fleet Street I should rather avoid,' admitted Charlie.

'You owe money?' Maria's mouth drew in tightly.

'No,' said Charlie, pulling her into a tight warren of alleyways, 'but some do not like my luck at cards.'

'How do you get your customers?' asked Maria, as Charlie wove them through the labyrinthine back streets. 'Surely commoners cannot afford a thief taker.' She was looking at his bare feet.

Charlie ignored the slight. 'During Cromwell's reign I ran secret masked balls for the aristocracy in Covent Garden,' he said. 'They were very popular and I made good money for a time. All else around was grey and Puritan. I made good enough noble acquaintances to be trusted as a thief taker.'

He felt a sudden pang of sadness, remembering how his wife had loved the masked balls.

'Here,' said Maria, turning a sudden corner. 'The house is just ahead.'

Charlie was relieved to see it looked to be a good sort of street, with none of the ominous red crosses which peppered the east of the city.

Then he saw the slogan, written up in chalk.

'REPENT,' read the letters. 'THE END IS NIGH.'

Chapter Six

Maria's house had leaded diamonds of real glass for windows. It was made in the half-timbered style, with an overhanging to counterweight the second storey floorboards and prevent them from bouncing underfoot. Bonfire smoke and mud stained the once-white walls, but besides these unavoidable scars of city living it was a clean residence.

Charlie eyed the exterior. Usually his thief taker clients numbered the common sort, who lived in backrooms and squats. Or aristocrats, who met with him in the nicer sort of ale-houses and taverns. The idea of entering a domestic home was a novelty.

He had often tried to imagine what it was like inside walls built for no other purpose than living in.

There was no red cross to show it was a plague house. And Charlie felt a stirring of unease. Something about the situation didn't add up.

'Why is there no plague cross?' he asked.

'Good fortune,' said Maria. 'We were sure they would find us out and shut us up in the house. But the constable never did.'

She used her hip to give the wooden door an extra shove.

'We have been burning hops and brimstone to fumigate the house, and the heat warped the wood,' she added, nodding to the door.

Charlie felt his lungs spasm in a quick succession of sneezes as they entered. The smoke seemed to have got into the very walls and the air smelt of dry bonfire.

A kitchen made up almost all of the downstairs storey with hanging fabric dividing a further portion which Charlie guessed to be a small larder. Probably the house did not extend to a garden and so they bought their meat and vegetables from stalls and used the Thames as a washroom and toilet.

There was no body here, and they stood for a moment.

'The scene is upstairs,' supplied Maria.

Charlie had a sudden feeling of the entire second storey bearing down on them both. With difficulty, he stopped himself from staring towards the ladder which led to the upper rooms.

Instead he let his gaze sweep around the room in which they stood. A large cauldron hung from the hearth, shining in a manner which suggested it was proudly cared for, with vegetable and pudding nets hung above it. The kind of rooms Charlie rented wouldn't have housed a cauldron even if he could have afforded one, and he mostly lived on bread and cheese when money was tight and pies and baked potatoes from street-stalls when he had the means.

He thought for a moment, trying to imagine how he might approach the situation if it were a simple theft.

'Did your sister have any possessions of value?' he asked, weighing up the circumstances. 'Something it might be worth murdering her for?'

Maria shook her head slowly.

'Most of what we had was sold, when we moved to London,' she said. 'Eva had some trinkets. Earrings from my mother. But they were not taken.'

'No clothes removed? No money?'

'No.'

'Was anything else removed from the house?'

'Not that I know of.'

'Did your sister have any enemies?' he asked, after a moment. 'Can you think of someone who would want to harm her?'

Maria shook her head. But Charlie thought he caught a flash of something in her expression.

'Jealous lovers?' he pressed, 'rejected suitors?'

In his experience, this tended to make up the mainstay of London violent crime towards women.

A flush appeared on Maria's neck.

'She was popular with men,' she admitted, after a moment. 'But none of those who liked her would want to hurt her.'

Her face had closed down, and Charlie decided to change the line of questioning.

'Did you notice anything about the man?' he said, 'When he entered the house?'

'Besides his being dressed as a plague doctor?' Her voice had a note of sarcasm.

'A stutter in his voice? A limp? Something to mark him out.'

'No. But likely we were too overawed by the spectacle. Plague doctors are fearsome-looking.'

'Did he do or say anything, before he went upstairs?'

'He asked Eva's age.'

Charlie logged this. 'How old was she?'

Maria swallowed at the past tense.

'Twenty-two.' Her voice quavered, and then her face hardened again almost instantly.

'Younger than you?'

'Two years older.'

Maria seemed older than twenty, thought Charlie. She had a prudent competence about her. The kind you might find in a housekeeper.

'Do you remember anything else?' asked Charlie.

She paused for a moment. 'He put a toad in a jar. He said it would purify the air,' she added. 'Do you have the toad still?'

This was the kind of evidence Charlie could use. It might tell him what part of London the murderer came from.

But Maria shook her head. 'We threw it in the Thames.'

Charlie was silent for a moment, knowing the next move should be to wherever the body lay. His mind drifted to the last time he had stood alone with a girl and he felt his cheeks redden.

'Would it be easier if the murderer had taken some property?' asked Maria, giving no indication she was thinking the same.

'Yes.' Charlie's eyes were drawn to the hatch in the ceiling where he assumed the body lay. 'It is goods I find. And from them people.'

'So you would ask around and see who had bought up the stolen goods?' asked Maria.

'In a way. The way I find people out is not by what they sell but how they sell it.'

Charlie frowned.

'I think I should see the scene now. I mean not to offend you but I had rather not stay longer than I must in this house.'

'Yes.' Maria collected herself.

A few little beds were arranged downstairs, presumably for the younger children and perhaps Maria herself.

The uneasy feeling stirred again in the pit of his stomach.

'Where is the rest of your family?' he asked.

'They have fled London,' said Maria. 'Father travelled with the children to an aunt in Clapham. To stay safe from plague.'

'But you did not go with your family to refuge?'

'No. I stayed to attend to . . . To this injustice.'

For some reason, her choice of words sounded alarm bells in his mind.

He looked back at Maria. She seemed so respectable. Was there something she wasn't telling him?

'I have the money,' she said, sensing his sudden mistrust. 'Here.' Maria pulled out a purse and selected a guinea from its jangling contents. 'For seeing the situation up there,' she added, placing the coin meaningfully on the small table.

Charlie looked away from the money and up towards the ceiling. Upstairs would be a further few bedrooms. And the body.

'It is up that ladder,' said Maria, pointing to the entrance to the second level. They both stood for a moment, looking at the opening.

Charlie paused. A strong instinct was warning him not to go upstairs. He pushed it down, attributing it to the prospect of viewing gory remains. But every sense in his body was suddenly telling him to run as far and as fast as he could.

Maria turned to face him, and her blue eyes had become dark with feeling.

'Please,' she said.

Her devastation set his resolve. She'd lost a sister. The least he could do was try to help.

'I know not what information I might give you,' he said slowly. 'But you have my word I will try my hardest to read the scene.'

He took a step towards the ladder, forcing his legs to move. Then, bringing his lavender posy closer to his mouth he walked back towards the stair and began to climb. *Think of the guinea,* he muttered to himself. Behind him he heard Maria's sigh of relief.

'I will wait down here,' she said. 'I cannot bear to see the scene anew.'

The words buzzed meaninglessly as a fresh flood of unease swept through Charlie. Maria's good looks had helped blind him to the danger. But now reality was hitting him hard.

His feet felt leaden as he took his first step onto the ladder, and then the next. He concentrated on the wooden rungs, the whorls and lines of the wood, polished to a dark shine by constant use. One hand followed the next, with the reluctant rest of him following on behind.

Chapter Seven

The landlord of the Old Bell on Fleet Street gave his guest another uneasy glance. Plague doctors always made him nervous. But this one was worse than most.

To begin with he'd not taken the time to remove his unwieldy beaked mask or take off the flat crystal goggles. Instead a portion of a pale neck had been unswaddled for eating while the disc eyes stared out over the table.

Then there was the sheer size of him. The bulk beneath the canvas covering was so enormous the landlord found himself wondering how the hulking body fitted beneath. It was as though a monster had come to dine.

The landlord watched in undisguised revulsion as the cloaked man forced down his third plate of gizzards. He didn't seem to have the usual manners of the physician class. Despite his huge frame, the man attacked the food as though he were starved. He had already devoured the remains of a rabbit stew and a joint of meat which had been expected to last the week, along with two bottles of cheap Canary wine.

The landlord had wanted to deny him entry but by law he was obliged to serve plague doctors. So he kept as far as possible from the monstrous guest, lest he breathe infected air. Besides, his ale-house was completely empty. He supposed he should be grateful for the custom.

Working the tavern the landlord had become an expert in gauging background. As more food disappeared down the gullet of his ravenous customer the more convinced he became that the man was not of a medical kind. Perhaps he had stolen or bought the costume to earn money from unsuspecting dupes.

And there was something . . . *unwholesome* about the way this man forced down plate after plate of food. As though he were feeding some demon as opposed to a grumbling stomach. The act of eating had greased the small exposed portion of his lower face with whitish sweat. And in his haste to despatch the gizzards he had missed his thick lips, smearing a daub of bloody entrails on the mask.

The landlord suppressed an involuntary shudder and forced himself to pick up a flagon and approach the visitor.

'Small beer?' he hovered uncertainly.

His attentions were rewarded with the wave of a bloated glove, strained to bursting point with its load of fat fingers. As he moved closer to the figure he noticed there was something unexpectedly solid about the shape. From the size of him the landlord had imagined rolls of fat, but now he was closer he could see the bull-like neck was muscular. There was a smell too. A strong musky scent emanating from the body which the man had evidently tried to mask with lavender. But instead of disguising the odour the cloying floral acted as a conduit, throwing the hot stench wider from the perspiring body. Turning his head away the landlord leaned in and filled the tankard.

'Do you treat plague nearby?' he asked.

The head shook, but the mouth kept chewing.

'These are dreadful times indeed,' said the landlord conversationally. 'For nothing that is done in the city can seem to stem the tide.'

The monster said nothing.

'You must be right hungry,' tried the landlord with a little high laugh, gesturing to the pile of empty plates. This time the iron mask swung so that the glittering crystal eyes were full on his face.

'Before Cromwell won the Civil War I was a soldier,' came the voice in a rumbling growl. 'They held us under siege for three long months and we starved to yellow skeletons. Since the horrors of that time I have a healthy appetite.'

The landlord swallowed, wishing he hadn't raised the issue. He had heard enough tales of Civil War atrocities to last a lifetime.

'Shall I take these for now or should I take a name and charge you later?' He pointed to the empty plates.

'How much?' The response was grunting, begrudging.

'Six shillings,' said the landlord. It was the most he'd charged for a single guest's meal in quite some time.

'I will pay half now. Send for the rest.'

The doctor withdrew a fat purse but to the landlord's dismay it was only filled with small coins. This did not bode well for extending credit. Three shillings in groats were counted out in neat rows and the mask turned up expectantly.

'What name?' asked the landlord, extending his arm to pull the money towards him whilst keeping as far as possible from the plague doctor.

'Thomas Malvern.'

'That is your name?' The landlord was confused. It sounded like an aristocrat's surname. Commoners had names like Tanner, or Fisher or Goldsmith after their family trade.

'It is an old family name,' said the man. 'But our house and lands were confiscated by Cromwell after the Civil War.'

The landlord nodded, only half hearing. It was a familiar enough story. Those who had fought on the side of the old King were mostly aristocrats. When Cromwell won he had first beheaded

King Charles senior. Then he had rewarded his own followers with the lands and titles of the old aristocratic order who had fought against him.

The landlord put down a slate for the man to scratch his address and was surprised to see the hand write a local residence. He didn't know any plague doctors who lived nearby.

'Will you take anything else?' By now the landlord was willing the guest to depart, although heaven knew he could do with the extra money with the city emptying out by the day.

In his discomfort the landlord picked up the flagon too quickly, spilling a little beer on the costume.

'Here, I will make amends,' he said, unthinkingly grabbing for the canvas to prevent the liquid soaking into it further. Thomas grasped for the cloak and as he did so the mask shifted to reveal his face.

The landlord's face registered dawning recognition and then horror.

Their eyes locked, and the landlord felt a surge of fear.

The doctor clamped the disguise back down again but the landlord had already seen. It was a face he knew well.

'*You.*' As the words sprang unwittingly from his mouth he knew he was a dead man. Whatever the reason for travelling in disguise and under a false name, this man should not want his secret known.

'I did not think you were permitted to practice as a physician,' gabbled the landlord, fear making his speech into nonsense.

'I am not permitted to do anything much at all.'

The landlord nodded as he retreated to the further side of the inn. He feigned turning one of the barrels whilst he rummaged for the loaded pistol he kept hidden.

He heard the scrape of a sword being drawn but he didn't have time to turn. The heavy butt of the handle splintered the side of his skull, felling him in a single blow.

Thomas leaned over the twitching body to assure himself the life's light had gone out of his erstwhile host.

He returned to his seat on the rough bench and unfurled a map of the City. Then taking a stick of charcoal he made a careful cross on the alehouse where he currently sat.

The charcoal paused for a moment, as Thomas noted with pleasure the other crosses.

Pleased with his progress he drew the remaining dish of food towards him. And with a shovelling stoicism, he finished his plate of gizzards.

Chapter Eight

Charlie's gaze was fixed on the shrouded shape of the corpse. It lay on a plain cot-bed, atop a straw mattress. Blood had leaked through the rust spattered straw, forming a dark pool on the floorboards below.

The girl's body had been wrapped in a winding sheet, gathered in a crown of linen at the head. The winding sheet covered almost all of the face, leaving the eyes, set in their slice of death-pale skin, all that was visible of the dead girl's features.

Downstairs a door closed, but he hardly heard it.

His mind had already ticked into thief taker mode and had been framing possibilities as the blood-stained bedroom had come into view.

The floorboards were poorly fixed and afforded ample sound and light to travel up from below.

The murderer must have been able to hear the family below, as he worked. Committing the crime with her family downstairs suggested he was brutally callous, as well as calculating.

Charlie returned his attention to the girl's remains.

The dead face lay bloodless and pale. It seemed to be taking up the whole room.

Two silver groats weighed down her eyes, giving the face an inhuman quality.

Charlie guessed some mutilation must have been made to the lower face and was now respectfully concealed.

He took a step nearer the corpse and a choking stench arrested his nostrils.

Charlie drew the lavender nosegay tightly against his nose. His insides swirled bright and cold. In his experience deadly illnesses had distinct odours. Was it plague he could smell on the body?

From what he could see the upper features gave no indication that death had involved a struggle.

He considered this. Maria's sister had either known her killer, or believed him a real plague doctor.

'Bring out your dead!'

The loud ringing from the outside street jolted him out of his thoughts. And a hoarse cry announced the rumbling approach of a dead-cart. Since the pestilence had risen the burial wagons now patrolled London regularly. Plague victims could not be buried in proper graves, and their families were often too poor to pay for a coffin.

To Charlie's mind the cart sounded ominously close and a sudden fear flashed through him. What if the dead-cart arrived here and shut him up inside?

Since April anyone found in a plague house was imprisoned there until they died or survived six weeks.

Instinctively he stepped out of sight of the window. And then he noticed that the winding sheet which swaddled the limbs tight was woollen.

This wouldn't be strange in many parts of the city. King Charles had decreed all burial materials to be made of wool to bolster the country's sheep trade. But in wealthy Holbourne he would expect householders to pay extra to avoid such a vulgar burial.

So the family did not have enough money to wrap their beloved daughter in linen. He logged the fact against the fee which Maria had offered.

Something wasn't right.

The same uncomfortable feeling crept through him.

Softening his tread Charlie stepped from the room and back to the opening. He froze.

The ladder leading back downstairs had gone.

He was trapped.

Maria must have removed his means of escape almost the moment he'd stepped onto the landing.

Charlie tried to stem his racing thoughts and quickly distilled them to one. He had to get out. Now.

First he needed to know if Maria was still below. Perhaps she could be reasoned with.

He moved back into the bedroom. His mind was whirling with reasons why Maria might want to trap him here. Had she gone mad with grief? Was it an innocent relocation of the ladder? Nothing plausible sprang to mind.

'I have seen the body,' he shouted, keeping his voice casual. The rumble of the dead-cart echoed ever closer over the cobbles. 'What more would you have me do Maria? For I should not like to take away the winding sheet.'

There was no reply, and he called again.

'Would you have me know anything else?' he said. 'Or shall I come back down?'

Again he was greeted by silence.

So Maria had gone. Or was waiting silently downstairs for him. He made a quick assessment. The door had slammed.

So she must have stolen the ladder and left the house. And that could only mean one thing. She was bringing someone else back with her. Someone who she didn't think he would have agreed to meet unless he was trapped on an upstairs landing.

This was bad.

He made a quick assessment. Two escape routes. The first posed two possible problems – the distance between the upstairs and the landing and the possibility that the front door had been bolted from outside.

The second was the bedroom window. One problem only. The distance of the fall.

He stepped around the bed and to the window.

The house was high, and the road beneath was cobbled rather than dirt track. He judged it was an ankle at least he risked by leaping. He struggled again to make sense of the situation.

Why would she have trapped him here?

He looked down again. If he made anything other than a clean break or sprain an amputation was unavoidable. Half the regulars at the Bucket wielded wooden limbs of some kind, and he had no intention of joining them. He didn't have twenty shillings for the surgeon in any case.

It was then he saw Maria walking back down the street towards the house.

She was accompanied by two burly looking men whose uniform Charlie recognised as from Newgate Prison.

Guards.

His hand dropped to the bag of counterfeit groats in his pocket. Owning forged coins counted as treason and was punishable by being half hung before having your heart ripped out and shown to you. Less fortunate counterfeiters were boiled in oil.

He stuttered out a silent curse. The men at Newgate tended to use a hands-on approach to questioning and would certainly empty his pockets.

Charlie swore. This ruled out escape by the window or the landing. If he fell badly the guards would easily catch him.

He scanned the room. Nothing. Only the bed and bare floorboards secured with thick nails. The few handfuls of straw inside the mattress offered nothing to break his fall.

Think. Why has she trapped you here and brought guards?

If he could work out the reason, perhaps he could talk his way out of danger.

His eyes flicked to the corpse. Maria had said her sister had been brutally murdered. Had she been telling the truth?

The winding sheet was not quite finished at the neck and Charlie took out his knife to slice open the wool.

He paused for a moment and then gripped the blade more determinedly. Maria had, after all, tricked and trapped him for no reason he thought he deserved.

'Bring out your dead!'

The call galvanised him to a decision. Newgate guards would soon be in the house and if he wanted to avoid a traitor's execution he needed to act. Ignoring his finer instincts he forced his attention back to the body.

His knife sliced the first inch of winding sheet and he paused for a moment.

The dead girl's coin eyes glared at him accusingly.

Images of the last traitor's execution swam before him. Twitching eyes. Shining intestines.

Charlie firmed his grip and slashed down. The wool winding sheet parted inch by inch, giving up a powder of woollen dust.

Voices floated up from the street below. Maria and the guards were closing in.

Turning back to the body, Charlie continued to cut.

An arm. A leg.

Pale and bloodied skin.

His hand began to shake.

A sharp pain bit into his arm. He jerked the knife down in shock, tugging and tearing the cloth fully away from the corpse.

It was just a flea bite, and he raised the injured wrist to rub the rising red weal, allowing his juddering heart to dance its rib-bruising beat.

He turned back to the bed, and the full vision of the murdered girl was before him.

His dagger clattered to the floor in alarm.

The corpse was now naked and exposed from neck to calf. And Charlie was confronted with the full madness of the murderer's work.

Maria's sister had been decorated all over in flowering branches of hawthorn and white ribbon. Each finger and toe had been carefully tied and long lengths wound up each leg.

Her brown hair was knotted all over with fabric and foliage. The dead mouth was stuffed with it. Thorns from the branch sliced at her lips.

His eyes skittered over the rest of the body.

Dripped over the pallid torso was white candlewax. It seemed to have been arranged in the shape of . . . *letters*. Charlie struggled to make out the words.

'He Returns'.

He returns?

His eyes slid to the throat. The girl's neck had been cut down to the spine, and cream vertebrae were visible against the blackening meat of butchered tissue.

On the lower torso a livid red mark stood out against the rivulets of blood which had dried all over.

The killer had branded the girl.

The burned mark blazed out from the cold dead body. And the crimson lump of burned skin was raised in a shape he was only too familiar with.

It was a crown, over three knots.

Charlie's hand flew to his keepsake, fingers tracing the identical pattern on his key.

For years he had searched for the meaning of the symbol, and he had never found any indication that it meant anything to anyone. But here it was, burned into the body of a dead girl.

It was then he realised why Maria had brought him here. The shock shook him so bodily he spoke out loud. 'She does not want a thief taker,' he said. 'She thinks me her sister's murderer.'

Chapter Nine

He returns. Charlie turned the phrase over in his mind and the key in his hand.

He checked again for plague marks on the corpse. There were no ruptured veins. No swellings. The neck had been cut in a single deep slash which went nearly to the spine. Though the arrangement of the dead features suggested the girl had died without much struggle.

Then there was the hawthorn which decorated the body. On May Day young men hung hawthorn on the door of the girl they hoped to marry. But now was July and the thorn bush had no obvious use.

Think Charlie. Your life could depend on this.

With effort, he compartmentalised his thoughts, forcing his attention away from the approaching guards.

Branding. Words. Hawthorn. Candlewax.

It was a sacrifice, he decided. The more he thought about it the surer he was. The body had been laid out like some gruesome ritual.

But for what? 'He returns'? Something to do with the new King?

Charlie sifted through his thoughts on who might be motivated to kill in this way.

Witches, perhaps. There were a few in the countryside. And since the King had returned, some had risen up in the city. They were known to sacrifice victims. Was this a witchcraft killing?

But something jarred at his deeper instincts.

What is wrong with the picture?

Somehow, something was missing. He didn't quite know what. The murder scene felt unfinished. It was a nagging feeling that he couldn't quite resolve.

He shelved the idea for a moment, turning to the matter of the guards. He was imprisoned on the upper floor, with a bag of forged coins, wearing a key whose symbol marked a dead girl. Even if he managed to convince the guards of his innocence it would likely follow some interrogatory procedures. London's condemned criminals were often wheeled through the public streets, and Charlie had always held a cold terror that he might one day join the mangled wretches on the hanging cart.

You need to solve this crime. The thought spiked him, urgently.

His eyes settled back on the branded corpse. There was no mistaking it. The crown over three knots. The same Charlie had carried since he could remember.

Never in his life had he seen the symbol anywhere else. Something stirred in him. That this could be a chance to find out his own hidden past.

Forcing his mind to be calm Charlie let the facts settle in.

The murderer used a knife to cut the throat.

He took hawthorn from somewhere. Likely Kings Cross where it grows most freely.

Candlewax. White. It can be got anywhere.

The crown-and-knots mark. He would have needed a special brand.

And suddenly he knew how to catch the killer.

The brand.

Only a few in the City could have made it.

'All I need do is find the right blacksmith,' Charlie was so struck by the simplicity of the plan he spoke aloud. 'Find the blacksmith, find the killer.'

If not for the guards outside it would have been easy. But the Newgate men would never allow him to hunt out the murderer. They would take him straight to prison and ask questions later.

After weeks in Newgate, Charlie would be tortured to confess and executed as a counterfeiter and murderer. And as far as he knew, guards didn't allow their victims out into the City, to gather evidence of their innocence.

The idea of losing a limb on the cobbled streets suddenly seemed more manageable, and he moved back to the window. Out on the street Maria and the guards had stopped. They were waiting for the dead-cart to trundle past them.

Her choice of Newgate guards brought with it an idea of how Maria had connected him with the key. Charlie occasionally reported to the prison with criminals. The Newgate magistrate must have recognised the shape on the body and told Maria that a thief taker wearing the same sign could be found in the Bucket of Blood.

The thought that he might be known as a wanted man in Newgate prison filled him with a bursting dread.

A kind of horrible inspiration dawned. The dead-cart was making its way towards the house. When the wagon drove under the window he might be able to jump on the back – into the mound of bodies. If he judged it right they would cushion his fall. It might give him a headstart outrunning the guards.

He stared out at the street, judging the distances involved. If he could get enough distance from the house as he fell, he would make it. His gaze fell on the piled-up corpses.

Ordinarily he crossed the road to avoid dead-carts. But what choice did he have? Given an opening Charlie knew he could outrun the guards. He took work as a sedan-chair carrier to keep him primed for chasing criminals through London's twisting alleys. Few could match his speeds.

The only other option was to stand and fight.

His eyes settled on the approaching men. They had not yet thought to look up towards the window. From his vantage point Charlie could make out the weathered sword hilt of an ex-Civil War soldier.

Despite now being in their thirties and forties, those who had fought the Civil War made superb guards. Having survived the atrocities they lacked the rational fear of the average person and were battle-hardened in violent combat.

Charlie's thin chest was latticed in hard sections rather than slung with heavy muscle, and his legs were slim. Carrying the sedan-chairs had added bulk and prominent veins to his forearms, but he was no match for the two Newgate guards. Charlie rated his chances in the average street brawl. But he was astute enough to pick his fights.

It was typical, he thought, that it had come to this. One minute he was happily selling forged certificates and making good money and the next he was forced to choose between torture, amputation or leaping into a pile of corpses. It was the kind of thing which always seemed to be happening to him.

His head span with trepidation as he put one foot up on the casement, and then another, splitting the dry wood as he heaved his weight into the space.

A cry came from the street. Maria had seen him and was pointing.

Beneath him the driver of the death cart urged his horse forward, and the wheels turned over the uneven street. The vehicle began to roll past the house until it was almost directly under the window.

Seizing his chance Charlie flung himself from upper storey.

Chapter Ten

Charlie landed almost square on his face, clamping his mouth shut against the unwholesome load. Most of the corpses had been stacked face down and his cheek was pressed against the cold greasy hair of an uppermost body.

Feeling a jolt the driver looked around, his face setting in anger as he spotted the unexpected passenger. 'Hi there!' he called. 'What do you mean by it lad? There could be plaguey infection in those dead!'

Charlie placed his hands gingerly on the stiff cargo and heaved himself upright.

In the middle distance he could see his plunge into the dead-cart had unsettled the guards. They stood uncertainly, wondering whether the risk of chasing a criminal who had mingled with plague bodies was too great.

Maria's voice echoed thin and high, berating the guards. 'This is your *duty*! It is a murderer you let loose for the sake of your own skins!'

The rest of the street had stopped to watch the strange scene now, with Maria's loud petition and the presence of guards all alerting them to the drama. A few had also noticed Charlie standing on the funeral pile and were staring at him aghast.

Ignoring the stares he positioned himself to jump from the cart. As he leapt from the mound of bodies onto the cobbled street a corpse shifted beneath him, making him twist and land awkwardly.

He felt something in his ankle wrench and gingerly tried a little pressure on his foot.

It hurt enough to slow him down, but he could still run.

Ahead on the street the guards had begun heading his way. But slowly. Anxious to keep well clear of the cart of bodies.

'I know nothing of how the symbol came to be there and have nothing to do with the crime!' He shouted, gritting his teeth as he took a few steps on the sprained ankle.

When the guards saw him step away from the dead-cart they broke into a run.

For a brief moment Charlie caught a glimpse of Maria's face. Her drawn features looked sorry.

Then he turned and fled as fast as his injured foot would allow.

Charlie turned at the end of the cobbled street, heading towards the East of the city. The pain in his foot pulsed in electric jolts.

'Hold! Arrest that man!' He heard rather than saw the guards give chase.

Holbourne Bridge jerked hazily before him and he tried to force his mind away from the agony and to the practicalities of escape.

The Bridge connected the newer London town to the medieval city over the Fleet River. If he could get inside the London Wall he could vanish into the warren of ancient backstreets. But this meant passing through either New Gate or Alders Gate.

In a flash decision he made for Alders Gate, which was further but easier to vanish through.

He raced towards it, hoping for heavy traffic on Charterhouse Street. With his practice weaving through carts and riders at speed it might earn him greater distance from the guards.

But as the route hove into view he saw the usual thorough-fare had been vastly thinned. Plague had decimated the mayhem of jostling carts and livestock drawn to nearby Smithfield. A quick glance over his shoulder revealed the two guards were pressing their advantage. Both were heavily dressed in thick woollen jerkin-coats, leather shoes and felt hats, and the youngest was clearly feeling the strain, his sword knocking clumsily against his legs. But the elder appeared to experience no such encumbrance and was tearing over the cobblestones on powerful legs.

His more experienced pursuer was gaining fast, and on the empty road with his damaged foot Charlie was losing ground.

Charterhouse Street seemed to yawn as an immense distance.

Up ahead three farmers had blocked the road completely with a vast gaggle of geese which they were herding into the city through Duck Lane.

Charlie slowed. Behind him the soldier-guard drew his sword and turned it expertly, angling the heavy handle forward so as to smash it down like a club. It was a manoeuvre so practised he didn't even break his stride. Clearly he was planning to split skulls first and ask questions later.

Setting his mouth determinedly Charlie ran straight at the flock. The herders turned in alarm and then outrage as the birds squawked and flapped, filling the air with an explosion of downy feathers and beating wings.

Charlie caught a quick glance of the farmers' furious efforts to bring the flock back under control. Then the geese were behind him and the heavy towers of Alders Gate came into view.

If he could make it through he would be safe. As soon as he passed through Alders Gate he could easily disappear and decide his next course of action.

The gate joined the City by a wooden bridge, crossing over the scrubland which had once been a moat.

Too late he realised his mistake. Plague times meant that Alders Gate was now guarded. And since it was made of two wooden doors rather than the metal grill at New Gate, each could be swung closed far faster than the portcullis could be lowered.

The approach was crowded with people, but Charlie could make out a sleepy-looking guard behind the crowd.

A shout came from behind.

'Close the gate!' The ex-soldier had made it past the teeming geese and was calling to the men at the gatehouse.

The sentinel guarding the Alders Gate entrance straightened from his previously slumped posture and stared.

'Close it!'

Recognising a Newgate uniform the sentinel swung down his pole and disappeared behind the entrance. The vast door began to close.

Charlie slowed, his mind racing through escape opportunities and finding none.

'Have a care!' came another voice. It came from the younger guard who had now caught up with the first and was standing hatless and panting. 'He may have the plague!'

His colleague turned to him in disbelief, but it was too late.

Screams and gasps went up from the people crowded onto the Alders Gate approach. Then chaos broke out as they began to scramble for a way off the bridge.

The sentry who had been in the act of closing the gate dropped his pikestaff and ran backwards into the city.

Charlie raced towards the entrance. Frightened citizens threw themselves bodily into the scrub as he passed. With a growl the soldier-guard had shoved his younger companion and was racing in pursuit. But Charlie had already made it through the London Wall.

Sanctuary and squalor closed around him simultaneously as his feet hit the soft mud track of the Old City. But the landscape of the

East had changed. When he had last seen it the plague was spreading fast. Now it had been declared a thiefdom.

Cheapside still bore sedan-chairs carrying noblemen who wouldn't risk their footwear on the muck roads of the City. But not a single pedestrian walked the streets. Stalls which had once sold second-hand clothing had been swept away. In their place were sellers of plague protection. Phials of plague water, cloves of smoked garlic, nosegays and facemasks now formed the thin trade.

Normal families had fled. The only residences still populated had opened up as fortune tellers and astrologists. Painted signs of Merlin's head were everywhere. As were the ominous flashes of red. Plague crosses. Infection was all around.

Charlie took a moment to stare open-mouthed at the transformation. Then he caught a glimpse of what he was looking for.

A familiar sedan-chair in the traffic. And with a brief glance over his shoulder he plunged towards it.

Chapter Eleven

The vast Royal bedchamber was traditionally in name only – designed to allow His Majesty to hold court in comfort whilst he slept elsewhere.

No previous monarch had included the actual furnishings of sleep, but the restored monarch's habits had gauged it necessary.

The bed itself was an imposing swathe of royal-blue silk headed by a towering edifice of carved oak which swept high up to the swooping ceiling and jutted over the bed in a shower of gold-threaded tassels.

The room was festooned in pillows and sofas of the same fabric, alongside acres of sumptuous rugs, a library's worth of gold leaf and a small forest of oak, all of it set to glint and glisten as the sunlight streamed from gigantic windows of real glass.

Against the morning light, King Charles II, ruler of England, Scotland and Ireland, stared at the floor. If he kept his eyes down his hangover was easier to bear.

From the other side of the room came the sawing sound of Amesbury snoring. The war general was some ten years older than the thirty year old King, but they'd forged a camaraderie in strong drink.

Charles made a cautious peek into the pounding dark depths of his head. Last night they'd transformed this official room into a haven of drink and song.

He hadn't counted on having to make policies from it this morning.

Somewhere in the middle distance he heard a door slam and wondered what the servants were making of their new ruler. Likely they were attending to the Queen, who was an early riser, having been raised in a convent in Portugal.

He heard footsteps, and two pairs of shoes stepped into his eye line. The first were sensible, black, cut in simple shapes from thick leather.

The second were blue, embroidered with gold thread and tied with fat loops of silk ribbon.

Charles allowed the information to compute. The beribboned pair belonged to the Mayor of London. Which meant the plain pair belonged to his overworked aide, Mr Blackstone.

Steeling himself Charles raised his eyes to his guests, wincing at the lightning bolt of pain the gesture brought.

'Gentlemen.' He gave them a weak smile.

The two men bowed.

Blackstone was undoubtedly the fatter, but he held his bulk in a masculine assuredness beneath his smart black attire. Mayor Lawrence's chubbiness was of a womanly sort, folding in a double chin and making tentative little breasts under the elaborate gold stitching and buttons of his suit.

'What can I help you with?' asked Charles.

'We fear, Your Majesty, that a feeling of witchcraft has risen up again,' said Mr Blackstone choosing his words carefully.

Charles rubbed his head, allowing his gaze to drift around the room. To his relief it looked as though only Amesbury had slept here last night.

'Wine.' Charles held out his hand.

There was the sonorous sound of an eased cork. A gurgle of liquid. And then a chalice was slid into his ringed fingers.

Charles took a grateful sip. The sound of Amesbury snoring still echoed through the room.

'What do you mean, again?' asked Charles, raising his dark eyebrows to better take in his guests.

'We had great problems with witches during your exile,' said Mayor Lawrence, who could always be relied upon to undo Blackstone's careful tact. 'It was a time of darkness for the country. Cromwell had taken power from your father the King. He told the people they must keep the strict Puritan religion. But many would not. And some evil people returned to . . . the old ways.'

'What old ways?'

'Devil worship and witchery,' said Lawrence. 'There were murders and sacrifices, and dissenters rose up. Cromwell put them under by brutal force. He hung twenty men as witches only weeks before his death. And since your return we have had nothing of that nature to trouble us.'

In his long black curls Charles noticed something sticky, by his ear. They had called for some sweet liquor, he remembered, just before dawn.

The King caught the eye of the nearest servant.

'Give these gentlemen wine. We have a very good Burgundy. Or a Bordeaux if they prefer.' He paused for a moment, making a mental examination of his stomach.

'What does the kitchen have?' he decided.

'We have a pheasant done in Claret, with bacon lardons,' said the servant. 'That is very good. There is a rabbit made with chicory which the Queen ordered. The cook roasts beef on the spit, soft inside, as you like, with French herbs, and there is roast chicken or a fresh turbot with lemon if you would take something lighter.'

Charles nodded.

'Is there any of the soup from last night? The bean potage?'

'I believe there is Sire.'

'I will take a little of that,' said Charles. 'And a few slices of beef I think I could manage,' he added. 'Would you gentlemen care for food?'

Blackstone and the Mayor shook their heads.

'So, you fear that witches have returned?' asked Charles, forcing his mind to the task. Somewhere beneath the hangover he felt a spark of anxiety. He drained his cup. On cue, a servant stepped forward to refresh his wine.

'There was a murder, in the city,' said Lawrence. 'It looked to be a sacrifice of sorts.'

King Charles took a deep mouthful of Bordeaux and swallowed.

The sound of loud snoring sawed through his thoughts.

'God's fish can someone wake Amesbury?' he said, raising a sudden hand to his pain-wracked head. 'We can none of us think with that din.'

A servant gave the slumbering Amesbury a rather disrespectful kick, and the military-cloaked body rolled over and ceased to snore.

'What kind of sacrifice?' asked Charles.

'A witch's sacrifice Sire,' said Lawrence. 'The body was covered all over in hawthorn, and words were written on the body and a symbol. Like a spell had been cast,' he added.

Charles pondered this.

'What did the writing say?'

'It said 'He Returns', said Lawrence.

The three men were silent for a moment.

'What do you think it means?' asked the King finally. He was looking at Blackstone, having judged him the more intelligent of the two.

The Mayor opened his mouth, but the King raised a finger and gestured to Blackstone.

'We . . . we do not know what it means,' said Blackstone, taking a slight step forward. Of course we fear it may relate to your return to the throne.' Blackstone paused for a moment.

'And what should be done about it?'

'We think it wise that the killer is swiftly caught and put to death harshly,' said Blackstone. 'The people . . . they are easily swayed. It would be unwise to let this murder go unpunished. More witches may rise.'

Mayor Lawrence made to speak again, but as he did the huge door banged, and his mouth dropped open. The King's mistress Louise Keroulle was walking across the room. Besides the flowers in her curling chestnut hair she was completely naked.

Mr Blackstone blushed scarlet. His eyes dropped and began frantically following the swirl pattern of the nearest Persian rug.

With barely a glance at the two officials Louise deposited herself into Charles's lap.

Blackstone snuck a sideways look at the Mayor. The ordinarily pompous face was mesmerised, his mouth slightly ajar.

'And you know the murderer?' Charles was saying, moving his head to be clear of Louise's naked torso. 'The witch who made the crime?'

Blackstone looked up a fraction to see the King's hands were roaming Louise's bare skin. He quickly blinked down again, waiting for the Mayor to answer the question.

There was an awkward silence. Mr Blackstone cleared his throat.

The Mayor, he knew, would be annoyed with his outspokenness. But needs must. Lawrence was beyond articulation.

'We think we know the man,' said Blackstone. 'The crime may have been committed by a commoner. A thief taker by trade. They perform services which The Watch are too old for,' he added by way of an explanation.

The King gave a heavy kind of shrug which almost dislodged Louise from his lap. She overbalanced, righted herself gracelessly with a hand between his legs and then began animatedly fondling his groin as though that had been her intention all along.

Charles hardly noticed. Then as an afterthought he moved a hand towards her nipple.

'Well then,' he said finally, 'do what you must to find him.'

'We need men to bring him in,' said Lawrence, jogged suddenly out of his trance by the affront of being ignored.

'My guard then, speak to Mr Chaffinch in the Palace. He will give you as many men as you need. Tell all the gatekeepers, and spread this thief taker's description to every plague checkpoint. To move around the city he must have a certificate bearing his name. Bring this man in. If he is guilty we will hang him as a witch. Set an example.'

Mayor Lawrence gave a grateful bow.

'Surely you are not expected to attend to every petty crime in the City,' demanded Louise, in her heavy French accent. 'That is for the Royal Guard.'

'Ah,' said Charles, with the faintest of smiles, 'but my guard is not allowed in the City. The people fear I will turn dictator as my father did, and they do not have the stomach to behead another King. Not since the brutalities of the Civil War.'

He gave another little shrug, but this time Louise was ready for him, anchoring her hands in fistfuls of his linen shirt.

'Where is my brother?' demanded Louise. 'He should be here to advise.'

Blackstone and the Mayor exchanged glances.

Louise had brought her whey-faced brother along with her to court. And rumour had it that she wanted George Keroulle to be given some royal appointment. As a younger man George had fought for King Charles I. Now he had been reduced to currying court favour through his younger sister and was suspected to be a spy.

'You can be sure this thief taker is the right man?' asked the King, ignoring her.

'We have strong reason,' said the Mayor. 'He carries this symbol.' With a flourish Mayor Lawrence pulled out a slip of paper and held it up.

A crown and knots danced before the King's drooping eyelids.

He stared at it for a moment and then looked questioningly at Lawrence.

'This same shape was found burned into the body,' concluded the Mayor.

The King frowned, then raised an eyebrow.

'This is the sole reason you think this man a murderer?'

Blackstone stepped a little forward and coughed politely.

'It is something of a political matter,' he admitted. 'We must be seen to act on witches. That the thief taker carries the murder symbol is enough to convince the public.'

'Arresting this man will show the mob that we strike hard and fast against devil-raising,' added Mayor Lawrence. 'It is important, Sire, in protecting your glorious reign from those godless factions who might oppose you.'

He did not add what they all knew. That dissenting groups, of all creeds and religions, were all over London. The slightest upheaval could galvanise them to rise against the new King.

Charles considered for a long moment.

'Then do what you must,' he said finally. 'Now. Is there any other matter I can help you with?'

Louise gave a little gasp of annoyance, and the King laughed.

'Forgive me,' he added. 'I was not raised as a King. Louise reminds me I should not demean myself with courtesies.'

Mayor Lawrence gave a little nod.

'The plague is outrunning us. We have not enough pits now to hold the bodies. Corpses pile up and rot in the streets.'

Louise wrinkled her nose. 'Do you see now why we must leave the city?' she hissed.

'There are common lands in Shoreditch and Moor Fields,' continued Lawrence. 'Peasants raise the odd pig or cow on them, or grow nut trees. By law they are protected. We would like permission to dig them up.'

The King nodded. 'Granted.' He thought for a moment. 'I will send Amesbury to help you see it done,' he added.

Blackstone raised his eyebrows. Amesbury was generally held to be a spectacularly effective general, but completely without morality. He chose whichever side paid the most, and whichever army he led won. Since Charles's return Amesbury's war talents meant he was kept as a close advisor. But like many Londoners, Blackstone doubted his integrity.

Louise leaned in and whispered something in the King's ear.

King Charles sighed and gave a sweep of his palm, signalling Blackstone and the Mayor should leave. Then he turned to his French mistress with a half-smile.

'Please be sure to take a dish of the pheasant on your way past the kitchens,' he called after the retreating officials. 'Louise has brought her own chef from Versailles and he prepares it in the French way. It is excellent.'

⁓⁓⁓

Blackstone and the Mayor walked carefully out of the Palace, both deep in thought.

'Did you see the harlot's nipples?' asked the Mayor, as they cleared the Palace gates and rejoined London's muddy chaos. 'She had put rouge on them. They were not a natural colour at all.'

But Blackstone had other things on his mind. As Mayor Lawrence's aide he had learned to keep silent. But in his silences he had become a great observer. And he had seen what Lawrence had missed.

The symbol of the crown and the looping knots.

He had seen something in His Majesty's face, when they'd shown him the symbol. King Charles had known what it meant.

Chapter Twelve

From inside the velvet-lined walls of the sedan-chair Charlie breathed a sigh of relief and leaned forwards towards the viewing hole.

The guards were just now coming through Alders Gate and could not see him concealed inside the sedan-chair. But it wouldn't be long before they started asking questions and someone pointed out where he was hiding.

'Can you take us to the bear pits Marcus? And make sure we are not followed?'

The carrier's amber eyes widened.

'The bear pits?'

'I cannot risk we are overheard.'

'You must pay me back if I am shaken down by bandits.'

The chair lifted and set off at speed. And they made a series of dizzyingly expert turns and feints along the maze of backstreets.

The chair pulled up at a bear-baiting pit and Charlie ducked gratefully out and into the jostling pack of men shouting their bets.

Moments later the chair carrier slid in next to him.

His working clothes could not disguise that he lacked the scabbed legs and wasted arms of other sedan hustlers.

Marc-Anthony, known to his friends as Marcus, ran an ingenious trade smuggling goods through London in sedan-chairs, which unlike larger wagons were never searched. His shining brown curls, glowing skin and sturdy limbs attested to his earning many hundred times more than most chair carriers.

'Trouble Charlie?'

Charlie nodded, keeping his eyes on the ragged-looking bear chained to a wooden post. The keepers were bringing the dogs into the scruffy dirt arena and they began to snarl at the chained bear. A couple of shouts went up from the excited crowd.

'Did the guards find you with the forgeries?'

Charlie had forgotten he had been selling Marc-Anthony's forged Health Certificates less than an hour ago.

Ordinarily the smuggler brought in tobacco, wine, lace and silk to avoid paying duty at Tower Bridge. But ever the entrepreneur he had deftly shifted his business to black-market Health Certificates as demand soared.

Charlie shook his head. 'It is nothing to do with the certificates. I am wanted Marcus, for some murder I know nothing of.'

Marc-Anthony's amber eyes widened. 'You are wanted for murder?'

Charlie nodded quickly, outlining the morning's events.

Marc-Anthony gave an obliging whistle.

'You of all people,' he said after a moment. 'You do not even believe in witchcraft.'

'The Newgate guards know my face,' continued Charlie, acknowledging Marc-Anthony's observation with a wry smile. 'And the girl has money. She's probably paid every grubbing vigilante in the City to chase me down.'

'Any bets! Any bets! Any bets!'

The pit-keeper held out his hand for their penny bet to stay and watch the action.

Charlie raised his hand and gave over two pennies. 'For the bear,' he said.

Marc-Anthony raised an eyebrow. 'I do not want to draw attention to myself by winning,' explained Charlie.

The bookie palmed the money with practised ease and raised a hand, signifying to the keepers that the dogs could be released.

'So what will you do now?' asked Marc-Anthony, raising his voice against the shouts of the crowd. 'You cannot go any further east. The plague is bad here, but deeper in is horror. The streets are deserted, and the only sounds are the shrieks and the moans of the dying. I mean to sail up the river as soon as I get a chance,' he added. 'I mean to wait out the plague on my tall-ship anchored on the Thames.'

Marc-Anthony seemed so urban in nature that Charlie frequently forgot he had a cottage in the little hamlet of Greenwich. He commuted once a week into the City by rowboat through the marshlands at Deptford Creek.

Charlie shook his head. 'I have to clear my name Marcus. I have no wish to be jumping at my shadow for the rest of my days, fearing being gutted at Tyburn.'

A low growling started up. Four dogs had been released from their chains and were circling the bear, teeth bared.

'Is it possible, to prove your innocence?'

Charlie nodded. 'Yes. If I find the murderer. To do that I must find out the blacksmith. A brand marked the corpse. Only a skilled blacksmith might have made it. When I find that man I think I might readily find facts which will lead me to the killer.'

Marc-Anthony was shaking his head. 'You cannot get to the blacksmiths Charlie. Have you not heard? They have all left town.'

Charlie's heart sank. 'Every one of the blacksmiths has left?'

'All Thames Street has been sealed off,' said Marc-Anthony. 'Plague has made it a ghetto. None are allowed in or out, and the blacksmiths are long gone.'

Charlie frowned, unwilling to give up.

'It is a witch killing,' he said, thinking aloud. 'Everything about the murder looked to be a sacrifice.'

'A witch was recently released from Wapping prison,' said Marc-Anthony thoughtfully. 'There is much talk of it in the town. Perhaps there is your murderer.'

'Perhaps. I think the murder is something to do with this.' Charlie's hand closed around the key at his neck. 'The mark on the murdered girl. The brand. It was made in this shape.'

'Sure but this could be good news for you. It might be a chance to discover where your key came from.'

Charlie laughed a little too loudly.

'That is the stuff of orphan's dreams,' he said.

'Yet that key must open something,' said Marc-Anthony.

Charlie looked away. As a boy he had thought his mother might have left him the key to find him again. Women left all manner of strange objects in the hope of retrieving their babes once they had the means. Little pieces of fabric, paper scraps, sketches, marked coins, playing cards, charms, shoe buckles and clothes pegs were all part of the medley.

But it was equally possible he had found the key somewhere between being orphaned as a small boy and left with the nuns. After all, Rowan had nothing. It made no sense for a mother to give one child a memento and not the other.

Growing up, Charlie had made his own investigations. The key was some odd shape it transpired – double-sided and not like an English key at all. Rather than having one blade it fanned out like a pair of wings and looked suspiciously foreign to most Londoners.

Nor did it seem the right shape to fit any known lock. Too big for a chest and too small for a door. Even what the key might open was not apparent.

In his more honest moments Charlie acknowledged he kept a secret faith alive that working as a thief taker could one day lead him to some window of his past. A fact which Marc-Anthony was one of the few to discern.

'I can ask Rowan,' Charlie decided. His brother tended to know too much of London's dark doings.

Marc-Anthony snorted. 'Your brother? When has he ever helped you Charlie?' he shook his head. 'One brother catches thieves and the other gets away with murder. Is that not how it is?'

The bear howled as the first dog leapt, bit sharply into its chest and dropped back down to avoid the swinging paws. Rising on its haunches the bear launched forward, but the chain caught sharply. A second dog attacked from the side, drawing blood from the thick neck.

Charlie thought for a moment, trying to manoeuvre the facts. It was a theft of sorts, he reasoned. The girl's life had been stolen.

He replayed the scene in his mind.

The coin eyes flashed at him. They had not been made by a coin house he recognised which was odd. He turned the fact over and logged it for later consideration.

Hawthorn on the body. The shrub grew in hedgerows all over London. It thrived mostly in Kings Cross. But hawthorn could have come from any part of the city.

The brand. That had been his greatest clue. If only the black-smiths were still in London.

The crowd were baying for blood now, shouting for the bear and dogs alike. And the bear dropped back to all fours, eyeing the dogs warily. The snarling pack huddled together, then one pounced.

Like lightning the bear's claw shot out. And suddenly the dog's intestines lay outside the ring. In a flash a second dog lay disembowelled at the bear's feet.

A great roar went up from the crowd. The canine bodies lolled glassy eyed, but only their owners showed any concern. Everyone else was waving and shouting.

'I hear your Lynette made a visit to the Bucket of Blood,' said Marc-Anthony, watching his face carefully. 'You could ask her for help. She could shelter you, at least.'

'She is not my Lynette.'

Marc-Anthony nodded tactfully. 'You have both decided on it then? To say that your marriage never happened?'

Charlie nodded.

'And she agreed to it?'

The two remaining dogs seemed to have lost their motivation for attack. Almost half-heartedly the first jumped to its death, eyes spinning in shock as the heavy paw thudded it back to the ground. The bear leaned down to rip out the throat of the stunned animal and then raised its bloody maw to issue a chilling growl. The last living dog whimpered and retreated. The crowd cheered.

'We did once love each other, despite everything,' said Charlie, 'But I have come to the end of my patience with her.'

Charlie had a sudden image of his estranged wife, her eyes glittering, standing in the whirling centre of a storm of fights and bitter words.

He took in the expression on Marc-Anthony's face and clarified slightly.

'Of course I still have feelings for her,' he said. 'But she needs much money for her happiness.'

'Do you still plan to open a gaming house?'

Charlie smiled. Marcus knew him well enough to take his ambition seriously. Most other people thought it a pipe-dream.

'Plague times have set me back,' admitted Charlie. 'Perhaps, in two years, I shall have funds enough.'

'It would be better to strike soon,' observed Marc-Anthony. 'Or others will discover the same cheap land as you and press their advantage.'

'Plague slows all business the same,' shrugged Charlie. Though he had been thinking the same thing himself. 'Perhaps I shall come into a fortune.'

The key seemed warm against his skin suddenly.

'You always were the very devil for good luck,' agreed Marc-Anthony.

The bear-handler moved in, both arms raised aloft in triumph. Hands began to shoot up in the crowd, from those who had betted on the bear. The bookie strode amongst them, matching the memorised faces to the winnings owed.

'You collect the winnings,' said Charlie. 'I do not wish to attract any more attention today.'

'What do you mean to do?'

Charlie thought of what scant clues he had left.

In his experience, the best way to catch a man was not to go where he had been. It was to predict his next move and arrive there before him.

'What do you know of witches and their spells?' he asked Marcus.

'Not much.'

'They call the corners,' do they not? Charlie urged forth a childhood memory. 'Hail to the spirits of the north. Spirits of mother and earth,' is that not how it goes?

Marc-Anthony was looking at him strangely.

'It was a play chant, was it not?' asked Charlie. 'The kind of thing children sang.'

'I know not what songs were sung at the Foundling Hospital,' said Marc-Anthony. 'But I never sang that as a child.'

'Before the Foundling Hospital, I think we sang it,' said Charlie. 'Witches call each corner. North, East, South and West. Such are spells made.'

Marc-Anthony frowned. 'This is the power ritual of witches,' he said. 'But it would be strange to hear on a child's lips.' He gave a little laugh. 'Are you sure you were not secretly raised to the dark arts? It would explain how you find villains so easily.'

The look on Charlie's face told him instantly it had been a joke too far.

'But you would need four witches,' Marc-Anthony added quickly. 'One to hold each corner.'

Unless . . .

'Witches use death magic, do they not?' asked Charlie. 'They believe it is all powerful.'

Marcus nodded. 'They are greatly feared for it.'

Charlie pictured the dead girl.

The hawthorn. It was suddenly taking on a new meaning. Hawthorn grew in the ground. In the earth.

He brought Maria's house to mind. Her front door faced away from the river. Towards the north.

Something else was urging forward too. He suddenly knew what had been missing from the murder scene.

The other elements.

Charlie had seen witch spells before. Before Cromwell began hanging witches in earnest, it was common to see a ritual scratched in the dirt, to protect a home or reverse a fever.

But pagan spells always represented all four elements.

The killer had only used one.

'I think the killer calls the corners,' said Charlie slowly. 'But one by one. North for earth.'

'What do you mean Charlie?'

'I mean, I think the murderer makes a master spell. But he uses death, to mark the corners.'

The facts were ordering themselves now. And Charlie had a feeling. The same he always got, when a case was starting to open itself to investigation.

'Why do you think so?' asked Marc-Anthony.

'Maria's Holbourne house was north for earth,' said Charlie. 'Her sister had been bound in hawthorn, to represent the element.'

Marc-Anthony shrugged. 'It seems a leap.'

Charlie's eyes flashed. 'Call it a thief taker's intuition.' He paused for a moment. 'And besides,' he admitted, 'it is the best theory I have. I can hardly go back to the scene and gather more information.'

Charlie's face was grim. 'If I am right, then he must make the other corners,' he said. 'He would need four deaths, to complete his spell. Though what he hopes to conjure, I know not.'

White ribbons. Candlewax. He returns.

He turned to Marc-Anthony.

'What comes after north for earth? It is east, is it not?'

Marc-Anthony nodded. 'East for air.'

Air. Charlie's mind raced over what might be needed for such a ritual.

Feathers. Birds.

'I will go to the bird market,' decided Charlie. 'I know people there. Someone might tell me something. Perhaps they even sold feathers for spells, before it became too dangerous.'

'Your Health Certificate is not good enough to get you into that part of London,' said Marc-Anthony. 'If you try a forgery in Regent's Park you'll be arrested.'

'Perhaps the checks are not so strict everywhere,' said Charlie, sounding more confident than he felt.

'But how will you get back into the west?' asked Marc-Anthony. 'Every gate will be guarded now. You'll be arrested the moment you step across London Wall.'

Charlie gave Marcus a hopeful smile. 'I need to borrow your boat.'

Chapter Thirteen

Charlie rowed the boat carefully away from Blackfriars slums.

The slum was the only part of London where even mercenaries would not venture. Squalor and desperation was such that residents would slit a throat for a halfpenny. Blackfriars operated as its own lawless hell, and no sane man ventured beyond the outlying filthy refuse which delineated its borders.

Keeping a careful eye on the bank Charlie rowed on, past the public boat-docking steps at the Strand and Charing Cross.

Slum-dwellers sometimes swum out and stole boats from solo rowers, and he couldn't risk Marc-Anthony's craft.

The Thames was London's lifeblood, and every citizen depended on river water to drink, cook and wash with. But for slum dwellers it was also their trade.

He docked at Horseferry, handing a penny to the waterman to guard the row-boat. Then he set off north.

The bird market was unusually subdued as Charlie approached. Around half the stalls were absent, and those who still traded held only a few birds.

He passed a wooden cage, which held a handful of twittering starlings. The birds were caught in Hyde Park, and when he and Lynette had first fallen in love Charlie had bought her a starling, so they might free it together.

Lynette had wanted to keep the creature. He should have known then.

Halfway along the dirt-track market was a wooden desk with an officious-looking clerk behind it and two heavy-set guards.

Charlie swallowed. The clerk was scrutinising each Health Certificate, comparing each stamp carefully.

To get to the rest of the bird sellers he needed to pass through.

Charlie's hand slid to his coat. Here the checks were far more thorough than in the East. The name on his certificate was false. He had to hope his description hadn't been circulated to the guards.

'Psst!'

A sudden noise drew his attention. He cast around in confusion and then he saw the source.

At a nearby stall Charlie spotted someone he recognised, a fellow ex-foundling. Changing direction he made for the familiar face.

'Oliver!' He began to raise his hand in salutation, but his old friend shook his head.

Confused, Charlie drew closer.

'What are you doing here Charlie?' hissed Oliver in a whisper. 'Do you not know you are a wanted man?'

'What?'

'It is all over London,' said Oliver. His stall held a few pitiful cages, and he settled himself down onto his haunches in the dust, gesturing Charlie did the same.

'The Mayor himself has got funds from the King to bring you in,' Oliver explained.

Charlie felt his stomach plummet in fear.

'They say you are connected to a witch-murder,' continued Oliver. 'And they are careful to put down such things quickly, for you remember how things were with Cromwell.'

'I am innocent,' said Charlie. 'You do know I am innocent?'

'Of course.' Oliver rested a hand briefly on his forearm. 'But your description has been put about at every checkpoint in the city.' He shook his head. 'It is a shame you are so good at your thief-taking Charlie. Many know your face. And with the fear of witches and plague in the city they will not hesitate to turn you in.'

Oliver glanced about nervously. 'This part of town is worst of all for dark rumours,' he said. 'The physicians are here, and they are all in fear. They say something is happening with the bodies.'

'What do you mean?'

'Bodies are not being buried where they should be. And some of the physicians say there are more bodies than dead people. They think something dark has come to London,' he added.

'Oliver,' said Charlie, keeping his voice in a low whisper. 'I am trying to clear my name. So I am come for information.' He hesitated, thinking of the easiest way to phrase his question.

'Would a witch buy feathers for a spell?' he asked finally, opting for the most straight-forward question.

Oliver frowned.

'Some silly girls did come for dove feathers and the like,' he said. 'But that was long ago. No woman should risk her neck for a love spell.'

'What of . . . A different spell?' pressed Charlie. 'A dark magic?'

Oliver visibly shuddered.

'Think you such a thing takes place in the City?'

'Perhaps,' admitted Charlie.

'Then they would not use feathers from the bird market,' replied Oliver with certainty. 'They would use an evil bird. A rook or a raven. We do not sell such things'

Charlie felt disappointment run through him.

'People used to buy ravens to clip their wings and leave them at the Tower of London,' continued Oliver. 'But no one bird seller will keep ravens since the plague. They are a bad omen. And unless you are allowed in the Tower,' he added, 'You cannot keep a raven in the city.'

'Why not?' Charlie couldn't imagine why the bird couldn't stay hidden.

'They are not like a starling or a nightingale Charlie. Ravens make a horrendous noise. When you cage them, they are loud enough to raise the dead. And you must know they are terrible luck. A neighbour would hear and make some complaint if you kept one.'

Charlie considered this.

'You must beware, if it is dark magic you track,' warned Oliver. 'There is all talk from the astrologers that some evil thing has arisen,' said Oliver. 'Signs and portents have been seen. Comets. Things of that kind.'

He squinted up into the summer sunshine.

'London is an ancient city,' he added. 'She holds bound in her belly the bones of giants and her soul is of old magic. Some wicked thing is abroad with this plague Charlie, all of us feel it. Perhaps something terrible has arisen with the King's return. A long-sleeping demon awoken and now stalking among us.'

Charlie considered this. Many peasants and poorer sorts turned to witchcraft for treatment. Particularly now plague made them desperate.

He thought of Maria and her country family and their dislike of doctors. Perhaps they were backwards enough to visit a witch.

Beside him he felt Oliver tense suddenly.

'There are two vigilantes at the checkpoint,' he hissed. 'And one is looking straight at you.'

Charlie looked up. His gaze met with a notorious hired thug. And as their eyes locked he knew they were here for him.

His heart sank.

Jack Tanner was the most brutal and determined tracker in the city. In an instant the many hiding places usually available to him evaporated. Jack would know them all.

There was only one place in the City too dangerous for the men to follow him. Crossing himself Charlie leapt to his feet and set off at a run for Blackfriars slum.

Chapter Fourteen

The knock sounded, and Antoinette trooped obediently downstairs to meet Thomas. For five years he had paid for her modest room in a good part of the city. In return she was available when he wanted to indulge his strange sexual demands.

She caught sight of her reflection in the glass near the door. The once beautiful face had aged rapidly on its daily diet of London living, but she still commanded enough of her youthful looks to be attractive.

Antoinette was a London cliché. She had been a country girl, come to the city to find maid's work and fallen for the wiles of one of the many London madams who lay in wait for the stage-coaches arriving from the provinces.

Now she was getting older and having failed to snare an aristocrat as a protector had settled for Thomas – a man of adequate if not illustrious means.

Her dress was new, in the style of the King's court favourites. Thomas didn't visit often, so she felt she owed him a different outfit for each occasion. The red material made a reasonable show of being silk. It fanned out in a style which she knew Thomas liked to lift up and over her head during 'The Act' as she'd come to term it.

She opened the door.

To her dismay he had come in his plague-doctor disguise. It was a habit he'd grown a taste for recently. And there was something else. He carried a squawking bird in a cage. A raven.

She felt a shudder, wondering what he had planned.

Pushing the distaste away from her face, she gave what she hoped was a seductive smile, keeping her lips together to disguise her mottled teeth.

'Come up.' She took up her dress with one hand and, holding the candle in the other, made up the stairs. Behind her she heard him follow. She held her skirt up a little higher, so he could see flashes of the naked skin underneath as she ascended.

Antoinette was no fool. She knew that to keep a man prepared to pay her rent required work. Particularly with one obliging enough to make rare visits. Some of her friends in the city were kept by young men who visited several times a day. For double the money they made she had her time mostly to herself.

Besides Thomas's occasional brutality it was an acceptable arrangement. But she didn't want it to last forever.

Without his knowledge she had taken on extra work at a gambling club. It was strictly against the rules of their arrangement. But in his line of work Thomas would never mix with the aristocratic high-rollers at Adders. She felt confident she would find another protector at the club.

Only a few more months of deceit and she would be free.

'I have poured you a cup of your favourite wine,' she said, leading him into her single bedchamber where candles had been lit.

Thomas grunted in reply. He placed the cage with the raven onto a table. Antoinette swallowed. Clearly he was eager to get down to things.

It was easy to forget, in the weeks between visits, what happened when they came around again. And recently Thomas had started to frighten her more and more.

Antoinette made herself a sudden promise, that this would be the last time she submitted herself to the ordeal. She would take a new protector, even if he paid less and visited more.

She paused to take a much-needed swig of wine and then moved to the four-poster bed, spreading herself out obligingly on the sheets.

Thomas approached, his ugly beaked hood looming over her, his blue eyes winking behind the crystal goggles.

Antoinette swallowed and forced a smile. There was something different in the expression behind the hood. Did he know she was working at the club? Impossible, she decided.

'I have missed you,' Antoinette lied as he moved closer.

She noticed a flash of metal. He was wearing a sword.

'Why did you bring that?' In her fear the words came out louder than she had intended. Thomas was much too real in his play-acting. She would not be able to explain away cuts so well as she could bruises.

In answer Thomas turned to the birdcage.

Chapter Fifteen

Charlie fled along the muddy banks of The Strand past knife-grinders, coopers and cork-cutters making their noisy trade.

Then the squalid tangle of the Blackfriars slum was before him.

Behind him he heard the two men stop as they realised where he was headed.

'Let him be murdered in there then,' he heard Jack Tanner say, spitting onto the floor. 'I'll not be beaten to death by slum rats for a shilling reward.'

As the thick of wood-and-cloth makeshift homes closed in around him Charlie made a few feints right and left before sprinting quickly into the depths.

A feeling of unease tightened in his stomach. Though a few slum residents were known to him, there were too many desperate people squatting here to make the journey alone. In the rest of London Charlie was considered poor. But in this lawless half-mile the clothes on his back were valuable enough to murder him for.

His plan was to head dead through the centre and come out by St Paul's Cathedral. Forced to take the winding route around the outskirts there would be no way Jack Tanner and his friend could get there before him.

Then he would head north to Moor Fields where his brother might be able to help him access his usual sources. He was betting that someone, somewhere, had seen a plague doctor with a raven.

Towards the edge of the slums lived the newest of residents. They slept in rickety tents of sacking and hemp.

But as Charlie headed further inwards the homes became more established. Temporary camps gave way to stranger permanent shelters fashioned from London's leavings. Broken cartwheels and stolen shop-signs made walls, reeds from the river improvised thatch, and sticks impaling found objects staked out muddy little gardens.

Trees in the slum had long since been pillaged for fuel, so burning horse manure and damp straw fed fires. The sweet fumes hung in the air.

Outside their homes the starving slum dwellers stared at him silently, marking him out as a non-resident.

He tensed, seeing a sudden faster movement. But it was only a slum boy heading south to the tanneries. The ulcers burned into his legs showed him to be an apprentice.

There but for the grace of God, thought Charlie. At the Foundling Hospital all the children were given away in apprenticeships at age thirteen. Ever the nun's favourite, his brother Rowan had been given choice work as a grocer's boy, but had soon been laid off.

Not wanting to risk a second apprentice fee with his younger brother, the nuns had promised Charlie to the leather tanneries in Bermondsey – the cheapest of all the placements. Apprentices to this trade worked in a waist-deep solution of corrosive lime and urine, flesh dissolving from their bones as they laboured. The work he'd done for Mother Mitchell had taught him some basic carpentry and domestic work, but not enough to earn a living. With no choice other than beg, Charlie had fearfully awaited his first day in the tanning pits.

To his great amazement Mother Mitchell had arrived at the Foundling Hospital the day before he was due in Bermondsey. The nuns watched open-mouthed as she swooped in like a great exotic bird, face loudly painted and silk dress spanning six foot wide. Her eyes were slitted from the unaccustomed daylight but she still managed to pack them with disdain as she considered the dour nuns.

The boy, she had said, *will not be put to work in stinking piss pits. Whatever the apprentice fee is I will pay it. He has some writing and a little music and is well enough in intellect besides, to have a better place.*

The foundling children had huddled in, transfixed by the unfolding drama. Sister Agnes, the reigning terror of the Hospital, pursed her lips so tight they disappeared into two bleached lines of outrage. Her reply came as a low hiss.

We do not take money which has been earned by sin.

If you are too holy to attend to the future of your charge I will see to him. Mother Mitchell had said. *The boy can come with me as my apprentice.*

It is not so simply done, Sister Agnes countered. *You are not recognised by a guild to take a foundling as an apprentice.*

Mother Mitchell had dropped a purse of coins on the table. It rattled.

If that is not enough, she had said with the smallest of smiles. *Send your creditors to my house in Mayfair. We have ample girls to entertain them.*

And sweeping Charlie into the great bright folds of her arm she led him away from the Foundling Hospital. One of the smaller orphans had begun to applaud. Sister Agnes slapped the clapping hand back down, spat into the dust and hastily crossed herself.

Charlie had worked in Mother Mitchell's bawdy house for three years and learned everything about how to get on in the tumultuous, heartless, thriving City of London.

And now, without looking, Charlie's hard-learned sense for danger alerted him to the fact he was being followed. It was a slum dweller, a teenage boy, barely clothed in stinking rags and bearing a scar which ran from his groin to under his chin. He was a distance away, but his intention was unmistakable. The boy was marking him.

Charlie varied his pace, to check the boy was matching his speed. There was no mistaking it.

The boy was scrawny and no match for Charlie. But there would be others, working with him.

As Charlie considered his best plan of action a high-pitched sound came from the boy's throat. And suddenly he was flanked on the far left and right by two other slum boys.

The first wore nothing but a grimy flour sack which skirted his filthy thighs. The hair on his head grew sparsely, in clumps, with angry bald ringworm circles covering the rest. The second had only one eye and was bare-chested, but wore a pair of trousers which had once belonged to a far larger man.

At first they tracked behind, and then the boys divided. For a moment two of them were out of sight. And then Charlie caught a glimpse of them blocking the path ahead. One held a squat length of wood, and the other wielded part of a cart wheel.

Behind him another two boys had joined with the first, like wolves closing in as a pack.

Charlie slowed, silently running through his options. Five. If it came to it he knew he could fight off three.

One of the boys peeled off seamlessly, and vanished into the slum. Presumably, the tactic was to station himself further ahead and block the route.

Mentally, Charlie assessed the pack's movements, searching for a weak spot. He scanned ahead. The rickety slum dwellings were low and crumbling. Nothing to afford much of a hiding place for a slum boy to jump him. And then he saw how the path passed by two close houses, with enough space between for a boy to hide.

It was hardly a military-grade ambush. But Charlie caught a flash of movement and knew he'd guessed right. This would be the place where they would surround him.

Charlie slowed, and then sprinted suddenly. The boys flanking him took a moment to realise what had happened, and then they were running flat out over the uneven slum ground.

But Charlie was too fast. He sped past the back of the close-together buildings and grabbed hold of the boy wedged in between them.

The slum attacker had just enough time to shout in high alarm, before Charlie dragged him out into the open by his neck.

'I have your friend,' he called, in a calm voice, as the other would-be attackers filtered into view. 'I want to see all four of you retreat to beyond the broken wheel in the far distance.'

He indicated with his head, as the slum boy in his grip writhed and bucked.

The nearest boy had the emotionless expression of someone with nothing to lose.

'And what if we do not?' he countered.

'If you do not, I will snap his neck,' said Charlie. He twisted his elbow to show he was serious, and the boy let out a squeal of surprised pain.

'Kill him then,' said the first boy, in a bored sort of way. 'There is more money for the rest of us when we rob you.'

Charlie retained his grip on the boy and tried for a different tactic. 'I have only a few coins,' he said. 'But you may take it as a fair toll for passing through.'

The other boys had gained confidence now and were beginning to move towards him as one. The first bared brown teeth in an evil grin.

'We do not want to tax you,' he said. 'You might easily return with friends for your revenge. We mean to kill you.'

Chapter Sixteen

Willing his heartbeat to slow, Charlie reached into his pocket. His hands closed on a few forged groats.

'I have here five guineas,' he lied, 'one for each of you.'

The boy with the brown teeth hefted his timber, considering.

Charlie loosened his grip on the slum boy's neck and set his feet. 'Here,' he said, 'you may have them if you can find them.'

And in a clean movement he released his prisoner and threw the coins towards the nearest house. They hit the canvas wall and fell to the ground.

The sound of the money had an electric effect on the boys. They sprinted headlong in the direction of the coins, pushing and grabbing at one another as they ran in an attempt to reach them first.

Charlie had already broken away, pounding along the dirt tracks of the slum, focusing on the fastest means of escape.

But all too quickly he heard the sound of the boys behind him. They had regrouped and were in hot pursuit. And though Charlie was fast, his knowledge of the labyrinthine slums was no match for the slum dwellers.

He turned sharply into a little encampment and found himself surrounded.

The boys circled him, several still with their weapons.

'It was a bad trick for that was only groats you threw,' said the boy with the brown teeth, wiping a line of blood from his nose where he'd fought with another boy to reach the cash.

'And you will pay for it.'

He eyed the lump of wood in his hand with a smirk.

The boys inched forward, each waiting for the other to strike the first blow. And Charlie readied himself for the attack.

Out of the corner of his eye, he made out a red plague cross, painted clumsily onto a nearby shack. If he could get close enough, he could pull down the nearest wall. It was a long shot, but the threat of plague might be enough to scare the boys away.

A blow came unexpectedly from behind, and Charlie fell sprawling into the dirt. He felt the hands reach inside his coat and pull out the forged Health Certificates.

'We can sell these,' he heard a voice say. 'Take his clothes next.'

In a last, desperate move, Charlie twisted his body towards the plague shack and grabbed at the makeshift wall.

He felt hands grab at his clothes, and he tightened his grip and pulled. He heard hessian tear. And then suddenly, like magic, the assault on his person stopped.

There was a low moaning sound and it took Charlie a moment to see his assailants had frozen in horror.

He risked a glance up in the direction of the noise. His plan to reveal the plague house had worked better than he could have hoped.

The plague shack was now open at the front, where one of the driftwood walls had fallen down.

And inside was the horrendous sight of a dying man.

Charlie and the boys stared.

The man squatted naked inside the broken slum house and beside him was a rail-thin woman, wearing the blue sash of a municipal nurse. Her patient was gripping the rusting end of a sheep-trough to hold himself upright, and every breath he took was a laboured groan. Dark red marks peppered his legs and black veins branched from his collar to his cheeks.

Charlie froze. Fear swarmed so thick and fast that his ears rang with it. He was only a few feet away from a plague carrier.

The slum boys scattered.

'Let him some dignity,' said the nurse, tossing a filthy string of hair from her face as she spoke. 'Do not stare.' She moved on limbs no thicker than broom handles and her withered face drew her lips up over a single tooth.

A terrible screaming howl went up from the man.

'It is the insides coming out,' explained the nurse. 'That often happens. The pain of the illness does it.' She stepped outside the exposed confines and started trying to heave up some fallen driftwood to form a partition between the dying man and the outside world. 'Help me then,' she said.

Charlie knew he should run away, but he couldn't bear to leave the man exposed and ashamed.

Rising painfully to his feet he pulled at the driftwood, keeping as far back from the victim as he could.

'Why has he no family with him?' Charlie managed, pulling his coat collar to cover his mouth.

'Ran away,' said the nurse, grunting with the effort of restoring the home. 'They talk very brave in the beginning, but when they see the agony of the disease they do not stay.'

'Why should you stay when you have seen such things?'

'What should I eat without my shilling payment? Them that run have places to go to. I have nothing. I take this work or starve.'

They righted the driftwood. The last glimpse Charlie caught of the man was of him panting, dog-like, his mouth a ragged red hole of agony. He began to make a chirruping insect noise.

'Like he has another day of torture,' said the nurse, shaking her head. 'If they live the first hour their body is fighting it and they must suffer as no human creature should. He has still to have the swellings raise so high on his neck they split the flesh. That is when he will beg me to finish him.'

Not knowing what else to do Charlie pulled out his bag of forged coins. The boys had taken his certificates and they were all he had left.

Charlie placed it in her skeletal fingers.

'Buy him something,' he said. 'A draft of gin. A glass of wine. Something to dull the pain.'

The nurse nodded silently at the gesture and disappeared back in the house. And with his brain in a tumult of horrors, Charlie made fast towards the edge of the slum.

Money he could easily get by without. But he had no Health Certificate. Which meant there was almost nowhere in the city he easily get to. Not to mention he was a wanted man with Newgate guards and vigilantes on his trail.

He mentally mapped the route to Moor Fields. If he kept close by the Fleet River he could get north with no health checks. It would take much longer, but once he was in the country fields of Clerkenwell there would be no guards or trackers. He could at least make his way round to Moor Fields, where Rowan worked, in relative safety.

He sent up a silent prayer that his brother would still be there and set off towards the Fleet River.

Chapter Seventeen

Antoinette's friend Sophie knocked cautiously at the door. Hearing nothing she pushed and was surprised to find it nudge easily open.

Sophie sometimes worked at Adders Club. And the furious owner had sent her to discover why Antoinette was absent from work.

'Antoinette?'

A little stab of fear shot through her. If her friend had been burgled the men might still be in the house.

'Antoinette?'

Sophie moved up the stairs. All about were black feathers. She paused to pick one up. It was bloodied, she realised, dropping it in horror.

The feather floated downwards. Blood was all over the stair. She was standing in it.

Drawing her feet back in alarm Sophie cast about for the source. Her eyes settled on a sad feathered lump at the entrance to the bedroom. She swallowed. A dead raven had been mangled to a sad pulp.

Sophie felt her stomach turn. Antoinette had told her that her keeper was a man of bizarre tastes.

She had a powerful urge to turn and run. But the idea of explaining her behaviour to Mr Adders pushed her forward.

Sophie stepped slowly up, over the dead bird and into the room.

A single candle was guttering to an end. The final sizzle of wax gave out a thin and narrow light.

Antoinette's bedroom dipped in and out of shadow.

Sophie noticed in the flickering candlelight that her friend's new red dress was hanging from the top of the four poster bed.

The flame flickered, spat and went out, leaving the room in darkness.

Sophie started. For a split second she had seen a ghostly face, its eyes glued shut with tears of blood.

She shuddered and shook herself. Too many Civil War ghosts, she told herself, drawing her tinderbox with a shaking hand. They were all the old Londoners talked about and soon she would be just the same.

Sophie fumbled in the dark for a fresh candle from the supply she knew was kept on dresser.

The tinderbox flared.

Antoinette's face blazed into view.

Sophie's first sound came out choking, barely audible. Then she opened her mouth and screamed louder than all the tolling dead bells in the city.

In the shadowing candlelight Antoinette's body swung back and forth, her bloody feathers fluttering in the evening breeze.

Chapter Eighteen

Blackstone regarded the outside of the building.

Apart from a discreet sign announcing 'Adders Gaming Club', it looked like any other wealthy residence.

'Looks ordinary does it not?' said the Mayor, echoing his thoughts. 'Who would guess at the world of sin behind this smart door? Still we are here to shut 'em down and that's the main thing.'

'You are certain,' said Blackstone carefully, 'you wish to attend this business in person?'

Mayor Lawrence shot him a sharp look.

'I mean to say,' countered Blackstone quickly. 'You have so many important duties to attend to.'

'None more important than stamping out vice Mr Blackstone,' said Lawrence pompously. 'You must be guided by my great knowledge of these delicate situations.'

Blackstone said nothing. Lawrence's motives were pitifully transparent. He had decided to accompany his aide only after discovering the kind of girls Adders Club employed.

Mayor Lawrence brushed an uncomfortable hand over the red curls of his head.

'It is a pity we had to burn the wigs,' he murmured. 'I should have liked to make this business properly attired.'

'Better to go bare-headed than plague-ridden,' Blackstone assured him. 'I am sure if Mr Adders has any sense he will have done likewise.'

Lawrence grunted in response and knocked on the door self-importantly.

To their surprise it was not a servant but William Adders himself who opened the door of the club to them.

The gambling den master was dressed in his usual immaculate suit of a gold-stitched waistcoat and deep-burgundy frock coat. A froth of snow-white silk gathered in tumbling folds at his neck.

William Adders ran the city's most exclusive and notorious gambling club. It had been founded last year by a group of fantastically wealthy noblemen. And the club permitted entry only to London's most dedicated high-rollers.

'My Lord Mayor,' Adders bowed very low. 'And Mr Blackstone. Please forgive my bare hair. We burned all the wigs only yesterday.'

He tipped his hand just a fraction, towards his brown curly hair, which was neatly combed, but minus its usual stricture of a wig. Without the dark curls he looked younger, and his features were even more fox-like.

Lawrence made a poor job of concealing his delight.

'The most sensible men go bare-headed,' he assured Adders. 'I hope also you consigned your quill pens to the bonfire. For feathers too may hide distemper.'

'Indeed,' agreed William. 'Even my fine feather bed was sent to the pyre.'

He eyed the two men for a moment.

'Please,' he added. 'Follow me. It is better we speak inside.' And he turned gracefully on the perfect heel of his leather shoe.

Neither man had expected to be led inside the club, and Blackstone half thought the Mayor would refuse to go in. But it seemed Lawrence was as curious as he to see inside the notorious gambling club.

'I assume you are here because of Antoinette's murder,' continued William. 'News travels fast. I only just heard of it myself.'

Blackstone and Lawrence looked at each other. They had no idea what he was talking about.

Though Blackstone knew the girl he was referring to, and a cold chill swept through him. As a man of the city he knew and liked Antoinette. She was a kept mistress and occasional prostitute when the price was right.

With plague bodies mounting up they had enough terrible things to contend with. The current rumour was that the nurses hired by City Hall were murdering the plague sufferers they should be caring for and robbing the corpses.

They followed William as he led them through a hallway lined with dishes of marzipan fruits and colourful meringues.

Beneath their feet the floor was marble, Blackstone noticed. One square foot alone would have been enough to pay for three new plague pits.

The hallway opened into the dazzling light of a magnificent room. More chandeliers than Blackstone had seen in his entire life were burning as one. He calculated the City Hall annual candle bill would not be enough to fill a single round of so many glittering crystal holders.

Huge curtains of heavy silk covered the large windows, giving the room a night-time feel, despite it being a hot summer's afternoon.

Blackstone took in the sweep of artfully arranged walnut tables laid out in the enormous room. They were sized varyingly to

C.S. Quinn

accommodate different groups of gamblers, with the plush seats of the largest running to forty.

Each table had its own thick candles and a leather-bound book for logging bets. Adders was arranged on credit, Blackstone assumed. That was the thing with aristocrats. Their name was all they needed.

Today, only one group of gamblers was evident. Five men, each wearing a frock coat with silk enough to buy and sell Blackstone several times over, looking weary.

Servants fluttered around the gamblers like birds, trimming wicks and pouring wine.

'Please sit.' William gestured them to be seated on a sumptuous velvet coach at the edge of the room. A cherub-faced girl in a low-cut dress placed wine glasses and a china plate of confections on the table in front of them.

'Our wine is imported from Champagne,' said William, as the girl poured three glasses. 'And we have these chestnut biscuits made by the King's own patisserie. You'll find the two complement each other perfectly.'

Mayor Lawrence took a sip of wine and a clumsy mouthful of crumbling biscuit.

His eyes roamed the room, searching for the girls which Adders was famed for. Finding none he swallowed disappointedly and coughed, signalling it was time for business.

'We are here to demand that you close your doors,' he said. 'With plague so high we must shut down establishments where men mix in great numbers.'

William's brow crumpled in puzzlement.

'Surely you have heard?' he asked incredulously. 'One of my best girls has been found murdered.'

'No,' said Mayor Lawrence, choosing to bluster rather than admit his ignorance. 'The City Hall is not here to help with your

98

domestic troubles. We have come to ensure you present no danger of spreading plague.'

William raised a sad eyebrow. 'If that is all your business then the thing is already done,' he said. 'Most of our customers have fled to their country houses. We already plan to close.'

Mayor Lawrence nodded as though he had forced the decision himself.

'See that you do,' he said, unable to resist issuing an order. And he began heaving himself up from the couch.

'Wait.' Blackstone couldn't help himself. He had liked Antoinette. 'What is the situation with your murdered girl?'

William sighed. 'She was one of our best,' he said. 'Another girl found her dead. She had been strung up by a rosary, and her guts were cut out. I assume it was some reference to my being a Catholic.'

Blackstone considered this. He hadn't known Adders was Catholic. Certainly the gambling master hid his religion well. Catholics were very unpopular, since the last King had been executed.

'And the monster had branded her with some symbol,' added William.

Mayor Lawrence froze.

'What kind of symbol?'

William drew out a piece of paper. 'I had it drawn,' he said, 'so I might better find her killer. For believe it when I find him he will suffer.'

He unfolded the page to reveal a crown with a loop of knots underneath.

Lawrence snatched it. 'You are quite sure?' he said. 'This was found on the body?'

Adders nodded. 'Burned into her flesh,' he said. 'I assume the deed was a message from a rival club. I am yet to discover what they mean by the symbol.'

Lawrence was opening and shutting his mouth like a fish.

'There was another girl killed with the same mark on her. We think the crime involves a local thief taker, by the name of Charlie Tuesday.'

Now it was William's turn to gape. 'You are quite sure?'

'We have the King's authority to hunt him,' said Lawrence. 'The man carries on him a key with the branded symbol at the head.'

'Has he been arrested?'

'He has evaded capture. We have put guards and a few vigilantes to the task and expect to find him soon.'

William was shaking his head. 'Guards? In a plague city? If this man is a thief taker he will run rings around them.' He thought for a moment. 'I will send my men to find him.'

Blackstone swallowed, thinking of the kind of men who were employed as William's security. The men had been employed as torturers by Cromwell.

'Perhaps we are best leaving things to the guards,' he said.

'My girls are important to business,' said William. 'Our policy is to put down hard anyone who would hurt them. What do you know of this thief taker?'

'We have gathered what we could from our informants in the City,' said Lawrence. 'Blackstone personally visited the Foundling Hospital where the man was orphaned.'

Lawrence glanced at Blackstone to confirm he had permission to relay his findings.

'He was raised by nuns,' said Blackstone. 'Most spoke of him as a good and gentle boy.'

'But one nun saw his true nature,' interrupted Lawrence, 'A lady by the name of Sister Agnes confirmed that he had consorted with whores from a young age. She thinks it likely twisted him. All that beauty paraded before him, but his lowly wage ensuring he might never enjoy it. We also know that his wife left him earlier this year to become an actress. Perhaps that was what finally charged his mind to revenge against women.'

'He is an orphan then?' asked William, quietly assessing.

'He has a brother,' said Lawrence. 'Both boys were committed as foundlings. Something strange in them,' he added. 'The nuns say both the boys could speak fluent Dutch when they were taken in.' He nodded as though the curiosity were a vital clue to the thief taker's deadly nature.

'Where was his brother seen last?

Lawrence shrugged. 'The brother is a petty criminal of sorts. He was last seen selling quack cures near Moor Fields.'

'And the brother has been questioned strongly?'

Lawrence shook his head. 'Our work is not to find murderers Mr Adders. 'At present all of our resources go to finding men and women willing to work as nurses and gravediggers. Most of those mad enough to take the first shift have died. And you can well imagine the type of person who will risk a plague death for a shilling a week. The city is staffed by desperate criminals, and we run short even of those. As their employers and their undertakers our work is constant,' he added.

'Then there is talk of the King leaving town,' Lawrence was on a roll now. 'If Charles deserts us the people will panic, and the streets will turn to anarchy.'

Blackstone thought of the King recognising the strange symbol. Now another girl had been murdered. Perhaps he should share his thoughts with the Mayor.

William nodded. Then he knocked on the table with the palm of his hand. Almost instantly an impossibly beautiful girl appeared.

Blackstone's eyes slid to the Mayor. Lawrence's tongue had crept out of the corner of his mouth, and he was staring unapologetically at the full breasts pressed upwards from the girl's tight dress.

'Have Jack and Robert come up with two chests from the store-room,' said William. The girl nodded and then vanished in a waft of rosewater perfume.

'I will see to it that the brother is questioned,' said William. 'If he knows where this thief taker is then it will be found out.'

Two men arrived, each dragging with them a heavy chest.

They wore the Adders livery, but it strained against their bulk. Blackstone recognised the cruel features of both men from Cromwell's prison.

They men stopped by William, leaving the chests in front of him.

The gambling master leaned forward and flung them both open.

Both were filled to the brim with pure gold coin.

Mayor Lawrence leaned forward. It was a great deal more money than either official would earn in their entire lives.

'One of these chests shall go to your recruitment of watchers and nurses,' said William. 'And the other shall go to finding out this Charlie Tuesday. And believe it gentlemen, he shall be questioned to the utmost of my men's powers.'

Chapter Nineteen

Charlie passed from dense streets to the wide expanse of Moor Fields. In the cloying summer heat the green moors had turned to yellow hay.

This was where London's laundry women usually laboured away in the sweltering sun, manhandling cumbersome water butts and pounding clothing.

But since wealthy households had left London the fields were now mostly filled with a carnival influx of stands and handwritten banners.

Chemists, apothecaries and quack doctors had crowded in with their pitches and were vying enthusiastically to sell plague cures.

Charlie caught sight of his brother. Rowan was barefoot but wearing a battered tricorn hat and standing by his own small stall of remedies.

As he drew closer he heard his brother's familiar voice shouting out a sales patter.

'Good people! The plague is one of the easiest diseases in the world to be cured. Take this physic within four hours of the first invasion and it will drive out the distemper before it can take a hold!'

The key had always separated them, even as boys. And sometimes Charlie thought that the resentment struck deeper than he realised. Rowan had always preferred to wallow in his abandonment rather than make a real attempt at fending for himself. He oscillated from tavern to money-making scheme, borrowing cash from whoever would lend it and bleeding dry any woman unfortunate enough to fall for his charm.

Rowan was similar in appearance to Charlie, with the large brown eyes, rounded nose and dark eyebrows which tapered expressively around the full arch of his sockets. But his dense hair sprang chestnut brown rather than dark blonde. He had not shaved the thick crop but let it grow long to conceal where he'd lost an ear in a knife attack.

Charlie had for a time covered his own dusty-blonde hair beneath a wide-brimmed hat, which he'd found only slightly damaged in a gutter. He fancied the headgear had given his soulful eyes a gentlemanly quality. But the headgear attracted fleas and he preferred going bare-headed than itchy.

'Charlie!' Rowan hopped down from his little stand.

Charlie smiled slightly as his brother slapped his shoulder.

'I'm in trouble,' admitted Charlie, speaking in Dutch, the code language they had used since they were children.

Understanding immediately, Rowan gestured they should step back from the main drag.

'I heard you and Lynette have parted ways,' he said, as they moved away from the crowds.

Charlie nodded.

'She'll come back for you and fool you again,' said his brother. 'Once a whore always a whore.' Charlie flinched. Rowan and Lynette had always hated each other.

'It is not Lynette that is the trouble,' said Charlie continuing to speak in Dutch, though they were now out of earshot.

He quickly outlined his status as a wanted man.

'So it is finally you who comes for my help,' said Rowan with a little smile.

Charlie nodded. 'I have no Health Certificate, and I need to move around the city to gather information.'

'I would give you the one you gave me, but I sold it last week,' admitted Rowan with a shrug. Then catching his brother's expression he added, 'You need not fear for me. This a good place for selling. People come from all over London for remedies, and the laundry women are always looking for fresh piss no matter how slow their trade is. That one pays me a groat a day to fill her barrel.'

He gestured with the cone of paper he held for the purposes of broadcasting a sales pitch to the wider audience of Moor Fields.

Charlie glanced back towards his brother's little stand. Selling quack cures to those dying from plague was dangerous. He felt the usual fear rise up, that he would one day find his older brother imprisoned or beaten to a pulp.

Rowan thought for a moment. 'You should think about fleeing the city,' he said. 'The villages outside the city fear Londoners will bring plague. Vigilantes have begun rising up to block passage. If you wait much longer you could find it is impossible to get out at all.'

'I want to solve this crime and prove I am no murderer,' said Charlie. 'I have a good lead on the villain. But there is not much time. I think he means to kill again. And soon.'

Rowan scratched his chin. 'What do you know of this man?'

'He is a plague doctor Rowan. And if my guess is right he may be carrying a caged bird – a raven. I can hardly think of anything more conspicuous. If I ask the right people he should be easy to find.'

His brother shrugged at the truth of this.

'But I need to find him soon,' added Charlie. 'Or he will kill again, and the clue will be lost.'

'How could you get information Charlie? You say you are wanted.'

'I was hoping you might find it out for me,' admitted Charlie.

'Are there other clues?' asked Rowan, reluctantly.

'I could likely have traced the brand to the blacksmiths, but they are all fled.'

Rowan was shaking his head.

'Not all the blacksmiths Charlie.'

'What do you mean?'

But Rowan twitched suddenly, staring into the middle distance.

'That is the signal,' he muttered.

Charlie groaned inwardly. Rowan was always in some kind of trouble. Though at least he took precautions. Spanning his daily operations were an orbiting cloud of street boys and informants, who reported any approaching danger.

'Come with me,' Rowan began dragging Charlie away from the little stand and back towards the hedgerow.

'There are a few people in the city who think I owe them money,' he explained, 'Best we get out of sight.'

Chapter Twenty

Charlie and Rowan lay concealed behind a large row of lavender bushes towards the back of Moor Fields.

'Rich folk pay extra to have their clothes dried on these,' explained Rowan. 'They make perfect hiding places. For we can see out through the branches, but with the sun in front none can see us.'

'Which men are looking for you Rowan?'

'You do not need to worry Charlie. I will soon pay them off.'

A tiny boy, around seven years old, ducked into the bushes with them.

'He has the sharpest eyes of them all,' said Rowan proudly, slipping the boy a coin.

The boy mumbled something. Charlie strained to hear.

Rowan turned to face him. 'You must find this villain with the bird before he kills again?' he asked.

Charlie nodded.

'Then things have turned worse for you. For he has already struck.'

'There has been another murder?'

Charlie felt a twist of despair. He had been sure the murderer would at least wait until sunrise.

'The boy says there are men from Adders Club, here about one of their girls who was killed. A girl named Antoinette. She was stuck with feathers and branded with the symbol same as the first. Some dreadful thing was done to her head, but the boy knows not what.'

Rowan put his hand on his brother's shoulder.

'I am sorry Charlie. It seems you would be best to flee the city. Those men are here to question me about your whereabouts. Rest assured they will never find me out to do so. But if Adders sent them he will not rest until they find you.'

Charlie closed his eyes, feeling a pang of terrible guilt. Another girl murdered.

'Listen Charlie,' added Rowan. 'This might not be such bad fortune. There is talk that the King might flee the City. If he does all will be chaos. There will be no order at all. Likely you can wait it out in the country for a few months, and this business will be forgotten.'

A surge of anger shot through him. He was determined to bring this man to justice.

Charlie addressed the facts as they now lay. Based on this recent killing the man was an inexperienced witch. Or a poor one. From Charlie's understanding, observing the right conditions for a spell was important.

Perhaps something had happened to force the murderer to move more quickly than he'd have liked.

And what of his choice of victims? Antoinette and Maria's sister. A prostitute and a middling sort of woman. Did they have something in common?

He turned it in his mind.

Earth and air. North and East. South would be next. Fire.

Charlie pushed away the creeping despair. Air had been his best clue. If the murderer meant to use fire there were tinderboxes and candles and fireplaces everywhere in the City. He could think of no clear way to track him that way.

The he remembered Rowan's remark about the blacksmiths.

'Why do you say there are still blacksmiths in the city?' Charlie asked, clinging to this fresh hope.

'Some of the blacksmiths work in naval contracts,' said his brother. 'It is treason for them to leave the city. I would bet my purse a few work at Thames Street still – unless they are all dead of the plague.'

'How do you know?'

'I lived at Thames Street for a month or so,' said Rowan. 'When I was with the shrimp-seller girl.' He smiled at the memory. 'It was a pity it turned sour,' he added.

Charlie thought about this new information.

'A naval blacksmith might not know anything,' he said. 'The blacksmith who made that brand did intricate work – not anchors and ship nails.'

'Those fine blacksmiths would have long fled or died,' said Rowan.

'Yet it is the best clue I have,' said Charlie. 'Perhaps I will have a little luck, and a naval blacksmith will know something. It is worth going to Thames Street,' he decided. He would need to plot a careful route, away from the checkpoints.

'You cannot get in,' said Rowan. 'Thames Street is closed. By royal decree.'

'I have heard.' Charlie peered carefully out through the bushes. He recognised the two Adders men, making their way slowly around the stalls.

'Then you have not heard it told strong enough,' Rowan was saying. 'It is death to go there. The district is gripped in infection so foul that not even dead-carts go there. I spoke to a searcher only today who refuses to do his duty in the area. He told me of dreadful sights. Suicides. Stinking corpses stacked by the roadways.'

Charlie's fingers moved to the key on his neck.

'I think this crime could tell us something of our mother,' he said, his eyes pleading.

Rowan's face instantly shut down. He had never quite forgiven Charlie for having the key.

'Why should you want to do that?' His brother's eyes had already veiled themselves.

Charlie shrugged helplessly as he watched the wall between them descend. They'd had the same conversation in different ways a hundred times. 'I just . . . I just would like to find her that is all,' he said. 'To know her.'

'Nothing to know,' said Rowan shortly. 'Likely she found some maid's work and left us to hang. Or took up with some rich man and we were a burden to her new ways. I would she is dead now of disease. If you wish to go to Thames Street and chance your life for such a woman then good luck to you.'

'What of the lady-in-the-hidden-room?' pressed Charlie. 'Would you not know more of her?'

The lady-in-the-hidden-room was the single pre-orphaned memory on which Charlie and Rowan both agreed. The boys had often been in a large house, or something like it. Charlie had a shifting, uncertain picture of a big stairwell.

Somewhere in the house Rowan had found a lady, secreted away in a dark chamber. Not a prisoner, but sad and frightened. They had visited her. Maybe many times. She had been kind to them.

'The lady is a lovely mystery,' admitted Rowan, 'but I like to keep her like that. I have so few memories I would not risk tainting them with the cold facts of truth.'

Rowan paused for a moment, his voice softening. 'It is most dangerous Charlie. Watchmen have been hired to guard Thames

Street. Even if you manage to get inside, if they catch you they will imprison you in the nearest house for six weeks – if you do not die of plague first.'

Rowan sighed, seeing his brother resolved. 'Wouldst you have me go along with you?'

Charlie smiled. In his perpetual annoyance with Rowan he often forgot his brother's loyalty.

'There is no reason for both of us to risk our health. Point me out some good protection instead,' he added, trying to sound braver than he felt.

The men from Adders' club had headed away now. Their receding figures were moving in the direction of Bishops Gate.

Rowan pointed across the tumult of sellers. 'Him over there. The chewing tobacco. It is the real thing he sells, but will soon run dry and he means to leave town today, so go quickly.' He rummaged in his purse and pushed a few coins into Charlie's hand. 'Or the husband and wife to the back of the field sell very good Venice Treacle. Strong. You can smell it from over here when the wind is right.'

'What is in the Treacle?' Charlie was intrigued. He had only heard of plague water sold.

'Viper flesh, opium. They put iron filings in it also.' Rowan began to tick the ingredients off on his fingers. 'It is sold for a shilling, but that is cheap if it keeps your life in your body.'

Chapter Twenty-One

The last time Charlie had walked along Thames Street it had been a hive of industry. Thick-skinned blacksmiths sweated over their fires, throwing out so many sparks that horses had to be blinkered. But today was eerily silence. Everything was locked, boarded and deserted.

A hastily erected barricade was made of a rope and hessian sacks. On one of them was scrawled: *Lord Save Us.*

The blacksmiths had expanded their trade from the back alleys of Blacksmith Lane to Thames Street during the Civil War. Large forges made pikestaffs and anchors, and smaller works were hammered out in the alleys alongside.

Between the forges were half-timbered houses in various states of disrepair. They ran back into greater disarray in a labyrinth of grim alleys, punctuated by mouldering lock-ups.

Now the only people were hired watchmen, ensuring no one went in and no one got out.

Charlie took careful stock of the building frontages. Though Thames Street's half-timbered residences all looked to be domestic, some were stables, with haylofts which provided easy access to the streets behind.

The watchmen had been recruited from poorer districts, and Charlie doubted they knew the difference between a stable and a house.

He watched the men on duty for a few minutes. He was right. Several of the stable fronts were out of eye-line. All he need do was climb up into the hayloft above and drop down into the warren of alleys beyond.

Flattening himself against the nearest building he cut a quick and silent path across the building shadows.

Then he hauled himself up using the blackened half timbers of the building and slid into the hayloft at the top.

A watchmen strode past on the street below, and Charlie tucked himself quickly out of sight, in amongst the piles of straw.

Once assured the danger had passed, he slipped carefully out the other side and landed in a dark alleyway.

Charlie paused to gain his bearings. A disused forge and a boarded up house. Everything was smaller than he remembered.

His eyes adjusted to the gloom, and he caught his breath. Red crosses ran like a rash across all the little doorways.

Charlie tore off a thick strip of his only shirt and wrapped it so tight around his head that his nose was pushed flat. He took a tight breath, staring ahead at the empty street. Then he pulled up his collar, twisted his head into it and stepped quickly into the grimy backstreets.

The houses behind Thames Street were built with overhangs, closing alleys below into gloom. Ordinarily urchins offered flaming litter for a groat. Whilst soup-sellers added light from woodstoves.

Today not a soul was in sight. All ahead was black.

And then from deep in the tangle of dark alleys came a long moan.

Charlie's heart picked up to a drummer's pace. The darkness would make navigation difficult. He'd been in the district a handful of times but always paid one of the barefoot children to lead him.

He crossed himself, raised the key to his lips and made a fervent prayer. Then he closed his eyes briefly, pushed his head further into his collar and pitched forward into the dark alleyway in a run.

The fetid gloom coiled around him. With nothing and no one to light the way the putrid odours of the alley took on an extra dimension. He was moving in a shambling half-jog, arms tight against his body, breathing shallow in his terror. But the hot weather had dried out the mud road into jagged ruts. He staggered, crashed into the nearest wall and frantically brushed at the dust where his shoulder had touched.

Another low agonised howl of anguish went up suddenly, echoing like a siren along the forsaken alley. For a moment Charlie was a lump of pounding heart and pulse of static brain. Then his stomach took on its own thudding beat.

As he tracked deeper the ground became soft again and his throat tightened. The streets seemed deserted but the damp earth told a different tale. There must still be people in these houses throwing their refuse onto the street, hidden away in the throes of death. He tried to remember what the alleyway looked like under fire and lamplight and marry it to the changing consistency of sludge beneath him.

Something heaved itself over his feet and jerking in reflex Charlie recognised the winking red eyes of a rat. He kicked it away. The bloated creature lolled, belly exposed before slowly righting itself.

Charlie watched it lope away. He remembered the plague protection he'd brought with him. Groping for the pouch of tobacco he rammed a tight plug into his dry mouth. Then willing his pounding insides to calm he stumbled on.

He turned into the next lane and in the gloom picked out the soft shape of a person. The first he had seen since setting foot in the district. It was a man. A broken figure sitting in a doorway. Charlie froze, and then he recognised the outline of a cloak and hood.

It was a watchman.

The man was sat on the muddy ground, his upper half propped against a doorframe.

A ragged wheezing sound echoed through the alley, to the time of the watchman's rapidly beating chest. He looked injured.

Charlie fed in a cautious extra few strands of tobacco. 'Do you sleep?'

As Charlie crept closer the head turned up. The lower face was swathed in grubby bandages. Two bottomless eyes were the only visible expression.

Charlie was close enough now to pick out a few features. The man had been badly beaten.

A shattered nose was joined by one eye, closed up and shining. Yellowed skin was scattered with deep bruises.

The makeshift face mask was soaked with a black stain. It was through his own blood that the man issued his rattling gasps. He must have been attacked, Charlie realised.

He paused for a moment. Watchmen usually worked in pairs to protect each other. His second must be nearby.

'Could I bring help?' asked Charlie, risking a few steps closer.

The man shook his head.

Charlie dropped to his haunches so as to be level with the cowed shape.

'Does your other man come?'

Again the watchman shook his head. 'He died. Few days ago.'

'Do you guard a household in there?' Charlie gestured to the doorway on which the watchman lounged.

'They escaped.'

It was a young voice which didn't match the heavy hood. 'Broke my face and arm both.' The watchmen took in a shuddering breath. 'But I shall wait here until the relief comes, and with some luck I shall still have my shilling.'

Charlie looked into the depths of the alley, wondering if the escapees were still roaming around.

'I am in search of a man,' he said, 'a criminal. Dressed as a plague doctor. He has murdered innocent girls, and I seek information to find him out.'

'You had better get off these streets, unless you want to be shut up,' croaked the watchman, giving no indication he'd understood. 'If they find you they will lock you in one of the houses and leave you to rot.'

Clearly the young guard figured himself long removed from such enforcement duties.

'Do any blacksmiths still work here?' asked Charlie. 'Do any still live?'

The watchman shook his head. 'They are all dead. You should not be here, roaming around,' he said. 'This district is closed. Go back into the city.'

He paused to issue a wheezing cough. 'In the finer parts of town they shoot themselves, those as have the means,' he confided in a whisper. 'But here they throw themselves from the windows. It is a fearful agony that would see a man chance his immortal soul.'

Charlie looked along the dark alley, assessing his next move. Clearly there was no information to be got from this poor watcher. And others could arrive at any moment.

Feeling for the injured man, he reached for his tobacco pouch and pulled out a generous handful.

'Here,' he said, kneeling to push it into the man's bloodied fingers. 'Take some tobacco. It will help protect you from the foul air, until they find you.'

The watchman nodded his thanks, and Charlie rose, trying to stop his legs from trembling.

'God save you,' Charlie muttered, wondering what he should do. It looked as though Thames Street was a dead end. And a dangerous one at that.

'Wait.' The watchman was holding the hem of Charlie's naval coat with limp fingers. 'There was a man,' he grunted, 'dressed as a plague doctor. We heard rumours that he visited the torturer's blacksmith.'

Charlie knelt down again quickly.

'What is the torturer's blacksmith?' he asked urgently.

'Hidden.' The watchman coughed again, a disconcertingly liquid sound. 'The blacksmiths are a good sort of men,' he managed. 'None of them think well of the dreadful things that are done to men in the Clink and the Tower. The blacksmith who makes tools for torture hides his identity from the others.'

'And this plague doctor visits him?' Charlie gripped the watchman's hand.

'I do not know for certain,' said the watchman. 'But there has been talk. A devil man. Dressed as a plague doctor. He visits with the torturer's smithy, and they say he carries death with him.'

'Do you know where this torturer's blacksmith may trade?'

The watchman shook his head. 'He was hidden. They say his shop may be in Swan Court.'

Charlie brought his London map to mind. Swan Court was small, but it was rammed full of smithies. Twenty or thirty at least.

'Thank you,' Charlie patted the watchman sincerely and rose to leave.

The watchman grunted. 'If you are fool enough to go there, then you will not last long. Swan Court was one of the first to get plague. It heaves with infection. If this torturer smithy was ever there, he is long since dead.'

Chapter Twenty-Two

Thomas stared out from his plague hood. Through the crystal goggles Thames Street looked even more hellish than he remembered.

The wide through-road was all but abandoned. Besides the little troop of terrified watchmen keeping guard.

He approached the nearest two, taking out his Health Certificate.

They were already moving aside as they recognised the shape of his plague-doctor costume. But a flash of the official certificate meant they fell back all the faster.

Thomas had the highest possible authority to move around the city.

He made his way quickly through the familiar alleyways. It was a route he'd taken countless times before. The blacksmith had sold him torture tools for years.

Thomas made a left, and then he was outside the sealed gate of Swan Court.

Removing a key from his cloak he opened the door carefully and locked it again behind him.

The blacksmith opened his front door warily. The look of caution failed to fall from his face when he recognised Thomas's costume. But he moved aside, gesturing the plague doctor should enter and looked nervously out into the courtyard before closing the door.

'I have come for the last consignment,' said Thomas. 'I trust they are ready for me.'

'Do you have the money?'

Thomas dropped a bag of coins on the table.

The blacksmith pulled back a thin partition which sealed the back of the room. Inside, three small barrels were filled to the brim with the rifle mechanisms.

'There are four hundred snapchances,' said the blacksmith. 'They will fit to the rifle butts you already have.'

Thomas picked one up. The metal snapchance was a little smaller than his hand and curled like a tadpole. At the end was the lever which joined musket with trigger.

'These are good,' he nodded in approval, turning the snapchance. Each had been printed with the sign – the crown with the looping three knots.

'You have wondered at my purpose for having these made?' he asked the blacksmith.

'I have made my trade on not asking questions.'

'I fought in the Civil War for the late dead King,' said Thomas. 'And after we lost the war Cromwell took my lands.'

The blacksmith nodded warily. He'd guessed that Thomas had been one of those cavaliers who had lost to Cromwell's roundheads. But having the information confirmed made him uneasy.

'Now King Charles II sits on the throne,' continued Thomas. 'And you might well think I would receive my dues. My lands back again. Rewards. Instead His Majesty's coward son spends all the Crown money on his mistresses. And he is too frightened of parliament to reward the loyal subjects who fought for his father.'

Thomas held up the snapchance to the light.

'So I mean to make my own justice,' he said. 'And your work has been very helpful in arming those who would follow me.'

The blacksmith gave a little nod, keen now for Thomas to leave.

Too late he saw the sword handle heading for his face. He staggered as the heavy handle connected. His hand shot out, grabbing blindly at a tarpaulin which had been strung into the low eaves to keep out the rain.

The tarpaulin ripped from the ceiling as the second blow twisted his jaw.

———————

The blacksmith came to consciousness to see a gigantic metal bird peering over him. His hands and feet had been bound tightly enough to draw blood, and he was lying on the hard dirt of his own floor. His mouth was stuffed with rags.

The bird's metal beak pulled back. Underneath it was a familiar face.

The blacksmith made a strangled sound through the rags.

'Surely you must have wondered why I came in disguise?' said Thomas. 'I would not have needed to do so if I were a common man.'

He moved to the little doctor's bag he always carried and opened it up. Inside, neatly arranged, was an assortment of bloodied objects. The blacksmith knew with terrible certainty their usage.

'You recognise your own work?' asked Thomas, gesturing to the tools.

The spiral of fear twisted deep in the blacksmith's stomach.

Thomas leaned closer. 'When I first came here, to buy these tools, do you know how I knew what to request?'

The blacksmith shook his head in mute terror.

'I was imprisoned in Wapping,' said Thomas. 'You would shudder to see what brutalities went on, with so many men crammed into the cells.'

He paused for a moment, his eyes selecting a tool from his array.

'I was tortured by Cromwell's men,' he continued, easing a thin set of pincers from the bag. 'That is why I am so adept with these tools.'

He locked eyes with the blacksmith. 'You will soon discover how talented I am,' he added.

On the floor the blacksmith tried to shake his head.

'I need to be sure you haven't told another soul about my visits here,' continued Thomas. He eased open the blood-stained pincers.

'I must be very, very sure,' he said. 'And after I am sure I will be kind and let you die.'

Chapter Twenty-Three

Charlie sent out a heartfelt jumbled prayer and tightened a fist around the key.

Entering a rough-cobbled street he risked quickening his pace in haste to get to Swan Court, breathing hard against the stale sweat of his coat.

Then his foot tripped on something yielding and his face met with a great buzzing swathe of flies. He swatted them back and his eyes dropped down to what he had just stumbled over. Charlie's stomach lurched. It was a corpse.

Picked out in shadows against the dark ground he could make out the face smashed against the cobble. The man had flung himself from the window above and lay with skull splintered and arm twisted under him.

Charlie's head dropped back to the corpse at his feet. He was holding the key so tightly his nails cut bloody crescents into his palms.

Enormous purple swellings bulged at the throat. One of the buboils had burst on impact and a thick mucus rolled forth, mixing with the blood from the cracked skull. The noisome fluid was dappled all over with a black army of flies.

A sudden light went on in a diamond-leaded window in the distance.

Charlie paused, transfixed for a moment. Someone had lit a candle, and the yellow light shone warmly through the glass panes. Then with a terrible slowness he felt strong fingers close around his foot.

It took him a long moment to digest what was happening and then it hit him with full force. The corpse he'd stumbled over was not dead and had tightened its fist on his ankle.

Shouting aloud he made to tug himself free but the grip was solid. A face had lifted up from the floor now and was raised towards him with filmy eyes. With a terrible deliberateness it began to heave itself nearer towards him, leaving a liquid trail as it moved.

Instinctively Charlie ducked down to grab up a loose cobblestone and hammered it with all his strength into the skeletal arm of the corpse. The bony fingers released and he ran headlong along the road and back into the winding dirt alleyways.

He stood for a moment, panting, and realised he had lost sense of where he was. Thoughts of finding the blacksmith had dulled in his panic. For a moment all he cared about was escaping this festering core of horrors and getting back into a safer part of the City. If he escaped this alive, he swore to himself, he would never put himself near a plague district again. And he would go straight, he threw in for good measure. No more forged Health Certificates or counterfeit coin trafficking. Honest thief taking would be his only business.

His mind tumbling with the living corpse he grabbed a fistful of tobacco and jammed it in his mouth. Acrid saliva filled his jaw and his lips shaped themselves in a rigid spasm of nausea. Unable to help himself Charlie bent double and heaved. With shaking fingers he pulled out another tuft of tobacco and pushed it between his dry lips.

Then he heard it. The steady sound of a blacksmith's hammer. Charlie swallowed hard.

Someone was still at work here. They might be able to tell him how he could find the torturer's blacksmith.

Charlie turned towards the dark beyond where the noise was coming from. Then he twisted through an alleyway, back out onto a small street, listened and made another cautious turn.

The hammering grew louder. Gaining confidence Charlie made towards it.

He turned into the alley where the sounds were the loudest and recognised the barrel makers. Swan Court was only a few streets away.

But a working blacksmith would have useful information.

The forge must be in a hidden enclave, thought Charlie, seeing no sparks spurt from the street.

The hammering came louder, and he cast about for the source.

The realisation came all too suddenly. There was no forge on this street. Only a house which had been locked full of plague sufferers.

The noise was an ulcerated hand banging a metal plate across the window casement.

Too late Charlie made the connection. A house with live occupants meant there would be a watchman. And he had walked right into their path.

Charlie's focus snapped to the doorway of the house to see a guard staring back at him. Then another stepped into view.

'Hold!' the first watchman was picking up a vicious-looking cudgel.

But Charlie was already racing towards Swan Court.

Chapter Twenty-Four

The heavy gates of Swan Court were locked, and Charlie could hear the shouts of the watchmen behind him.

Willing himself to keep calm, he slipped out the piece of earring he used for lock-picking.

He slipped the wire earring deftly into the keyhole, eased it up towards where he judged the bolt-hook would be.

Behind him the watchman's feet thudded down on the wet mud.

The catch slipped open.

Charlie caught a final view of the first watchman's outraged face as it barrelled down the alley towards him. Then he was through the door, letting the heavy lock click back down.

Charlie took in the little courtyard as the watchman hammered on the thick door.

Without a key they would have to get some better implement than the cudgels they carried to open it.

He calculated he had less than ten minutes until they returned with reinforcements.

If he was to make this risk worthwhile he needed to identify the torturer's blacksmith, and quickly.

Inside the yard were the blacksmith forges for smaller implements, and their forges were crammed into every available space. But no blacksmiths were at work.

Above each was hung a clustered display of metalwork advertising the skill of the occupant. Everything from fire pokers to metal hinges were strung up to the eaves. Some blacksmiths had a talent for delicate items, with ornate buckles and buttons, thimbles and tinder boxes, whilst others specialised in sturdier keyholes and door handles, fire gratings and gateposts. Behind the dangling displays stood decrepit wooden buildings, each hardly larger than a hut, for the purposes of sleeping. But as far as Charlie could tell the area was deserted of live-in occupants. All the blacksmiths had fled.

He scanned the assortment of empty workstations wondering how on earth he could narrow them down. There seemed to be nothing to suggest one blacksmith made tools for torturers.

Cries echoed around the wider area, and Charlie realised the watchman were trying to find other men to help them bring him in.

Carefully he pushed down his panic at the thought and began making a slow circuit of the forges, taking in the abandoned anvils and ironwork. Whoever supplied London's prisons had made a good job of staying hidden amongst his colleagues.

Charlie twisted his mouth in annoyance. There must have been over forty blacksmiths working here. Even with the courtyard deserted it would take him days to search every residence. He forced himself to think calmly, unwilling to accept the situation was hopeless.

He tried to focus.

Think Charlie. You see things others do not.

There must be something here that the blacksmiths who lived in the area had failed to notice. Some clue a fresh perspective could discern.

Charlie thought carefully. The blacksmith couldn't be working openly on the torture tools. He would easily be seen by his fellows. All the forges were in full view of one another.

A gust of wind swirled into the little space. The location had been designed to make the most of river air for sweltering work. There was a low ringing melody as the collection of hanging metal work chimed in the breeze.

In the waving iron something occurred to him. The suspended metalwork represented the height of each blacksmith's skill or specialty. But what if a blacksmith didn't need to advertise? What if his customers were of the kind whose purchases were paid for generously and in secret?

If that were the case he would have no need to demonstrate the latest heights of his skill by updating his wares. His display might be older than the others.

Where once had been countless blacksmiths Charlie now suddenly only saw one. The dangling metal on display was several shades darker than the surrounding forges. As though it had been a long time hanging without replacement.

Charlie walked towards it and noticed cobwebs and patches of rust were woven in.

His eyes dropped to scan the forge below. It looked ordinary enough. But there was a slight change in colour on the side of it. Barely discernible to the naked eye were scant white markings. He crouched to run his fingers along them.

It was taper wax.

The residue had melted and then cooled in tiny rivulets along the side of the anvil. Charlie tapped it as he considered.

This blacksmith has worked at night. When even the light of the forge is not strong enough to work by. He makes metalwork under cover of darkness.

Then he saw the red cross on the door.

In the distance the relentless tolling of funeral bells sounded out like a warning. A padlock had been nailed to the entry. The blacksmith had been shut up.

Charlie knew now would be the time to leave. He could escape the district, flee the city and hope the murders were forgotten.

Weighing the key in his hand Charlie cast his eye over the exterior of the house. The chimney wasn't smoking, so the occupant was either absent, or incapable of caring for himself.

Before he could change his mind Charlie dropped to his stomach and, covering his mouth, peered through the gap at the bottom.

Inside all was still.

Rising to his knees Charlie studied the padlock which had been fixed to the outside of the door with heavy nails.

He slid in the earring wire, and after a tense moment the padlock fell open. Charlie caught it with his free hand and hung it loosely back so that any returning watchmen might not immediately see which residence he had entered.

The door opened easily and Charlie stopped to check the security of his mouth covering. Then he waited in the doorway, listening for any sound inside.

His heart stopped for a moment. A crashing noise was coming from the room. As though a huge wild bird were caught inside.

Then he saw the source. A tarpaulin which had once lined the roof flapped free. In the breeze it slapped loudly against the wall and floor.

Inching slowly into the house Charlie took stock.

Inside the windowless wooden walls it was mostly dark.

He tied off the tarpaulin so as to better hear any occupant.

Then Charlie paused again, ears straining.

Silence. The room was empty.

He stepped further into the dark, floor creaking beneath him. *Wooden floorboards, an expensive choice for a poor blacksmith.* There was a real bed too, with a frame of netted ropes. He could just make out that papers were strewn about the floor and a barrel of half finished iron-work upended. It looked as though someone had been here before him.

The residence had been ransacked.

A sour smell washed over him. A smell of dead things.

In the gloom he could make out a hanging brace of pigeons under the chimney. It smelled as though the meat had begun to turn in the thick summer heat.

He knelt at the upended barrel and picked up one of the metal objects from the floor. It was a snapchance – the firing mechanism for a musket.

Charlie sat back on his heels to consider. The floor was strewn with them. Fifty at least. Far more than any domestic purpose might need.

So this blacksmith was making weapons.

Charlie thought about this. Close to the overturned barrel he could make out damp rings on the wood floor where other containers had been sat. He made a quick calculation. Three barrels. Four hundred snapchances. Four hundred muskets.

The blacksmith had made enough to equip an army.

He let his thumb travel over the snapchance and it picked out a familiar shape.

Burned into the soft metal on the underside was a symbol he recognised. It was a crown, over a loop of knots.

Charlie held the snapchance to his arm, considering its size against the image he held of Maria's dead sister.

One of these snapchances had been used to brand the body. He was sure of it.

Charlie turned the possibility in his mind along with the musket part.

Then against the soft tolling of the death bells his ears suddenly picked out a different sound. A noise like someone close-by.

A dog or cat, he reasoned. Then it came again. Louder this time. Too loud for a creeping animal.

Before he could make a decision to hide the door creaked open behind him and a pallid face swung suddenly into view. Silhouetted against the frame the figure held aloft an iron bar. It inched through the doorway with an assassin's assurance.

'Tell me what you know,' demanded a muffled voice. 'Or I shall stove in your skull.'

Chapter Twenty-Five

Blackstone and the Mayor were ushered into a low room which smelt of unwashed bodies.

Inside, lit by the smoky light of a whale-oil lamp, Amesbury was laid almost horizontal on a chaise lounge. The soldier of fortune had his great brown leather boots stacked in front of him. And he wore his usual heavy army cloak – lest anyone forget his military brilliance.

Amesbury wore his brown hair long and curled like the King, with a dandyish little moustache. His large body he held comfortably, like well-worn armour.

A gaudily-painted woman lay against his shoulder, whilst another dangled grapes towards his mouth, giggling affectedly. His pet monkey skulked about the floor snatching up scraps of grape skin.

Amesbury sat up very slightly as Blackstone and the Mayor entered. The women fell back a little, clinging to him protectively.

The monkey sat up on its haunches as though joining the conversation. No one knew exactly where Amesbury had found the pet. But he'd spent time in the navy and the rumour was he'd won it in a game of Hearts.

'Welcome,' said Amesbury. 'This is a little place I come sometimes. We may talk here privately.'

'It stinks of sin in here,' announced Mayor Lawrence. 'Could you think of no other place we might meet?'

Above them a rhythmic thumping started up. The two women smirked at one another.

'I wanted to be sure we were not overheard,' said Amesbury.

As he spoke the door broke open and a half-dressed aristocrat fell into the room. Three laughing girls came rolling after, each in various states of undress.

'You must keep your promise!' said one, attaching herself to his boot. 'The whole barrel or the old madam.' And shrieking with merriment the little group fell back into the room they'd come from.

Keeping his expression neutral Blackstone crossed the room and closed the door they'd fallen through.

The loud laughing and shouting grew slightly quieter.

'Amesbury,' Blackstone bowed only slightly. He did not trust the King's advisor, who had switched sides several times during the Civil War.

'What is it you wished to discuss with us?'

Amesbury shined a buckle on his military cloak with a calloused thumb.

'I hear there has been another witch-murder,' he said.

Blackstone was silent for a moment. He had no idea how Amesbury had gained his information.

Mayor Lawrence made a little huff of annoyance.

He had recently purchased a pair of spectacles from Cheapside and his pallid eyes were horribly magnified behind the scratched round lenses. The leather arms struggled to reach around the bulky face.

'We have put the King's money to find the thief taker,' he said. 'You can be sure he will be found.'

'Can you be sure it was the thief taker you suspect in any case?' asked Amesbury.

Blackstone had always wondered the same thing himself. The country was overrun with religious fanatics since the upheaval of Cromwell's Puritan ways. Many had far greater motive than the thief taker.

'This spell seems to have been made against His Majesty,' continued Amesbury. 'And we know King Charles has many enemies. Many who fought for his father in the Civil War had their lands confiscated and were disappointed when his son did not return them.'

'You were one of those men as I remember,' said Mayor Lawrence.

Amesbury smiled. 'I am hardly concerned with that,' he said. 'I busy myself preventing uprisings. Every day we put down some faction or another.'

'The second murder was made with a rosary,' he continued. 'An implement of Catholic prayer. Is the thief taker Catholic?'

'It doesn't signify,' blustered the Mayor. 'There are hundreds of Catholics in London who keep their faith secret.'

Amesbury considered this. 'Yet Catholics are those who have lost the most,' he observed. 'That would be motive enough, to cast some unholy spell against His Majesty, would it not? Perhaps it would be sensible to widen our net.'

'And do you have any suspects of your own in mind?' asked Mayor Lawrence sarcastically. 'The King's mistress for example? For all the people say Louise Keroulle and her brother are witches.'

At the mention of Louise and her brother, Blackstone noticed something in Amesbury's face shift. Then the expression had passed, and he wondered if he had imagined it.

'The dead girl worked at Adders Gaming House,' he said. 'I have spoken to Mr Adders and am told a new member joined only a few days before her death. A Thomas Malvern.' He paused for a moment.

'Adders is of the impression that Malvern is not their usual sort of member. He had no family estate and was extended no credit. But Malvern had plenty of ready money, and so they were happy to let him bet.'

'That does not sound so suspicious to me,' said Lawrence. 'Surely those clubs will allow any inside, who have the means.'

'Malvern wore a plague doctor habit,' continued Amesbury. 'Which he refused to relinquish, even after Adder's girls requested it. They thought Malvern played a trick to disconcert other gamblers. But the costume, of course, would also hide his face.'

Blackstone and the Mayor waited patiently for Amesbury's train of thought to conclude.

'It seems to me strange that a suspicious kind of character should join the club only a few days before one of their girls is murdered,' he continued. 'I would have you both find out more about this Thomas Malvern. Visit some other gaming houses. See what you might discover.'

Mayor Lawrence had screwed his fat face in indignation. 'We do not have the resources to make these kinds of enquiries.'

Amesbury smiled. 'I would count it as a favour,' he said, his tone making it clear there was no compromise on the issue.

Blackstone bowed. 'It will be done.'

'I have also heard that a witch was released from prison in Wapping last month,' continued Amesbury. 'This would seem worth pursuing.' He raised his hand as the Mayor began to protest.

'This I shall do myself Lawrence. You need not trouble yourself. Save your energies for bringing us the thief taker.'

'Why did this require us to meet secretly?' asked Blackstone. Though he knew the answer. Amesbury did not have the King's permission to be making enquiries.

'It is better not to trouble the King with such things,' said Amesbury dismissively. 'And there is another matter.'

He rang a little bell and a boy-servant came in with a bowl of drinking chocolate. He began whisking it manfully.

'Would you gentlemen care for a little chocolate?' asked Amesbury. 'It is a little affectation I picked up in the colonies.'

The Mayor shook his head vehemently, and Blackstone, though tempted, gave his own shake of decline.

Amesbury picked up the cup, tiny in his calloused soldier hands, and took a draft.

'His Majesty asks that coin counterfeiters be looked to.'

Lawrence gave a gasp of frustration. 'Coin counterfeiters? The city is on the brink of riot. Mobs have come from the country-side and run half mad with terror that Londoners will infect their villages. What does it matter if a few forged groats are spent?'

'I only extend policy from His Majesty,' said Amesbury. 'Counterfeit coins are so widespread they threaten to ruin the economy.'

Blackstone privately doubted that the King had much say in the policy Amesbury circulated.

Amesbury was made for Civil War and political unrest. Armies led by him were virtually indestructible, but he was utterly without loyalty. King Charles had only made him a close advisor in a bid to keep him Royalist.

'There is talk His Majesty might desert the City,' said Blackstone.

'Morality costs money,' shrugged Amesbury, 'and King Charles has very little. Parliament makes sure of it.' His expression was blank, giving no indication he'd advised the King one way or another.

'But how are we to enact any policy without funds?' demanded the Mayor. 'Already we run short of wages for the gravediggers and nurses. We need more fires to clean the air and more pits to bury bodies. How is such a thing to be done?'

Amesbury took out his eating knife and began picking his teeth.

'My great fear gentlemen,' he said. 'Is that they cannot be done.'

Chapter Twenty-Six

'Tell me what you know,' demanded the voice. 'Or I shall stove in your skull.'

The raised iron bar was silhouetted in the blacksmith's doorway.

Several thoughts merged in Charlie's head at once.

'Maria?' he said. 'Is that you?'

The iron bar raised a little higher.

Charlie was so shocked he said the first thing which came into his head.

'You still owe me a guinea,' he said.

The iron bar lowered fractionally, in confusion, and then she rallied.

'What do you know of my sister's murderer?' she demanded, raising it up again.

He eyed the iron bar. 'There is no need for your weapon,' he said. 'I come to clear my name, that is all. Why are you here?'

'The same reason as you. I thought a blacksmith might have made the thing which marked Eva. So I waited and watched for you to arrive on Thames Street. Then I followed you.'

'And did you realise then that you wrongly accused me of your sister's murder?' That I was an innocent man trying to clear my name?'

Maria waved her weapon, stepping closer. Like Charlie she had made a mask of linen to protect her face and kept a hand covering her mouth. She shut the door behind her with a single hand.

'Where did you get the key?' She wielded the weapon menacingly.

'Peace!' Charlie raised his hands. 'It was left to me as a found-ling! I know no more of what the mark means than you.'

Charlie voice rose in exasperation.

'I do not even believe in the power of witches!' he protested. 'I am a rational man. I think those who buy spells and potions are foolish.'

Maria let the weapon fall a little.

'Why do you carry the key?'

Charlie's free hand moved to it defensively. 'It was left to me. That is all. It was the only thing I was found with when I entered the Foundling Hospital.'

Maria seemed thoughtful for a moment, and then her brows knitted in understanding.

'Then you have your own mystery to solve,' she said. 'That is what brings you here. You think to find your mother or something like it.'

'I come to clear my name, that is all. From the wrongs you have done it.'

But Maria seemed to have an unerring ability to know he was dissembling.

'You also must wonder why that key was left to you,' she repeated. 'Do not think me a fool Charlie Thief-Taker. If you only sought to evade capture you could escape whilst plague rages and be easily forgot. You have as much reason as I to find out this man who left the mark.'

She looked suddenly guilty. 'I confess I may have been mistaken for bringing the guards. Though you cannot think too ill of me.

I want to see my sister's murderer brought to justice and I feared you might run before information could be got of you. That is typical of the common sort.'

'And accusing innocent men and trying to have them arrested and tortured, is that the way of the finer sort?' retorted Charlie. 'I have the whole city on my tail Maria! The King himself has sent men to bring me in.'

'It matters not in any case,' said Maria. 'We are here to the same purpose. We might help each other,' she added.

Charlie eyed her suspiciously. The last time they'd met she had tricked him with embarrassing ease.

'Why should I trust you? You might have guards ready to pounce as we speak.'

'No more than I should trust you,' said Maria. 'You bear the mark of a murderer, and your soft-hearted story could be nothing more than a feint.'

They glared at each other.

'I give you my word,' said Maria finally. 'I do not try to trick you. Only to find out my sister's killer.' She stooped to put the iron bar on the floor. 'See?'

Charlie stood for a moment, weighing up the options. He had to concede that it would take two people less time to make a search of the premises than one. And with watchmen headed back anytime soon it seemed sensible to use her help.

'We make a quick search,' he concluded. 'Watchmen saw me come into the court and they will soon return. But after we leave you must promise not to follow me from here.'

Maria gave the tiniest begrudging incline of her head.

'And you must agree to believe me that I am innocent of any murder,' he added.

'I have no choice for now. Though if I find some evidence you have lied to me you shall be sorry for it,' she concluded.

Charlie resisted a retort, returning his attention instead to the task at hand.

'I found something,' he said, pointing. 'That barrel was full of musket firing parts. A hundred at least. And by the looks of things there were many more. And they bear the mark. The same that was made on your sister.'

Maria was silent for a moment.

'Someone making muskets?' she said finally. 'An uprising?'

Charlie nodded. He was impressed. She was more perceptive than he had given her credit for.

'But why should such a man want to harm my sister?'

'I know not. But I thought to make a search,' he answered. 'Though it seems as though someone has been here before us,' he added, looking at the ironwork flung carelessly across the room.

'I have a tinderbox,' said Maria, striking the flint as she spoke, 'and this little candle stump. So we might see better.'

Walking towards the edge of the room she held her candle over the strewn objects. Then Maria stopped suddenly by the bed.

'It is sticky here, underfoot.'

Charlie knew before he reached her.

'Here,' he said, stepping forward and taking the lighted candle from her. 'Let me attend to the looking of this.'

The slick of dried liquid flashed ominous red in the flame and joined a dark shape under the bed. Charlie turned his head up to Maria. Her face had a faraway look about it and her mouth was set downwards.

'Is it the blacksmith?' she whispered.

Charlie nodded.

He inched closer holding his hand steady. Keeping his distance he extended his arm towards the body.

Charlie swallowed as the leather-like skin came into better view.

The blacksmith had been tortured. Part of his lip and nose had been cut away and dark blood blisters were all that remained of his fingernails.

Half his head was missing where a heavy metal hilt had splintered his skull.

'Someone has swung some heavy thing into his head,' said Charlie, straightening up to block Maria's view of the extent of the blacksmith's injuries.

'I think the person who had those rifle parts made wanted to cover his tracks,' he added.

'Might it not have been a simple robbery?' asked Maria.

'No,' said Charlie. 'There are torture marks on him. A burglar would not have done that.'

Maria was silent for a moment, and Charlie regretted telling her the details.

'We should keep looking,' she said. 'The killer might have left some clue.'

'These are likely our best clues,' said Charlie, holding up a snapchance. 'Guards are headed for the house Maria. Better we leave now.'

But as he spoke he spotted something. The pigeons trussed in a row to the fireplace. A single wing of one was lolling free.

The sight roused his thief taker's intuition.

There was something about the injury which did not tally with the way dead birds usually hung.

He walked over to inspect the broken wing.

'Someone has cut a quill for a pen,' he murmured, looking at the neat incision. 'That could hardly have been the blacksmith. A man such as he does not write.'

The feather had been cut adeptly by someone literate enough to carry their own pen knife. An educated man. He logged the fact.

'What of those firing mechanisms you spoke of?' asked Maria, interrupting his thoughts. 'Might they not lead us to him?'

Charlie nodded slowly. 'For muskets he will need gunpowder.'

A man's voice on the street brought their conversation to a standstill.

'Which house is it?'

They both froze.

'That one seems to have its padlock hanging free.'

Charlie glared at Maria.

'You did not put the padlock back!'

'How was I to know you were not clever enough to stay free of the watchmen?' she hissed.

'There is a plague cross on the door!' shouted one of the guards.

Charlie and Maria exchanged glances.

Another voice sounded out from the street.

'Then take a quick look within and we can both be free of this hellish place.'

'I do not mean to take long about it.'

Charlie darted forward and, slipping a quick hand through the door, relocked the padlock.

'He is in there!' came a shout from the street. 'His hand just locked the door!'

There was a heavy sound of metal. Someone at the front door was loosening the padlock.

'Come quick for I should not like to go within alone!' shouted the guard.

Charlie turned quickly towards Maria and back to the door.

'They will be armed and will not stop to question.'

'What can we do?' whispered Maria. 'They will think us plague thieves and arrest us for certain.'

'If they do not kill us first.'

Chapter Twenty-Seven

Amesbury lay on the silken covers of the King's four-poster bed. He had removed his cloak, revealing a soldier's shirt banded around his wide girth, with an orange sash. But his legs, crossed in front of him, were still clad in long leather boots.

The servant had brought him a little breakfast. Some fresh bread, butter and a pint of cream were by the bed. And the first girl had also been ushered in.

Amesbury considered her.

The girl wore a red silk dress which she was slowly inching off her white shoulders. Two dark nipples peaked into view, then the curve of her stomach, a patch of chestnut hair and two shapely thighs as the dress amassed in a pile at her feet.

He waved his hand that she might turn a circle for him.

The girl obliged, keeping her expression seductively angled towards the bed.

Amesbury nodded. The King liked that kind of thing. She might do very well.

'You understand how this would work?' he asked the girl. 'I will pay you a fair salary. And you will ask His Majesty for nothing. No trinkets, no property. Not even if he offers it.'

The girl nodded.

'You will offer no opinion on politics. And you will report to me on his other mistresses,' Amesbury added. 'Tell me what they ask of the King and what he is likely to give.'

She nodded again, but more slowly this time.

'Very good,' said Amesbury. 'Have you had the pox?'

The girl shook her head vehemently.

'Show me.'

For a second the girl hesitated.

'Show me between your legs. I would like to see for myself.'

The girl clambered up onto the bed. Kneeling in front of him, she spread her legs.

'Wider, so I might see.'

She spread them a little further. Amesbury noted several mercury scars, where she had been treated for syphilis.

He shook his head sadly. She had looked so promising.

'You are no good to me if you give the King the pox,' he said. 'I mean to help him keep his country, not to give the man a life of pain.'

He signalled the girl should get up.

'You are a handsome girl and will do very well in the City,' he said, holding out a coin. The girl rewarded him with a wide smile. She folded the money in her palm and climbed off the bed to retrieve her dress from the floor.

She was exiting just as Louise Keroulle, in a rare state of full dress, exploded into the room.

'What are these girls who wait outside in the corridor?' she demanded, fury thickening her French accent.

'Come now Louise,' scolded Amesbury, 'we are neither of us children.'

'You look to find my replacement!' she raged. 'You will not do it. You think I am a spy. But I am not!'

Louise stamped her foot. Then she ripped the tortoise-shell clips from her curling brown hair and launched them at the bed.

Amesbury was on his feet.

'Do not think you might have your tantrums with me as you do with the King.'

At his full height Amesbury still cut an intimidating figure, despite being now over forty.

'How dare you employ whores to turn His Majesty away from me!' returned Louise. But the fight had gone out of her voice.

She stood, for a moment, her bosom heaving in and out of her dress. 'You have no right,' she hissed, 'to treat me this way. It was France who sheltered him in exile. My brother fought for his father.'

'What is happening Louisie?'

Another French accent sounded, and Louise's brother George entered the room. He was only a few years younger than Amesbury and treated Louise more like a daughter than a sister.

George, with his pronounced widow's peak, flamboyantly French gold-embroidered coat and beribboned stockings, came closer.

'He tries to find women, to take the King's heart away,' said Louise, pointing a trembling finger at Amesbury.

'And why should I not?' retorted Amesbury, his temper rising. 'Do you have any idea, you foolish girl, the trouble you cause?

'Do not dare to speak badly of my sister,' blustered George. 'I fought for your King and for your King's father.'

'As did I,' said Amesbury. 'And now women like your sister spend the King's money on clothes and jewellery. Money which should have gone to repairing the wounds of the Civil War.'

Louise looked uncertain.

'Some think you are a spy for the French, the harm you have done His Majesty's rule,' continued Amesbury, his voice steady with anger. 'But I think you are just greedy. Greedy and foolish.'

He pointed at Louise. 'The King's money should have been paid to the Catholics who defended his father,' he said. 'Those men fought for him. They suffered greatly under Cromwell. Now there is nothing to repay them. And why? So whores like you can have a bejewelled dress and a fine country house for your parties.'

Louise and George stood open-mouthed now, as the storm of Amesbury's rage descended.

'You pretty girls,' he continued, 'with your clothes and diamond rings. You take, take take. And it is *men* who go to war for it. Have you any idea what happens on a battlefield? What is necessary?'

Louise's face was fearful.

Amesbury shook his head. 'The King was not brought up a ruler,' he said. 'He comes to it later in life. Who can blame him now he has the money and women like you cling to him like leeches? What man wouldn't make poor choices, under the circumstances?'

He nodded towards the white lace and pink silk fitted around Louise's small waist and flaring to a costly expanse.

'You came to seduce the King, knowing him to be married. And you dare question my morals for finding a girl who will tax our country less than you? A girl who does not try and make him leave London, for her own selfish ends?'

George stepped protectively towards his sister.

'We should leave London,' he said, 'for our own safety. In France when there is plague . . .'

'This is not France!' interrupted Amesbury. 'This is England. And the English expect more from their King. If he leaves it will let all those who might form uprising know that their King is weak and absent.' Amesbury gave a great heaving sigh. 'Do you have any concept of politics at all? Every day we hear of more uprisings. The moment the King deserts the city they will have their reason to strike.'

A little brown body bounded into the room, ran up Amesbury's leg and wrapped its tail around his waist.

Louise gave a hiss of disgust. She'd always hated Amesbury's pet monkey.

The animal had bitten her more than once and seemed to have been trained to pickpocket her. Though Amesbury swore it was not an intentional education.

'The court must leave London,' she said. 'These whores outside risk us all. Any of those girls outside could be carrying plague.'

'If the King leaves London,' said Amesbury, 'then the city will fall to chaos. Already order is worn thin.'

'Then we all face death!' replied Louise, her cherub features contorted in rage. 'You pretend you love the King. You are only bitter because you were one of those who did not get his land back. We must leave. Soon!'

'You must listen to her,' agreed George, who always sided with his sister. 'You risk us all if you do not convince the King to leave London.'

But Amesbury wasn't listening. His monkey had tugged something free from Louise's pocket. A letter inscribed with a symbol.

Mesmerised, he watched as the animal delivered it to his hand.

'What is this?' Amesbury demanded, waving the paper at Louise, 'where did this symbol come from?'

Louise shrugged. 'The King was reading it. He asked me to put it safe for him.'

In a single bound Amesbury had her by the throat, pressed against the wall.

George sprung towards his sister, but Amesbury's huge hand shot out and sent him flying. George fell sprawling on the far side of the chamber.

'Where,' hissed Amesbury, 'did you get this?'

Louise's face had reddened under the pressure at her throat. Her voice came out in thick gasps.

'The King,' she managed. 'I swear it! Put me down. Please. I know not anything more than that.'

Amesbury stared closely at her face, determining whether she was lying.

After a second he released his hold. Louise fell away, gasping and clutching her throat.

'You have made an enemy of me Amesbury,' she whispered, backing away. On the far side of the room George had righted himself and moved to join his sister.

'The King will leave London,' she snarled, 'I will be sure of it. And believe it, there will come a day when you will be sorry. It will come sooner than you think.'

Louise backed carefully out of the room, still rubbing her neck, and George followed after.

Amesbury stood alone with the letter. His fingers traced the symbol at the bottom.

'A crown,' he muttered, 'over three knots.' His hand had begun to twitch. An old habit from the Civil War.

'I thought they were all dead,' he whispered.

Chapter Twenty-Eight

Charlie looked up appraisingly. The roof was of thin thatch. It had been made cheaply from the reeds of London's nearby marshlands. He reached up and snatched an experimental handful. The thatch had not been well maintained and was mouldering.

'We can pull it down and get out through the roof,' he said, gripping another handful of reeds and tugging them free. 'It is not more than a few inches thick and weak in places. If we both work fast we may be able to escape.'

Maria stood immobile looking at him, and then she leapt into sudden action. 'Where is the best place?'

'There,' said Charlie. 'The thatch is much looser here. You can almost see daylight in places.'

He led the way punching in his fist and tearing away clumps of thatch as fast as he could. The sharp material sliced into his skin and it took all his strength to break the strongest reeds.

Outside he heard the chink of wood on metal. The watchman was smashing at the padlock with his cudgel.

In desperation Charlie returned to the task of destruction with renewed vigour. Sunshine shone through a fist-sized hole. Fitting together the backs of his hands he ploughed up between the reeds and wrenched them into a larger opening.

He looked down to see Maria seemed to have stopped work on the roof and was staring back towards the door.

'Help me!' hissed Charlie. 'Make haste Maria, they will soon be in the house.'

From the other side of the door a voice shouted through.

'Hear this you thieves! I am bringing now justice, so do not think you may flee, for I and my friend are both watchmen and are armed besides.'

The smashing sound at the door grew louder. It sounded as though the padlock had begun to give way.

Another voice echoed along the street.

'Which house?' It was a second watchman. 'I have a master key.'

The second shout galvanised Maria back into action, and they both scrabbled desperately, hands colliding as they pulled at the fibres. The reeds opened out into a hole large enough for a person to squeeze through.

'It looks very dirty,' said Maria uncertainly, looking at the dusty opening.

Ignoring her and readying himself for the impact Charlie shut his eyes, bent his knees and pushed his shoulders with all his strength into the gap.

It held at first and then split and tore, allowing his chest to break through.

Taking a deep breath of the London bonfire smoke Charlie opened his eyes at the welcome daylight of his city. He drew first an arm and then the rest of his body through the hole.

Out on the roof the sense of freedom was overwhelming. He looked back to Maria below.

She called nervously up to him. 'I do not think I will fit through there.'

There was a different sound at the door. The second watchman had arrived and was fitting a key to the lock.

Charlie bit back retorting that she could stay in the house for all he cared. He wouldn't like to have her imprisonment on his conscience but her freedom was not worth risking his own neck for if she wouldn't even try for it.

'Put your arms up,' he said, grasping her long fingers as she obeyed and pulling as hard as he could.

'The key won't fit,' he heard the watchman shout. 'The lock is too badly damaged.'

'Then smash it in. It will only take a few more blows,' said his companion.

Charlie turned desperately to Maria.

'You have to push with your feet,' he said. There was a sudden jolt of pressure as she deigned to assist her own escape. Then something stuck at the hips. Maria's hooped skirt had stuck in the gap.

A shuddering blow smashed at the door. The wood splintered.

'Take it off,' he said in exasperation.

'It cost me three shillings!'

'The thing is no use to you if you are killed by plague watchmen,' he hissed. 'I do not have to help you Maria. You may stay here and die in high fashion if you prefer.'

Another blow split the door nearly in two. Behind it the watchmen could now be seen kicking their way into the house.

Her face twisted in annoyance, Maria slipped off the hoop underskirt and let it fall to the floor.

Bracing his legs against the roof he wrapped his arms under hers.

'What is it you wear?' he complained as the rigid garment pressed into his skin. His experiences with women involved fabric underclothes, but she seemed to be dressed in some kind of armour.

'It is the reed you feel, for strengthening my bodice,' said Maria. 'The shape keeps the figure upright and proper,' she added with considerably more loftiness than the situation entitled her to.

Below her the two watchmen barrelled into the house.

Shaking his head in disbelief Charlie made a final heartfelt tug, wrenching her slim shoulders through the opening and onto the roof.

He pulled her through just in time to see the first man make a snatch at her leg.

Charlie set off racing along the City thatch. And with a final sad glance in the direction of her abandoned hoop underskirt, Maria followed after.

Running over thatch was hard work, and every footfall sunk and caught a little in the reed, taking twice as much effort as the ground. Charlie found himself out of breath and sweating by the time he'd run the length of the street by the rooftops.

To his amazement Maria arrived next to him almost immediately, looking flushed and determined.

'I'm from the country,' she said, by way of explanation, 'when piglets and lambs escape you must be fast over rough ground.'

'They will give chase along the street,' said Charlie. 'Likely they may stop to take hold of weaponry. We should get down from the roofs.'

They both slipped down from the roof to the deserted pavement and strode in silence onto the wide streets of Cheapside.

Charlie realised his hair was stuffed with the broken splinters of thatch and dug his hand through the thick mop, restoring dark blonde to places.

'So this plague doctor kills an innocent girl and looks to equip an army.' He said, finally taking a moment to understand what they had found at the blacksmiths.

'You said we must talk to the gunpowder men. They might know something.'

Charlie shook his head. 'My connections are not so high. But to make gunpowder you need saltpetre.'

There were eleven saltpetre men scattered around the City, and he had no idea how he might get to each with no Health Certificate and half of London in pursuit of him. But it was the best lead they had.

Maria's nose wrinkled. 'We must go to the saltpetre men?'

'You must think yourself very fine indeed,' said Charlie. He didn't bother to keep the disgust from his voice. 'It is only your sister's murderer we seek Maria.'

'I would do anything to find her killer,' said Maria, 'But I cannot help that my sensibilities are finer than yours and I do not relish the smell of saltpetre. Or throw myself in cartloads of dead bodies at any opportunity,' she added haughtily, tossing her hair.

Something about the gesture reminded him of Mother Mitchell's girls. And then it occurred to him. The second dead girl. Antoinette. She was a kept woman. And most women of that sort had some dealings with Mother Mitchell's network at some point.

'There may be something else,' he said. 'Mother Mitchell. She might tell me something.' He thought of the plague ravaging the city. 'That is if she hasn't already left,' he added.

'Then we must go there now,' decided Maria.

'We?' Charlie looked at her. 'You will not be coming with me. The last thing I need is some fool girl slowing me down and troubling those I need information from. Besides, you made me a promise that you would leave me be.'

Maria shook her head obstinately. 'I promised I would not follow you. But that does not stop me telling the Newgate guards where you go.'

'You would not.' He stared into her face, horrified to see she was serious.

'I would do anything. Anything to bring my sister's killer to justice. Do not test me Charlie Thief-Taker. I would see you swing with a smile on my face, if it brought me one step closer to justice for Eva.'

Charlie was lost for words.

'We must go then to this . . . this Mother-Mitchell-courtesan of yours,' said Maria, stumbling over the words, 'and see what she might tell us.'

'You give me no choice,' said Charlie. 'Only make sure you say nothing when we arrive, Maria. For I would not want anyone offended by your high-handed ways.'

'Then better you stay silent as we walk there,' she said, 'in case some person I know hears your gutter accent and thinks you my husband.'

Chapter Twenty-Nine

Thomas unlocked the door to the cellar.

He lit a candle and the damp room swelled into light.

Teresa was sitting silently on a chair. As he took a step towards her she held up her hands, shielding her face from the candlelight.

Thomas stooped down, placing the candle on the floor.

'Teresa,' he said, 'why do you sit here in the dark?'

She gave him a faint little smile. 'Some of my memories pain me less in the dark.'

He bent down to be at the same level as his wife.

Despite everything that had happened to her, Teresa was still a beautiful woman. Though her long blonde hair was now finally turning to white.

Thomas took her hand. She let it rest limply in his, but did not turn to face him.

'You must try to eat a little more food,' he said, picking up the bread which he had brought her that morning.

He broke off a piece and offered it. But when she did not take it he rested the loaf back on the floor.

Even in the semi-gloom of the cellar the sadness in her lovely blue eyes broke his heart.

'Ik bit wilhom,' she said, reverting to Dutch.

He translated the words into English. *I am sad today.*

Teresa had never told him what Cromwell's soldiers had done to her. He had returned from war to find she was too terrified to go outside. The doctor told him she could no longer have children.

She still stitched his clothes and mended his boots, but had reverted to speaking mostly Dutch and would not come out from their cellar without heavy persuasion.

Thomas took her hand and stroked it. She was a statuesque woman, standing nearly as tall as Thomas himself, with broad shoulders. But sat in the dark of the cellar she seemed hardly larger than a child.

'We will have to leave this house again soon,' he said, stroking her hand faster. 'But you will not be outside for very long.'

Teresa was shaking her head. Since the war she suffered strange breathless attacks around male strangers. She had told Thomas the fits felt like dying.

'You will stay in the special room I got for you,' he continued. 'Do you remember it? You will be all alone and safe there. No one can get to you. And there are no windows to trouble you with the sunlight.'

Since the soldiers had got to her, Teresa had an abhorrence of daylight. He had never found out why. Though parts of their house had been set alight.

He squeezed her hands tight. 'I will make sure justice is visited on those men that hurt you,' he said. 'I left you alone once but I will always care for you now.'

'Danke Thomas.'

Thank you Thomas.

Teresa gave another thin little smile.

Thomas turned his head away from the candlelight so she couldn't see his face.

As a young soldier cavalier serving his King, Thomas had been naive. He had promised his wife no harm would come to her. But his promise had been broken.

Thomas ascended the staircase leading from his wife's dank room and made his way to the back part of the house where the pigeon croft had been built.

The plague-doctor costume hung on the wall. A streak of gore still winked out accusingly on the bottom skirts.

An image of Antoinette's face rose up, and he drove it down.

Thomas looked into the blank eyes of the mask for a moment. Then he unfurled a large lunar chart and studied the movements of the planets carefully. Full moon was less than a week away. The power would be at a height. Perfect timing to complete the first stage of his plans.

A flutter of wings drew his attention away from the charts, and he turned to see the arrival of his carrier pigeon. He had learned from his days as a soldier to keep a little stock of the trained birds, and they had proved invaluable to send his messages.

Thomas frowned to see the pigeon had been injured. It had caught itself in something and was missing a leg. Mercifully the message had remained attached. He looked accusingly at the animal and roughly tugged the roll of paper free.

'Confirm contamination. Wapping awaits your arrival.'

Taking out a quill he scratched out a new message.

'London contamination almost complete.'

For a few moments he enjoyed a delicious feeling of divine providence. Then the familiar pain returned in his belly and the smile slid from his face.

He studied the paper again, trying to focus his attention on the message instead of the tight gripe in his stomach. The nagging hunger never abated. A platoon of starved soldiers trooped forever in his mind. And the day he returned home from Cromwell's torturers to find his beautiful wife brutalised.

Thomas shook himself out of the revelry. Memories had been coming back to him thick and fast recently, spurred on by the hunger which seemed to be growing daily.

Distracted he turned to the injured pigeon which flapped on the floor of its cage. He reached in and took it out.

The bird flicked its head back and forth, considering him rapidly from every angle. Taking it in his strong grip he wrenched it bodily open, splitting the delicate bone and gouging through the soft breast with his fingers.

The animal gave a strange gurgling shriek, and all the other pigeons began to coo and flap urgently in their cage.

Thomas pulled at the bird, letting the blood run over his fingers and gazed at the beating heart of the animal.

Once, when he had been under siege and starving, Thomas had eaten the entrails of rats, mice and cats. And the food had quelled the burning void.

He paused, staring at the bloody insides, waiting for the moment when the emptiness was filled and the suffering lifted.

It never came.

Casting the twitching bird disconsolately to the floor Thomas stalked from the building. He was still hungry.

Chapter Thirty

Mother Mitchell was huffing a huge chest from her front door with the aid of an elaborately attired young woman.

Charlie sighed in relief.

In the huge span of her silken dress, Mother Mitchell was quite a sight for the daytime. Next to him Maria was staring with undisguised curiosity.

'This is the last of the clothes Sophie,' Mother Mitchell was calling back into the Regent Street townhouse. Then she caught sight of Charlie and gave a rare beam of pleasure.

'Well now boy, this is a surprise to find you still living, for I would have thought you to be dead with the rest of London. Come and give me a kiss, for I am truly pleased to see you.'

Charlie obediently bobbed her a quick kiss and turned to see the cart which was groaning under the weight of the household possessions.

It was strange to see the nocturnal Mother Mitchell out of doors, and the fascinated locals clearly thought the same. Many had come out of their houses to gawk at the girls in their sumptuous dresses and high-wrought hair.

'I need some information,' said Charlie.

'What is it you want to know?' she asked, extracting a slim white pipe from the folds of her gown and seating herself at the side of the cart.

'I want to know about a dead girl.'

'So you attend to murders now?'

'Not exactly.' Charlie made a quick glance at Maria.

Mother Mitchell laughed her creaking phlegmatic laugh. 'But of course it is always a girl with you, Charlie Tuesday,' she said, tugging out a pinch of tobacco and pressing it into the silver-edged mouth of her pipe. 'This is your new wife?' she asked, pointing with the pipe at Maria.

'Were she my wife it would be a hard life indeed.'

'Yes it would,' said Maria. 'For if I had cause to marry so low it would be sad for myself and my family besides.'

Mother Mitchell looked at Maria and back at Charlie, amused. As though she saw something they did not.

'So who was murdered?' she asked Charlie.

'A girl named Antoinette. She was a kept mistress near Cheapside. Did you have any dealings with her?'

Mother Mitchell rocked back and forth as if trying to urge a memory forward. Then her face broke with sudden enlightenment.

'I never did employ Antoinette,' she announced. 'But you will thank me dearly Charlie. For I employ the girl who found her body.'

Maria hustled forward.

'Is she here? Can we speak to her?'

Mother Mitchell appraised Maria with a practised eye.

'I will call her out,' she said, her eyes roving Maria's attractive face and figure. 'Sophie!'

She fumbled with her pipe as they waited for the girl to emerge.

'The lad thinks to charge me four guineas for a wagon,' said Mother Mitchell, conversationally, pointing to a sour-looking adolescent in the driver's seat.

159

'I said to him: 'Boy. I have more say in this city than the King himself, and if you do not drive me and my girls at six shillings I shall see you at Newgate Prison when this sad plague is over and your thumbs broken besides.''

She raised her voice to include the driver in the conversation. 'So he takes us now for six and he shall be lucky to get that if he does not take good care of my girls. For they do not like to be moved from their fine rooms,' she added.

A blonde girl in silk skirts emerged from the house and approached them warily.

'Sophie,' said Mother Mitchell. 'This man here is a thief taker. He wants to help find Antoinette's killer. You must tell him all you know.'

Sophie had turned pale.

'Tell the man,' prompted Mother Mitchell. 'No harm will come to you.'

'She was murdered,' started Sophie uncertainly.

'How did you find her?' asked Charlie.

'I went to the room where she stayed. She was . . . hanging . . . when I found her.'

Charlie and Maria looked at each other.

'What do you mean hanging?' asked Maria.

Sophie looked at Mother Mitchell to confirm she might speak with the second stranger. Mother Mitchell nodded.

Sophie swallowed. 'She was hung up,' she repeated. 'Her body was. But her head . . . .'

Sophie's eyes started to roll and she swayed a little. Mother Mitchell leapt forward and shook her by the shoulders. 'God's fish don't faint again girl!' She rummaged in her purse for smelling salts.

But Sophie was already recovering.

'Her head was in a cage,' she managed, her voice stronger now. She swallowed again and tears sprang to her eyes. 'Like what you would keep a bird in. It had been wrapped in white ribbon. And her body had been stuck full of feathers. All over. Black feathers.'

'Raven's feathers?' Maria sounded uncertain. Ravens were thought to house the souls of dead people.

'All over,' continued Sophie. 'They'd been pushed into her. Into her chest and arms.' Her lip trembled. 'There was a cup too. As though someone had drunk her blood.'

Even Mother Mitchell had turned a little pale.

But Charlie's eyes had widened.

'A raven,' he muttered, remembering the information from the bird market. 'Then he must be a high-up man. With permission to enter the Tower of London.'

Maria looked at him uncertainly.

'Who was the last person she saw?' asked Charlie.

'Her keeper,' said Sophie. 'It was him that must have done for her. Antoinette was no fool. She would not have let anyone else up into her house when she was alone. London is dangerous for girls such as us.'

Charlie logged the fact. 'Would her keeper have been capable of murder? Did he love her?'

Sophie licked her lips. 'She often had bad bruises after he came.'

'Then why did she not stop his visits?' demanded Maria. 'Why should she endure such treatment?'

Sophie gave a hard little laugh. 'It is not so strange or bad as many men do. Many of us thought her lucky. For her man came to her rarely and paid her full board.'

'Did you know his name?' asked Charlie, 'the man who paid her keeping?'

Sophie shook her head. 'Not his real name. Antoinette told me he used an alias. Thomas Malvern.'

Maria gasped.

'What is it?' asked Charlie.

'I . . .' Maria swallowed. 'I know that name,' she whispered.

They waited for her to continue, and to Charlie's surprise Maria's face began to darken into a blush.

'I think Eva mentioned him,' she said. 'Malvern, or something like it.'

'How did she mention him?' asked Charlie.

Maria's mouth twisted, and the blush deepened. 'She had a few men, who she thought might buy her into keeping. She would . . . boast about them.'

Her eyes turned to Charlie, imploring him. 'She was not a bad girl,' she whispered. 'Only she drew men's attention, without meaning to.'

'Why did you not say this before?'

'I . . . I did not think it mattered.'

'You did not think it mattered? That your dead sister had a host of strange men, who wanted to buy her as a mistress.'

'It was not like that!' retorted Maria hotly. 'It was *nothing* like that. You make it sound . . . You make her sound like a prostitute. A few innocent flirtations, that is all. Men loved Eva. You could see it in their eyes. None would have hurt her.'

'And yet one did,' said Charlie darkly.

Maria had turned pale and her hands were shaking.

Charlie wondered if Maria could really believe her sister's innocence. It was typical of her high ways, he thought, that she would withhold valuable information which might reflect badly on her family's morals.

'Do you know anything else about this Malvern?'

She shook her head. 'His name stood out, that is all. The others were ordinary common names, and I have long forgot them.'

'A man named Malvern wanted to buy your sister into keeping?' confirmed Charlie. 'As his mistress?'

Maria flushed. 'Such terms are often bandied in flirt, or jest,' she snapped. 'Eva always looked to end our poverty. And perhaps some men took it more seriously than others what could be for sale. I might have understood her wrong, when she mentioned Malvern,' she added in an embarrassed mumble.

'Can you tell us anything else about Antoinette's keeper?' asked Charlie, looking at Sophie.

Sophie nodded slowly. 'She said he had talked of spreading some infection. To take revenge on the King. At first she thought it was play-acting, but towards the end she thought it might all be real.'

'What kind of infection?'

'I do not know. But there is plague all around.'

They looked at one another uneasily.

'What of Antoinette,' pressed Charlie. 'Can you tell us anything of her?'

'She was a good friend,' said Sophie, the tears rising up again. 'And she deserved better than she got in this City.'

'Antoinette was working for William Adders,' offered Mother Mitchell. 'I do not trust that man Charlie. He is not all he seems.'

'What do you mean?'

'Something wrong with the way he treats his girls from what I hear,' she replied, taking a deep drag on her pipe. 'And he is one of those that is bitter of the King's return. Thinks things were better under Cromwell. I would not be surprised if all that money he makes from his gambling house goes to ill ends.'

Sophie had fallen silent and was staring at Maria.

'What is it?' asked Maria, discomforted by the girl's gaze.

'Antoinette looked like you,' she said, raising a finger to point. 'The likeness is very strong. They could have been sisters,' she added, turning to Charlie.

Charlie felt a chill sweep through him. He risked a glance at Maria.

She had turned silent.

The revelation had clearly shaken her badly.

'It is another witch-murder,' said Charlie slowly. 'I think perhaps we should see what more we can find about this witch who was released from Wapping.'

'Why should you wish to do that?' asked Maria.

'That man might be our murderer,' said Charlie.

But Maria was shaking her head and staring at him in surprise. 'The witch who was released from Wapping is not a man,' she said. 'She is not even a witch.'

'What do you know about it?' asked Charlie in confusion.

'I told you our family are from the country,' explained Maria. 'We do not like city physicians. The witch imprisoned at Wapping is a woman. A wise woman. She comes from our village,' she added, 'and she healed the sick before they threw her in prison for not attending church.'

Charlie felt his heart sink as another avenue of investigation closed.

'He is no commoner, your man,' ventured Mother Mitchell, her eyes flicking between Charlie and Maria. 'Antoinette was not good enough for a lord, but she could command a fair enough sort. A man high up in a guild, perhaps, or a physician.'

Charlie looked at Maria. 'The physician's college. Perhaps someone there can tell us something. He wore one of their costumes after all. And then we should find a way to question this William Adders. Perhaps he knows something more about Antoinette's keeper.'

'My Health Certificate is not good enough to get into that part of town,' said Maria.

'And there are guards all around who want my head,' said Charlie. 'But if we had good enough certificates it would be worth the risk.'

He thought for a moment. Marc-Anthony would have long left town. So his usual avenue of forgeries was closed. Who else did he know? Methodically, he tracked through everyone who owed him a favour. No certificates to be got that way.

He frowned, letting his mind instead loop over the way the documents were got officially. Surely there must be some flaw in the system?

His mental map of London reordered itself until finally he hit on a route and a destination where they could avoid the health checkpoints.

'I know where we can get certificates,' he said finally.

'If you think to go to Guildhall it is a bad plan,' snapped Maria. 'We do not have time to wait to buy certificates.'

'We are not going to buy them,' said Charlie. 'We are going to steal them.'

Chapter Thirty-One

The Royal Exchange was jammed full of shoppers jostling for a bargain amongst the enthusiastic attentions of the shop girls and apprentice boys. Plague had not come to this part of the City, and citizens were enjoying an opportunity to shop without risk of infection.

'I think you should like it here,' said Charlie, eyeing Maria's fashionable dress. 'Since this is a place for shopping.'

Two broad galleries ran the length of the Exchange, walled on either side by arched columns with shops in between them. And in between the bustle of bargain-hunters the shouts of retailers attempting to lure customers were deafening.

Maria glanced at the cheap drapers and costume jewellers. A curds and cream shop was making a lively trade.

A shop girl grabbed her arm, dragging her towards a fabric shop. 'This colour is a good cloth for you,' she said, pointing to the thin red material which made up her own low-cut dress. 'I make the best price of any here.'

Maria wrenched her arm free and the girl drifted away towards other shoppers, unperturbed by the slight.

'Why are we here?' she asked as more hands assailed her. 'This is not a place for certificates.'

'I know an astrologer who has a room here,' he explained.

'You would have our fortunes told?'

'Not exactly.'

His eyes drifted upwards, scanning for the name. And then he saw it, almost entirely hidden amongst other painted advertisements for astrologers, fortune tellers, dentists and apothecaries on the second level of the Exchange.

'William Lilly,' read the worn and peeling sign. 'Astrologer'.

'Here,' he pulled Maria towards a set of stone steps leading to the next storey. They emerged onto the open second floor and a run of dusty small doors took the place of the large shops below.

'Is he a friend of yours, this fortune teller?' asked Maria.

'No, I would not call him a friend.'

'Then why do we go to him?'

'Lilly has an arrangement with Guildhall,' explained Charlie. 'They send him copies of the Health Certificates.'

'What for?'

'To help him make better predictions. Plague certificates hold information on birthdates and occupations. That is useful to understand how the sun and stars make us who we are.'

Maria nodded, understanding. 'So we steal two copies of Health Certificates?'

'Exactly. We'll find some husband and wife of similar ages.'

'And the copies will pass checks?'

'They are exactly the same as the real thing. Not many people know copies are made,' he added.

'And how are we to steal them?'

They had reached an ageing door. Large chalk letters covered it proclaiming: 'Predicted the return of His Majesty in 1660 ten years before the event!'

Charlie lowered his voice and pointed. 'See that storeroom next door? I can pick the lock and get in. These rooms are divided by partitions which do not meet the ceilings,' he added.

'So you will break in and climb over.'

'Yes. And you will go in and have Lilly read your fortune. To distract him.'

Maria looked uncertain. 'Is that not a godless business? Having your fortune told?'

'So says the girl who visits a witch, when her family is ill.'

Maria coloured. 'Very well. But I have no idea what I might say.'

'He likes pretty girls,' said Charlie. 'Pay him your penny and he will do all the talking.'

As Maria approached Lilly's door, Charlie slid carefully onto the partition and surveyed the room below.

Lilly's room was decorated in faded wall-charts. Rotations of the sun, movements of the planets and arrangements of the stars were all documented.

Heaped everywhere were piles of paper. Health Certificates.

William Lilly sat behind a fat-legged table where the papers grew to almost a man's height. His thick legs filled white silk stockings and his bulky body filled the black and gold breeches which had been fashionable before the Revolution.

He was scratching away with a feather quill. Charlie recognised something on the page. It was one of the noble crests, from before the Civil War.

Charlie swept his memory. He had seen the emblem by chance, over ten years ago, on a military banner. Why was Lilly using it now?

There was a knock at the door.

Lilly started and swept the papers hurriedly into his desk drawer.

Then he looked up from behind a pair of small gold binoculars. 'Come in.'

Maria entered and Lilly's face brightened slightly.

'Hello my dear,' he announced. 'What can I do for you?'

Curtseying politely Maria came into the room. 'I would like my fortune told,' she said. And then, uncertain what was expected, she produced her penny and pushed it nervously towards him.

Lilly slid it into his desk drawer, never taking his eyes off her.

'Of course. Please sit,' he assessed her carefully. 'I imagine with a healthy lady such as you are, it is a matter of love?'

'Yes, that is it,' Maria stammered, her cheeks getting pink.

'I thought so.'

From the partition Charlie slid down silently, landing behind Lilly's desk.

He waited for a long tense moment, hoping Lilly hadn't sensed or heard him enter. But for the time being at least, Maria was doing her job. The astrologer's eyes were all for her.

Charlie squatted down, hardly daring to breathe. Lilly was only a few feet away. He lowered his head, passing his eyes over an untidy pile of handwritten certificates.

Two leapt out at him. A man and wife aged seventeen and twenty-seven. That would work, he decided, sliding them into his shirt.

'Are you to be married?' he heard Lilly ask.

'I am betrothed,' said Maria. 'Well,' she added, 'he will ask soon.'

'And where is your betrothed?'

'He left London a week ago. He has relatives in Sussex who might shelter him from plague.'

Charlie shook his head, wondering what kind of husband-to-be would leave his future wife to the mercy of the distemper. This was the first Maria had mentioned of a betrothed, and he did not think she was the type to make things up on the spot. Likely she had no strong feelings for the poor man and was marrying him for some family advantage.

Charlie was about to haul himself back over the partition when he noticed a feather quill.

The image of the lolling pigeon wing in the blacksmiths suddenly came to mind.

Something about that bird still troubled his thief taker's intuition. And now an idea presented itself.

What if Thomas Malvern had taken a Health Certificate? If he had planned to get one from Guildhall he would have needed his own pen, to fill out his details.

Quill feathers weren't widely available currently, for fear they carried plague. So Thomas might well have cut himself a feather at the blacksmith's, for the purpose of writing a certificate at Guildhall. If he had, then a copy would provide invaluable information.

Behind Lilly he saw Maria's eyes flick urgently. Questioning why he wasn't leaving.

The astrologer turned to follow the direction of her gaze.

'My betrothed wanted me to go with him,' blurted Maria, 'I had rather stayed.'

'I see,' said Lilly, his attention back on Maria. 'It is to be a marriage of convenience then?' he added.

The certificates seemed to be arranged alphabetically. Charlie's eyes roamed the piles. The 'M's were on the other side of the room. He caught Maria's eye and silently pointed.

'My betrothed is a good man,' said Maria a little too loudly. 'And he will care for me. Tell me,' she stood, 'what does the map show Mr Lilly?' She walked to the opposite side of the room and pointed to the colourful counties of England criss-crossed in blue and red lines.

Charlie had to hand it to Maria. She caught on fast.

Lilly moved out from his desk with effort to join her. The astrologer was heavy now, Charlie noticed. Lilly had gained considerable bulk since the war had ended. A diet of cheap pies had not agreed with him.

'It is the Civil War campaign young lady. That map shows the paths of the Royalist and Parliamentary troops in the last months of war.'

His eyes followed the trails over the nation and he shook his head. 'The armies were most evenly matched. Had one or two battles ended differently this country would have retained its King, and Cromwell would never have seized power.'

'And this is a birth-sign chart?' Maria pointed to another wall chart.

'Ah yes,' said Lilly. 'You are Virgo are you not?'

Maria nodded.

'The sign of the good wife,' nodded Lilly, 'but with hidden passion.'

Charlie smirked to himself. It did not surprise him that Maria's marriage had been arranged. She didn't seem too troubled with feelings. Probably it would keep her happy enough. There were times when he even envied people who could make such logical stock of their emotions.

Carefully he flicked through the 'M' pile.

Merryweather, Morris. The names hadn't been put in any order besides first letter.

'I am sure my feelings will grow for my future husband,' Maria was saying.

'Well,' said Lilly, 'let us find out. Come sit and I will read your palm.'

Charlie froze. If Lilly turned he would see him stooping above the pile of certificates.

'What do you think of this Mr Lilly?'

Charlie looked up in amazement to see Maria had pulled down the top of her dress to expose almost all of her left breast. Only the position of her hand concealed it from view.

Lilly's attention was riveted to where she was standing.

The astrologer opened and shut his mouth, craning forward for a better look. For a moment his hand moved of its own accord towards Maria and then he snatched it back.

'I have had it since birth.' Maria wore an expression of innocent curiosity.

'I think it is only a mole,' managed Lilly. 'But perhaps the shape means something.' He tugged at his shirt, as if uncertain where his hands should be.

Mercher, Marrow, Charlie continued to flick.

'A crest of sorts,' Lilly was saying hoarsely. 'Perhaps you have some noble blood.'

Malvern!

Charlie could hardly believe his luck. He rolled it up and slid it carefully into his shirt. Then he stepped back carefully to the partition and hauled himself over it.

'Oh that is true to be sure,' Maria was saying. 'Our family were of a far finer sort, before misfortune saw us move to London.'

Her eyes followed Charlie over the partition.

'Thank you very much Mr Lilly,' she announced suddenly. 'It was a very good fortune.' And she swept suddenly out of the room, leaving an open-mouthed Lilly in her wake.

Chapter Thirty-Two

'What were you doing in there?' Maria was outraged. 'We were nearly both caught.'

'I was enjoying your birthmark.'

Maria's face turned to outrage. 'How dare you? It was to save your skin.'

'And hearing about your future husband,' continued Charlie, with a roguish grin. 'He sounds like a lucky man if you might calculate a way to fall in love with him.'

'I was just saying anything that came into my head. I meant nothing by it.'

'I hope you never try at cards,' said Charlie, 'you are a bad bluff.'

He held up a certificate. Maria snatched it.

'Thomas Malvern!' She gave him a sudden smile. 'He has taken a certificate. That is very clever of you to think of it.'

She frowned at the paper.

'He writes his religion as Catholic,' she observed.

'Which means he fought for the old King,' said Charlie. 'Look at his date of birth. He would have battled in the civil war. And he was a Royalist.'

Maria looked confused, and he realised she was too young to remember the Civil War.

'The last King Charles turned Catholic,' he explained, 'that faith allows Kings to rule as tyrants. They believe man-made laws need not apply to Kings.'

'So the old King acted tyrant?'

'Yes. And England is a Protestant country. Most people believed that they should be ruled by parliament as well as a King.'

'And they fought about it?'

'For years. It was ugly and brutal. And the old King's followers were aristocrats, Catholics or both,' added Charlie.

'So this Malvern supported the King?'

'Without a doubt. And if he seeks to arm an uprising, he is probably one of those many poor Catholics who have been betrayed by King Charles II. For none of them got their lands back when he returned.'

'And he makes some witchcraft to see his plans succeed?' asked Maria, frowning.

Charlie thought about this. It was the part of the plan which made the least sense to him.

'Perhaps,' he conceded. 'Though it is a strange mystery. Everything we know about Malvern suggests he is high born. Or at least was once. He must have access to royal places in London. For his raven was likely taken from the Tower. He can cut his own quill. And his writing is educated.'

Charlie pointed at the certificate.

The writing had the confident shape of a man who wrote often. Unlike the careful loops on Maria's Health Certificate, which suggested she'd paid close attention to a writing tutor, but didn't apply the skill in practical frequency.

'The certificate tells us something more important,' added Charlie. 'He is leaving London. See you his destination.'

Maria's face fell. 'Wapping. That place is deep in plague,' she whispered.

Wapping had been one of the first places Londoners had fled to when plague had broken out. It was a few miles away from the infected city. But now the small town was thick with the illness.

The plague stories which came from Wapping were so terrible that many dismissed them as make-believe.

'That date is today,' added Maria, 'he leaves town today. Why should he want to travel to Wapping?'

'Why should he want to leave at all?' asked Charlie. 'It makes no sense. This man makes careful murders. North and East. Why should he suddenly halt his plans and leave the city?'

Maria shrugged. 'Perhaps Wapping is South. Is that not next? For fire?'

Charlie was shaking his head. 'It does not feel right.' He frowned. 'These murders. They would not happen close together in London and then far apart.'

'Something has upset his plans then?' asked Maria, hopefully.

Charlie frowned. 'Perhaps.'

He thought for a long moment.

'Or.' He said slowly. 'Something has happened to speed his plans.'

'What do you mean?'

'What if some event has occurred, which makes his invasion suddenly more achievable? What if he hurries now, to complete his scheme?'

Charlie swallowed, remembering Rowan's warning.

'The King. There is talk he will leave London. What if this Malvern, this high-up man, what if he knows more than us? What if the King flees soon? And Malvern rushes now, to make his uprising?'

'Then why go to Wapping?' asked Maria.

Charlie thought for a moment. 'There is a port at Wapping.'

He grabbed up the certificate. 'Which gate does he leave from?'

Maria peered to where he was pointing. 'Bishops Gate,' she said.

'That is the large gate for wagons and carts,' said Charlie. 'There is no reason to choose that gate were he on horseback – it would be far slower. Perhaps he uses a wagon to make some delivery of his weapons to a foreign enemy.' Charlie was thinking out loud, but none of the reasons were striking him yet.

'Malvern could not import anything,' he added. 'All water routes are closed since plague came. Even a high-up man could not use his influence to import goods.'

Maria's face was shining with hope. 'If he travels by cart we can outpace him,' she said. 'We can take horses and make the journey faster.'

Charlie nodded, making a quick calculation. 'Even if he drives the smallest wagon with good horses we should be twice as fast,' he acknowledged. 'And we may take smaller roads where he must stay on the larger.'

Maria's gaze settled on Charlie. 'So we must determine to be better friends,' she said.

'What?'

'Because we need each other, Charlie Thief-Taker.'

'Why should you think, Maria, that I might ever need something from you?'

'Because I have money to hire horses and know the ways of the country besides. I'll wager you have never even left London.'

Charlie felt his jaw tighten. The truth of the statement made it no less irksome.

'And I cannot easily travel alone as a woman. I need protection. You might do very well for that.'

'Besides,' she added, seeing him still hesitate. 'I will pay you very well. A guinea a day and a further five if we catch him.'

She drew out her purse. 'Here is two in advance,' she added.

Charlie hesitated. His hand moved to his key.

'Take it,' she said, pushing the coins into his other hand.

'Wapping is not more than a few miles,' said Charlie, as his fingers slowly closed on the money. He was trying to calculate how much time he could spend with Maria without doing her bodily harm. 'But the route is no longer direct. Vigilantes seal the roads to the south. We must head north and take the long way around the countryside to get there.'

'If we set off now and travel by horseback we should be there within two days at the very most,' said Maria, ignoring his attempt to show local knowledge. 'More likely one and a half. His wagon would take three days if he makes right good time.'

'Then that is what we must do,' said Charlie, his stomach tightening at the thought of leaving London for the first time in his life. 'We will journey ahead of this Malvern and lay an ambush.'

Her eyes were shining with the prospect. 'Then,' she continued, 'he shall answer for what was done to my poor sister.'

As they left the Exchange Charlie noticed a monkey was snaking around the market stalls. That was very strange indeed. Such an animal was valuable. What was it doing in Cheapside?

Chapter Thirty-Three

The girl smiled, swinging her cup so the wine inside sloshed back and forth.

'I have seen you in a different club before,' she slurred.

'I have taken up gambling as a recent hobby,' said Thomas drawing out the heavy keys to the church.

The girl followed him in, leaning on his arm.

'What is your name?' he asked, as he unlocked the heavy doors to the chapel.

'Jenny.' She was staring through the drunken corridor of her vision into the church.

'How is it you have keys to the church?' she asked.

'I have a little influence in the city.'

She giggled, hiccupping slightly.

'Of course you do. Is Malvern an old family?'

He tensed. It was a gesture Jenny would normally have picked up on. But the wine had dulled her senses.

'How did you know my name?' he asked.

Jenny tried to shrug. But the restraints of her dress made it difficult. She settled for a lopsided sway of her arm.

'I have a little reading. More than most girls. I saw you sign your name in the gambling book.'

Jenny was hoping her ability to read might appeal to him. Though now she thought about it, perhaps he wanted to be anonymous. A far-off part of her brain nagged she might have said the wrong thing. But she couldn't make it mesh with the wheeling drink-soaked part.

Thomas was silent, fiddling with the lock on the door.

She leaned in close. 'I am pleased you have such influence in the city,' she said, opting for the flattery which she assumed would work on a powerful man.

Jenny had been working at Smith and Widdle's Club for two months now and was growing tired of it. She was a seasonal worker, making embroidery and shoes when there was a market for it and doing maid's work, laundry or prostitution when the economy was down.

She was nearly eighteen and had decided it was time for a steady job. She was angling for a man to buy her out of the club and into keeping. Thomas would do for her first protector, after which she would seek out a duke or an earl.

The door of the church fell open, and the first thing that hit Jenny was the smell.

She coughed and gagged.

Thomas looked around at her in surprise.

Jenny coughed again, her eyes watering. He hadn't noticed the smell, she realised.

Perhaps it was best not to mention it.

'I am not used to churches,' she told him, to distract from her reaction. 'For they chase away girls such as I. You must think me a great sinner, for I cannot even name the London churches.'

She had meant the remark to lighten the mood. But the confession drew a glower of disgust from Thomas.

Clearly he was a deeply religious man, thought Jenny, swallowing.

Thomas lit a candle, and they walked further into the depths of the church. Beneath the drunken fug an instinct sparked at Jenny that the door was now uncomfortably far away.

Thomas stopped. The candle rested on a small back portion of the church swelled into yellow light, casting the rest in dancing shadows.

'You store food here?' asked Jenny after a long moment, forcing her stomach to calmness. She was staring at the inside of the church.

Food was stacked neatly all around. Enough to feed an army. It covered almost every wall and was arranged on the floor and the tombstones.

'I was held under siege in the war,' explained Thomas. 'I like to be sure there is plenty stored should times of need arise. This plague might see London cut off from food supplied from the country,' he added.

Jenny nodded, trying not to retch.

The food was all spoiled. Putrefying sausages, mouldering bread, stale casks of ale and joints of meat rotting to a dripping liquid on the bone. The source of the terrible smell had become clear.

She suddenly felt very sober.

Thomas picked up a bag from the floor.

'What is that?' Jenny rearranged her features into a smile, hoping he would not notice the dead horror in her eyes.

'Something that we might entertain ourselves better,' he answered.

A sudden fluttering sounded loudly around the church.

Jenny started.

'There are not bats in here?' she asked. 'I am all a fear of bats.'

She was hoping the lie might form a reason for her to leave. Following Thomas to this deserted church now seemed a very bad idea.

Thomas shook his head in annoyance. 'It is a message,' he said. 'A carrier pigeon. Wait here,' he added, 'I will only be a moment.'

He vanished into the shadows, leaving Jenny standing alone in the small circumference of candlelight.

Her gaze cast about for some excuse to leave. It settled on his bag.

Some little part of drunk curiosity remained, and she stooped down to open it. If it was full of jewellery or some other gift, she might consider staying.

The catch was rusty, and her cold fingers struggled with it.

At the back of the church she heard more feathers flapping and the urgent coos of pigeons.

With a click the bag fell open. Jenny's hands flew to her mouth.

She stepped up, staggering backwards under the weight of her skirts, and fell.

The bloody torture tools winked out at her.

Scrabbling backwards she heaved herself up on the nearest pew and bent double for a moment, heaving.

Then her eyes darted desperately for some escape.

The door was too far. And outside the church were two deserted alleyways. In her heavy skirts she wouldn't stand a chance of outrunning him.

Her eyes fell again to the torture tools. An evil-looking curved knife glinted back.

Moments later Jenny eased herself into the hiding place, just as Thomas returned.

He stood for a long moment, staring at where she had been.

From her tiny peephole Jenny watched, willing the shuddering gasps of her breath to come silently.

He picked up a sword.

'I know you are still here,' he called. 'If you reveal yourself now it will be easier for you. I will only toy with you a little.'

Jenny bit her lip, feeling the blood well into her mouth.

Thomas stalked slowly around the room. His gaze settled on a hanging tapestry bulging obviously from the wall. A blue skirt was peeking from the bottom.

Smiling he walked towards it.

'Since you did not reveal yourself your punishment will be very great,' he said. 'I have kept people alive for weeks. Perhaps you will become my longest living experiment.'

Jenny screwed her eyes tight shut and prayed. Silent tears of pure terror ran down her face.

Thomas drew nearer.

She held her breath.

Then he strode past her hiding place, using his sword to lift the tapestry hanging a few feet from where she stood.

Under the tapestry lay the ragged remains of her dress. Thomas regarded it for a long moment. She'd somehow managed to cut it away from her body and stuff it here to mislead him. His eyes settled on his box of torture tools. A knife was missing.

Hidden a few feet away Jenny let out her breath in a slow measured stream. The curved blade was gripped reassuringly in her palm.

She knew enough about the Civil War to remember all churches had spaces for the priests to hide and had sought it out just in time. Jenny's fingers reaffirmed their grip on the knife. She was fast enough to stab his eye, she thought. And that might be enough to escape.

Girls raised in St Giles knew how to handle knives, and for the first time in her life, Jenny was grateful for her gutter upbringing.

There would be repercussions. He was rich, she had seen from his gambling, and could pay men to come for her. But one problem at a time. First, she meant to escape with her life.

She steeled herself, waiting for the little door of her hiding place to fly open.

The moment of attack never came. Thomas turned and stared towards the door of the church. She realised with fast-flowering relief that he assumed she had already left the building.

Thomas stalked out of the church, leaving Jenny alone with the piles of rotting food.

It was hours later that she risked scaling the bell-tower and climbing down the roof. Then she ran sobbing back to safe squalor of St Giles, in the tattered remains of her fine dress.

Chapter Thirty-Four

Charlie tried unsuccessfully once more to loop his foot into the stirrup and tumbled headlong into the mud.

Clicking her tongue Maria steered her horse expertly around and assessed his failure.

'He knows you are afraid,' she said, sliding from her horse. 'He will not hurt you. But you make him fearful when he thinks you know not what you do.'

'I do not know what I do!' protested Charlie. 'I think this a bad plan Maria, to take horses when I cannot ride.'

The horses were rented until the next roadside stables, at which point they would be swapped for fresh mounts. And having never done anything as expensive as hiring a horse, Charlie was terrified he would inflict some costly damage on the animal.

Maria blinked in calm assessment of the situation. 'Here, I will hold him,' she said finally, reaching for the reins.

She was, it transpired, highly skilled with horses. So much so, in fact, as to have no understanding that it might be difficult for someone else. She'd roundly dismissed his protestations that he'd never ridden a horse, waving her hand and declaring it easy. 'You will learn it quickly,' she said. 'There is nothing to know – mount up and sit still whilst it moves. Is that how you marked your nose and lip? From a horse?' she asked, peering up at him in sudden realisation.

'Yes.' Charlie scowled to deter further questioning. He liked to let people assume he had gained the kink to his rounded nose and sliver of scar on his lip in a knife fight.

'It hasn't marked you too badly,' she said, peering at his face. 'You are still a handsome man.'

She stopped, suddenly, embarrassed by the remark.

'Enough practise,' she announced. 'Time to find us some good horses for the road.' And waved her hand for the ostler to approach.

Charlie watched as Maria busied herself with buying the horses, rejecting two with broken knees.

'They could have thrown their riders and he has not ridden before,' Maria said, pointing at Charlie and raising her voice accusingly on the ostler.

'You know as well as I that the roads are thick with vigilantes, and the wrong horses could have us both killed.'

The ostler raised his hands in defeat, but Maria kept talking.

'Our lives are worth the same in the eyes of God no matter what the clothes on our backs,' she said, 'just because we do not dress so fine as some we are still entitled to the respect you would show a richer sort.'

She walked past the two horses which had been led out and tucked her hand under the chin of another animal reined further from the path.

'That is a mare,' said the ostler uncertainly. Maria turned to include Charlie in the choice of what was evidently to be his horse. He looked at the animal uncertainly. There seemed to be something haughty in its expression.

'What about that one?' asked Charlie, pointing to a horse with a kinder face.

'Mares can be temperamental, but they are faster,' said Maria, ignoring him and trotting out the animal of her choosing. As if in answer the animal reared up to its hind legs, towering above them. Maria laughed and pulled it back down by its reins, patting the flank approvingly.

Charlie's mouth dropped open in sheer unadulterated terror.

'If she rears up you must lean back and grip with your knees,' explained Maria conversationally. 'Else you will be thrown.'

As a lowly city dweller Charlie's sum knowledge of horses was to get out of their way fast. The prospect of getting astride left him in a cold sweat. But he accepted his fate dumbly. Trepidation had rendered him silent.

'You will do better with fast animals,' conceded the ostler. 'This is the only road out of London where you have a chance of getting through alive. But vigilantes have sprung up here too. A traveller and his wife were beaten to death last night.'

The ostler went to bring them saddles and to Charlie's great surprise came back holding a tankard of plague water.

'It is made local,' he said.

Maria hesitated at the strong sulphur stench which wove up from the cup and then evidently deciding it would be bad manners to refuse, took a deep swig. She passed it to Charlie and he did the same, wondering where on earth the water had been found to make such a foul-tasting drink.

Maria swilled and spat.

'There is something sharp in the water,' she complained, rubbing at her teeth with a finger.

'They use iron filings in plague water,' explained Charlie. 'You should try and swallow them down. They are good for you.'

He sucked back the liquid, feeling the ground iron catch at his throat.

Maria and the ostler disappeared to settle the payment, and she returned minutes later, shocked to find Charlie not in his saddle.

'I did not wish to risk hurting the horse,' he lied.

'You have seen such a thing a thousand times over in the city,' she said. 'Hook your leg and mount up. It is simple enough.'

And so began the process of his mounting the horse, which ended in success only after three humiliating tumbles.

'I asked the ostler as to the route, and he told me there is only one road large enough for a wagon,' said Maria. 'Yet many smaller roads can take those on horseback. We must ask people on the route for the fastest path.'

Charlie tapped his head. 'I have Lilly's campaign map memorised from when we visited his room.'

'In your head?' she regarded him suspiciously.

'Yes,' Charlie found it hard to explain how his mind could grab pictures and hold on to them. That was just how he had been made. 'I do not read and write so well as some. But I have a good memory for pictures,' he explained.

Maria seemed to accept this.

'That will certainly make it easier for us to outrun him,' she said.

Charlie nodded. 'The safe way to Wapping is long. The route we must take is thirty miles.'

'Then we should easily be there by tomorrow evening,' said Maria. 'That should give us a whole day to convince the justices in Wapping to detain and question Malvern.

Without waiting for his agreement she reached out a leg towards Charlie and spurred his horse with an expertly judged kick before taking off at speed ahead of him. Charlie, who had only just adjusted to the new mode of transport, found himself tossed about at every angle as his horse charged forward.

Chapter Thirty-Five

Charlie and Maria's spurt of speed was short-lived. As soon as they met the open road they hit the throngs of frightened refugees fleeing London.

The way was thick with riders, walkers and carts weighed down with possessions. Some carried enormous packs containing all their worldly belongings, whilst others had little hand-carts and still more rode horses.

The crowd were skittish and their eyes roamed the fields for attackers.

In the far dusk-distance torches were being lit. Charlie peered for a moment, wondering if it was some archaic country tradition.

'Why do they light torches?' he asked Maria, presuming she would know about country traditions.

'I do not know.' She was frowning at the horizon.

Then Charlie realised.

Across the countryside vigilantes were setting out from their villages.

A chill of fear shot through him.

Maria, sharp as ever, had also made the connection.

'They are at least ten miles away,' she said. There was a little shudder of terror in her voice.

'Best we try and get on as far as we can then,' said Charlie. 'And hope they head in some other direction.'

Some others in the crowd had noticed the torches too, and a swell of unease rippled through the travellers.

They were all trapped, they knew. This road was the safest track. But being part of the multitude made them a target.

Charlie stared at the unfamiliar landscape. Leaving the path meant they could easily be picked off.

To the side of the highway stood the occasional ramshackle hut with a few chickens pecking in the yard outside. The rickety dwellings had weeds growing through the rush roofs and the occasional goat grazing atop. Each had a neat beehive of hay stacked outside the front. Some had dug makeshift toilets for passing travellers to deposit their sewage as fertiliser.

For the most part the householders couldn't be seen, but occasionally some woman sat outside spinning, glaring at the passing crowds.

He didn't imagine any shelter would be forthcoming from the locals.

Charlie snuck a glance at Maria. She had a faraway expression, her broad mouth set level and blue eyes making starker relief of the strong nose. Her long body bobbed effortlessly along to the rhythm of the horse. It reminded him of a taut-strung longbow. Charlie saw her suddenly as a warrior queen, riding into battle.

She looked nothing like the other frightened women riders.

'We can outpace Malvern and soon you will have your revenge,' he said.

She looked at him curiously. 'It is not revenge I seek,' she said. 'It is justice.'

'Is there a difference?' Charlie was confused.

'Yes,' she said with certainty. 'Yes there is. For I have seen people poison their lives with revenge. And I should not wish to follow that path.'

But she did not elaborate further and Charlie was left to puzzle over what justice was if it wasn't revenge for crimes done to others.

Certainly, he thought, if someone murdered his brother it would be revenge he wanted.

Charlie looked out into the middle distance. The vigilante torches looked closer now. Maria was evidently thinking the same. She scanned the route ahead, looking for openings through the crowd.

Seeing none she turned her clear blue eyes towards him.

'Are you married Mr Thief-Taker?'

'I was,' he said. The question took him by surprise.

'She is dead then? Your wife.'

'No,' he answered.

Maria's voice raised an octave. 'You made a divorce?'

Charlie gave a hard laugh. 'That is for rich kings. We agreed to forget the marriage ever happened. Now she can discover a rich man and not have a husband to stop her.'

'But that was a pact before God,' said Maria.

Charlie shrugged. 'Tell Lynette. I do not intend to take another wife. My promise is true. What she does is the business of her own soul.'

'Does she work a trade?'

'She is an actress.'

Maria assessed this for a moment, weighing whether he meant 'prostitute'.

'Does she take Lynette as her stage name? After the famous lady?'

'She is the famous lady.'

'The actress Lynette? *She* is your wife?'

'*Was* my wife.'

'But she is known all over the city.'

'We met when theatres were still banned under Cromwell.'

'And none of her wealth goes to you as her husband?'

'Are you always this curious?'

'I only seek to talk of other things than those torches,' she said, nodding into the distance. 'For it is best not to take fright too early. And I look to know a little more of the man I am to be travelling with for two days,' she added.

There was a shout in the distance. Charlie and Maria looked at one another. The throngs of people burst into a chatter of animated fear.

'They are still far away,' said Maria, but she didn't sound so sure.

Charlie had never been out of the comforting confines of London, and he was disconcertingly rudderless in the wide open country. In the City he could always get a meal or a place to hide. Here he had far fewer resources.

His eyes roamed the horizon again for the vigilante torches. They were undeniably closer. But they seemed to have stopped moving.

'Do you remember anything about your mother?' asked Maria.

'No.' Charlie realised he sounded abrupt and adjusted. 'Not much in any case. A face, maybe. But it is hard to be certain it is her.' He frowned.

'Faces fade,' agreed Maria. 'I am sometimes surprised at how fast.'

She stopped suddenly, as though she had said too much.

'It is not that,' said Charlie. 'There was a lady. My brother found her, hidden away in a room. Very beautiful. I sometimes think I am confusing my mother's face with hers.'

'Hidden away?'

'I do not really remember. Only that she was sad and lonely, in a secret dark room. I think she played with us.'

Maria considered this. 'It sounds very mysterious,' she said finally. Her face suggested she was thinking deeply on it.

'Do you remember anything else about her?' she added.

'I wish I did.'

'Are you angry that you were left orphaned?' asked Maria. She was looking at his key now.

'Why should I be?' He pushed the key inside his shirt.

'That you were left in the Foundling Hospital,' said Maria. 'I have been only once to give some alms, and it looked a dreadful sort of place with children of skin and bone. I felt great pity for them.'

Charlie bristled.

'The Foundling Hospital is well enough,' he said.

Maria hissed in annoyance as her horse was forced to a slow trot, hemmed in by the trudging Londoners. The fear of attack had panicked some and mobilised others, and the shifting crowd had begun to move forward and back on itself in a rising gridlock.

Maria sat up high on her horse, looking impatiently out into the distance.

'The crowds will slow us,' she said. 'But this Malvern must travel under the same restraints. And once we get onto the back roads it will make us even faster again, for they will have no such burden of travellers.' Her hand slid to her stomach suddenly, her face twisting in pain.

'I think there was something bad in that plague water the ostler gave us,' she said, catching Charlie's expression. 'My belly complains of it.'

Already the sun was beginning to set. And the sides of the road had begun to fill up with makeshift tents as people drifted from the path and set up camp for the night.

Most seemed to have decided to brazen it out for the night and hope for the best.

Charlie raised his arm to point, slipped and quickly grabbed the reins again. He looked over to Maria to see if she had noticed the indignity of the manoeuvre. But she was looking to the edge of the highway, at the travellers setting up camp.

'They do not know country ways,' she observed. 'They hope that if they set up camp and are not found travelling the road, they will be safe from the men who come for them.'

'Country ways are not so different from city ways,' said Charlie, darkly. 'Once the mob sets up they must have some violence.'

Chapter Thirty-Six

'We should go on in the dark for a few miles,' said Charlie. 'If vigilantes come we will be sitting ducks amongst these fires.'

He glanced at Maria. Her mouth was clamped tight as though in pain. She still sat upright, but given that she wore a bodice stitched with reed he suspected she had little choice in the matter.

'It is nothing,' she said, noticing him looking at her. 'I have a headache from the hard riding in the sun.'

She had begun to look increasingly ill as the day wore on. Charlie had tried to pretend to himself it was just the heat. But in his deeper self, he knew. Something was wrong. Her face was so pale it had turned almost blue.

'Perhaps we should stop now and take some rest,' said Charlie uncertainly, but as he spoke Maria tumbled lengthways from her horse.

'Maria!' He dismounted, half falling from his horse, and ran to where she lay.

Maria was curled into a close ball of agony. The smell hit him immediately and he recognised it from some dark forgotten place of his childhood. It was the unmistakable stench of dysentery sweat. Even in the dusky half light of nightfall her face had a ghostly-blue pallor.

The bloody flux wiped out entire slums in London. And Charlie, having survived the illness, was immune to the infection, but not the horror of it.

He looked at the various camps. Round their individual firesides the little parties of families and travellers looked almost cheerful. One man was playing a pipe whilst his daughter cooked sausages over a fire. Other groups passed flagons of ale back and forth.

Each encampment sat firmly divided from the other. And Charlie knew no one would help a sick girl in plague time. He could hardly blame them.

But Maria would die if she was left exposed out here.

Charlie's mouth turned down in a tight, frightened line.

She would not survive the infection unless she were got somewhere warm and properly nursed.

He remembered the bog-water smell of the Venice Treacle from the stables. If that had been the source she must have taken the bad air deep inside.

Stumbling he pulled her upright.

Maria scrabbled with her feet, trying to help him. Then she heaved and vomited onto the roadside. 'I am sorry,' she whispered. 'Leave me here. If vigilantes find you with a sick girl they will kill you.'

'I will get you somewhere warm and you can sweat it out,' said Charlie, trying to sound convincing. None he knew had survived dysentery without immediate access to a bed and a fire. They were miles from anywhere in the exposed countryside.

Maria was weak and fainting as he led her to the horses. Not knowing what else to do he slung her bodily over the first animal and grabbed the reins of the second.

With his thoughts a mad buzz of terror, Charlie began to walk with the horses back out on the track.

He contemplated mounting, but he knew he wasn't a good enough rider to hold the other horse.

From her position laid over the saddle Maria's prone form lay disconcertingly motionless. Charlie had no idea of where he was going or what he was going to do.

'A warm bed could save her life,' he reasoned out loud, trying to make himself believe it.

Maria stirred a little, causing the counterweight of her legs to shift and sending her slipping down the side of the horse. He grabbed at her, finding himself torn in two directions as the second animal took the chance to veer away.

'Walthamstow,' said Maria, as he held her desperately by the top of her dress. 'It is only a few miles from here. There is a wise woman there. She can help.' And then she drifted back into unconsciousness.

Charlie managed to haul her back over the horse. Her long torso flopped easily across the animal.

He replayed her words. Wise woman. *A witch.* Then he remembered. The witch who had been released from Wapping prison. Maria had said the woman was from her village. He shuddered. No Christian visited witches.

In the dark he tried to quell his rising panic. Vigilantes were on every horizon, and he was travelling with a sick girl. Whatever he decided it must be fast.

He called the map to mind. Walthamstow was the nearest town. Strange that she hadn't mentioned where she was from when they were passing so close.

He did not expect that the locals would let him and a sick girl into their village during plague times. But he hardly had a wealth of other options.

Charlie took the reins and tugged at the horses. Then he set off as fast as he could with the animals reined in behind him.

As he made towards the witch vigilante torches winked closer on every horizon.

Chapter Thirty-Seven

Mayor Lawrence pushed opened the door to his half-timbered house on Fen Church Street. The summer day had drooped to night, and he thought he was not too late.

Sounds from inside confirmed his hopes. His maid-servant was home. He felt his body react before he had seen her.

In his dining room was an expensive table which had come with his wife's dowry and six cheaper chairs of his own.

Lawrence ran his tongue over his lower lip. His wife was out, visiting her sister.

Behind the table Debs was on her knees, cleaning the fire grate by candlelight. He watched the swaying of her hips as the brush moved over the hearth tiles.

Even the way she worked was provocative.

When Lawrence had hired the fourteen-year-old maid his wife had insisted the girl dressed more modestly. But everything Debs wore hinted at the tantalising figure beneath.

The bulge of her brown hair beneath the pink cotton cap. A border of white lace framing the exquisite youth of her skin. Linen cloth draped to cover the tops of her breasts, but managing somehow only to highlight them further.

He crept into the room and knelt silently behind her, lifting her skirt and running a hand up her thigh.

Debs jerked around, her hand catching his in reflex.

Then she saw Lawrence and her shocked expression changed to something smiling and shrewd.

The sight of her face brought another electric shock of lust. Her large green eyes dropped a little at the corners, giving Debs a permanently smouldering expression.

She had neat brown eyebrows and a tiny straight nose, like an artist's pencil marks. Her neck could be considered thick. Chubby even. But to Lawrence it was voluptuous. A gateway to the hidden paradise below.

Debs had once shown him her breasts and the image was burned in his brain.

His hand was still trapped under hers, halfway up the silky skin of her thigh.

Lawrence pushed a little upwards.

Her hold on his fingers tightened.

Desire for her gripped him. Every sense in his body screamed to wrench aside the skirts, before she could push him away.

But Lawrence knew Debs well enough. She would never let him have her like this, on the floor.

He pushed his hand up again, using more force. The tip of his finger slid further up between her legs.

She squealed and twisted away, turning backwards to face him as she lounged on the wooden floorboards.

The linen cloth covering her chest had come apart in the middle, just a fraction. Beneath it the line where her breasts met moved in time to her breathing.

Lawrence made another move to get under her skirts, but she was too fast for him, scrabbling away and raising a finger to her lips.

'Mayor Lawrence,' she whispered in the sultry tones he often replayed in his fantasies. 'What if your wife were to come?'

She stood up, dusting herself down.

Lawrence raised himself from the floor.

'Please Debs,' he said, 'I cannot bear it.'

The memory of where his hand had been moments before was torturing him.

'Then you must find a place where we might enjoy each other's company.'

She folded her arms.

'It is not easy Debs, when you are so high up in the city as I am. People recognise me. And I am so busy with the King's missions besides,' he added, seizing the chance to try and impress her.

Deb's eyes registered interest.

'Do you still seek the witch-murderer?'

'We know it to be this thief taker,' said Lawrence. 'But I have been asked to investigate another man. Someone who calls himself Thomas Malvern. They think he might be involved.'

Lawrence gave a heavy shrug to denote the foolishness of majesty.

'They have me visiting gambling clubs and following bets this man has made. And all of it has come to nothing of course,' he continued.

Lawrence took out a little ruby ring.

'I have a gift for you,' he said.

The expression of delight on her face was worth the torment of the last few hours waiting to see her.

'You must not wear it when my wife is home,' he added.

Debs nodded, and Lawrence seated himself on the nearest chair.

'Come sit on my lap and I will put it on you.'

She hesitated and then seated herself. He wondered if she could feel the heat rising up from his thighs in waves.

'What does this man bet on?' asked Debs as she settled herself on his legs.

'Malvern bets large sums on the plague and where it might spread,' said Lawrence, shifting so she tilted back further towards his groin. 'All perfectly innocent.'

'Where does he think it will spread?' Debs shuffled a little forward.

Lawrence shrugged. 'To the rich parts of town. It is not a bet he is likely to win. The rich can afford to protect themselves with guards in the west.'

Debs nodded, gratifyingly interested in his business.

'Surely the gambling house must refuse to pay his bet if he wins?'

Lawrence grunted. 'A lawless place such as that? They will pay out bets, under any circumstance. It is a kind of honour amongst thieves I suppose,' he added, begrudgingly.

'Perhaps this Malvern knows something more about plague than most,' she observed.

Lawrence gave a hard laugh. 'He is a fool Debs. Talk at the club is Malvern boasts of spreading some infection himself. He will get himself hanged in due course, whether he is guilty of murder or not.'

The Mayor shook his head. 'We are better to forget Malvern and find out this thief taker.'

'You might ask my father for help,' suggested Debs, tilting her pretty head. 'All kinds of men visit an astrologer. Perhaps he could tell you something.'

Lawrence smiled. Debs's loyalty to her family was admirable. She was no ordinary common girl. Her father was William Lilly, who had once been astrologer to the old King.

It was a shame, thought Lawrence, that such a beautiful daughter did not have a better dowry to raise her above maid's work.

Though it suited him well enough. Just a few more weeks, and Lawrence felt certain he would enjoy every part of Debs Lilly on his own terms.

'Put out your hand,' he instructed.

She proffered her fingers and Lawrence found himself marvelling at the youth of her white skin and the perfect pink scallops of her fingernails.

He dug a hand up under her skirts. She flinched, but did not object.

'Let me see a little further,' he whispered hoarsely, his mouth flat against her ear. 'Let me see more than I have done.' He held the ring out in his other hand, like bait.

Debs smiled and inched up her skirts over her knee.

Lawrence hardly dared breathe. She pulled them up higher.

The ring in his outstretched hand began to tremble.

She gave another final flash. More than he would have ever hoped to see. Lawrence stared, trying to brand the sight in his mind for later use.

Then he noticed something besides the dizzying allure of her nakedness.

'Are you bruised?' he asked in sudden confusion. 'You have a mark there.'

Debs frowned, rearranged her skirts in confusion.

'There is no bruise,' she started to say. And then she saw the purple mark, feathering down from her groin in a network of raised veins.

It was a plague token.

As her skirts fell back down she was already screaming.

Chapter Thirty-Eight

Pain had tightened Charlie's awareness to a narrow dim tunnel. It throbbed through his savaged feet, bit at his strained muscles and pulled down at his eyelids. Ahead the slice of dark highway jarred in his vision as he took step after exhausted step.

'Hold!' A frightened voice sounded from up ahead, and Charlie realised that he had reached Walthamstow and the village was guarded through the night.

In the dawn light Charlie made out the weary face of a young man. He was staring at Maria's lolling body and blue face.

The guard's eyes bulged and he kicked a sleeping form lying out on the grass. A second sentry looked up blearily then rose to his feet.

'He tries to bring with him the plague,' he said.

'No, no,' Charlie held up tired hands. 'It is the bloody flux she has. She is from your village. I only ask you to let her rest somewhere warm.'

Maria was unconscious and her skin had turned an even paler blue. Her breathing came in short rapid breaths.

'Get back!' shouted the first guard.

'Please,' said Charlie. 'Her name is Maria. Anna-Maria. She used to be of your village. She has an older sister, Eva.'

The sentries exchanged glances and receded into muttering. Eventually one disappeared back towards the village and the other spoke up.

'We have sent for the wise woman,' he said cryptically.

Charlie's mouth set tightly, realising what they meant. They had called for the witch.

His mind raced. Likely the villagers thought to have him cursed.

Before he could make up his mind to turn back a female voice rang out. He squinted into the gloom to see a tall woman stalking towards the gate.

She matched the height of both guards, and her simple wool dress was crowded by the jumble of scissors, knives and leather pouches strung from a belt on her hips. Her hair was like an explosion. Coarse red curls corkscrewed down to her waist and out at the sides in munificent chaos.

Charlie momentarily forgot the peril of Maria's health to regard the statuesque woman with undisguised fear. He had never seen a witch before and wondered what she was capable of.

Herbs and greenery were stuffed beneath her belt beside the assortment of cutting implements.

The woman sniffed the air and gave a quick nod. Her sun-dappled face and bright brown eyes settled on Charlie.

'It is dysentery that she has,' she confirmed. 'Bring her through.' She turned quickly without any notion her orders would not be immediately attended to.

One of the young guards stepped forward to take the reins of the horse, holding a handkerchief over his mouth. Charlie made to go along behind it, but the other guard stopped him uncertainly.

'Have him bring her through,' called the woman without turning around. 'If he has made it this far then most likely he has not taken the bloody flux.'

———

The wise woman's cottage was set a little apart from the other smaller huts. It was made of wattle and daub and perfectly round with a hole belching chimney smoke through a blackened circle of thatch.

A glimpse of white flowers brought a sudden image of Maria's slaughtered sister. There was a hawthorn tree growing in her garden of odd-looking plants.

'Bring her in,' came the command from in front, 'and we will see what can be done.'

Charlie carried in Maria's slumped form. Her face was flushed now and her breathing was laboured.

The wise woman worked quickly to spread a thick hessian sack on the floor and lay Maria gently onto it.

'What is this?' she tapped against the solid bodice. 'Better to do without foolish clothes of this kind. Look away,' she added, gesturing to Charlie, 'I will take off this rigid thing so she might breathe more easily.'

Looking around the cottage Charlie had the strangest feeling that he had been there before. The cottage was lined at the sides with three enormous tables, each packed with a chaotic array of containers.

There were large flagons from which leaves and branches poked, ceramic dishes filled with different coloured grease, lolling heads of opium poppies, thickly-tied clusters of liquorice root and many pestle and mortars in various stages of pounding.

Charlie had heard of witches who lived in the country, riding pigs and worshipping the moon. But there was also talk of magical folk who could cure with potions and spells. This must be what she was about to perform on Maria.

'The pulse of the blood is steady and that is a good thing,' said the woman. Charlie turned back to see Maria dressed in a white shift, her thick bodice lying beside her. The wise woman had moved to a table.

'But her breathing is bad,' she concluded, cutting up herbs and garlic with a rapid hand and throwing them into a pot with a pinch of salt and a spoon of honey.

Charlie watched her with disappointment. So far her potion had been pitifully peasant-like. He'd expected a few shavings of unicorn horn at least. Even the lowliest alchemist in London had a dried lizard to stir the pot.

'Do you not have any special ingredients for a cure?' he asked, looking at the basic contents of the cauldron bubbling away. The woman shook her head. 'If there was a cure for bloody flux then all would know of it,' she said. 'It is the body that fights the illness and all we can do is give it the means to clean itself.'

She handed him the cup.

'Have her drink all of this in little sips,' she said. 'She must drink all, no matter how difficult it is for her. Then she will rest a little and in an hour we will give her another cup to drink.' The woman looked at the ill girl. 'We will try our best to keep her alive,' she said. 'Anna-Maria's family has a sad enough history.'

'What do you mean?' Despite the circumstances, Charlie's curiosity was piqued. He'd always assumed Maria to come from a family of plenty.

'She was bedded with a local boy, but the marriage did not take place,' said the wise woman, frowning at the half-conscious girl.

'Bedded?'

'It is a country practice. The young people who are betrothed spend a night together before they are wed.' She pointed. 'Give her the liquid.'

'But what if the girl becomes pregnant?' said Charlie, half distracted from the task. He set the cup against Maria's lips. To his relief she opened her mouth a little.

'They do not make relations of that kind,' explained the wise woman patiently.

'Of what kind then?' Another tilt. Another sip.

'Of the kind which a couple might like to know before they are wed.'

Charlie let his eyes fall on Maria's face, trying to imagine her as the kind of girl who would roll around in a country grope. He found that he couldn't.

'So why did they not marry after they were . . . bedded?' he asked finally, letting the final few dregs of the cup tip into Maria's soft mouth.

'No one knows. They were betrothed even as children. It would have been a good match. Here,' she added, taking the cup and refilling it. 'Give her this as well, if she will take it.'

Charlie took it, feeling his throat grip into a tight fist as he looked on Maria's face.

In sleep her perpetual expression of disdain had vanished. The oval of her pale face looked like an ink-drawing, with eyebrows and nose sketched straight and lashes curved in dark semi-circles. Her wide mouth looked smaller. It was strange, he thought, to notice these details when they mattered least.

The eyes slid open a crack to reveal a mass of burst vessels.

'Eva?' she whispered.

Charlie shook his head. 'Try to rest,' he muttered, feeling like an impostor suddenly. Someone else should be at her bedside. A friend or relative.

He brought the cup again to her mouth and she took a little mouthful. Then her head slumped back, letting the broth trickle out down her chin.

Suddenly the woman was by his side.

'You should rest again now,' she said. 'Things will look better in the morning.'

He moved to a corner of the hut where the woman had laid down some straw for him to sleep on. Charlie slumped back down, falling into a dark slumber where images of Maria's pale face slunk through his mind.

Chapter Thirty-Nine

Charlie awoke to find a pair of light-brown eyes staring down at him and blinked awake in shock.

'You snore very badly,' said the wise woman. She stood, unleashing the clattering sound of the implements at her hips. 'But you may go and take your thanks from Maria, for you saved her life.'

'She is . . . she is well then?'

'Not yet well. But she is out of danger. She was asking for you. Come.'

The wise woman walked away from his makeshift bed, and he stumbled up to follow.

Maria's skin had changed from blue to white, and her eyes were open and alert. A half finished dish of soup by her side suggested she'd been able to take some food.

To his great surprise Charlie felt the breath rush out of him in relief.

'Joan says you saved my life by bringing me here,' she said in a tight little voice. 'And so I suppose I owe you great thanks.' She clenched her eyes shut as if the admission pained her. 'For you might have left me on the road.'

'Is she . . . is she a witch?' Charlie lowered his voice. As far as he could see the woman had brought Maria back from the brink of death, but if Satan had been involved in the process he'd rather know sooner rather than later.

'I am a believer in God just as you are,' came the voice of the wise woman. 'But I choose to listen different to some, for I do not like cold churches. Though they put me in prison for it,' she added.

'Can you tell us something of Wapping?' asked Charlie, thinking the information might be useful.'

The wise woman shook her head. 'I saw only the prison,' she said. 'It is a dreadful place.'

'Could you not use your magic to enchant the guards?' asked Charlie.

'It is no dark thing we do here,' replied the wise woman. 'Herbs and roots and berries. That is all.'

'The Church would not agree with you,' said Charlie.

'No they would likely not,' she said. 'And I tread a careful path. For if the wrong person takes a dislike to me I might still be burned as a witch. But I find I have a gift for healing and so I take the risk to share it.'

Charlie considered this. Mother Mitchell's words came floating back to him.

See you lightning strike me down or the ground rumble beneath me when I enter a church? A woman works the laundry, she sells her body. Men beg on the streets, they sell their bodies. God minds not which part you sell boy. The only disgrace to Him is not being paid enough for it.

'Whoever gave you that key knew something of the old ways,' the wise woman was saying.

Charlie's hand moved to his neck in surprise.

'It is tied in the colour of enchantment,' she added, indicating the aged purple ribbon looping through the key. 'It was a close friend who gave it to you?'

'I was found holding it,' said Charlie, 'as an orphan. I think my mother gave it me.'

'Did she wear willow?' the wise woman tapped the plait around her neck.

A sudden, unexpected image forked into Charlie's mind. A purple ribbon. A voice.

The willow is a maiden whose tresses sweep the water. From it she takes great powers. A magic tree.

Charlie shook the image away, feeling an urgent need to change the subject. He didn't want his scant maternal recollections to be muddied with ideas of witchery.

Something else occurred to him suddenly.

'I want to know about something which grows in your garden,' said Charlie. He had remembered the hawthorn growing outside. 'I will fetch it to you.'

Crossing the cottage he ducked out through the little door, and spotting the hawthorn waving in the wind he tugged free a little branch of it.

As he returned to the doorway a blood-curdling shriek went up and he froze in his tracks. The wise woman stood guarding her door. Her hand was struck out towards him.

'Do not bring it within!' she bellowed.

Charlie paused looking to the hawthorn branch.

'It is the smell of death!' she shouted. 'It is bad luck to bring it within the home!'

In his shock Charlie dropped the branch entirely, and as the wise woman was still frozen in the attitude of pointing he kicked it away for good measure.

'But. You grow it in your garden,' he returned uncertainly.

'Did you not know that hawthorn should not be brought into the home?' she said. 'Is this something Londoners know nothing of?'

The wise woman shook her head as if in pity at the ignorance of city dwellers. She disappeared momentarily and reappeared with a bowl of salt and sage leaves.

'Clean your hands in this before you come back within,' she said. She was still shaking her head at his idiocy.

He followed her to where a wide-eyed Maria was still reclined in bed.

'I . . . I wanted to ask her about the hawthorn.' He explained, feeling he had been caught committing some kind of crime.

Maria's face set quickly in recognition.

'It was found on my sister's body,' she explained.

'I heard about Eva,' nodded the wise woman. 'We lit candles for your poor sister. And we heard rumours of another death,' she added. 'The witch-murders, people are calling them. We hear talk of nothing else but the dreadful details.'

'We think he makes a master spell,' said Charlie. 'A death for each corner. Hawthorn for earth.'

'Hawthorn can mean earth. But it has many good magical uses besides,' said the wise woman. 'They are under the May moon. The moon of disenchantment. The moon of hindrance. It brings with it the corpse smell which is bad luck.'

'But what does it mean?' persisted Charlie.

'Disenchantment can be used for many things,' said the wise woman. 'To turn away the desires of a suitor. To thwart the power of a great enemy, or halt some event. Those with proper knowledge would never make the spell indoors,' she added.

Charlie gave a half smile, not really understanding.

'Are white ribbons part of the spell?' he asked, remembering the decorated corpses.

The wise woman nodded. 'White ribbon is to bind tight and to hinder.'

'Then we thought right,' said Charlie. 'He makes some spell against the King. To aid an uprising.'

'Only the person who has cast the spell would know their reasons,' said the wise woman. 'They will carry with them an emblem or a charm that the spell had been accomplished. Some charm or other thing to keep the magic alive. If you found that it might be possible to know what the spell was for. But without it the reason is a mystery.'

The wise woman's expression hardened.

'Death is a powerful seal on a spell. But it is for dark ends only. This is an older magic.' She looked thoughtful. 'The second girl was found with a birdcage was she not?'

Charlie nodded. 'With feathers on her.'

'Then I agree that there is some master spell at work,' said the wise woman. 'Hawthorn is of the earth. And birds are of the air.' She counted on her fingers. 'Fire and water are left. He means to make some powerful spell of the elements. And for that,' she added, 'two more must die.'

'We must make haste to get back on the road,' said Maria. She was struggling to sit upright. Sat on the edge of the bed she leaned forward for a long pain-wracked minute. 'We have lost half a day, but we may still reach Wapping ahead of him.'

'Maria you cannot think to travel?' Charlie looked at her in alarm.

'I am quite well now.' She was looking straight ahead, but had not yet attempted the move to stand. Leaning on her hand she pitched forward slightly and then staggered upright. To his amazement she reached to scoop up her reed bodice which the wise woman had cast onto the floor beside her bed.

'It is better we wait,' protested Charlie. 'And you cannot think to wear that ridiculous bodice?'

Recovery from dysentery could be rapid. But taking a rough horseback ride on a dusty track seemed reckless.

Maria gritted her teeth and began to strap the rigid garment around the outside of her shift. She tightened the laces single-handedly, with a gasp of pain. 'I am practised enough with horses to sit easily for a few hours,' she said, battling to control a grimace. 'We can still overtake him if we ride hard. But we will lose any advantage if we do not go now.'

Maria clambered to her feet. The wise woman rooted around in her store of herbs.

'Here is a little parcel of food and a flask of ginever to protect you from plague,' she said, stuffing a flask and a bulging handkerchief into Charlie's hand.

'Plague is thick in Wapping. It roams the streets and all is deadly. You must be most careful,' she added. 'Maria is not yet well. And the way from here is thick with men trying to kill Londoners.'

Something else occurred to her, and she stooped to retrieve it from underneath a table.

'This was left by a Civil War soldier, and I have never had a use for it.' She was holding out a heavy looking pistol.

Charlie took it.

'It only has one shot,' she explained. 'But one shot could be all you need if those vigilantes get hold of you.'

'Thank you.' Charlie handed the gun to Maria. 'Best you have this,' he said. 'I have other ways to defend myself.'

Maria took the pistol uncertainly.

'Then you must have something,' insisted the wise woman, looking at Charlie. She unhooked a pair of scissors on her belt and passed them to him.

'They are for trimming candlewicks,' she said, 'to light your journey.'

Charlie nodded his thanks, wondering where on earth he would be lighting candles.

They both headed for the door.

'God Bless your father Anna-Maria,' said the wise woman, 'and his forgiveness to your mother.'

Charlie saw something inscrutable pass through Maria's eyes and then it was gone. She kicked open the door harder than he'd thought possible in her feeble state and made out ahead of him.

Chapter Forty

Dawn was breaking as the wagon jogged uncomfortably over the rough track. Under his plague hood Thomas was already sweating in the heat of the day.

He smiled to himself. As plague savaged the east, the west of the city still traded. Soon his infection would explode across the city, spreading it widely and quickly throughout England.

His final plans were almost in place.

A turnpike loomed ahead on the road and he readied himself.

He turned his head to check on his wife. Teresa was sat at the back of the wagon, her arms wrapped around her knees, her blonde hair falling like a curtain over her shoulders.

He knew she must be anxious to be outside.

Pulling at the reins Thomas brought all six horses to a standstill with difficulty. He reached into his canvas cloak and drew out two Health Certificates, holding them aloft.

His status in the city had ensured him the highest possible authority to travel. And the royal crest sped him through country outposts where others would be stopped.

The turnpike man was keeping a long distance and had swaddled most of his head with his own shirt.

'You may not pass.'

Thomas peered closer in disbelief. The turnpike man was holding a pitchfork in an unconvincing attitude of confrontation.

'Move aside,' called Thomas from the driver's seat.

'You may not pass.' The man gave a little frightened dance, clearly concerned to come nearer. He caught sight of Thomas's wife sitting in the wagon and he stood staring for a moment.

'My wife does not like the dust of the road,' explained Thomas.

The turnpike continued to gaze at Teresa, clearly wondering how such an attractive woman had ended up travelling with this monster.

Teresa pushed her head deeper into the cradle of her arms, so only her eyes could be seen.

'Move aside,' repeated Thomas evenly.

The turnpike's voice swelled, finding courage in the announcement. 'We know what you are about in these parts and we'll no more of it. Travelling when the moon is full. Bringing back dead bodies in that wagon,' he pointed the pitchfork. 'No more will a devil's consort travel near our village,' he concluded, puffing his chest out. 'The men have settled upon it and will drive you out by force if needs be.'

'And yet you have not men with you now.' It was a statement rather than a question, and Thomas made it with his head cocked to one side in amusement. He knew his passage to Wapping had begun to draw attention from the locals, but since this would be his last trip it was of little concern.

'They are not yet out 'o their beds,' admitted the turnpike, with an anxious glance over his shoulder. 'But soon they will be.'

Thomas made a deliberate show of tilting his beaked mask to look into the empty fields beyond the turnpike. He lowered his voice.

'I will give you two choices.'

The turnpike took a stronger hold on his pitchfork.

'You may live,' continued Thomas, 'and let me pass. Or you may die, and let me pass. It matters not either way to me.' He unsheathed his sword and regarded the blade lazily.

The turnpike had begun to tremble, but he held firm. It was only when Thomas made to descend from the wagon that he backed away towards his gate.

'You must sign your name in the book,' he said, keeping his eyes on Thomas. 'All that pass must sign their names. King's orders.'

Thomas slid from his horse, approaching the turnpike and taking a cautious look at the wagon. Teresa had ducked out of sight.

'For your trouble,' said Thomas, tossing a coin towards the turnpike.

The man caught it in an easy movement and examined it, looking up in surprised gratitude.

As Thomas predicted, the cash calmed the man. He stopped inching away and waited as Thomas approached to sign the book.

The turnpike never saw the sword flash out.

It sliced open his belly before he had chance to scream.

He gaped down at the mortal wound, his face taut in silent amazement.

Thomas allowed his sword to fall with a thud on the grassy ground. Flexing his gloved fingers he stepped towards the turnpike's open wound.

In a practised movement Thomas's hand plunged in and up through the intestines and into the ribcage.

The turnpike tottered, suspended on Thomas's bloody hand. His mouth opened in a choking sound.

'Do you feel that?' asked Thomas. 'That is your heart I squeeze at.'

A curtain of blood was pouring from the turnpike's severed stomach.

'This was how they killed my father,' continued Thomas. 'After they burned his hands to black stumps.'

Thomas squeezed his fist.

'You are all of you traitors,' he said. 'And I will see your King die a traitor as he deserves.'

The turnpike continued to choke and gasp.

In his gloved hand Thomas felt the final little shudder, the last effort of the heart to live.

Then the turnpike's head dropped, and Thomas knelt, laying the body on the ground.

He wrenched his bloodied forearm from inside the man's remains. The heart in his hand was a dishevelled lump of tissue. They didn't always come out whole.

Thomas looked at it for a long moment.

This would be the last visit to Wapping and the last load. Infection would soon be impossible to halt.

They'd told him at the port that he would never find men to load his dreadful cargo. Not at any price. But they were wrong. Men could be got for a price. It was simply a case of knowing where to look.

Thomas picked up the quill by the turnpike's book. He wetted the nib in the bloody heart. And smiling under his mask he wrote his alias.

In these parts fear was useful currency. The locals should know who they should be afraid of.

Chapter Forty-One

The land around London was a wild sort of place. But despite the unruly fields the air was fresh. Golden-green crops grew either side of the hard sun-beaten track. But the road was almost deserted.

Charlie and Maria passed a huge stage-coach inn with a bread-baking oven, brewing barn and smokehouse, but it was all boarded up.

Maria wheezed and wavered atop her horse, but refused to stop. 'It is only the dust,' she said, in a tired voice. 'I am quite well.'

Charlie was building a grudging admiration for her. He knew she must be feeling weak and ill. She was certainly tougher than he had originally supposed.

'Not that way,' Maria was shaking her head as he attempted to steer his horse onto a smaller lane.

'That way goes through Hackney marshes,' she explained. 'It is dangerous for the horses.'

Charlie consulted his mental map. Avoiding the marshland meant they were a day's ride from Stratford. Besides that they needed to get as far ahead of Malvern as possible, they only had a little parcel of food from the wise woman.

He caught sight of a snatch of grey in a roadside gully. It was a canvas tent. Someone had made a little camp, but it was now deserted.

'Wait here,' he said, sliding down the side of his horse. 'Maybe there is a little food which has been left.'

'Wait!' said Maria. 'It could be dangerous.'

'If there is something in there which can help us then we should use it,' said Charlie. 'This looks to be a fortunate find.'

He scrambled down into the gully and approached the tent. It had been hastily constructed from canvas and trees branches in a circular wigwam shape. Taking up a stick from the ground, Charlie lifted the flap at the entrance.

Sunlight shone into the tent, lighting the faces inside.

Lying in the tent were the bloody remains of a husband and wife.

He fell back, covering his mouth. The canvas dropped down and Charlie leant heavily on the verge for a moment. Then he scrambled back up the gully as quickly as his legs would take him.

'What was it?' asked Maria, seeing he had turned pale despite the heat of the day.

'Bodies,' he mumbled, scrabbling to get back on his horse. 'It looks as though the vigilantes have been here recently.'

Maria was pointing uncertainly towards the fields.

In the middle distance were three nut-brown farmers. They hefted farm tools in the unmistakable stance of men bent on violence.

Charlie grabbed hold of Maria.

'This way,' he said fiercely, pulling her and the horses towards the waving grassland of the marsh.

'But that is swamp,' protested Maria.

'Those are likely the same men that killed the people in that tent,' hissed Charlie. 'They have come back to hide the bodies so they cannot be hanged for their crime.'

He tugged her off the road and onto the marshland.

Hackney marshes stretched before them. Islands of tall reed and grass grew in a patchwork of waterlogged soil. It was impossible to tell how deep and boggy it ran.

But the marsh grass grew waist height and was relatively soft and green.

'They will see our movement from the grass,' said Maria uncertainly. But she took the reins from Charlie and led the horses gently into the swampy soil, making reassuring clicking sounds to guide them forwards.

The horses stood a foot taller than the waving grass.

'We need to get over there,' Charlie pointed to a denser higher patch in the marsh, 'where the shrub can hide us and the animals both.'

He took a few steps towards it and his leg sank knee deep into the swampy land.

The men were near enough to hear their voices now.

'Hurry!' urged Charlie, wrenching his foot free from the mud. 'They will see the horses.'

But Maria had stopped to listen. 'Wait,' she said. 'They said something about a wagon, I am sure of it.'

'Perhaps wagons pass through here Maria. It hardly matters if they kill us.'

The two horses were standing prominently above the marsh grasses, and the screen of scrubland looked far away.

Then Maria, displaying a talent for horsemanship which bordered on the supernatural, coaxed both animals to kneel and then lie on the marsh floor.

Realising it was too late to run, Charlie knelt beside them, praying the animals didn't give them away.

'You are sure it was him,' sounded a voice, 'you are sure it was the plague doctor?'

Charlie froze. His eyes flicked to Maria, who was straining to hear every word.

'Aye,' came another voice. 'The last name signed in the tollbook was Thomas Malvern.'

There was a hawking sound as the speaker paused to spit.

'Malvern's last mockery of us, I reckon. Letting us know it were him that killed that poor turnpike.'

'We should have been braver on the last full moon,' voiced the third man. 'We should have put a stop to it then. Him coming through with his dread load of dead bodies.'

'Aye,' agreed the second man. 'For whenever the corpse collector comes then young girls die.'

'You are sure he killed the turnpike?'

'There was blood everywhere. And no turnpike. What else do you think happened?'

'We should be glad of one thing,' said the second man. 'If he did for the turnpike then he must mean to make this his last journey through these parts.'

Maria caught Charlie's eye and frowned meaningfully.

'What do you think he did with the body?' asked the first man.

There was a long pause. One of the men spat again.

'God save us we never find out,' said the third man. 'Come now,' he added. 'Let us deal with these battered bodies. We can sink them in the marsh and they will never be found.'

One of the horses shook its head and let out a loud *harrumph* of air.

'What was that?' asked one of the men.

'What?'

'That sound! Be quiet. Listen!'

There was a long agonising silence. Charlie held his breath, looking to Maria and willing the horses to stay still.

'Maybe more city folk hide in the edge of the marshlands. We had best sweep the edges.'

Charlie picked out a stone from the grass and, gauging his shot, skimmed it across the marsh. Moments later an outraged bird flapped out squawking from the grass.

'It is only a marsh bird you fool,' said the first man. 'Now let us get these bodies hidden before we are all hanged for it.'

* * *

It was almost an hour until the men departed, heaving away the evidence of their crime to another part of the marsh.

'Did you hear that?' asked Maria. 'Thomas Malvern. He travels with corpses by the full moon.'

Charlie nodded, more concerned with their immediate escape.

'And he was there only this morning,' continued Maria. 'We may outpace him still.'

Her eyes were shining as she thought through the options.

'Stratford is close, and he must pass through it. With luck we might be able to get to some justice there before him and have them make his arrest.'

Charlie began heaving himself upright in the mud, thinking they would need a lot more luck than she realised to convince the Stratford guards to let them in.

And at the moment they had a far more pressing problem.

'We cannot risk going back onto the main road,' he said. 'Those men are policing it and there could be others. If we are to go on, Maria, it must be through the marsh.'

Chapter Forty-Two

Amesbury checked the information on his paper.

Shadwell harbour front, red door.

He turned to Blackstone.

'We should find her in one of these brothels,' he said.

'And you can be sure this is the same Jenny that met with Malvern?'

Amesbury nodded. 'She left the gambling club with him. Then she fled to her mother's bawdy house. That is on this road.'

Blackstone wondered how Amesbury had gotten hold of this information. But since it was likely to be from his elaborate spy network, thought it politic not to ask.

The two men scanned the dilapidated array of bawdy houses and taverns which were crushed along the waterfront like bad teeth.

'I remember this place from my seafaring days,' said Blackstone. 'Even after months fighting battles at sea, we avoided brothels here. They are for men too drunk to value their lives.'

'It will not take long,' said Amesbury, 'and then you may return to your plague duties as promised.'

Blackstone nodded, not relishing the thought of returning to the Wapping Road. 'That one,' he said, pointing to a red door.

The two men approached the house. Amesbury raised his hand to knock and then, thinking better of it, pushed the rotting door and walked in with Blackstone following after.

Inside the house was gloomy, with dusty floorboards and a plain table with a half empty bottle of wine.

Three women sat a little apart from the table on a long bench. Each had their skirt hitched high to their waist and sat splay-legged in demonstration of what could be paid for.

One seemed slightly better off than the rest, Blackstone noted. Perhaps she had been a kept mistress recently abandoned by her suitor. Shadwell was for sailors, and every London prostitute with a choice in the matter avoided sailors.

The better-presented woman wore a pink silk bodice which had been cut to expose both her breasts. She had curled two tendrils of dark waxy hair to fall on either side of her cat-like eyes and looked to be in her mid-twenties.

The arrangement of her hair and features reminded Amesbury of Louise Keroulle, the King's mistress. Amesbury had told Blackstone that he did not trust Louise. He had recently found her rummaging through the King's private documents. And Amesbury was fast subscribing to the belief that she and her brother George may be French spies.

The prostitutes on either side of the better-kept woman looked ten years older. One had glued false eyebrows of mouse fur to her face, giving her an expression of permanent outrage.

The other had an enormous bosom, its ageing shape inexpertly bundled into her tight blue dress. A network of white stretch marks dappled her cleavage and, Blackstone guessed, ran to the corpulent belly bulging below.

The most attractive of the three moved to pour wine from the bottle, but Amesbury held up his hand. Blackstone guessed he had not brought enough ready money to risk the fees the house might try to extort for a glass of wine.

The woman sat back down, her eyes roaming his face with a mixture of curiosity and annoyance.

The door banged and an enormous man lumbered into the room. At first Blackstone assumed him to be a customer. Then he caught sight of the fear in the women's faces and realised the man must be in charge.

The owner had a slick of greasy black and grey hair and a sad tug of skin where his left eye had once been. His shirt was dirty and hung loose, but his breeches were new, stitched in the longer style of sailors.

The man's remaining eye flicked accusingly over the two men and then the women.

'Why have our guests not been offered wine?'

'They offered,' said Amesbury. 'I declined.'

Rage animated the bawdy-house owner's features. He moved to the table and picked up the bottle.

'A man does not come to a bawdy house and refuse a drink,' he said, sloshing the thin red liquid into a tankard. He thrust the vessel at Amesbury.

'Take it,' he demanded, tipping out a second drink and foisting it on Blackstone.

Slowly Amesbury wrapped his calloused fingers around the tankard. Watching him, Blackstone did the same.

A little of the anger seemed to go out of the bawdy-house owner.

'You came from the city?' he asked suspiciously.

Amesbury nodded, taking a sip of the thin wine.

'London is a foul place,' opined the man, tipping a cup of wine for himself and drinking. 'I was there only last week. To buy ointment,' he added, cupping his testicles by way of explanation. 'For sailors are a dirty breed, and it passes to me, by way of the women.'

He scratched his head, philosophical on this point, and took another swig of wine.

'I will go no more,' he continued, 'for I hear dread things. A thousand corpses turned up overnight in Fen Church graveyard. No one knows from where. The locals are in terror, for the devil must have a hand in it.'

'The locals exaggerate,' said Amesbury with a dismissive wave of his wine. 'Plague makes them as giddy as women.'

'I saw it myself,' glowered the bawdy-house owner, 'a great pauper's grave. Empty one day. Filled to the brim the next.'

'Such a thing is not possible,' Blackstone reassured him. 'Even if half the city had died overnight . . .'

'I tell you I saw it!' shouted the man, wine sloshing from his cup. 'And a great beaked monster visits the church at night. That is what the people say. The devil himself is filling London's graves.'

Amesbury glanced at Blackstone.

'Perhaps something worth investigating,' he said finally.

Blackstone nodded. 'I shall visit the graveyard on my return.'

The bawdy house owner appeared to be wrestling with this information.

After a moment he nodded at the women, evidently deciding the conversation to be concluded. They sat up a little in their seats.

'Do not be fooled that she looks a little older,' the bawdy-house owner said conversationally, gesturing at the face with the mouse-brows. 'She will do anything you ask. Anything.'

He turned to Blackstone. 'You seem a proper sort,' he assessed. 'She will do for you. Very good proportions you will find on her. I know them personally.'

A barking sound which could have been a laugh came from the owner's mouth.

'We have come looking for a different girl,' said Amesbury carefully. 'Someone who I was told worked here.'

'A man does not come into my house, drink my wine and ask for a different girl,' said the bawdy-house owner. His anger was rising again.

'A girl named Jenny,' said Amesbury.

The owner's face tightened, and the name brought a jolt of recognition from the woman with the mouse eyebrows.

'You want to know about Jenny you ask one of the whores,' said the owner. He snatched up the bottle again and filled Amesbury's already full tankard to the brim.

'Two guineas for the wine,' he added, thrusting out his palm, 'unless you want to add a bloody nose to your bill.'

Amesbury dug in his purse, and Blackstone was relieved to see it heavy with coins.

'One guinea,' said Amesbury evenly, dropping a coin into the man's grubby palm.

The brothel owner gave a grunt of acceptance. The coin was enough to buy several cases of the wine he served, Blackstone judged.

'You want to ask them something you have to pay for their company,' the owner said, glowering.

Amesbury turned to the women. They looked frightened.

His eyes rested on the mouse-brows.

'Her then,' he said.

'And you?' the brothel-keeper turned on Blackstone.

'I will keep them both company.'

'Very well,' the owner's face made some complicated expressions. 'As I said, she will do anything you ask of her. But you must pay a tax for heavy usage.'

Amesbury dug in his purse and dropped more coins on the table.

The women's eyes grew large. Hurriedly, the owner swept the money into his hand.

'Leave your swords,' he added.

Blackstone shook his head, with a little smile.

'It will be safe,' said the owner. 'There are no thieves here.'

'We have drunk your wine,' said Blackstone. 'We will not leave our swords. We are not young sailors of sixteen.'

Amesbury smiled approvingly. He had suspected there was something steelier in Blackstone than was obvious as the chubby Mayor's overworked aide. The man had a soldier's fearlessness beneath his black robes of office. Amesbury could always see courage in a man.

The owner twisted his mouth in annoyance, but seemed to accept this. It was common practice to steal swords, guns and anything of value left downstairs in a bawdy house.

'In there.' He pointed to a door leading to the back.

The woman rose from her chair, spitting on her hand and rubbing between her legs. Then she ambled ahead of the men keeping her skirt held high above her naked bottom half.

They followed behind. Blackstone's gaze dropped to her naked buttocks, which bore a deep red impression from where she'd been sitting.

She led them into a room with two sagging hemp sacks filled with straw and an open box of pig-bladder condoms. Several still held the contents of previous visitors.

The woman fished around in the box for the cleanest and laid it over her forearm.

'Front or back I do not mind. I charge the same for both,' she said, addressing Amesbury. 'You may put your mouth where you like. But I cannot have you in mine, for I have an ulcer.' She dragged down her lip at the side to show them both an open sore at the side of her cheek.

Having finished the explanation she settled herself with her legs apart on the crackling hemp sacks.

'We are looking for a girl named Jenny,' said Amesbury.

'You do not want business first? He will not like it if you do not,' she added, jabbing a finger towards the front of the house.

Amesbury shook his head. 'She ran away from a gaming house where she worked,' he explained.

The mouse brows drew together.

'She owed no money,' added Amesbury. 'But the man she was last seen with, we are trying to know a little more about him.'

The woman huffed out a long breath, and Amesbury tossed a handful of coins onto the sacking.

The woman regarded them, but didn't scoop them up.

'We mean her no harm. Truly. We are to catch a murderer,' said Blackstone. The woman stared at him for a moment, as if assessing his sincerity.

'What kind of murderer?' she asked.

'A murderer of innocent girls,' said Amesbury. 'A butcher.'

The woman's eyes flicked back and forth, between the men.

'She was here,' she said finally, 'for a little time. That man she met at the gaming house. He greatly frightened her. She said he meant to kill her.'

'Did she say anything else?' asked Blackstone.

'She said he took her to a church filled with rotting food.'

'Did she say which church?'

London had over fifty churches of all sizes.

The woman shook her head slowly.

'Where is she now?' asked Amesbury.

'She's gone,' said the woman. 'The plague is coming to these parts. She went where she might stay safe.'

'Where?' Amesbury pressed.

'She boarded one of those ships,' said the woman. 'The ones that float out on the Thames and wait for the plague to pass.'

Blackstone felt the hope of finding Jenny vanish. Tens of boats had taken to the water and all fiercely deterred boarders. Finding her aboard would be impossible.

'You will give her a message if you see her?' the woman was saying.

'I will if I can,' said Amesbury.

'Tell her to stay safe and away from those dangerous clubs in west London,' said the woman. 'I am her mother, you see,' she added.

'Then that man is your husband?' asked Amesbury, gesturing out beyond the room, towards the thickset man who had harassed him to drink the house wine.

'My third,' said the woman. 'He is not Jenny's father. But I am fortunate for he takes good care of me. Before he came and we were married I was beaten black and blue. Sailors you see,' she added with an explanatory shrug at the docks beyond the house. 'After months at sea they have more enthusiasm than they do money. And they do not take kindly to a refusal.'

She gave them both a plaintive look.

'I hope you catch this man,' she said. 'I thank God daily my Jenny escaped. It breaks my heart to think some other mother might not have my fortune.'

Chapter Forty-Three

Charlie and Maria wove deeper into the marshland, with the terrified horses sinking and splashing at almost every step.

Aside from their movements the marsh was silent. Eerie. The occasional squawking cry of a bird and the buzzing hum of insects were the only sound.

In London Charlie had thought to be free from the constant bell tolling and dead-carts, the splatters of red crosses, choking bonfire smoke and cries of mountebanks would be a relief.

But he would rather the din of the ailing city to the ghostly whispers of the marsh.

The rotting ground beneath them belched up a bog stench, and Charlie wondered how many bodies had been sunk forever here, during the Civil War.

The grasses formed a passage of sorts through the marsh. But there were still swathes of land where they had to risk passing over water-logged areas of indeterminate depth.

They came to the end of a grassed section and stopped to look out at the festering pond-land ahead.

'Over there,' said Charlie, uncertainly. 'I think I can see the bottom, and it is not so deep.'

He shielded his gaze from the sun.

'It is only this last stretch of water Maria. I can see the road from here.'

Maria nodded, her face slicked with sweat. It was hard work trudging through the boggy ground and she made each laboured step in pale silence.

Charlie put a tentative foot into the stinking water. It sank up to his thigh, and he staggered and almost fell into the cloying mud.

Twisting backwards he grabbed hold of the tall grasses and wrenched himself back onto firmer ground.

His heart was pounding.

'You have hurt yourself.'

Maria was kneeling at his side. Charlie realised that blood was running from his mud-slathered leg.

He looked down in surprise. It was straight slash, like a sword or a knife wound.

'Perhaps there is some sharp stick sunk deep in there,' he said, shrugging. The wound was not bad, and he held a hand to it for a moment, testing it.

'Better hope this mud does not infect it,' murmured Maria. Then her eyes settled on something further out in the water.

'That is what wounded your leg,' she said, pointing. 'Look. You must have dislodged it when you stepped in, and now it rises to the top.'

Floating face down in the marsh was the tattered dun-coloured remains of a corpse.

It held a rusting sword which now pointed straight up through the water. But the body was badly decomposed, and only a few ragged pieces of fabric still clung to what was mostly skeleton.

'It must be an old Civil War soldier,' said Charlie. 'Perhaps he meant to escape out here and drowned.'

But Maria was shaking her head, looking at the water. 'I think there was a battle near here,' she said.

The first rising body had set off a chain reaction, and one by one, body after body rumbled up from the stinking depths. An entire troop bubbled slowly to the surface.

Charlie swallowed.

'We must think at which point we should turn back,' he said.

'Turn back?' Maria looked at him in disbelief.

'This is swampland Maria. I know little about horses and how far they may travel through it, but if they drown we must go on foot. And with no provision to eat or drink that would be very hard. We could die on the road, of starvation or worse, and people would not come to our aid,' he added.

'You may go back whenever you wish,' said Maria. 'I mean to carry out what I started.' She choked out an involuntary cough and looked annoyed with herself. 'My family might not be so wealthy now, but we deserve justice as well as when we were a rich sort. It will *not* be forgotten, her death.' She glared ahead at the corpse-filled pool.

'Those that are in poverty they allow themselves to be crushed by it. They lie down and accept the law will not defend them. But I will not accept it. Do you hear? I need only three men. One man to read the rites, another to tie the noose and a third to loose the trap-door. And *I will see justice done*.' She was glaring furiously at him.

Charlie looked at Maria for a moment. He had made her a promise. His hand slid to the key around his neck.

'I think they would take our weight,' he said, finally, pointing to the floating remains of the dead soldiers.

Maria said nothing, but her eyes registered silent assent.

Charlie stuck out a foot and kicked the nearest body. It moved only a little. He stepped on to it, waving wildly off balance for a moment, and then finding his footing. He felt some delicate bones crack beneath his bare feet. But the body held firm.

'They will hold us,' he said. 'But I am not so sure about the horses.'

'Let me worry about the horses,' said Maria, and she led them behind her, clicking her tongue.

Charlie put out his hand and helped Maria stumble onto the first floating body. She fell forwards into his arms, and for a moment he could smell the perfume of her hair and skin. Then she righted herself.

'They are firm enough,' she agreed. 'I think the horses can make it.'

They stumbled forward, a few feet at a time, into the wide pool. Beneath them the bodies shifted and twisted in the water. But they formed a firm enough structure to walk on.

The terrified horses plunged and whinnied, but Maria managed to calm them sufficiently to follow behind.

Charlie pointed to a fresh water stream leading into the pool they were wading through.

'The bodies must have floated in from there,' he said. 'Likely there is a river where the bodies were dumped.'

He shook his head. 'So many dreadful deaths in the name of war. God knows how these poor men died.'

As he spoke he saw a dark shape, near the mouth of the stream.

It was another dead man. But unlike the others, this had a trail of bright red drifting out accusingly from where the body had washed up.

'Look,' said Charlie. 'That is not an old corpse. The blood is fresh.'

Maria stared. 'Do you think it is another vigilante murder?'

Charlie shook his head. 'Look at how he is dressed. He is a turnpike.'

They looked at one another.

'The men talked of Malvern having murdered a turnpike,' said Maria.

Charlie nodded. He began wading over to where the body had washed up.

'Be careful,' called Maria, staying where she was. 'The ground looks more boggy where you step.'

Charlie approached the dead man.

The turnpike's white face was twisted in surprise. Most of him was sunk deep below the surface. But his clenched fist was peeking out of the water. Charlie moved a little closer. He caught a flash of silver in between the fingers.

'There is something in his hand,' muttered Charlie. 'It looks as though it could be a coin.'

He peered closer.

'I am sure of it. He has money still clutched in his grip,' he called to Maria.

Stooping carefully Charlie inched apart the cold dead hand.

'What are you doing?' called Maria in horror, as he extracted the coin. 'Surely you do not take money from a dead man?'

'All London coins are made in token houses,' said Charlie, straightening up and bouncing the coin in his palm. 'Each token house makes its own mark.'

'What good does that do us?' asked Maria. 'There are over a hundred places in the city that make coins.'

'And I know them all,' said Charlie. 'I am a thief taker Maria.'

He splashed back over to where she was standing.

'And where were these coins made?' she asked.

'Not around these parts,' said Charlie. 'I think these must have been Thomas Malvern's last payment to that poor turnpike.'

He held up a shilling. 'But they are not made in a London coin house either.'

'What do you mean?'

'These coins are forgeries.'

He thought for a moment. 'A man high up in the city, but poor enough to be paying in forged coins,' he said. 'Something doesn't feel right.'

There was a sudden splash of water, and Maria's horse gave a blood-curdling scream.

Its hindquarters sunk fast into the bog.

Charlie and Maria lunged for the rein simultaneously. But the horse was already up to its belly in the mud.

'Come forward!' shouted Maria, dragging at the reins with all her strength. 'Kick yourself free!'

They both pulled, but the terrified horse twisted its head and fought against the reins.

It sunk another foot.

'Get the other horse!' shouted Maria. 'It will panic and run itself into mud too!'

Charlie grabbed at the reins of his horse and attempted a soothing pat on its neck.

Maria was struggling with the sinking horse, shouting and pleading with it. But inch by inch the animal was disappearing into the marsh.

She turned to Charlie, tears streaming down her face.

'We can't leave her to drown,' she sobbed. 'She will sink piece by piece and all the time in terror.'

'Is there any way to get her out?' asked Charlie, scanning his memory for what little he knew of horses.

Maria shook her head. 'No. Not even if we had a wagon and other horses to drag her. We are too far into the marsh.'

Maria stopped pulling at the reins and knelt by the frightened, drowning horse. She rested her cheek on its nose.

The horse stopped tossing its head and stared at her through sad eyes.

'She knows,' whispered Maria. 'She knows she is going to die.'

Charlie swallowed. He took a few steps closer, with one hand still holding his own horse.

'What about the gun Maria?'

She turned to look at him through tear-filled eyes. After a moment she nodded and fumbled in her dress for the heavy pistol the wise woman had given them.

'Here,' she held it out to him.

Charlie was about to protest, and then he saw the helpless look on her face.

'Come away then,' he said. 'Look to this horse and I will do it.'

He felt the cold metal press into his hand as she dragged herself over to the second horse.

Then he knelt by the sinking animal and stroked its nose.

'It is for the best,' he whispered. 'You will suffer less this way.'

Maria gave a sob and turned away.

As Charlie pulled the trigger the explosion drove every marsh bird for a mile shrieking into the air.

The horse Maria was holding tried to rear up, but she tugged at the reins expertly, bringing her back down.

'We'd best move quickly,' said Charlie, as the horse's eyes slowly drooped shut and the surrounding water pooled red.

'That gunshot will have alerted every vigilante for miles around. And now we only have one horse to take us both. And no bullets.'

Chapter Forty-Four

Thomas sat patiently outside the booth. He could hear every word of his wife's earnest confession.

'We have sinned in our marriage,' Teresa was saying, as Thomas strained his ears to hear better.

'How have you sinned?' asked the priest.

'We do not have relations such as a husband and wife should.' Teresa's voice was barely more than a whisper. 'I have not given my husband children.'

The priest paused for a moment.

'It is your wifely duty,' he said.

Teresa was silent in reply.

Outside the booth Thomas felt the familiar guilt. Teresa had been married to him so her dowry might help the war effort. But it had all been spent, and the cause lost. After his release from prison Thomas would not defile his lovely wife with his dark appetites. That he reserved for Protestant girls.

His encounters had started as a release. A revenge of sorts on the fathers and brothers of Cromwell's England. In the beginning it gave him great pleasure to defile the heretic women. But soon it wasn't enough to demean and degrade. Thomas's liaisons sunk to ever greater depths of depravity. Until one day he discovered that bloodshed brought a new dimension.

Thomas shook himself out of his personal hell of self-disgust and shame. The priest was still taking Teresa's confession.

'Does the devil speak to you often?' the priest was asking.

'He told me to take my own life,' admitted Teresa, 'after the soldiers came.'

'But you did not succumb to temptation?'

'Never. Though I was tempted many times. I was sent to Holland, so the soldiers might not get to me again,' she added. 'But still I feared they would come.'

There was a pause. 'Keep to your prayers Teresa. I will speak with your husband and offer advice to protect your soul.'

After a moment Teresa emerged from the little confessional booth. Thomas pointed she should climb back into the wagon and stood to address the priest.

Instinctively the holy man took a little step back as he approached.

'She is frightened to be outside,' explained Thomas, ignoring the reaction. 'Since the war she is afraid of men she doesn't know. It is only because you are a holy man that she can bear to have you talk to her,' he added.

Thomas eyed the priest. Like most Catholic holy men he had seen an unnatural share of violence. Several bad breaks had spread his nose at an angle. And he was missing half the fingers on his left hand.

The priest was looking to where Teresa was angling her slim waist to clamber back into to wagon. His face fought a peculiar battle, fear eventually outmanoeuvring hatred, as he turned back to Thomas.

'You treat her well? You are not violent to her?' his voice was thick with suspicion.

241

'No.'

There was a pause. Thomas could feel the priest's distaste coming in thick waves. On his last journey Thomas had not been able to resist indulging himself with a local girl. The holy man had heard the confession and many worse before it.

'Perhaps the hot summer has made her worse,' said the priest eventually. 'Have you anywhere suitable for her when you reach your destination?'

Thomas nodded. 'I know Wapping well. During the war I helped build the prison there. There are old cells that are never used, and she might stay very well in one of those.'

The priest blanched.

'Teresa would be most afraid in a hostelry or tavern, where any strange man might come in and out,' explained Thomas. 'You and I might think a cell is a sad place to stay, but she is much comforted by the security of such a place.'

'Surely you do not mean to lead your wife past the guards and rough convicts?' protested the priest. 'For that must fright her greatly.'

'There is a secret way in,' said Thomas, 'only I know of it. She will not be faced with any scenes from the prison at all.'

But as Thomas said the words an uneasy feeling flitted in his stomach. A memory of Civil War ghosts and ghouls.

Thomas's wagon pulled away, and the priest waited on the dirt road, staring after it. As the vehicle rumbled off he relaxed his clenched fist. The slow opening of his fingers revealed a paper, folded tightly in his palm. It was damp with the sweat of clutching it. But the moisture had not affected what was written there.

There was some kind of map – London – the priest assumed, with a scatter of crosses dotted across it. And a roll of paper which he recognised as a carrier pigeon message.

They had slipped from Thomas's clothing, as he took off his heavy cloak to enter the confessional booth. But as the wagon turned a corner and rolled on out of sight, the priest made no move to return the papers.

Chapter Forty-Five

Charlie and Maria reached the justices in Stratford only to find that Malvern had outrun them.

They had entered the little village of brick and half-timbered houses easily enough. Plague had now broken out in Stratford and its few remaining inhabitants no longer cared who came and went.

And they had been fortunate that the constable had not yet fled. But after that their luck had run out. A man wearing a plague costume had driven his wagon through the village hours ago.

'I do not know how he could have outpaced us,' repeated Maria, her eyes imploring the village constable for a different answer. 'His wagon was only a little ahead of us this morning. We should be hours ahead of him by now.'

'I know not how he travels so fast by wagon,' said the constable. 'But we hear reports that this monster and his wagon disappears and reappears from the roads. We like it not.'

Charlie was shaking his head furiously.

'He is clever,' he said to Maria. 'Malvern has found out some faster way. A path where he cannot be followed so easily.'

Charlie's mind was tracing out the map in his head. There was something other than roads, he remembered. Lilly's map showed the marching route of the Royalist army where it had been marked in red.

'What about the old military marching routes?' he asked the constable. 'Could a wagon take those instead of roads?'

'The old ghost routes?' replied the constable. 'He would be a fearsome sort of man who would go those ways. For they are haunted by the dead soldiers of the Civil War.'

'But a wagon could easily travel on a wide marching route,' said Charlie, thinking out loud.

He turned to Maria.

'That is what he does. I am sure of it. He takes the old army routes. And that tells us something else about him Maria.'

'What?'

'Firstly, he is clever. Very clever. And he guards against being followed. Second, that he fought in the Civil War and had a high position in the guard. For a foot soldier would have no reason to memorise a marching route. That would be for generals and commanders.'

'Sure you do not mean to head to Wapping?' the constable's face was a mask of horror. 'Have you not heard? It is a ghetto of disease.'

Charlie nodded. 'We have heard. But our business means we must risk it.'

The constable was shaking his head. 'It where the first plaguey Londoners fled,' he said. 'The whole town is riddled and it is dangerous even to walk the streets.'

Maria looked at Charlie uneasily. 'Surely if plague is so bad then the people keep to their beds?' she ventured.

But the constable crossed himself and looked to the floor.

Charlie called the map to mind again.

'We still have a chance,' he said. 'We too have a map of the army route.'

'But we only have one horse between us,' said Maria.

'If we ride hard and our horse holds out under such treatment we may yet gain on Malvern before Wapping.'

Maria was looking at their beleaguered horse.

'Then we must make haste,' she said. 'And pray the horse understands our purpose. If she does not collapse beneath us, then maybe we will have some luck. We are faster yet than a wagon.'

On the horizon the sun was setting.

'We may be in Wapping by morning,' she said.

Chapter Forty-Six

Charlie regarded Maria carefully from the corner of his eye. Her long limbs had lost their poise and were waving about the sides of the horse. Her breathing was laboured, and she leant low towards the neck of her animal.

As they rode deep into the night the horse was panting with exhaustion, and Charlie walked alongside to lighten its load. But as the stars twinkled above, both the animal and Maria were teetering on the brink of collapse.

So far they had avoided the ominous groups of torches which swept the night landscape. But with the horse so exhausted Charlie knew they would have little chance of escape if they were cornered.

'We will rest for an hour or so,' he decided. 'It is dangerous to go on with the horse so tired.'

Maria did not object, sliding silently from the horse with her eyes drooping.

'Here,' said Charlie. 'Sleep for an hour and I will keep watch.' He looked around him. 'It is high enough ground,' he decided. 'We should be able to see anyone approach long before they see us.'

Though they had Maria's tinderbox he didn't dare light a fire.

But he prepared what little food they had left, and then taking out his knife he cut down a few leafy tree branches and laid them out.

'You can rest on these,' he said, cutting away the thicker braches so the leaves fanned out in a makeshift bed.

Maria smiled. 'You should teach the man I am to marry,' she said. 'He can hardly use a knife to spread butter.' Then she looked down in embarrassment, as though she had admitted too much.

They made a little picnic with the remains of the food and Charlie brought out a flask of ginever.

Maria took a heavy draught before passing it back.

'Tomorrow we will finally arrest this Malvern,' she said sleepily, 'and see what kind of a man he is.'

They sat in silence, passing the flask back and forth between them. Charlie let the warmth of the gin seep into him. In the moonlight Maria's handsome features looked gentler and more girlish. She was beautiful, he thought, as the drink flushed through him.

Maria also seemed softened by the gin. She smiled at him in a fuzzy sort of way.

'When I first met you I thought you a low sort of man,' she said. 'But I see different now. You are not so bad Charlie Thief-Taker.'

Charlie allowed himself a half smile, realising Maria had probably not drunk spirits before.

'You were clever,' she continued, 'memorising the map from Lilly. And you saved my life. Were it not for you I would have died on the road for certain.'

'You are not so bad either,' he said, 'for I thought you right high-handed and proud when we first met.'

They looked at each other, smiling, and then the silent moment turned suddenly awkward.

'The constellations are brighter in the country,' said Charlie, turning his attention up to the star-filled sky.

'Know you anything of astrology?'

He nodded. 'I taught myself all the constellations as a boy.'

'I did not think you the kind of man who would be interested in the makings of the universe.'

Charlie smiled. 'They all have stories. See there, where the bright star meets four faint ones? That is Perseus. That collection there is Andromeda, his mother. In the legend Perseus rescues her from a rich evil King. It was my favourite story as a boy.'

Maria studied his face. 'The son rescues the mother?'

Charlie looked away.

'Tell me about your wife,' she said, leaning closer, 'the actress.'

She was close enough now that Charlie was breathing in the perfume of her skin. It was a disconcertingly sensual smell, and he had to force his attention back to the conversation.

'Lynette was one of Mother Mitchell's girls,' he said, suddenly finding thoughts of his estranged wife were the last thing on his mind. 'We fell in love. Then the King returned and the stages reopened and women performed for the first time. Lynette would come away from the theatre with gloves stuffed full of money from noblemen hoping to be her patron.'

'And you were jealous?'

'I fought many men for the things they spoke of her,' said Charlie.

'So you drove her away?'

Charlie's mouth twisted, trying to think of the best way to describe Lynette.

'She is a woman of changing feelings,' he settled on eventually. 'And she does not always behave honourably. But it is impossible not to forgive her.'

Maria let out a surprisingly unladylike snort.

'It sounds as though your wife is a selfish woman, with a beautiful face,' she said.

Charlie was silent for a moment, struck by how very close Maria was to the truth.

'We often argued. Over money especially. And we agreed to say our marriage never was,' he replied.

'So how does the story end Charlie Thief-Taker?'

'What do you mean?'

'Do you get rich and have your wife return to you? Is that the plan?'

'Maybe a little in part,' he admitted.

He paused for a moment, deliberating. Then he reached into his naval coat and extracted a dog-eared folded up paper. Charlie smoothed it out.

Maria's eyes settled on the sketch of a building and then looked up at him questioningly.

'I mean to build a gaming house,' he said shyly. 'South of the river.'

'It is grand,' she said, sounding surprised.

'Land is cheap, south of the river,' said Charlie. 'People think it a flood plain. But this year they build a waterwheel. The river is being diverted.'

'So your plan is to buy land there?'

Charlie nodded. 'I will build cheaply. And when it's finished, I can employ my brother and keep him from his dangerous practices.'

'It is a good plan,' she said after a moment. 'If your ambition is to make money.'

She paused. 'Is that your reason for seeking out Malvern?' she added. 'You think your mother has left you a fortune?'

Charlie thought about this.

'No. But I want to know what became of my mother,' he replied. 'Rowan thinks there is nothing to tell. But I cannot shake the feeling . . . .' He struggled for a moment, looking for a less childish reason. 'I would take my revenge if some man or woman forced her to give us up,' he concluded.

'Then it is a poor ambition you have set yourself,' she said. 'For you might forget your revenge and simply be happy.'

Charlie shook his head. 'I could never forgive if I discovered my mother was made to abandon us.'

'My mother left us,' said Maria.

Charlie sat up a little in the dark.

'She took all our money and fled,' continued Maria. 'And after that the boy I was betrothed to would not have me. For his father advised him not to take a girl without a dowry. And he was a coward, as it turned out.'

'What of your betrothed now?' asked Charlie. 'The one who you do not live safe with in plague time?'

Maria shrugged. 'I have tried love matches and they will not do. So I have finally learned to decide with my head. My betrothed will care for me and keep me.'

He noticed that her hands were shaking. She saw him looking and folded them quickly into her lap.

'But you do not love him?' Charlie surmised.

'No. But love can grow. That is what they tell me. I respect him, that is enough. And when the children come that will be something as well.'

In the half-light Charlie felt her shoulder settle against his.

'It is a nice that we are now almost friends,' she said sleepily. 'I am sure your wife misses her husband.'

Charlie put his arm around her and when she didn't resist he rested his mouth in her hair.

'The world is harder than you think for women,' she murmured. He felt her sag against him. Then her hand moved to hold his.

'Charlie?' She turned, so that their faces were almost touching. There was something in her eyes he'd never seen before. 'I feel safe with you,' she said.

Charlie moved his hand to cup her jaw, and she didn't resist, closing her eyes, leaning onto it.

He could feel the warm current of her breath on his face.

She opened her eyes again, and slowly Charlie moved forward to kiss her.

Their lips met, and suddenly Charlie was lost in the smell and the taste of her. His arms were at her waist, pulling her close.

Maria pressed against him, as he wound his fingers deep into her hair, moving his mouth and body tight to hers. Then his hand came up against the barrier of her thick bodice. And suddenly she was rigid in his arms, pulling back.

Charlie stared back at her, confused. Her sudden passion had taken him by surprise. How could it have evaporated so quickly?

'It is not that I do not like you as a man,' she said. 'But I could never . . . Not with a man who couldn't . . . You are married,' she finished, finally.

'I am separated,' said Charlie. 'There is nothing to stop me being with someone else.' His arms were still around Maria's waist, and her pounding heat was palpable.

He leaned in to kiss her again, but she twisted away, and his lips grazed her cheek.

'I am betrothed,' she said, wriggling out of his embrace. 'And my future husband is a good person. I could not betray him with a man like you.'

Her face had now hardened back to the serious expression he was more familiar with.

'A man like me?' Charlie's voice came out choked.

'I did not mean it quite like that,' said Maria, 'But I have been bred to marry sensibly.'

'So you have,' said Charlie, not bothering to keep the contempt from his tone. 'And I wish you well of it. For I know of many happy girls who seek a man for his money and position.' He stopped short of saying there was a name for that kind of woman.

'I have my family to think of,' said Maria, 'I do not mean to offend you. But you must see we could hardly make a match.'

Charlie didn't answer her. Instead he shuffled a few feet away, and pulling his coat over himself lay down to sleep.

More than anything he was offended by her self-deception. Only moments ago the desire had come off her in waves. Now she was trying to pretend her chaste persona had never been breached.

'There is no reason to behave foolishly,' said Maria. Charlie ignored her, and getting no response she lay down on the damp grass.

He could tell by her ragged breathing that she was not even close to falling asleep. Laying his coat across her he stared back up at the stars, trying to ignore the sudden wakefulness the situation had created.

In the night sky a cloud had moved over Perseus. So he let his eyes drift around the stars that formed Virgo. The good wife.

Charlie's annoyance with Maria rose again.

He closed his eyes and tried to let the darkness envelop him. Tomorrow would bring the morning and with it Malvern and his thief taker fee.

As his mind dropped into sleep his thoughts were still on Maria.

There was no reason why he should care that she thought herself above him.

I do not even like her, he muttered to himself, *she is proud and rude and asks too many questions besides.*

But it hurt all the same.

As sleep washed over him, Charlie drifted into a flashing circuit of jarringly familiar images. Maria's sister, covered in bloodied ribbons. And then another set of ribbons, from long ago, tied around a book. Herbs thrown, candles lit.

A voice he thought was his mother's, telling him she would keep him safe.

And then he was in a low, dark room, with a shuffling, animal shape in the corner. The lady-in-the-hidden room. Beautiful. Her blonde hair a waving curtain.

She smiled and beckoned him.

Come Charlie. I will tell you all the secrets.

Her voice was wrong. Croaking and hard. Then snakes came from her eyes, and her white face dissolved into bloodied thorns and feather.

Chapter Forty-Seven

Charlie awoke to the smell of smoke and knew instantly something was wrong.

Rolling over silently in the dark, he nudged Maria awake, putting his finger to his lips as her eyes blinked open.

Men's voices echoed out over the night air.

'Vigilantes,' hissed Charlie. 'They sound close. We have to go now.'

Maria nodded and moved to saddle the horse. But Charlie shook his head.

'She is too exhausted to move quickly,' he whispered. 'The horse will slow our escape. We have to leave her here.'

'But it is miles to travel on foot!' she protested.

She was the most ridiculous girl he'd ever met, Charlie thought to himself, still stung by her rejection. Despite her airs and claims to high-breeding she came from a tumble-down rented house in a bad part of the City. And here she was insisting on a horse to carry her.

The shouts and waving torches broke over the crest of the hill.

Charlie grabbed Maria by the arm before she had a chance to reply and dragged her towards a nearby copse of trees.

'Over there,' he said, 'we must get out of sight.'

Dawn was breaking and a crest of searing orange light had appeared on the horizon.

Charlie and Maria fled, stumbling in the dark and into a little copse of trees. Outside they heard the men and saw the waving fiery torches.

The vigilantes had settled around the horse and seemed to be arguing amongst themselves.

'With any luck they will think she has slipped away from her rider,' Charlie whispered.

Amongst the trees was all half-light, despite the glimmer of the breaking sun in the fields beyond.

Charlie stepped carefully through the shadows, tugging Maria behind him.

His eyes swept the canopy above looking for clues as to how deep the wood ran.

Then, in the dawning light, he noticed something.

A pathway of branches had been broken, as though something large and lumbering had passed this way. And the damaged trees stretched up to the height of two men.

The height of two men, thought Charlie, *or the height of a large wagon.*

He dropped to the floor and tried the earth with his fingers. It was hard, compacted. But he could just make out where wide wheel ruts had trundled through the leafy floor.

For a moment the shouts in the distance faded into nothing as Charlie thought what it might mean.

'A large wagon has been this way recently,' he whispered to Maria. 'It must have come up the same road as us and then veered off on this pathway.'

Without waiting for an answer he began tracking forward through the trees, following the path of broken branches the wagon had made.

There was a stumbling sound behind him, and Maria gave a stifled yelp of pain.

'Shh!' he whispered. 'They'll hear us.' He stopped for a moment to check they hadn't been heard. 'What is it?' he asked finally, after he was certain they were still well hidden.

'On the ground,' said Maria. 'There's something sticking out. I walked into it in the dark.'

She paused for a moment. 'It's a cross. We must be on some local burial ground,' she said.

In the dawn sun Charlie picked out, not just one wooden cross, but tens of them.

The wagon trail had led them into a hidden graveyard.

The crosses had been made from simple branches from the nearby trees and stood at waist height all around.

'Honest people do not hide their bodies away in woods,' he said. 'This burial ground is meant to be secret.'

Then he saw a dark shape in the trees. 'Someone has built something,' he said, 'like a hut . . . or a church.'

The building was the height of a half-timbered house and had been crudely fashioned from interwoven branches covered in badly-woven thatch. Heavy logs formed the side walls, with only the smallest holes for sunlight.

Charlie could not tell how far back it ran into the trees, but from the height of it the makeshift building was an appreciable size for the country.

'I think it must be a secret church,' said Maria. 'I have heard about them,' she added, as Charlie frowned in confusion. 'They are built by Catholics. For they are not allowed to pray in England. If their priests are caught ministering they are hanged.'

'Then these graves must be Catholic Civil War soldiers who fought for the King,' said Charlie.

Their eyes swept the collection of waist-high wooden crosses.

'I will look inside the church,' said Charlie. 'Thomas Malvern is a Catholic. Perhaps he stops here on his way to Wapping and has left some clue.'

Maria clutched at his arm.

'Don't be a fool. If those who built this church were to be caught they would be hung and worse. You cannot just step in for a look around. They will think you bring the law and fight you to the death.'

'It looks deserted,' ventured Charlie. 'And I am practised at slipping into buildings unseen. Wait here. I will only be a moment.'

Charlie crept carefully towards the open barn doorway of the church and then slipped inside, keeping his back against the wall of logs.

The smell of the forest floor was amplified inside, and the damp scent of leaves was joined by something else. Incense, he realised, catching sight of a large burner suspended from the ceiling. It was unlit, but the smell lingered.

A candle flickered on the far side, and Charlie's heart missed a beat. Someone had been here recently. His eyes scanned the empty interior.

Large logs formed the little collection of pews, but all sat empty. The building was not large, but the tiny windows meant most of it was in shadow.

His gaze settled on some kind of writing on the far wall, flickering in the candlelight. He made towards it, his head turning a quick left and right for any sign of movement.

A flat board had been made of yet more timber, and onto it was carved a list of names with numbers after them. Dates.

Whoever built this church must be very sure it would never be found, he realised, to risk writing up the names of those who attended its illegal services.

Perhaps they were all dead and buried. But the dates looked to come up to only a few years ago. Were they the dates of their deaths, perhaps? He couldn't be sure.

Peering up at the names he began the painstaking business of reading them, his lips moving with the effort. He reached the bottom having found no familiar names. Nothing which could be a clue to track Malvern.

The thick wax below the board began to gutter and spit. The wick needed trimming, and he wondered whether someone had left the flame to die.

Listening carefully, he assured himself there was no one in the church. He looked at the dying candle, debating. If it went out he would see nothing.

Remembering the scissors left to him by the wise woman he retrieved them from his hanging pocket and approached the candle.

As he closed the scissors around the wick the blades twisted in his hand without warning. Folding between them the flame died entirely. Suddenly the wall of names vanished to black.

Not as useful as the wise woman hoped, he thought.

Charlie felt his heart beat faster in the darkness. Then his eyes adjusted to the dimmer light.

The texture of the wooden noticeboard was thrown into better relief, revealing a mess of scarred hatchings partway up. Someone had scratched out one of the benefactors from the middle of the list. And bringing his hand to test the shape of the surface Charlie's fingers could just make out the letters which had once been written there.

It was a T, and then an H.

He let his hand glide over the other letters and suddenly he knew what the words were before his touch discerned it.

Thomas Malvern.

He pulled back his fingers in alarm and as he did so there was a sudden sound behind him. Charlie whipped around to see a shape move silently through the shadows.

Then there was a flicker and a candle on the far side of the church lit, illuminating a man holding a crossbow.

He was dressed in a priest's robes and pointed the arrow squarely at Charlie. The face was that of a boxer, his wildly broken nose spread almost flat.

'Have you come from London?' asked the priest, anxiety thickening his voice.

Charlie noticed the hand holding the crossbow was missing several fingers.

'That I do,' said Charlie, surprised at the deduction.

'Parliament has sent you then?'

Charlie shook his head dumbly in response. And then he realised what the priest was asking.

'I am not come as an official to find you out,' he said.

The priest raised the crossbow a little.

'I cannot risk that you would tell others of our existence,' he said. His face looked sorry and his finger began to tighten on the trigger.

'Wait!' Charlie held up his hands. In desperation he decided to take a chance.

'I am looking for the man whose name was on this wall,' he said. 'Thomas Malvern.'

The priest lowered the crossbow a fraction. Charlie saw a flicker of fear in his eyes.

'You come to make his arrest then?' asked the priest, dropping his voice to a whisper and looking about the dark church as if fearing they were being watched.

Charlie swallowed, keeping his attention on the crossbow. The wrong answer could send the bolt through his heart.

'He murdered a friend of mine,' he said finally. 'A young girl.'

The priest screwed up his face, and to Charlie's amazement his eyes had welled with tears.

'So many young girls,' he whispered. 'And nothing is done.'

'You . . . know him then?' asked Charlie.

The priest nodded. 'I take his confession every time he passes through.' He shook his head. 'You must understand. I am bound by a higher master than even the King. I cannot break the codes of the confessional. It is a holy vow.'

'But you must hear his crimes and do nothing about them,' said Charlie, suddenly understanding.

The priest stared back at Charlie. 'If you are to seek out his arrest you must be careful,' he said. 'He is a powerful man, and he does not travel by his real name. After the war he left these parts. But he established a trade of some kind between Wapping and London.' The priest paused for an uneasy moment.

'What kind of trade?' asked Charlie.

He hesitated. 'Some tell it that Malvern transports bodies.'

'Dead bodies?'

'It is not known for sure,' said the priest. 'Only that his trade had earned him a title in London.'

'And what title is that?'

'They call him the corpse collector. And there were rumours that he had not given up on the Royalist cause. That he had become obsessed with a Catholic uprising.'

The priest was choosing his words carefully, and Charlie wondered what more had been admitted to him in the confessional.

'He has some plans with the docks,' added the priest meaningfully. Charlie nodded, understanding the inference. As they'd suspected Malvern meant to import or export something dear to his cause.

C.S. Quinn

'I think he may be involved in . . . some kind of dark magic,' said Charlie, hoping to prompt the priest's religious obligations. 'I fear he plans another murder.'

But to his surprise the priest gave a firm shake of his head. 'Thomas Malvern would never do or say anything contrary to his Catholic faith. If you look for one involved in some unholy business then you have the wrong man.'

Charlie looked at him in confusion.

'During the war Thomas Malvern swum out to Royalist boats through cannon fire to retrieve the crucifixes of the dead men on board,' added the priest.

Charlie's mind was a blur. The murders, the journeys at full moon. Surely there had to be some dark magic at the heart of it? Likely Malvern's mind had become warped since the Civil War and the priest credited him with more religion than was now the case.

'From what I know Malvern does have some idea to make an uprising,' said Charlie. 'We found evidence he is making weapons.'

The priest considered this. 'I should like to help you more, indeed I should,' he said. 'But I am bound by my vows. There is one thing only,' he added, 'perhaps you might look to the confessional yourself.'

He gestured to a temporary structure of wattle and hemp-cloth in the corner of the church.

'Not to confess,' added the priest, seeing Charlie hesitate. 'Perhaps, from interest, to see inside the booth. It is over there,' he added. 'I will make sure it has no Catholic artefacts inside to disturb you.' And with that he turned and walked towards the back of the church.

Charlie looked at the retreating priest, trying to decide what he was suggesting. The priest ducked in and out of the booth before vanishing.

Charlie went after. He approached the confession booth and looked at it carefully, wondering if it would constitute a breach of faith to look inside. Deciding that it wouldn't he lifted the curtain.

Nothing inside suggested anything to him and he was about to let the curtain drop when he caught sight of a fold of paper on the floor of the confessional.

Had the priest dropped it there for him to find?

Ducking down quickly he picked it up.

It was a map of London, he realised, unfolding it. Annotated with a seemingly meaningless scatter of crosses.

His mind danced over the locations, searching for a pattern, but he found none. The crosses seemed to denote all kinds of places. A tavern here, a market there.

As he examined the map, his eyes caught sight of another piece of paper on the floor. Charlie stooped down to scoop it up.

It was tiny, no bigger than a finger's width. A few words were written on it in ink and it was curled as though it had been tightly rolled up. Slowly he read. And then drew the paper closer to better understand what he was seeing – and what the crosses meant.

The writing was in the same sloping hand which had been used to fill out Malvern's Health Certificate.

It was a message, he realised, designed for a carrier pigeon.

And the sentence was short but unmistakable.

'London infection will begin on August full moon.'

He checked the date against his own mental lunar calendar.

Full moon was tomorrow.

Chapter Forty-Eight

In the heat of the summer evening Thomas tossed in his bed, the sheets soaked with sweat.

The memories of his time after the war pierced his waking hours and wove into his sleep. The dreams drifted about him, of after the Civil War, when the Royalists were captured.

The Clink prison had been built for forty men. But after Cromwell's victory three hundred Royalists were forced into the confines. Men who had battled the roundheads wrestled each other for a patch of stone floor a foot across.

Those too weak to fight their corner stood for twenty-four hours a day. Whilst the sun was up screams of men being tortured echoed through the gaol, and the body lice writhed and bit in the warm conditions.

After six long months a guard picked out Thomas for a special task for Cromwell. He was to torture confessions from Catholic plotters against the Republic.

Thomas no longer had the heart to refuse or even care.

The eyes of his first victim widened in terror as the implement was drawn out, and his pleading changed to mumblings. And as the first agonised scream lifted Thomas felt something he had not felt in a long time. A tug, a feeling. As though the hunger at the heart of him had finally been fed a single mouthful.

He woke up with a jolt, realising he was not in his own bed. The rough linen sheets were those of the Wapping hostelry where he had bought a room for the night.

Thomas surveyed the unfamiliar room, willing his heartbeat to slow. He had died so many times in his dreams he was sometimes unsure if he were still living.

Through the floorboards of his upstairs room the sound of the landlord's conversation drifted up.

'The fat-guts is screaming in his sleep,' he announced. The landlord's wife sniggered.

Thomas felt a coldness coil around his heart.

The landlord was a fellow ex soldier. They had lasted the starvation of the siege together. And Thomas sought out his old comrade in Wapping now he rented beds to travellers. During plague time it was his only hope of a bed.

The reunion had not gone as Thomas had planned. Striding confidently towards his wartime colleague he had been met with a blank stare.

He doesn't remember me, thought Thomas. And then as he introduced himself by name the realisation came. *He doesn't recognise me.*

His one-time brother-in-arms peered at him, digesting the introduction, and then his face flashed as he fought to disguise the revulsion.

For a sudden, terrible moment, Thomas saw what he had become. The grotesque bulk of his swollen frame. Eyes flattened to reptilian cruelty.

He sees me from before, Thomas realised, with a jolt. *When there was some feeling left. But he does not see it now. He looks for something in me which is gone.*

An image of himself as a boy flashed before him. The straight-backed young man who had gone to battle for King and country. What had become of him? When had he slipped away?

'Thomas?' The man was peering intently into his eyes. 'It has been many years.'

Thomas managed a half smile. His practised emotions were manoeuvring beneath his initial shock. They hardened into place.

The man made a lopsided expression which Thomas was well used to. The mouth which tries to belie the fear in the eyes. He felt relief. This was a situation he was well used to. It had been foolish to try and dredge up some sentimental memory.

'What brings you back to the town?' asked the man.

'Trade I have here,' said Thomas. 'One last collection I must bring back to London. You rent these rooms alone?' he added.

'I took a wife. Towards the end of the war.' The man stood a little to the side of the entrance to his lodging as if protecting the unseen woman inside.

Thomas thought carefully. He had only vague memories of their last days in Wapping. The gunshots which echoed through the streets as their commanders were shot without trial and the groans of the prisoners loaded up for torture.

'Does your wife still live?' the man asked, his face struggling to decide whether his wife would be more fortunate dead or alive.

'She lives,' said Thomas.

The man frowned as if tugging at some distant memory. 'You married a Catholic heiress did you not?'

Thomas nodded. 'It was a marriage of convenience for us both, for her dowry would have been forfeit had she not married. But she has been a dutiful wife.'

'Would I had been so wise,' said the man, shaking his head. 'For there were enough dowried Catholic girls during those times to have made us all rich men.' He glanced over his shoulder. 'Though my Nancy keeps me happy enough,' he added, 'and she is a hard worker.'

'The dowry was all given up to the war,' said Thomas, 'the marriage gained me nothing but an unhappy wife.'

The man nodded sympathetically, having heard similar tales many times before.

'And do you bring your wife with you?'

'She . . . is elsewhere in town.'

'You would not lodge with your wife?'

'She has particular needs,' said Thomas. He saw a flash of her sad face as he'd brought her to the dank empty cell in Wapping prison.

The man gave his first easy laugh.

'Who would have thought it Thomas? You famed for battle and your wife makes you soft-hearted.'

The man shook his head. 'The young Charles has betrayed us again,' he said sadly, 'after all that was promised to us by his father.' His eyes flicked up suddenly. 'Did you gain anything back of your old lands when the second King Charles returned?'

Thomas shook his head. 'None. Though I petitioned for them. The new King Charles scattered a few lands to the highest born and left the rest of us to rot.'

'Like father like son,' observed the man.

Thomas nodded, feeling the familiar pang. It was a sensation that he was well used to. No matter how much he ate he could not chase away the pain of the betrayal. *Hunger. Hungry. Starved. Famished.* He found different ways to say it, but they all felt the same.

Thomas suddenly remembered seeing a group of women prostituting themselves as he entered the better part of Wapping.

There had been a tiny girl who was hardly bigger than a ten year old with the lined face of a much older woman. The green dress she wore blazed oddly against the muted colours of the town's female populace, and she had matched it with an enormous green bonnet which towered above her head in an assortment of ragged ruffles.

The girl had smiled as he passed and raised her skirts. As he walked by she simultaneously lowered her smile and garments without a change in emotion.

Something about the image had burned itself on his brain. And it reared up now, demanding to be satisfied.

'I have business in the village,' he said shortly, to his new host. Who only nodded in apparent relief at the announced departure.

And so Thomas set out in the direction of the girl in the green bonnet.

Chapter Forty-Nine

As Charlie and Maria trudged the last few miles to Wapping the dirt track was eerily empty. Not even vigilantes, it seemed, dared risk their lives near the plague town.

Charlie had picked up a strange noise in the distance and stopped for a moment, listening.

'What is it?' asked Maria.

'Do you hear that?' he asked. 'It has been getting louder this last twenty minutes.

'Perhaps someone is sawing wood,' said Maria, stopping to listen. 'That is what it sounds like.'

Charlie let the sound roll around his thoughts. It did remind him of wood-sawing. But he couldn't imagine this to be an occupation on the plague-road to Wapping.

Uneasily, he signalled they should keep walking.

'You may leave me here,' said Maria. 'I will pay you in any case, for you have more than earned your fee.'

Charlie shook his head. 'And what will you do then Maria? Stride unprotected into a plague town. Wapping is a port. It is dangerous even without plague. You would not last a single night.'

'Then what are your plans if not to enter the town and find this Malvern out?'

'I would find out more about what he is about and where he goes,' said Charlie. 'The priest suggested he has some business with the docks.'

'He travels under high authority,' said Maria. 'Do you think this man is known to the King?'

Charlie thought for a moment. 'The King has enough people close to him who might want to do him harm,' he said. 'There is much talk of his mistress Louise Keroulle and her brother – that they spy for the French. And many courtiers fought for his father and have not been rewarded.'

He let his mind range over what else he knew. 'It is possible he might be a physician,' he added, 'he wears their clothes after all. And that status would fit with a man who could afford to buy Antoinette.'

Charlie had a sudden memory of William Lilly, stuffing the documents into his desk. There were so many men like that in the city, who had suffered at the change in regime and might want revenge. And the forged coins. That would suggest a person who did not have the means of a royal consort. He could hardly imagine how Louise Keroulle would grow short of funds.

'But Malvern is spreading infection,' mused Maria. 'That is what you found in the confession.'

'We do not know that is his plan,' Charlie replied. 'The crosses on the map. They do not fit well with a disease. For he does not pick the most populated places.'

'He marks taverns and markets,' replied Maria. 'They have many people.'

'But no churches and no docks,' said Charlie. 'If I wanted to pick an area where many people gathered I should choose St Paul's Cathedral. Or St Katherine's dock.'

'Yet this Malvern deals in bodies and looks to be arming for some uprising,' said Maria. 'What dark business can he be doing? Surely he means to spread plague with his spells?'

Charlie shook his head. 'Such a thing is impossible Maria. None know what it is in the air that causes the plague. Even if a man wanted to commit such evil the thing could not be done.'

'Besides,' he added, 'the priest was adamant Malvern was a Catholic of the true faith and would never chance his soul with witchcraft. I think there is something here we do not see. Malvern is clever. Remember the roadways he took so he might not be easily followed? I have seen trials of people involved in witching and devil worship and the like . . . They always seem to have a foolishness about them, Maria. This Malvern seems harder, he seems more careful than that.'

'Money then,' she said, 'he must look to make money by some illegal means.'

Charlie felt a flare of annoyance.

'Not everything is to do with money Maria. Some people have a greater purpose in life than securing a rich husband.'

'Such as sending thieves to the noose?' She turned on him angrily.

'I send those as deserve it,' replied Charlie, 'but those poor people who you would have arrested for no reason, I do not send them to such a fate.'

'Then you are not even successful at the fool occupation you have carved out for yourself,' she said with a sniff.

'And what occupation awaits you?' He said, the anger rising up. 'You whose sister is fine enough to prostitute herself.'

Maria turned a deep shade of red. 'Do you *dare*? You are angry because I would not kiss you in some roadside field. Because I am bred to better than a thief taker.'

'You think too much of yourself. There are a thousand fairer women with better manners besides who I might consider before I deign to hitch myself to a harpy like you.'

'And you are the last man in the world. The *last* man. Who I would ever *consider* . . .' Maria took a breath to deliver the final invective and stopped.

Up ahead the reason for the strange sawing sound had become suddenly apparent.

A black mass of flies, like an unearthly thundercloud, buzzed ahead of them.

The swarming insects covered an area the size of a market square and circled up to the height of a house.

Maria's mouth dropped open in horror. She quickly clapped both hands over it.

Charlie too, raised his hand to his mouth.

'It is a plague pit,' he said. 'Someone has made a plague pit outside Wapping. But they have not finished it.'

Funeral pits were usually covered with shovels of quicklime for every corpse buried to stop the rot until the earth was put back. But this grave had been abandoned. The pit spanned the same width as the flies spiralling blackly above it, and Charlie estimated that at least a thousand bodies had been thrown to rot in the summer sun.

'If we mean to get into Wapping we must go past it,' he said. 'The town gate is on the other side.'

The summer breeze carried a waft of the putrefying bodies past them. Maria made a retching sound, turning away from the road, her eyes watering.

'You do not have to go on,' said Charlie gently. 'I can go into Wapping alone. I will tell you all I find.'

Behind her hand Maria shook her head.

'I think I can see a gatehouse of sorts,' continued Charlie. 'It may be that it is still manned, even in these times.'

'We will go then,' said Maria, taking her hand away from her mouth. She choked for a moment and then steadied herself. Charlie felt his own stomach turn as another wave of the foul air swept towards them.

'Come,' he said, 'we will soon be in Wapping.'

Chapter Fifty

Blackstone wetted his nib and began to write by the light of his stuttering candle. He and Amesbury had gone their separate ways in Wapping – the old general to track the thief taker and Blackstone to continue his official business for the Mayor. Lawrence had asked Blackstone to report on the King's movements, since the rumour was he was leaving the city for Oxford. And so Blackstone's new mission was to deliver what scant information he could find on His Majesty's likely return to London.

Mayor Lawrence had asked for a daily report, and though there were not postal services to deliver them, Blackstone did the best he could.

It has all happened as we feared. The King has fled London. And most think it the persuasion of Louise Keroulle. For she has the ear of the King and looks only to her own selfish ends. More than we realised, as you will soon see.

The King and his courtiers now hide in Oxford. And London has fallen to chaos. My real fear is some vengeful faction will take advantage of this dark time, to persuade weak minded men to rise up against the new monarch.

But there are bad rumours from the court in Oxford, where the King hides from the plague. A courtier who is a friend to me gives the most shocking information.

He had cause to visit the King's rooms, and he hears from them strange noises. The courtier knows His Majesty to be making a rare visit to his wife. And so he wonders what to make of it.

He enters the King's bedchamber, and what does he see but Louise Keroulle, the King's mistress.

At least, he sees part of her. The bottom half. And as she is all naked he does not know for a moment that it is her.

But he can hear now where the noises come from and he realises he witnesses a rape.

A woman is laid over the bed, her front half pushed in amongst the bedclothes. And pinning her down is a man, who has pulled down part of his breeches only. He is using her roughly from behind, so the courtier says, and with such force he must be hurting the lady very greatly.

From the sound of her screams he realises now it is Louise Keroulle, and the realisation sends fear through him. For having stumbled across the situation could be his death.

The courtier reaches for his sword, wondering how best to approach. If it is a nobleman who is committing the crime then he must tread carefully. For it would be treason to treat him with violence. Like most of the Palace he does not care much for Louise Keroulle and thinks her to be an evil influence on the King. But he knows any woman deserves aid at the hands of such a brute.

The courtier takes a careful step forward.

Louise's legs are stretched out flat and the man holds her head by a handful of hair, pushing her face into the bed to mask her screams.

Then, amongst the noises, Louise says something in French which enrages the man. And he goes about her with even more vigour.

The courtier unsheathes his sword, thinking the man in his violence may kill her. But like most who serve the King, this courtier knows a little French, and Louise's words suddenly make their English shapes in his head.

He realises Louise was not begging for mercy, but encouraging the man. And the knowledge comes to him, horribly fast, that he does not see a rape as he first assumed. He is witness to some barbarous act of lust between Louise and a member of the royal court.

But now it is too late to escape unseen. For the sound of the courtier drawing his sword has alerted the traitors to his presence.

Louise's lover turns. And the courtier sees it is none other than George Keroulle, Louise's own brother, who makes the act upon her.

Now the courtier knows he has seen his own certain death if he is not quick to deliver himself, and he runs headlong from the room.

Behind him he hears shouts in French and the stumbling approach as George makes after him. But the semi-clothing has slowed him, and the courtier makes his escape from the grounds at Oxford.

There he got on one of the smaller highways south and found a place safe enough to send me this information.

You may well imagine what effect this news might have on the court. So for now we must decide amongst ourselves what best use to make of it.

Certainly the public feeling is high that Louise and her brother are witches. And this does little to dispel the notion.

Blackstone raised his pen, thinking for a moment.

That is what I know of the court, he wrote. *For my task of telling you the news from the plagues districts I fear my report will be not nearly so lively.*

Since the King has left all is dark and there is no law at all. Men do what terrible deeds they will and fear not reprisal.

I find myself here near the London Wall, where once were market stalls. But all now has been picked so bare that not even an apple core remains.

Much of my finer feelings have been shocked to the core. Where the bodies mount up there are no pits to bury them, and people grow so used to corpses that dreadful things happen.

There is a body of men who roam the streets seeking the young female corpses, which they fight over and drag back to their homes for what awful purpose only God knows.

Now no food can get into London from the country, people have begun to starve. And there is no one who would sell provisions even if a trading route was established.

Blackstone rested his nib for a moment, realising the pen in his hand was shaking. He scratched out only a few more lines.

I hear it that the rich still make merry enough in the west. But day by day as this fearful infection grows, parts of London become cut away entire from the rest of the country.

Chapter Fifty-One

Wapping town gate stood open, like a great black mouth yawning out to the town beyond.

Charlie and Maria drew closer, but there was no sign of a gatekeeper.

'Shall we go through?' asked Maria uncertainly.

Up ahead was a cobbled main road through which grass and cow parsley had begun to sprout. It looked deserted. Eerie. Like a ghost town.

'There are some fresh wagon ruts leading through the gate,' Charlie pointed out. 'These are from a large and heavy vehicle. And they have not yet dried.'

'You think Malvern drove his wagon in here, even though the town is deserted?' asked Maria.

'I think someone drove a wagon in here recently,' said Charlie. 'We can only be sure it was Malvern if we go in and ask.'

They drew closer to the dark stone gateway. The wooden door hung half open.

'Any guard?' shouted Charlie. But he was greeted by silence.

They passed through the door and surveyed the main road beyond.

Beneath their feet the cobbles were loose and broken, where weeds had begun to grow up beneath them.

Charlie remembered Wapping when the docks had been clustered with ships loading in lumber and steel from Sweden to the harbour warehouses.

Now there was nothing, and nobody.

'Any guard?' Charlie shouted aloud down the street. Nothing but echoes answered him.

There was a sudden sound. A scratching and scrabbling from one of the alleys to the side of the road. Into the empty opening crept the shadow of a man.

'Who is there?' Charlie's voice tightened uncertainly. Beside him he heard Maria hold her breath.

A voice sounded out in reply. But it was unintelligible and he strained to hear.

The lurching shape became a staggering man.

'It is a drunk,' said Maria with relief.

But Charlie's hand was reaching for his knife.

The man began winding his way towards them.

'Back away,' said Charlie, keeping Maria behind him, 'he isn't right at all.'

The man began a mixture of mumbling shouts, and for a moment Charlie thought that he was a drunk after all.

Then the words began to make sense.

Please. Help. Me.

The apparition made a sudden spurt of speed towards them.

Charlie turned to run, grabbing at Maria's dress to pull her with him.

But she was rooted to the spot with fear. Charlie turned to drag her more bodily after him and caught a glimpse of the blistered neck, the blackened finger tips and the gaping pain-stiffened mouth.

'Maria we must get away!'

The words broke the spell of her terror and she twisted to run away, but she managed only a few blind steps before she tripped on the broken cobbles and tumbled down.

Charlie stooped to pull her back to her feet.

The man was clawing at himself, and his shirt hung in shreds. He was closing on them now, dragging the shattered pulp of a leg behind him.

His hand stretched out towards Maria who was scrabbling backwards over the cobbles. He held a palm of grubby coins.

'Please,' he gasped, 'A pistol . . . .'

Suddenly from behind a heavy length of wood connected with the head of the plague sufferer. The man went crashing to the ground.

Behind him, without his trademark wooden teeth, was Bitey.

He was wielding a two-foot lump of timber and had stopped for a minute to replace his dentures with his free hand. Dark oak grinned out.

Charlie blinked up at him in astonishment. He had never seen Bitey outside the dark confines of the Bucket of Blood. The old man's weather-beaten clothing, Cavalier hat and fierce smudge of beard took on an almost heroic quality. Particularly since he was now openly armed with a knife attached to either hip.

'Why are you out roaming the streets?' he admonished. 'Have you no sense at all?'

Charlie gaped up at him, and recognition set in.

'Charlie!' Bitey held out a hand and pulled him upright. 'I thought you were long dead!'

And who is this? The ancient face made a pantomime expression, and Bitey bowed to doff his dilapidated hat.

'A new wife, Charlie?'

'No,' said Charlie, 'this is Maria.'

Bitey's eyes roamed both faces and seemed to find some answer there.

'Very well,' he said.

Maria staggered to her feet and stared down at the felled body.

'I think you might have killed him,' she said.

Bitey shrugged. 'He was dead in any case,' he said. 'Walking dead. Twas a kindness.'

'What happened here?' asked Maria, 'what happened to the town?'

'Many poorer folk thought Wapping would be a safe place to hole up and wait out the plague,' said Bitey. 'I had the same notion myself,' he added. 'For I have no plague certificate which will get me into the west. But where you have many people in one place the plague will sure follow. One infected is all you need.'

Bitey hesitated for a moment. 'You are quite in health are you not?'

'So far as I know,' said Charlie. Maria gave a short little nod.

'Then all is well,' announced Bitey. 'Come then we shall get you inside and safe.' He put a paternal hand on Charlie's shoulder.

'Best you both stick with me for a bit eh? I have a safe place where I might find a stronger weapon than these knives. You cannot wander the streets alone during these dread times. Not with these walking men abroad.'

'Walking men?'

''S what I call them plaguey that roam the streets,' he said. 'Most of those with the infection take to their beds, stay there. Some die within an hour. For others it takes longer. Three days, four days. A week. But there is another kind, Charlie, as I like to see it. Walking men. They do not hole up and die but take to the streets and roam about in their agony. They are sent mad by it, the suffering. The illness drives them out to look for a holy man or some way to end their pain. They know not what they do, poor souls. For they will clutch at anyone and you cannot risk that they will not come at you and spread their foul air upon you.' He looked at his club appraisingly. 'Better you carry a weapon for that purpose,' he concluded.

'Come,' he said suddenly. 'We shall get off the streets and arm ourselves proper.' A sudden shriek rent the air. 'We should go,' he repeated. 'Best we be gone in case there are more of these roaming sorts.'

Chapter Fifty-Two

'The sounds you hear is the groans and sobs of those dying or mourning,' said Bitey, as he led Charlie and Maria through the Wapping backstreets. 'You get used to it. It is not dangerous. Only sad for the soul.'

'We need your help Bitey,' said Charlie. 'We're here in search of a man. Someone named Thomas Malvern. We think he means to start an uprising. He makes some business at the docks.'

'He could not do that from here Charlie,' said Bitey, as they broke out of the narrow streets and rounded on a part of the waterfront. 'The docks have been closed this month past. Because of the plague you see.'

Bitey gestured at the empty harbour front.

'Then what business could he have here?' Maria asked Charlie in confusion.

Charlie was silent, looking at the waterfront. No ships were docked. But the priest had told him Malvern had some business with a ship. It didn't make sense.

'Best come off the streets with me whilst you think it through,' said Bitey, pointing them to a courtyard reserved for the Royal troops.

Charlie nodded.

Bitey headed for a deserted stables block at the back, beckoning they should follow.

'Surely we break the law coming in here,' whispered Maria, looking at the grand buildings surrounding the dockside stables.

'The King is not in London to enforce his law,' said Bitey. 'Nor his troops neither. Along to the lofts and we are in a safe place.'

Charlie and Maria followed him across the empty courtyard. Grass had struck up amongst the cobbles here too.

'Here we are,' said Bitey, gesturing up. 'Through this gate and up that ladder and we are safe enough.'

'You are housed in the Palace stables?' asked Maria.

'It is a clever thought is it not?' Bitey tapped his nose. 'You have to keep your wits about you if you want to stay alive,' he said. 'Pick a place to sleep which is hidden from thieves and the plaguey alike.'

'Thieves?' asked Charlie.

'Robber, burglars,' confirmed Bitey, dragging himself with grunting effort through the bars of the stable gate.

They walked across the deserted yard and Bitey began climbing a ladder into the nearest hayloft. 'They are starved and desperate, and loot what they can to eat.'

'How do you find food?' asked Maria, gazing up the ladder after him.

'I creep into homes and take what I can,' said Bitey, apparently unaware of the contradiction. 'I have still half a large barrel of ale. For food I take what I can from the ground,' he added. 'Those who have fled leave little gardens in which grow a few vegetables.'

He heaved himself up with a grunt. Charlie slipped his slimmer frame behind and then turned to help Maria and her bulky skirts through.

'Those who stay to pillage are deadly,' said Bitey. 'They break into houses and will kill you fast and savage for the shirt on your back. For there are no laws any longer to govern what men do to other men. Not here in any case.'

Bitey was in the top of the hayloft now and Charlie let Maria go up first after him. Inside was a vast and empty loft, with no evidence of a bed.

'There are no rushes or straw or anything of that nature,' Bitey was saying. 'For straw attracts rats and rats bring cats, and they draw dogs. And all of those will carry the foul air with them.'

In the corner was an open weave basket under which clucked a single chicken.

Bitey reached a mottled hand under the basket to stroke the soft feathers. 'I found her wandering about,' he added. 'I get a few eggs from her, and I drink them off raw.'

'Why do you not light a fire?' asked Maria, who was struggling up off the top of the ladder with Charlie's assistance from lower down, and seeing the loft for the first time.

'Two rules in plague time,' said Bitey, counting out a single finger as Maria manhandled the last of her skirts through the opening. 'No candles, no tapers, no lights. Folk will see them and come to rob you in your bed or breathe plague upon you.'

'Would those with plague come to seek you out?' asked Charlie.

Bitey nodded, he was rooting around in a far corner of the hayloft. 'It is a fearsome agony they are in. They roam around in hope of finding a pistol, or a merciful soul who will stove their heads in. A young woman yonder risked lighting a fire a few days back. Her cottage was crawling with plaguey dead within the hour. And now she has plague herself. She will die today if she is lucky, for her screams are awful to hear.'

Bitey had unearthed a small barrel and rolled it over the floor to his guests.

'Made a trade for this earlier in the week,' he said. 'It is rum. And good for putting a fire in your heart.'

He held the barrel up for Maria to drink from, and Charlie realised she had likely never drunk straight from a tap before.

'Open your mouth under the tap,' he explained, 'Bitey will open it enough for a mouthful of rum to spill out.'

He thought she might refuse, but instead Maria opened her mouth wide and let Bitey unleash a generous flow of spirits past her lips.

She swallowed, gritted her teeth and shuddered bodily, shaking her head.

'That is good,' she said.

Bitey held out the barrel for Charlie, and then Charlie shouldered it so Bitey could take a drink.

'What is the second rule?' asked Maria, the flush of rum seeping into her face. 'You said there were two,' she added, turning to Charlie for confirmation.

'Stay away from Wapping prison. It is thick with plague. And the guards mean to imprison any who wander the streets. They call it a public service. To prevent the spread of the infection. It is over west,' he added pointing, 'away from the waterfront.'

'Can you think of any person who might keep track of who comes in and out of the town?' asked Charlie, whose thoughts had never left the possible movements of Thomas Malvern. 'This man we seek is a murderer and we mean to bring him to justice.'

Bitey threw his head back and laughed.

'You'll not find any justice here,' he said. 'If a murderer flees to these parts he is safe enough from the law.'

Maria's jaw had tightened. 'We *will* bring this man to justice,' she said. 'There must be a way,' she added, looking helplessly at Charlie.

'We can find out his identity,' said Charlie, looking at Bitey. 'He travels under a false name. But we think him to be an important man in the City.'

'If he is an important man then there is even less chance of justice for you,' said Bitey.

'Even so,' said Charlie, 'that is what we mean to do.' His hand was clutching his key tightly. Bitey's eyes logged the gesture, and he reached up to stroke his chaotic beard.

'How do you know he is not dead already of plague, this man you seek?' he said after a moment.

'From what we know he arrived only a few hours ago,' said Charlie.

'And he is important, you say.' Bitey thought for a moment. 'There are places in town which are better guarded,' he conceded, 'where perhaps a rich man might stay and be safer than most. But if you want information of new arrivals you must go to the Coach and Horses.'

'There is an open tavern?' asked Charlie.

Bitey shook his head. 'The landlord and his wife barricaded themselves inside a few weeks back, with their ale and food. They have weapons too, muskets, and will shoot any suspicious person who comes near. That whole quarter is thick with plague people who have been attracted by the sound of gunshot,' he added.

'Then how are we to get to them?' asked Maria, in dismay.

Bitey sat back on his haunches. 'I am known to the landlord,' he said. 'I have traded him food for his drink. He trusts that I am wise enough to stay well clear of those with plague. Perhaps that will be enough to get you inside.'

He surveyed the bare boards and then eased up one to reveal a little clutch of rusting swords underneath.

'I have a little stock of weapons,' he said to Charlie, 'perhaps enough that you and I might protect the lady. You are familiar with a sword?' he asked, hefting up a dusty scabbard and throwing it towards Charlie.

'I am used to a knife,' said Charlie. 'I think that will be good enough.'

Bitey nodded. 'All men of my age can wield a sword same as their own arm,' he said, with a touch of sadness in his voice. 'Civil War, you see. It made monsters of all of us.'

Chapter Fifty-Three

Bitey inched carefully along the Wapping streets with Charlie and Maria following behind.

On leaving the hayloft Bitey had insisted they take several more drafts of rum for courage. Charlie suspected Maria was drunk. He kept a close eye on her as she drifted behind, a faint smile on her face.

Bitey froze suddenly and Charlie saw his attention had been drawn to a door on one of the smart homes. It was opening slowly.

'We must be still,' Bitey pushed them both back against a wall and raised his cudgel.

Out of the doorway came a small boy. He was inching out slowly with his back to the street, and Charlie strained to see what made him move by slow degrees. As his arms came into view they saw him to be dragging something. A female corpse, finely dressed and grotesquely disfigured by disease.

'It is his mother,' said Charlie. 'The poor fellow removes his dead mother from the house.' He could see plague spots were already bulging behind the boy's ears.

Charlie felt a deep wave of sadness. Every instinct was shouting to help the boy bury his mother and give him some shelter and comfort. But they would be condemning themselves to almost certain plague death. And the child was good as dead already.

'What is it?' asked Maria, the rum working to pitch her voice loudly down the street.

'Sssh!' hissed Charlie.

But his warning came too late. The child turned to see them and dropping the arms of the corpse took a wailing step towards them, then broke into a trot.

'Stay back,' shouted Bitey, unhooking his sword and pointing it forward. The little boy stopped, and his face crumpled. He began to howl, his eyes and nose overflowing.

'I mean it lad,' said Bitey. 'I am sorry for you indeed. But there is no help for you here. You must go on back that way,' he gestured in the opposite direction. The little boy began a slow walk away.

Maria had now worked out what was happening and made to follow the boy.

'He needs our help!' she announced, outraged that neither man was offering aid.

Charlie grabbed her arm, pulling her back. 'Hold,' he whispered. 'I know you would give him comfort. But already the plague tokens are on him.'

'We have to help him!' Maria was suddenly furious.

'He is not long for this world,' said Bitey, his expression sympathetic. 'You must learn to do without that soft heart if you are to survive in these times.'

'Come,' he added, with a wave of his hands. 'The tavern is just up ahead.'

The Coach and Horses tavern was a half-timbered tavern made of three stories. What had once been leaded windows was now boarded up on all sides by thick planks. Huge ships nails had been hammered through into the walls and across the door.

Across the battered remains of the cobbled street was a church. And in front of the huge doors lay heaps of scattered bodies.

'Did they come to die in sight of God?' whispered Maria, looking at the corpses.

Bitey turned distractedly from his assessment of the building.

'They are not dead,' he said. 'People come in the hope that a minister will receive their last rites. Or some Christian soul will do what they cannot and end their lives,' he added, 'for even in the agony of plague many are still brave enough to stave off suicide and save their souls from the depths of hell.'

Charlie stepped protectively in front of Maria, who continued to stare at the mound of plague victims.

'Surely they must be dead,' she muttered, as Bitey sought the opening to the tavern.

'This board here is the one,' he said, reaching up to tug at a plank. 'They left it loose so those that know might get inside.'

Charlie moved to help him pull at the board, but as he grasped it the plank seemed solid.

'Bit stiffer than I remember,' said Bitey, gripping with his hands and leaning back to apply his body weight.

The wood gave a sudden shriek, and an arm-sized sliver sheared away. Charlie moved just in time to catch Bitey as he was thrown off balance.

'Mayhap that is not the plank,' said Bitey, staring at the damage they'd done accusingly. Perhaps the other side,' he added, straightening his hat.

But the sound of the rent wood had had an effect on the mound of plague bodies.

Groans and shufflings echoed out over the deserted street. People had begun to stir.

Charlie turned to Bitey.

'We must hurry,' he hissed. 'We have woken some of the plague people. They will come petitioning us to finish them.'

A single man had heaved himself up faster than the rest and was now righting himself on unsteady feet. Most of his shirt was torn away, but by his breeches he looked to have been a wealthy man.

His yellowed eyes settled on Maria, and he began loping towards her.

She gripped at Charlie's arm.

'Tell him to make haste,' she said. 'A plague man comes.'

Bitey had taken a step back from the tavern and was assessing it in confusion.

'My memory is not so good as it was,' he admitted.

The plague man was closing in now, and he was near enough they could see the balloons of purple skin which had risen up under either armpit.

'You look like my daughter,' he said to Maria, in a voice which came out as a croak. 'Surely you would take pity on me.'

'Get behind me,' said Charlie, drawing the rusting sword.

The man made two more staggering steps, and then an earth-shattering boom sounded, shaking the windows of the empty street.

The plague man fell down, and a growing pool of blood formed beneath him.

Another blast sounded, and Charlie felt a pain in his upper arm.

He looked to see he had been grazed by musket shot.

'They are firing at us from the tavern!' he said, pulling Maria and Bitey back towards the wall. 'They think we are plague people trying to get in.'

'There is not reason for them to think so,' said Bitey, scratching at his head. 'Wait, I will have words with them.'

Bitey swung back towards the aperture they had made, and Charlie grabbed him back just in time as a third shot went off.

Across the street the effect on the plague people was electric. The mound shifted. Bodies began to right themselves one by one.

Charlie leaned back towards the opening.

'We are not plague people,' he shouted to the unseen occupants, moving the side of his face as near as he dared to the open sliver of plank.

The barrel of a musket slid out within inches of his cheek.

In a single fast movement Charlie grabbed the gun with both hands and pulled it free. On the other side of the board he heard a man's voice curse.

'We are here with Bitey,' he added, checking the musket was loaded. 'He knows you.'

'Aye that I do!' called Bitey, from his position backed against the building. 'And I would take it well if you would let us in, for we have some plague people headed for us.'

Charlie's eyes fell back on the church. At least ten bodies had now mobilised. Some crawled and some walked.

'How do you know which plank it is?' Charlie asked, aiming the musket at the nearest plague sufferer.

'Three along from the top, west wall, the plank with the crotchet shaped knot,' said Bitey. 'I thought I had it right,' he added.

Charlie made a quick glance at the sun. 'We are on the north wall,' he said. 'We need to move around the building.'

He signalled with his arm and moved back, keeping the barrel of the musket pointed towards the plague people.

'Maria,' he called, 'can you count the planks?'

'Of course I can count,' she said. 'And I have music too. I know what a crotchet looks like.'

Charlie turned his head to see she was scanning the west face of the building.

'Crotchet shaped knot,' she muttered, running her hand along a plank.

An elderly man had made ahead of the rest and started up a shambling kind of run towards them.

Trying to keep his body steady Charlie aimed the musket and pulled the trigger.

The old man wheeled violently to one side and then fell.

'That was my only shot,' said Charlie. 'You need to get us inside.'

'I have found it,' said Maria. 'Here.'

'That's the one,' said Bitey delightedly, 'I remember it well now.'

'Then get it open, said Charlie.

'Of course.' The old man ran his calloused fingers over the plank and twisted. It dropped free revealing a wide opening.

'Get Maria through first,' he said to Bitey.

'Don't offend anyone inside before we get in there,' he added to Maria, as Bitey hoisted her headfirst through the gap.

She launched forward in a flurry of thick skirts and was gone.

'I hope you are right about this opening,' said Charlie, hefting the musket through the gap after Maria. 'They might kill her before we get inside.'

'They are kindly folk,' said Bitey, placing a foot on the plank to lever himself through the gap. 'You must not mind they shot at us.'

Several of the crawling sufferers were making good ground now. A young woman of seventeen or so with grotesque buboils either side of her ears, a middle aged man and a young boy were heaving themselves over the cobbles.

Charlie turned to see Bitey was still halfway through the gap and gave the old man a quick shove to push him the rest of the way through.

He heard a muffled cry of reproach and then the opening was empty.

The young woman was gaining ground fast. She had adopted a strange bandy-legged hobble, as though her muscles had given out, and the swaying of her skeleton alone was moving her forwards.

Unhooking his sword Charlie banged it loudly against the cobblestones and then threw it as far as he could over the heads of the plague sufferers.

The man furthest from him turned to make after it, but the young boy and the woman only watched it go, then continued their stumbling progress towards him.

The young woman was only a few yards away from him now. Her eyes were a mass of red blood vessels, and she was panting through slightly parted lips, like a long-distance runner approaching a finish line.

Charlie stepped onto the plank and pulled himself into the gap.

Halfway through he felt a hand with sharp fingernails on his bare foot. He kicked back and felt his heel connect with something hard. Teeth, and then his leg was free and he somersaulted forward into the tavern beyond.

'Close up the gap!' commanded an angry voice. And people either side of him hammered a plank into place.

Charlie looked up to see Bitey and Maria were being held with muskets pointed at them.

A man with buckteeth peered drunkenly at Charlie.

'Like I said,' he slurred. 'They have compromised our safety. We must kill all three of them.'

Chapter Fifty-Four

King Charles knocked on the door a little too loudly, then opened it in softer apology.

His wife's face showed surprise as he moved inside her bedchamber.

'Our appointment was arranged,' he reminded her, closing the door behind him.

She nodded, her face still contorted in confusion.

English was her second language and Charles was never sure what she understood. Though he knew she dreaded the fulfilment of their marital obligations.

Her room smelled of sealing wax. Queen Catherine of Braganza wrote many letters to her Portuguese family. Her room too, was a little enclave of Mediterranean gold and red in a Palace of English tastes. The four-poster bed was hung with tapestries stitched by nuns from the convent where Catherine had grown up. The rugs on the floor had been acquired on her pilgrimage to a favourite shrine in Lisbon.

Charles stepped towards her, and she held out her arms, childlike, ready to be undressed. He began drawing off her heavy clothes, starting with her uppermost dress.

'I hear things from the court,' she began in her stuttering Portuguese accent. 'That Catholics in England are unhappy with how they are treated.'

Catherine was a devout Catholic, a fact which Charles did his best to keep hidden from the English people.

'I have received letters,' she continued, 'from an astrologer. William Lilly. He asks for his position in the Royal Household to be reconsidered now you have returned.'

Charles tugged off the uppermost dress and laid it carefully on a chair. 'I remember William Lilly,' he said, 'I am doing my best to see he is rewarded for his loyalty. But parliament are all against me.'

'There is something else,' insisted Catherine.

Charles moved to loosen the dress at the front. He had tried to kiss her once, on the mouth. But she had twisted her head away and one of the ornaments in her elaborate wig had scratched his face.

'What is that?' he asked, stooping to roll down her stockings. He felt the muscles in her legs tighten.

Charles had experimented with ways to make his wife more complicit in their marital obligations. But so far all his efforts had come to nothing. Any attempt at intimacy set his wife rigid and twitching, as though she was being tortured.

He stood, and moving behind her began unlacing her stays with expert speed. This experience with women's clothing, he felt, was one of the few skills his wife enjoyed.

'This symbol,' she said. 'The one they say is used by the witch-murderer. You know what it means. I see you draw it.'

Charles's hand faltered for a moment. Then continued the practised unlacing. The stays came away in his hand, leaving Catherine in nothing but her white linen shift.

'It is a symbol from long ago,' he said carefully. 'From my childhood. Back in the days when my father was on the throne.'

He took her hands and guided her to the bed. She lay down obediently, and in an effort to make her comfortable Charles began to prop pillows around and under her. The expression on Catherine's face was unreadable.

She looked up at him uncomfortably from her position, prone on the bed.

'What does it mean?'

'It is the sign of the Sealed Knot,' said Charles, 'It was a group of Royalist noblemen who swore to protect the crown from Cromwell.'

Catherine's face showed confusion.

'They were all powerful men,' said Charles, 'Powerful, and skilled, and fearless. The kind of men you would want on your side. After my father was executed they worked in secret to return me to the crown. But then they fell to fighting amongst themselves.'

He began working off her shift. Underneath her clothes his wife's body was small, childlike even. With breasts like a partially-grown afterthought.

'Where are they now?' asked Catherine, drawing her arms tight across her naked chest.

Charles shook his head. 'Long gone. Dead.'

Stroking the shape of her body with his hand, Charles let it rest between her legs. The space felt parched, cold.

He worried he must hurt her.

When he had first experienced the tightness of his wife's body, he thought the other women had lied to him about their virginity.

Now he realised it was due to how much she hated her wifely duties. The thought was unsettling.

Resting his gaze on the space above Catherine's head, Charles summoned up an image of Louise's legs spreading slowly open. The picture allowed him to rally. He entered the reluctant body of his wife.

Catherine lay with her jaw clenched, her breath sounding fast through her pinched lips.

The smell from her mouth was of her orange-water perfume. And something else. Garlic, perhaps.

The thought sapped him of the thin enthusiasm he had managed to muster. He felt himself flag and wondered if she could feel it.

Charles trawled his memory for some scene to enliven him.

It settled upon Louise, her hand between her legs, her fingers working frantically, expertly.

The thought caught for a moment and then slipped from him. He tracked deeper, plumbing the depths of his fantasies in partial panic.

Louise with one of the maids, her little white hand deep inside, the maid's face contorted in ecstasy, Louise's white fingers thrusting relentlessly deeper.

To his great relief the image allowed him to finish. Though it was in a silent shame that the most debased prostitutes had yet to illicit from him.

Beneath him Catherine's eyes twitched back and forth, asking whether it was all over.

Charles rolled himself off his wife and sent up a short but fervent prayer that he had finally made her pregnant.

'What if any of those men still lived?' asked Catherine, her eyes still fixed pointedly on the ceiling.

'That,' said Charles, taking the hint to get off the bed and start dressing, 'would be very dangerous indeed.'

Chapter Fifty-Five

Bitey had negotiated an uneasy truce with the handful of inebriated inmates of the Coach and Horses. It had been mostly achieved by his revealing a clutch of hen's eggs he'd managed to transport ingeniously beneath his battered hat. But the locals were still uncertain. The tension was palpable.

The three men in residence, it transpired, formed what remained of the town's constabulary and prison guard. A fact which made Charlie nervous.

'Yon landlord's the only one who could tell you about the town's comings and goings,' confirmed a lanky man with pronounced buckteeth, who claimed to be Wapping's constable. 'He is gone for the moment, visiting the better part of town, where his daughter works.'

'What is the better part of town?' Charlie had asked Bitey, keeping a careful eye on the gaoler.

'The guarded part, as I told you before,' said Bitey, 'a few streets where rich folk might be safe from the plague. A handful of women are allowed in that part to work as prostitutes, and the landlord's daughter is one of them.'

'The landlord will be back within a few hours,' added the bucktoothed man.

He did not offer an invitation to join them. The three men sat a little apart, at their own table, looking suspiciously at the newcomers. They all smoked pipes, which was unusual, Charlie noticed. Normally tobacco was a luxury reserved for the rich.

He looked around the rest of the tavern.

It was basic enough, with several large barrels of beer from which drinkers helped themselves.

Bitey was already filling his cup.

One of the men raised himself to offer Maria a drink from a bottle of wine kept on the bar.

She nodded, not seeming to notice that he filled her a cup with his eyes riveted to her uncovered hair and fashionable dress.

'This is Burgundy, and far cheaper than any you might get in London,' she said, returning to where Charlie stood on the other side of the tavern. 'It is fine stuff.'

He privately doubted that the wine was genuine Burgundy. It would likely be some cheaper drink. Charlie wondered if the rum Maria had drunk earlier was still having an effect.

⌣‿⌣

Several hours later Maria had made her steady way through several cups of wine.

In the candlelight the sadness had fallen away from her face and Charlie noticed all the men were staring openly towards Maria.

Her smile blazed out at him.

'We should ask them what they know,' she announced. 'They cannot be so badly disposed towards us,' she gestured with the tankard towards the men.

Charlie assessed the buck-toothed constable who seemed to have been getting drunker at the same pace as Maria.

301

'Best we wait until the landlord returns,' he said. Though the gnawing thought of Malvern moving unchecked in Wapping was making his hands twitch.

Bitey nodded in agreement. 'They are rough men,' he agreed uneasily. 'And it will not take much to have them think us a threat.'

But Maria had risen uncertainly to her feet. And before Charlie could stop her she approached the three seated men.

'What do you know of witchcraft in these parts?' she asked, raising her tankard in salute.

The constable with the buckteeth assessed her with renewed suspicion.

Charlie moved quickly to stand beside her.

'She has an interest in country affairs,' he said lamely. 'And we hear that many witches stood trial in the country.'

'That they did,' said the constable, still staring at Maria. 'Thirty men and women were hanged only this spring for witchcraft.'

'And what spells did they perform?' pressed Maria, 'how did you know they were witches.'

The constable looked to the men next to him and then back to Maria.

'I conducted the trials myself,' he said. 'They confessed, under torture in Wapping prison. They had called upon Satan's powers.'

'But they had not made spells?' insisted Maria, 'with ribbons and candles and such?'

'Why do you want to know?' the constable's posture tightened in his chair.

'She is only curious,' said Charlie, grabbing Maria by the waist and steering her away. 'What are you doing?' he hissed in her ear. 'We are here by grace and favour and you make us sound as though we have come to town to devil worship!'

'There is no harm in asking,' said Maria, turning uncertainly back to the men. They glowered after her. The constable leaned to mutter something in the ear of his closest companion.

'They think we are husband and wife,' she added, laughing and looking out into the wider tavern. 'It would not be so terrible if we were would it Charlie?'

She must be drunker than he'd realised, Charlie decided.

'You told me not so long ago that I was the last man you would ever consider for such things.'

Maria laughed. 'Oh come now Charlie. Do not bear grudges for past harms. Women do not mean everything they say out loud. I mean to marry for security, it is not a slight on you.'

She said it with a finality which annoyed him. Charlie frowned, momentarily forgetting about the three men still staring out at them from their corner.

'That is the talk of old widows, not girls of twenty.'

'What do you think Charlie? That I should marry for love? That is the way for a life of poverty.'

He looked at her for a moment.

'I do not think you believe that,' he said. 'I think you have taken some hard luck and you hope it has made you hard. But it is a poor act.'

A flicker of pain passed over her face. 'You may think yourself a fine judge of character Charlie Thief-Taker. But you know nothing of me.' The words caught in her throat. 'I am to find out some other company.'

She made to move back to where Bitey was sitting, but in a sudden surge of feeling, Charlie grabbed her by the wrist.

'I know that you cannot look me in the eye when you talk about your future husband,' he said. 'I know you pull at the seams of your dress when you speak of having children. And I know the minute you have a drink inside you, you talk of your poor husband-to-be with nothing but scorn.'

She looked for a moment as though she might hit him. Then she wrenched her arm from his grip and stalked off to sit back with Bitey.

The three seated men looked on with interest.

A loud bang echoed through the tavern, and Charlie turned his head to see the plank entry had opened. Heaving his way through was the tavern landlord.

Bitey moved to help him in, and Charlie felt a wave of relief. The tension between them and the locals had been palpable. Now they could find the information they needed and get back to tracking Malvern. Before tonight's moon brought about some unstoppable completion to his plan.

'Do you know anything of a wagon that has newly arrived in town?' asked Bitey, as the landlord leaned on his arm and stood upright in the tavern.

But the landlord's face was twisted in distress.

'I know only one thing,' he said, his voice cracking as he spoke. 'My daughter. My beautiful daughter has gone missing.'

The landlord turned to the buck-toothed constable.

'You love my Lilieth do you not?'

The constable nodded, dumbstruck.

'Then you must help me find her.'

The constable was already rising to his feet. He cast a final malevolent glare towards Charlie and Maria.

'My great fear is that she has taken plague and gone off to die alone,' said the landlord, his eyes haunted with the notion. 'I should hate to think of her in agony in some lonely place.'

The constable extended a sympathetic pat on his arm. 'Your Lilieth keeps herself in good health,' he assured him. 'Likely she has met with some travelling customer, or takes a drink with one of the other girls.'

The landlord shook his head. 'Her green bonnet was found on the street,' he said. 'That is what puts me in the most fear. For she loved that bonnet and would not lose it.'

'We will go to where she worked,' said the constable. 'We might find something out there.'

And the landlord and constable slipped back out of the tavern, leaving Charlie, Maria and Bitey alone with the last two men.

They looked at one another uneasily.

Maria sat down heavily.

'It is hopeless,' she said. 'That was the only person who might have helped us. And he knows nothing.'

Bitey shrugged at the sad reality of this.

But Charlie's face was lined in thought.

The smell of tobacco sat heavy on the air.

Strange that so many of the town can afford tobacco.

His thoughts moved to the cut-price Burgundy wine which Maria had been drinking.

It must be a smuggler's town, he realised, thinking back to Marc-Anthony's imports. Tobacco and wine were all popular illegal imports.

Suddenly the facts slotted together.

The full moon. The docks.

Nothing can get out of those docks. But what about getting something in? That is why Malvern travels by the lunar calendar. It is not for reasons of witchcraft. He comes to town when the tide is high.

Slowly Charlie rose to his feet. His heart was racing.

So Malvern must be smuggling something, he thought. *Something that could aid an uprising.*

He turned to Maria. 'We need to get to the docks,' he said.

Chapter Fifty-Six

When the constable and landlord arrived outside Lilieth's working room there was a terrible stench of acrid smoke on the air.

They exchanged glances.

'I will go alone,' said the constable. 'If there is fire it could be dangerous.'

He had asked Lilieth to marry him several times and so far she had refused. But he always felt confident she would yield in the end. The constable crossed himself, assessing the haze of smoke in the air. He refused to believe anything bad had happened to her.

'It smells like someone left a spit of meat to char,' murmured the landlord.

The constable nodded.

'Likely she has fallen asleep and left some meat to burn.' But he couldn't keep the doubt from his voice.

'Wait here,' he added. 'I will shout down from the window if anything is needed inside. It may be faster to have a man on the street and one inside if something has . . . has happened.'

The constable pushed open the thick wooden door which led to three single rooms. On the ground level nothing seemed awry. But smoke was pouring from the second storey.

The constable pulled off his flammable shirt and jerkin.

He made his way up the creaking stairs to find the smoke was clearing. Whatever the fire was must have gone out. Likely it was as they presumed, a joint of meat which had been charred to a cinder and sent out smoke. A terrible waste in plague times. But better than a house fire.

He entered the single room of the second floor, a plainly decorated chamber which he'd seen many times before.

A single chair sat in the middle of the room.

The constable missed his footing and stumbled.

Sat on the chair, with her green dress burned to cinders, drooped the charred husk of a woman.

The fire had been started in her lap, and the remains of her head had slumped forward.

Thick lines of greasy soot ran over the holes where her ears had been. Her nose had melted to two jagged dark caves and the lips were scorched to nothing, setting the mouth in an endless silent scream.

The constable felt ice tunnelling through every vein in his body.

He staggered again, and then he fell to his knees. 'Oh God,' he said. 'Oh God.' Someone had ripped his heart out and in the empty space thick anguish took hold.

The constable moved towards the corpse like a sleepwalker, willing himself to be wrong. But there was no mistaking her.

Red welts shone on the scalp where her dark hair had been. The large blue eyes that he remembered had boiled in their sockets with the long lashes burned to a crust.

He thought for a moment that strange heaving sounds came from the chair where she sat. Then he realised it was the noise of his own wracking sobs which were shaking him bodily.

The constable was close enough to smell the acrid fumes which still came from the body, and he reached out and touched the charred shoulder.

In the tumult of his mind he thought for the villain who might have done this.

Wrapped around the body were ribbons. White ribbons. But all bloodied and not burned. Some words had been written on the floor in blood, but he could not read them.

A spell, he realised. Some unholy spell had been cast.

Then he remembered the two strangers from the Coach and Horses.

The harlot girl with her hair uncovered and the man she had come with. She had been interested in spells and witches. And he had stopped her asking, as though they had something to hide.

In the madness of his grief the constable felt both fists grip themselves. He would find out this pair, and he would see them stand trial.

Chapter Fifty-Seven

As the docks came into full view Charlie froze. Behind him he heard Maria suppress a little gasp.

The docks they had seen in the daytime were empty. All abandoned.

Now the thick stretch of water was covered in row-boats. There were over ten of them, their storm lanterns scattered in the dark like winking yellow eyes.

On the waterfront heavyset men were hauling loads from the boats into a single enormous wagon.

They had guessed right. Somebody was importing here. It must be Malvern.

'He brings in bodies?' whispered Maria, staring at the cargo. Charlie nodded. The cargo looked to be corpses, wrapped tightly in linen winding sheets.

'We must get out of sight,' he muttered. Charlie cast about for a hiding place and settled on an abandoned skiff by the side of the harbour.

'Behind here,' he said, pulling her by the arm.

Maria followed and they were quickly out of view.

Through the sails of the skiff Charlie let his eyes run over the operation.

The men doing the loading were a thick-skinned, tough-looking crew, and Charlie identified them immediately as professional smugglers. Most had the kinds of injuries which resulted from a lifetime's fighting on the high seas away from any hope of medical treatment.

Limbs had been replaced with everything from spade handles to broken oars. Many had the open ulcers of scurvy.

Charlie's heart was beating so hard he wondered that they couldn't hear him. Smugglers were the kind of men who drowned each other for sport.

He took in the shape of the row-boats, trying to gain a clue as to where they might be from. Tax evaders shipped whisky from Scotland and wool from Yorkshire as well as luxuries like lace, wine and sugar from all over the globe. Trafficking routes were well established to every country in the colony and pirates would import anything for the right price.

'Malvern!' a rough sailor's voice shouted up the docks.

Charlie stared in disbelief. Walking in amongst the men was a monster. There was no other word for it. The huge shape was swathed in thick canvas, with a long beak jutting down.

As it strode the docks a shaft of moonlight made a ghostly pattern on the head and, rather than revealing some gruesome spectre, Charlie saw it to be a man in a plague-doctor costume.

Malvern. So this was him. The man who had murdered Maria's sister, fitted out in his killer's disguise.

The size of him gave the shape an extra bestial quality. He was enormous – easily as large as three of his burly smugglers – and the effect of the huge figure beneath the thick canvas was grotesque. Its crystal eyes winked in the moonlight making it impossible to tell in which direction the figure was staring but giving the impression it could see everywhere.

'We have to leave,' Charlie whispered to Maria. 'These men will kill us if they see us. And we have seen all we might.'

Maria nodded, her face ghostly pale in the moonlight. Slowly they crept back from the skiff and slipped quickly into the streets which ran behind the harbour.

'We should go to where Bitey stays and hide there,' said Charlie. 'Then we might put together some kind of plan to see Malvern captured.'

They were already on the street where Bitey had made his abode.

Charlie felt a sudden pain and his hand went to his collarbone.

A line of blood ran down it. Someone had thrown a stone or a missile.

He looked about in confusion and too late saw Bitey signalling from the second storey stable-block.

Then the road crowded in with men bearing torches and pistols.

'Remember me?' asked the buck-toothed man. Beside him the other constables moved closer.

Charlie felt Maria stiffen.

'You are accused of being witches,' said the constable. 'And for the murder of an innocent girl. So we are here to take you to the prison so you might stand trial.'

'We have done nothing wrong,' said Charlie evenly, looking at the constable. 'You waste time imprisoning us. For the real murderer goes free.'

The constable pointed the pistol.

'We will discover if you are innocent or no soon enough,' he said. 'Country trials are not the same as those in the City. They are a great deal faster.'

'But how will you assemble a judge in plague times?' asked Maria in confusion.

'Our judge lives in Wapping prison,' said the constable, with an evil grin. 'In this town we believe in the old ways of trialling suspects.'

The men crowded in on them, and Charlie realised what the constable meant.

In London justice was of a more modern kind. But before judges and courts, innocence had been determined by ordeal. Convicts were tied up and dropped into rivers, had fatal wounds administered, or were made to drink lethal poison.

If the suspect lived then it was deemed that God had intervened and shown their innocence. But no one ever survived the trials.

'We will take you to Wapping prison,' said the constable, 'and there you will both meet your trial by Ordeal.'

Chapter Fifty-Eight

Charlie struggled as men grabbed his arms. He heard Maria shrieking in protest of her innocence.

Then they were dragged forward by their bound wrists, towards the part of town which held Wapping prison.

'We are innocent!' insisted Maria.

'We will find that out soon enough,' said the constable. 'A poor girl has burned and you will both meet the same fate.'

Charlie assessed their surroundings and the number of captors. Now was not the time to try for escape, he decided. The men held loaded pistols, and he guessed they would not hesitate to use them. And even if he could struggle free and run, he couldn't leave Maria.

He felt rather than saw Maria's fear build as they approached Wapping prison.

Dawn was breaking and the heavy stone walls of the building inched into view.

They were quiet, contemplating the approach.

'Do you think they mean to burn us?' whispered Maria in a quavering voice.

'Maybe they will find our innocence before they make us stand trial,' said Charlie.

Maria clamped her mouth shut and stared straight ahead. There were tears in her eyes.

Charlie thought back to what he knew.

The murdered girl had been burned, according to the constable. This was fire then. The third. He had assumed that the killing would stop outside London. It still didn't make sense to him. Malvern the avenging soldier was high-born, scheming and clever. Malvern as a witch-killer . . . . His actions were illogical and peasant-like. Something didn't fit.

Today was the day when Malvern's plan was due for fruition. Had he already planned for a fourth girl to die? A water death, to complete his master spell?

The guard waved them forward into the prison.

Thick walls were joined by a heavy wooden door. Inside was cold and a set of steps led downwards. The guard gestured they should descend.

And as they were led down further below ground the air took on an oozing damp which seemed to catch at the lungs immediately. Maria began coughing violently, and Charlie remembered her laboured breathing on the road to Wapping. He wondered how much she had been hiding her ill-health, brought on by the dysentery.

They reached the bottom of the slippery spiral staircase and the guard led them along the length of corridor. Impossibly thick stone walls encased them on every side and iron grille as thick as a man's arm enclosed the various cells.

At the end stood a dank open cell. In it were some thirty prisoners, standing or sitting dejectedly on the straw-strewn floor.

One man lay apart from the others, bearing unmistakable marks. He was in the dying stages of the plague. Even in the gloom Charlie could make out the distension at the neck. Plague buboils had stretched the skin obscenely taut, where it throbbed tight and shiny over deep swellings of hardening blood.

The shirt had been torn away to expose the map of infection across his tortured body. A network of bruises and raised claret-coloured veins twisted out from his armpits in heavy raised blisters and down to his groin in a web of black and green.

Maria froze and backed into the guard behind her.

'You cannot make us go in there!' she cried. 'It is certain death! That man has the plague. Where is your pest house?'

'This is the pest house,' said the guard. 'We are overrun with plague.'

'We have not been convicted of any crime!' said Maria. 'And you condemn us to death.'

'There is a barrel of plague water in there,' said the guard, as he threw them into the cell and closed the bars behind them. 'The constable will be along to begin your trial,' he added, pressing his face at the iron bars to deliver the news.

Maria flung herself at the door as the guard exited and began shouting their innocence. Then having assured herself he had left she leaned back against the bars, her face wrenched into an expression of hopelessness.

'We will stay back here against the bars,' said Charlie, putting an arm around her waist. 'As far back from the others as possible.'

He looked out at the dying man and the other prisoners, and then back at Maria.

Her usually tidy hair was in disarray and her dress was ripped at the collar where the guards had dragged her into the prison. Charlie had never seen Maria look so utterly defeated.

'Come,' he said, moving his hand to the fabric. 'Here is torn. Let me see if I can reattach it. There. Now you may face the guards in your usual style.'

He looked up at her with a smile, but something in her sad face made his stop, with his hand rested on her collarbone.

'It will be alright Maria,' he said. 'I will get you out of here.'

Her lips were on his suddenly, and he was kissing her back, pushing against the weight of her feeling. Steadying himself he caught her up in his arms. And for a long moment they were lost in one another, their surroundings fading away.

'I am sorry Charlie.' Maria pulled back, staring into his eyes.

'Sorry for what?'

'I wanted you. Back in that field. And my foolish thoughts of marriage stopped me. Now we are doomed to die and I will regret my pride forever.'

'Shhh,' he kissed her mouth. 'You must not talk that way. We will not die in here, I promise you.'

She looked so sad that he could almost feel his heart breaking.

'I swear it to you Maria,' he repeated, making his voice hard with conviction.

'They are going to burn us alive.' Her voice was barely a whisper.

'Look into my eyes.' Charlie took her chin in his hand. 'I will never let any harm come to you. Look at me. Do you believe it now?'

She blinked, swallowed and then nodded slowly.

'I do.'

'We shall escape it, Maria. And when we do, I shall hold you to that guinea you owe me.'

She laughed weakly, and Charlie smiled back. But in his heart he could think of no way they might evade the dreadful fate which awaited them.

A jangle of keys alerted them to the sudden presence of the guard. He had returned with the constable.

Reluctantly Charlie and Maria drew apart to face their fate.

'We must try you one at a time,' announced the constable as he drew back the bars. His eyes rested on Maria. 'She was asking about spells and the like. Her guilt should be determined first.'

Charlie's arms went around Maria. 'I shall go first,' he said. 'It is not right a woman should be tried,' he added, releasing her reluctantly and stepping forward.

'No Charlie!' Maria's eyes had filled with tears. She grabbed at his hand.

'I will be back soon Maria,' he said, with a half smile. 'And when I return they will know my innocence and you will not need to be tried.'

Maria's hand gripped his tightly. Then the constable and the guard grabbed hold of Charlie and manhandled him out of the cell.

'You are good men, I know it,' he said, as they tugged him down further into the prison. 'Let her go, I beg you. She is innocent and has money to pay for your kindness besides.'

The constable gave Charlie a rough shove.

'My Lilieth was murdered,' he said. 'And you will both burn.'

Chapter Fifty-Nine

'We reserve a special cell for our trials,' said the constable. 'It is not so fancy as London courts, but we find it serves our purpose.'

Charlie let the words buzz in his head, keeping his attention on the construction of the prison and possibilities of escape.

The corridor was dark, narrow and damp. It wound around away from the other cells and ended in a single thick doorway.

The constable moved ahead and unlocked the door with a thick set of keys. It opened an inch on ancient hinges, and the constable shouldered his weight against it.

Slowly the room beyond was revealed. A single torch burned, flickering on stone walls glinting with slippery mould.

In the centre of the room, like a monstrous metal bed, was the place where Charlie realised his trial would take place.

A large metal plate had been roughly shaped into the limbs of a man. But the space where the head should rest was unfinished, leaving a hole.

At the feet and wrists were thick metal manacles. And underneath the bed was a space for a brazier, already filled with fresh wood.

Charlie let out a slow breath, taking it all in.

The guard pushed him forward, and he stepped into the room.

It stank of burned flesh.

'Be quick about it,' said the constable. 'Get him in and the manacles on.'

'You're very quiet,' he added, as they pulled Charlie onto the metal plate and began binding his wrists. 'Usually they are all screaming and crying by now.'

Charlie let his wrists feel out the manacles and angled his hands so they might be secured more loosely. But the guard tugged them so tight they cut away the circulation to his hands.

The constable strapped down his feet. Charlie let them lie still, but he thought they might not be so firmly bound as his hands. He let the idea float like a little firefly of warmth in the cold tumult of his mind.

'The wood begins to burn by your feet,' explained the constable. 'So you might start to say your prayers when you feel it warm there. Then the flames will catch along your body,' he continued. 'When they reach your head there is a hole there, as you can feel.' The constable turned to include the guard in the conversation.

'If you are guilty then the fire will quickly burn away all your hair. And then your brains will be slowly cooked in your skull.'

He leaned closer to meet Charlie's eyes. 'If you killed my Lilieth then this is a merciful death for you. For you will be dead in a few hours or less. Though you will feel pain like none other on earth.'

'And if I am innocent?' asked Charlie, his voice steady.

'Then God will intervene,' said the constable. 'And we will come back here and find you alive, with no burns upon your body.'

The constable stood up and unhooked the burning torch from its holding. Then he bent and lowered it.

There was a crackling sound as the wood caught, and flames plumed up with smoke. Charlie felt the first warmth at his feet.

'We will return soon,' said the constable.

He stooped to dip his tankard in a barrel of plague water by the entrance to the cell and took a long sip. 'And if you are guilty I hope to God you suffer with your trial.'

The door creaked shut and Charlie was left alone with the growing heat.

He twisted in the manacles and pressed all his strength into tugging his hands and feet free.

He had already begun to lose sensation in his hands, and pulsing pain was juddering through his fingertips where the bonds had been made tight.

His feet had been bound tighter than he initially hoped. He kicked and pulled, but they held firm.

He could feel the fire building now. His face and body had broken out in a sweat, and the heat under his feet and calves had grown from a gentle warmth to a strong heat.

Charlie turned his legs as far as they would move in the bonds, to move the heat to a different stretch of skin.

The fire was building fast now, and it was only a few seconds before the newly exposed part of his leg became unbearably hot.

His eyes swept the walls of the cell for some way to escape. The stone walls looked mercifully cool in their glinting damp. But there was nothing to help him get free.

The fire had reached his middle torso now, and the pain was becoming unbearable. He felt a stretch of blisters bubble out along his spine and gritted his teeth to stop from shouting aloud.

There was a scrabbling sound in the corner of the cell. Rats. Charlie felt himself wondering hazily whether they might eat his remains.

He shook his head, trying to bring himself back to logical thoughts.

The manacles were his only hope. Again he began twisting and pulling. But his hands were now burning in their own fire of blood loss, and the pain of pulling them was almost as bad as the fire beneath him.

Ignoring the pain, he dug in and pulled. He thought he felt the skin drag a fraction and then it stopped hard against the metal restraints.

Charlie felt a sweep of heat flare against his shoulder blades and knew it could not be long before the fire reached his head.

His feet and legs were blazing in a world of agony. Moving them even fractionally wafted hot air over the screaming skin.

The fire seared the plate under his neck.

Charlie closed his eyes and pulled and kicked with his feet. The movement felt like boiling oil was being poured on his burning legs. And they were held fast. The heavy metal was unmoving.

There was a fizzing sound and Charlie smelled the first burning hair at the nape of his neck.

He knew it could be only moments before his head was consumed in a ball of fire.

Charlie let the pain roll over him.

There was a sudden pressure on his wrists. The heat, he assumed, was now scorching on the manacles which held him.

Then the pain lessened, and he suddenly found his wrists had sprung free.

Without pausing to think he sprang up, away from the bed. A jet of fire pulsed suddenly behind him, where his head had been moments before.

His legs still burned, and he saw the shape of a person by his feet, opening up the manacles at his ankles.

Charlie rolled himself free of the burning metal bed and fell heavily into the dirt of the cell floor, panting in relief.

His eyes scanned for who or what had allowed his freedom. The person was hunched over where he'd been lying, half visible in the flickering torch light and the glow of heat from under the bed.

Charlie tried to stand, but his feet gave way.

Then the person straightened, and Charlie saw female features. It was a woman, perhaps forty years old.

'Goid I nooit! Weinig Charlie Oakley,' came her low voice in Dutch.

In his head the Dutch words reformed themselves into English. *I cannot believe it. Little Charlie Oakley.*

Chapter Sixty

Another light blazed in the cell, and Charlie saw the woman was holding a little stub of candle. The flame fluttered and then grew to a warm orb.

'Little Charlie Oakley,' she repeated in Dutch. 'After all these years.'

Charlie stood in the semi-dark, shocked into silence.

'I was frightened when they brought you in,' explained the woman. 'No one is supposed to come in this room. It is mine alone. So I hid.'

The blonde hair had turned partially white and the large blue eyes were a little duller with age. But he remembered the lovely face so well.

'It is you,' Charlie breathed, speaking in Dutch.

Some faint details were coming back, that this woman had taught him and his brother Dutch. She was the mistress of a great house, where his mother had worked.

He fought for more memories, but there were none.

'Then I became braver and I looked and saw it was you,' continued the woman. 'And I recognised you from all those years ago.'

Charlie clung to this sudden revelation. His mother had worked in a large house. That was something.

And now he had a name. Charlie Oakley. He tried to feel something for the surname, but there was nothing.

This lady, he remembered, had lived in the cellar.

She raised the candle to consider his face.

'So Sally Oakley put you safe as she said she would,' she said, wonderingly.

His mind was churning at the strange familiarity of it all. Hearing the name was an electric shock of recognition. Sally Oakley. That must be his mother's name.

'Where is my mother now?' said Charlie, unable to keep his orphan abandonment from rising to the fore.

'Why she took you to put you safe,' said the woman. The musical voice brought with it a feeling rather than a memory. That as a boy he had sometimes been frightened of her.

'But where did she go?'

'My husband sent her away Charlie,' she shook her head. 'I did not want him to for it was a fine thing having a lady's maid.'

'Where? Where did she go?'

'I do not know.'

Charlie's mind was reeling, trying to think through what it meant.

'Why?' he insisted, unable to keep the desperation from his voice. 'Why did he send her away?'

'Your mother found his secrets and hid them,' she said. 'Secrets about my husband and the King. That no one can know.'

Charlie remembered the key. What if his mother had hidden these special papers away and given him the means to find them?

His gaze settled back on the woman. Teresa. Her name announced itself in his head from a long buried remembrance.

'How did you get here?' asked Charlie, his thoughts turning to escape and the returning guard and constable.

'My husband brought me here,' she said, 'I do not like to be near men I have not met before. So he keeps me here safe and alone.'

'But how did you get past the guards? Is he known to them?'

'My husband helped build this prison,' she said. 'They dug a secret way in. Only he knows of it now.'

Hopes for news of his mother kept forking into Charlie's thoughts and he drove them down with effort.

The guard and the constable must be planning to return soon. He needed to escape.

If there was a secret tunnel out he could hide in it and rescue Maria when she was put in the cell.

'Can you show me?' he asked, 'show me the way out?'

Teresa shook her head. But there was something disingenuous about the gesture. As though she was frightened of being left alone.

'Only my husband knows it,' she said. Charlie caught the tiniest flicker. Her eyes had moved just slightly to the wall behind him.

'Perhaps we could find it together,' he said carefully, watching her face and moving to the back wall.

Her features tightened. And he realised she didn't want him to get out.

Charlie considered Teresa carefully. She was tall and heavily made. But he could overpower her if necessary.

Perhaps she only wanted his company, he reasoned, trapped all alone in here, in the dark. He tried to remember what else he knew of her. A few Dutch words came.

The-lady-in-the-hidden-room.

He and Rowan still spoke of her. But she had faded to conversational currency, the origins of which were no longer solid.

Faced with the reality Charlie's memory of a lonely enchanted thing was superseded by something darker.

He tried to push the rising tumult of fractured memories away and concentrate on the necessity of escape. Maria. He had to save Maria.

Charlie let his eyes scan the wall. The heavy stones looked similar, and if there was a door he guessed the hinges must be hidden away in the dark mortar.

With only a small torch it was impossible to see where a door might start and end. It would take him too long to scan each section of stone inch by laborious inch.

The realisation brought with it a plan. He moved to the barrel of plague water in the corner of the cell and tilted it carefully into the light.

Plague water was made with iron filings.

A plan was forming. A plan of escape.

'What is it you do?' asked Teresa. There was a hint of fear in her voice.

Charlie lifted the barrel.

Iron filings. Iron was magnetic. It would stick to other iron.

If there were iron hinges or a handle hidden in the stone wall, the filings would find it out far quicker than the naked eye.

Taking careful aim he sloshed an arc of water towards a portion of the far wall.

Then taking the torch he swept it over the heavy stone.

At first he thought there was nothing. Then the flame glittered on a few fragments of iron, which clung to the dark iron embedded in the stone.

Scooping a denser hand of iron filings from the bottom of the barrel, Charlie spread them near where the first few had remained.

The shape of a hinge. He traced it down, spreading more filings, until the second was revealed. The hinges were only a few feet apart. A small door then, large enough to crawl through.

Taking the final part of the plague water, Charlie flung it towards where he hoped the opening might be. And there it was suddenly, framed by glittering iron filings. A tiny dark hole that had been indiscernible moments before.

An opening.

Taking one of the unburned sticks from the fire, Charlie prised it into where the door began. It resisted at first and then began to swing open in a dusty shower of mortar.

'Wait!' called Teresa. 'You must not open it!'

She caught his arm.

Charlie turned, pulling himself free and sent her staggering back a few steps.

His eye was drawn to a sudden flash of white at her chest. Something tumbled out of her dress.

At first Charlie thought it must be a handkerchief or little posy. Then his gaze settled on what had fallen. A flash of white and red. It was a little clutch of blood-stained ribbons.

White ribbons.

Charlie stared, his thoughts moving into place. The bloodied ribbons were wrapped around a doll made of sackcloth.

For a long moment they both stood staring. Then Teresa snatched them back and stuffed them deep into her clothing. But not before Charlie realised what he had seen.

White ribbons. Blood. A witch's spell.

Charlie remembered what the wise woman had said. That whoever performed the spell on Maria's sister would carry part of the magic.

The woman carried ribbons, like those found on the corpses.

A tangle of thoughts balled themselves into one.

'It was you,' he whispered.

Teresa stared back at him. A single hand self-consciously tried to push the blood-stained fabrics deeper.

'It was you who cast the spells,' said Charlie.

Chapter Sixty-One

Thomas usually had little call to enter the prison, and it was a practice he aimed studiously to avoid.

He hated the dungeons. They reminded him of his time in the Clink prison. Not to mention that plague cases had now been reported. He thought of his wife safely housed in her secret separate cell. Soon he would collect her and they could return to London.

But first he had cause to visit the lower dungeon. The gaoler had informed him that a woman had been imprisoned. A young girl named Maria.

Thomas enjoyed his ready access to any females imprisoned in Wapping. Usually he toyed with them inside the cell. But with plague rife he would rather take this girl back to London for longer entertainment.

Since the Civil War his tastes had changed, and pain had become inextricably linked with pleasure. He was careful only to indulge with Protestant girls. And it still surprised him how much some women would bear, for a few more coins.

Others were less willing, but he was not averse to capturing by force. The girls never told their tales. Not once they knew who he was. And what he could do.

Teresa.

He had a sudden vision of his wife, manoeuvring bloody remains. Lighting candles. Saying words.

Beneath his hot mask Thomas squeezed his eyes tight shut.

He hadn't been able to refuse his wife. Not after he'd failed her the first time. What else could he do, but give her the victims she craved for her witchcraft?

In the past he had delivered her animals. But when Teresa discovered his infidelities, her bloodlust had turned to punish him. She wanted his women as penance. The dirty Protestant girls who had tainted her husband.

Thomas, carrying a lifetime of guilt, married to a half-dead thing, searched his soul and found nothing left there to refuse her.

He never saw the spells and did not believe in their power. But he left her a trail of ready girls on which to work her horrors. And under the plague costume, charged with the prospect of casting her unholy works, Teresa was brave enough to leave their dark cellar and visit in person.

His beaked mask nodded in comforting protection from the foul air.

Then he saw something to take his mind off infection entirely. A flash of blonde hair.

He had arrived at his destination. And he moved forward to peer further into the cell. To his amazement the attractive face looked familiar. Who was it the girl reminded him of? Then memory of the meeting rushed back in.

Thomas had been deep amongst the throngs of Catholics petitioning for their lands to be returned when he saw her. Eva had worn her dress low enough to make it clear what was for sale but her face was haughty with her own self worth. She met his gaze with a challenging stare of her own, and when he approached her she turned and walked away. Though not fast enough that he might not follow.

He pursued her through the backstreets until she had stopped suddenly and turned.

'You needn't think I am for business,' she said, eyeing him in a manner which suggested the complete opposite. 'Here,' she leaned forward and pushed a scrap of paper into his hand. 'You might find me here, in the evenings, if your intentions are of a better kind than desire for a prostitute.'

She'd slipped away then leaving Thomas alone. The paper in his hand had been inked with the name of a tavern, suggesting the girl could read and write. And though in his heart he knew that the look in her eyes was acted, Thomas felt some feeling stir.

He'd found her out later that day. Eva was one of the many who arrived in London imagining their beauty to be a ticket out of poverty. Her family now languished in a cheap rented house in Holbourne. A situation she made clear she had no intention of remaining in.

'For gentlemen can be kind to poor girls,' she said, looking carefully up at him through long lashes, 'and I pray that some man might buy me up as a mistress so that I might live fine in the City.'

Thomas had let his eyes roam shamelessly over her as she talked. There was no doubt she was right for his purpose.

Thomas felt his stomach rumble beneath the heavy canvas. It was not Eva. He could see that clearly now. But in the dank dungeon the girl had much of Eva's attraction – she looked like an angel. He found his breathing becoming heavy and strained in the heat of the air.

Thomas signalled to the gaoler.

'Open the door.'

Chapter Sixty-Two

The angelic calm in Teresa's face evaporated. She shuffled back with a snarl, her hands clasped protectively towards the bloody ribbons now hidden in her dress.

'I know it was you,' said Charlie, 'those ribbons you carry are part of your spell. No one but the witch would own them.'

Teresa's eyes darted back and forth as if searching for a way to deny the accusation. Then she replied.

'Yes,' she hissed. All the music had gone from her voice. 'I decided to avenge myself.'

'But what revenge could you want?' whispered Charlie.

Teresa's face twisted. 'Those girls. For what they did with my husband.' She stared at Charlie for a moment as if daring him to answer. 'Thomas does my bidding, for he knows what sin he did. He has dishonoured me and must make amends.'

Charlie's brain was whirring, working it all out.

'Thomas brings you girls, so you might perform your spells?' he decided.

Teresa nodded, seeming pleased by his interest.

'Since the war Thomas has indulged his taste for Protestant girls,' she said. 'Why should he deny me the same?'

Charlie was silent with horror.

'The first,' she said. 'Such a greedy girl. She told her family she had plague, so Thomas might visit her more easily.' She moved a hand to her mouth, stifling a giggle.

'How people shrank from me, in Thomas's plague-doctor costume!' she gloated. 'Since the soldiers came I have been afraid of stepping outside. But cloaked and masked I grew bolder. And I roughened my voice with syrup of hellebore, so none knew me for a woman.'

Teresa's eyes glittered.

'Her neck was still warm, when I had the knife at her throat,' she crooned. 'Then all the blood flowed out. And I had all the time I wanted to cast my spell.'

Teresa seemed to be enjoying the revelations of her cleverness.

'I was sold like cattle for my dowry,' she added bitterly, 'and after the soldiers got to me my husband would not come to my bed. Yet those girls sought to make money from my misfortune.'

'So you made your spells against your husband?' Charlie had half his mind on the escape route and the other on keeping her distracted by talking.

Teresa gave an arch smile. 'Not against my husband. Against his return to *them*. The Sealed Knot. Those whose sign you wear.'

She pointed at the key looped around Charlie's neck.

'They were the men who sold me and spent my dowry. And now they rise again.'

Teresa closed her eyes, and her voice lowered, like a chant.

'I wrapped the ribbons. And I burned the candle to make the words. 'He Returns', to hinder his return to the Sealed Knot. I know my powers are true,' she added, 'for after I made the spell their traitor King was driven out of London. Blood magic is powerful.'

Her eyes flicked quickly to his neck and back again.

'You seek out your mother,' she murmured. Something of the musical quality had returned to her voice. 'I could call her to us.' Her eyes travelled over his face and then paused.

'We could summon Sally Oakley,' she said. 'With the blood in your veins it could be easily done.'

The tiniest spark of hope flashed in Charlie's mind.

What if her powers were real? He pushed it back, but it grew.

'I will make a plate of water,' she was saying. 'Just a few drops of blood and a candle. The right words. She will be revealed to us.'

Charlie knew he shouldn't be curious to see the spell done. But he found himself leaning forwards, hypnotised, to see what Teresa meant to do.

She was tugging free some bundle of artefacts from the corner of the cell.

Seeing the direction of his gaze the woman drew the bundle closer, hiding it against her body. Then she began shuffling back towards where he stood, eyeing him hungrily.

The movement called to mind something Mother Mitchell had told him when he first came to her house.

Do not be a fool man and imagine a beautiful woman must be harmless, she had said. *In this city a woman might hide a weapon as well as a man.*

His reaction came just in time. Teresa lunged at him, a long knife flashing in her hand. He deflected it just as the blade nicked his neck.

The rest of her bundle clattered to the floor. A blood-stained cup and a bell rolled in the dirt.

Charlie grabbed both her wrists but she was strong, and the blood which now showed on his neck had driven her into a kind of mania. Her blue eyes were slitted with intent, her words a babbling monologue.

'Blood,' she was saying, 'powerful blood.'

He raised them both upright still clinging to her wrists. The knife in her hand was pointed towards his jugular. Madness gave her an unnatural strength.

Desperately, Charlie kicked out with his foot, dislodging the heavy metal plate that had lain over the flames.

Sparks and hot tinder flew, and Teresa shrieked, shielding her face from the spray. Taking his chance, Charlie pushed her away and dived for the opening in the wall.

His shoulders grazed both sides and he landed on the other side of the cell in total darkness.

Chapter Sixty-Three

Maria awoke to find herself jolted painfully against a dusty wooden floor. She tried to move her hands and found she couldn't. They were bound tightly together, and as she tried to raise them up an electric pain stabbed in her wrists and arms.

Her mouth was dusty, dry and her head throbbed.

She tried to think back to how she'd got there.

There was the prison. She searched the jumble of memories. Even that was painful. Like prodding the place where a tooth had been with your tongue. *The cell. Plague.*

The memory thudded back.

The plague doctor.

Her stomach filled with ice.

The plague doctor.

Her last memory was of being dragged from the cells. She'd kicked and screamed, and the guards had let him take her. They seemed to think he was an important man.

Then . . . She struggled to remember.

He'd got her outside the prison and told her to sit still whilst he bound her legs and hands.

Numbly she'd watched as he wrenched the rope around her wrists and ankles.

Then he began pushing up her skirts, telling her not to scream.

She had tried to fight with him. But he'd reached out and gripped some part of her neck. The strength of his fingers was inhuman, and the grip found out some thick nerve, charging her body with excruciating pain.

'Do not struggle,' he'd said to her, 'this is only a tiny part of what I can do to you.'

The pain combined with her tight bodice must have been great enough to make her faint. Because after that there was nothing.

She moved her knees, trying to discover if anything had been done to her whilst she was unconscious. As far as she could tell it hadn't. Which meant he wanted her to be awake for whatever he meant to do.

And that frightened her far more.

Maria twisted on the wagon floor, trying to see some way to escape. The walls of the wagon looked thick. She moved experimentally on the boards beneath her.

The planks were immoveable, and thudding against the floor brought a searing paroxysm of pain to her hip and shoulder.

Her legs and shoulder must have been badly bruised from where he'd flung her in the wagon, she realised. Maria gave her shoulder another little twitch, and the pain flooded back, worse this time.

She thought it might be dislocated.

To the back of the wagon she could see a heap of shapes which came and went with the slices of sunlight flitting through the moving vehicle.

At first she thought her eyes had deceived her.

Corpses?

There was no mistaking them. Each wrapped neatly in a winding sheet. But the faces were covered. Which was unusual. And now that she thought about it there was no smell either.

Was it something other than bodies that he transported?

Maria inched painfully towards the shapes. Every movement brought a fresh pain to her injured shoulder.

Something pulled at her foot with an ominous clinking sound. There was some kind of manacle around her ankle. She was chained to the side of the wagon.

He must have a connection to the prisons then, she thought. No ordinary man would be able to lay his hands on irons.

The chain held firm, but she thought if she stretched out her damaged arm far enough she might be able to tug free one of the winding sheets and see what it was he transported.

She stopped for a moment, as the white heat shuddered through her shoulder. Then she gritted her teeth, willing herself to make the final distance.

Her hand touched the nearest body.

It was cold. Hard. And she snatched her hand back in alarm, gasping as the movement ricocheted through her shoulder.

Slowly, she reached out again. Her fingertips tapped the hard corpse. Then she realised. It was metal. Something metal she was feeling.

Maria scrabbled for a closer hold, but couldn't get one. This was the nearest she could get.

There was a sudden jolt, and she found herself sliding back along the floor of the wagon.

Her heart began to race. The wagon had stopped.

She heard the slow sound of the driver dismounting, his heavy tread sounding along the side of the wagon.

Her purse was still attached to her hip, and she mentally rummaged through its contents for something which could help her.

She could feel by its weight the pistol had gone. All she had were a few coins, and some wax cosmetic to make her cheeks look rosy.

She almost sighed aloud at her own vanity. Why hadn't she armed herself with a knife, instead of a useless cosmetic?

The tinderbox she had given to Charlie. Was there a needle? She thought there might be. That was something at least.

A key turned and a shaft of sunlight blinded her. She tried to throw up her arms, squinting in the unfamiliar light.

Peering into the dark was a great metal beak. The crystal goggles lay as flat and cold as the blue eyes beneath them.

The plague doctor began to heave his great bulk inside the wagon. And then he was standing over her. She could smell his sweat.

'It hurts,' he said, raising a gloved hand slightly towards her shoulder.

It wasn't a question, but she nodded anyway.

The plague doctor stood for a long moment, looking at her.

'I do not feel such things any more,' he said. 'But I like to see them in other people. It reassures me I am still alive.'

He stuck out a booted foot and pressed down on her damaged shoulder.

Maria felt white hot waves of agony course through her. She pressed her lips together, feeling tears roll from her eyes.

'Things were done to me after the war that cannot be spoken of,' he said.

Beneath his foot her whole arm had begun to pulse.

'After your body is used in such ways you feel nothing. Mostly nothing,' he corrected himself. 'At times like this I can feel a little something. Watching your face.'

He pressed down harder. Maria gritted her teeth.

'Yes,' he said, 'a little something.' He watched her with interest for a moment.

Carefully he drew up his foot. Then he leaned forward, wrapped a tight gag around her mouth and unlocked the manacle at her ankle.

'Soon we will be in London,' he said, dragging her upwards. 'First I must collect my wife. She will be very happy, when I deliver you to her.'

Chapter Sixty-Four

Charlie pulled the rest of his body through the opening just as the blade of a knife snickered across his bare ankle.

'Come back Charlie!' cried Teresa. 'I will tell you more of your mother.' Candlelight glimmered through, throwing her tall silhouette. The light revealed a tunnel large enough to stand up in, but gave no clue as to what might be ahead.

He straightened up, feeling with his hands for what he couldn't see, hobbling blindly into the darkness. The light was enough to see a man-sized tunnel had been dug and walled with tiny tiles, like mosaics. Then it died and all was black.

From behind he heard Teresa heaving herself through the opening, her knife scraping against the stone.

Throwing out his arms Charlie made a stumbling jog forward.

'Wait Charlie Oakley!' cried Teresa. 'I will share your mother's secrets!' She switched to shout after him in English. 'Come back and we shall find out where she is gone.'

Abandoning all thoughts of caution Charlie started to run. He needed to get to Maria. Fast. The ground beneath him was uneven and he lurched over mounds of ragged soil struggling not to fall.

He could hear the woman had broken into an ungainly sort of trot but it was impossible to judge how fast she was moving. His shoulders bounced against the tiled wall and he swore as the stone-work tore his skin.

Teresa's voice echoed along the tunnel. He staggered on.

Then with a cry of pain he thudded face-first into a solid wall of earth.

It was a dead end. The tunnel had been blocked. He cycled through his options. Despite her height he was stronger than her. But fighting blind and unarmed against her knife he might not avoid a chance swing of the blade.

He laid a hand against the wall behind him to steady himself, and as he did he felt a tangle of thin roots. Something was growing on the other side of the earth. That meant the end of the tunnel couldn't be too far from the surface. The delicate root structure suggested something which didn't grow deep.

He scrabbled to drive his hand into the soft earth. It broke out almost instantly into warm air on the other side, and as he pulled his arm back through a shaft of light followed the falling soil.

In the slim beam of sunshine the tunnel's end revealed itself. And to his amazement only a few steps from where he was standing was a wooden door with a latched handle.

A jumble of prayers caught in this throat as he raised his hand to the large latch, pressed it down and pushed with all his strength. Against the full weight of his body the door inched open, showing the thinnest crack of the outside world.

It must be of some hugely thick construction, thought Charlie, driving in with his legs to push it open further. The door creaked and rolled at agonisingly low speed, revealing as it did so the maddened face of Teresa bowling towards him from the gloom of the tunnel.

Charlie slipped through the narrow opening and let it slam back as Teresa hurled herself against it from the other side.

The door smashed into her wrist, turning the knife in on itself as her body fell forward.

The blade jackknifed back against the door and disappeared into some dark reach of her body.

A scream issued up and then a choking and a gurgling.

Charlie turned his body to hold the door shut, pushing it fast, not willing to risk that she was trying to trick him again.

The outside of the door was lined with a thick covering of turf and set hidden into a near vertical verge. He leaned against it.

Charlie paused to take a quick stock of his discoveries and surroundings.

The tunnel had brought him out by the waterfront. He was standing in a sunken grassed area, and behind him the entrance to the prison was now rendered almost invisible, set into the slanted slope.

Broken walls of the old port loomed above him, casting drawn-out shadows in the late afternoon light. His heart hammered as he assessed the situation.

Maria. He would have to get back in the tunnel somehow. It was his best hope of freeing her from the prison.

Stepping away from the door he stood for a moment. If Teresa was badly injured he could easily return through the tunnel. But it could have just as easily been a feint to lure him back.

His mind scanned the possible options.

Weakness flowed suddenly into his muscles.

Charlie willed himself to take stock of what had happened, driving down the pain from his burned back and legs which had suddenly reared again.

It was not Malvern who killed those girls. It was his wife.

Charlie tried to assess what it meant. If Malvern was not involved in some dark magic then his uprising must be more calculated, more logical than they'd given him credit for.

What was it he brought back to London by the wagonload?

A heavy form blocked out the sun, casting him into cold shade. Charlie looked up. His curiosity turned to instant fear.

A huge wagon, driven by six black horses, had arrived on the road. From his vantage point in the grassed trench the enormous hooves drew level with his head. Then slowly the vast turning wheels followed after.

Charlie waited frozen for a moment, wondering whether he could be seen. Then a shadow fell long across the grass beside him.

It was in the shape of a curved beak.

The plague doctor had arrived.

Chapter Sixty-Five

Taking a quick stock of his surroundings Charlie ducked low and sprinted towards the cover of a nearby hedgerow. He threw himself behind it panting and peered through the branches to assess whether he'd been seen.

The heavy vehicle stood motionless. It was a contained wagon – an enormous black chest on wheels with a separate driver's seat at the front. Malvern stepped down from the seat and moved to the back of the wagon. He opened the doors, and Charlie caught a flash of blonde hair inside.

Maria.

He stared out at the scene in horror. Malvern must have taken her from the dungeon. But why? The possible reasons made his stomach lurch.

He couldn't tell if she were alive or dead, but he could make out her hands and feet had been bound.

Charlie gritted his teeth. She could not be dead. He wouldn't believe it.

Malvern closed up the door of the wagon with a heavy padlock and then turned towards the hedgerow where Charlie was hiding.

There was a long moment as the beaked mask stared out towards him. Charlie stayed motionless, his breath held.

Slowly Malvern began to stalk towards him. As he drew closer the residue of rusting blood on the hem of his canvas cloak came into close relief.

Then he turned towards the place in the grassy verge that held the hidden door leading to the dungeon. Charlie watched as he slipped a short rod of metal from his cloak and inserted it into some secret part of the door.

Using both arms he pulled at the heavy opening, dragging it back to reveal the dark tunnel inside. Charlie saw the slump of the corpse first. Teresa fell forward glassy-eyed, the motion of her dead limbs rigid. A dark circle of blood stained her tattered white shift. Her gore-soaked hand had closed around the knife but she'd failed to pull it free. It was lodged in her stomach right up to the hilt.

Her scream must have been real then, thought Charlie. Teresa had run onto her own blade as the door slammed into her. He looked back to the wagon, fighting the instinct to run out into the open and wrench at the padlock. It was probably basic enough for him to pick. But he would need longer than a few snatched moments.

He stemmed his breathing trying to remind himself he could do Maria no good by dying.

Charlie's attention went back to Malvern. He had dropped to his knees and was examining the body of his dead wife. It was impossible to tell what he was feeling behind the mask.

Malvern reached forward and tugged out the knife. Then he held it up in the sunshine and looked at the bloody blade for a long moment.

A low growl of anguish went up.

Malvern was howling a strangled lamentation.

After a moment the sound stopped and he heaved up the body and began walking back to the wagon. Malvern was alert now, looking left and right.

Heaving the corpse of his wife into the wagon with more delicacy than he had Maria, the crystal eye goggles gazed unblinking into the dark interior. Charlie caught a glimpse of blonde hair and then the load of corpses, wrapped in their linen winding sheets.

Then Malvern shut up the heavy door of the back and bolted it with a thick lock. Returning to the front he climbed heavily into the driver's seat and urged the horses forward with a flick of the reins.

The wagon lurched into motion.

Chapter Sixty-Six

Charlie watched the wagon roll slowly away, trying to quell the rising panic that Maria could be dead.

He rose slowly from behind the hedge. The vehicle was not yet moving fast. It would take a good few minutes of open road to reach full speed.

The wagon was like a boxed-in shed on wheels, with a padlocked door at the back and a seat for Malvern at the front.

Charlie was sure that the back entrance of the wagon could not be easily seen by the driver.

And breaking into a jog he followed at a safe distance along the waterfront road. The wagon rolled through the unmanned south of the town and out onto the London Road.

On the wide dirt track Malvern gave another flick of the reins. The horses broke into a canter, bouncing the vehicle high on the rutted and unkempt highway.

Charlie dropped back to avoid being seen and then made his decision.

Under the padlocked back door was a thin lip of wood. If he ran and jumped, there might be just enough wood to get a toe-hold.

Then he could try and pick the lock whilst the wagon was in motion. It wouldn't be easy. But any chance to save Maria was worth the risk.

Charlie broke into a sprint. But the wagon raced ahead. He realised he had underestimated the pace which six horses could build. The wagon was ricocheting over the road at a rapid speed, spitting a slew of pebbles towards him in its wake.

He threw up an arm to keep the sharp missiles from his face and willed himself to run faster.

The padlocked door grew nearer.

Charlie slowed for a moment and then charged at the back of the wagon in a run. He leapt, planting one foot on the narrow ledge and gripping the edges of the wagon with his hands.

The support beneath his feet splintered away completely. His leg crashed painfully through the damaged wood. But he managed to scrabble with the other and gain the slightest of toe-holds. His hands gripped white to the side of the carriage.

The wagon began to slow. And he realised Malvern must have felt the impact and was stopping to inspect his vehicle. Charlie looked back to the road. He had no choice but to jump down and hide. But Malvern would see the damage and know he was being followed.

Charlie closed his eyes. He couldn't. He couldn't jump away.

'Maria,' he hissed, holding his mouth to the door. 'Are you there?'

No sound came from inside the wagon. The horses had slowed now to a trot.

'Please Maria. Please say you are alive.'

Nothing.

The wagon gave a sudden lurch. It was picking up speed again. Charlie held his breath until he was sure of it.

Malvern must have decided against delay and had urged the horses back to a faster pace.

Examining the lock Charlie struggled to pull out his pick whilst holding one-handed to the juddering wagon.

With the motion over the ragged road it was impossible. Lock picking required delicacy of movement and here he had none. He swung a hand to the keyhole and swore as the wire of his lock-picking earring sheered away.

Charlie held his arm steady and aimed again at the lock.

The wagon veered crazily to one side and his foot twisted downwards. Beneath him the last part of the ledge cracked ominously. In desperation he lunged towards the lock, and the wire slipped once more into it. The wagon bounced and jolted, but he thought he could feel the internal lever.

A rut in the road threw him a foot in the air, and he gasped, but managed to keep his arm tight to the lock.

There was only one lever to pick. Charlie twisted the wire to spring the lock.

Then the horses reared and gunned forward sending the wheels behind them careening back and forth.

His foot bore down hard on the remaining sliver of ledge. It split under his weight and twisted away beneath him.

Charlie's grip scrabbled at the wagon sides for a moment. Then he fell, hitting the dirt track face-first.

Charlie felt the breath knocked out of his body and then nothing.

And up ahead the wagon raced on to London without him.

Chapter Sixty-Seven

Mayor Lawrence gave a low exploratory cough. Over the past few days he had personally supervised the removal of six thousand corpses from the streets and homes of his city.

Probably he had been working too hard in the smoke of the many bonfires, he decided.

After the death of his serving maid, Lawrence's whole family had fallen in quick succession. Now he wondered why he had worked so hard for so long on matters of his own self-importance. He would have dropped every last chain of office in the Thames for one more day with his wife.

With no one to go home to, Lawrence had begun involving himself in things which were previously beneath his notice. At first he had merely been horrified that there were not enough staff to clear the mounting bodies. But with little care for his own life it had not taken long to take to the task in person.

The ragged and desperate men who still cleared bodies found the Mayor's involvement strange. But Lawrence did not care. The terrible work helped stave off the memory of his awful loss.

Sounds of a baby crying had been reported on Brewer Street, and Lawrence was making to investigate. He was dreading what he might find. Taking to the streets in person had been a revelation.

The house was of the fine brick sort, and the door was sturdily bolted from the inside. He tapped at a window and peered inside. A well-appointed reception room attested to the wealth of the owners. From what he could see it had been abandoned.

Then he heard it. The unmistakable sound of a baby crying.

Swallowing hard Lawrence returned to the front door. He knocked hard, and then heaved his bulky weight against it without waiting for an answer. On the second attempt the wood splintered and he shouldered his way in.

The crying was louder now, inconsolable. It was coming from the back of the house and Lawrence moved through the first reception room into a second smaller room.

He stopped suddenly.

Inside, stretched out on a chaise lounge, was a dead woman. She wore a fine silk dress which had been pulled down at the front. And wedged against one of her exposed breasts, in the crook of the cold dead arms, was a screaming baby.

Lawrence froze for a long moment. And then swallowed, heading towards the child.

'There, there,' he whispered, his fear temporarily bested by his need to comfort the child.

He approached the corpse, tilting his head to see how he might best extract the infant.

Up close he saw the plague tokens covering the breasts of the dead woman.

They served him a sudden haunting flash of how plague had decimated his own small household.

His maidservant Debs had died within hours of discovering the marks on her body. But his wife had taken four long days to die.

He drove the images back and addressed how best to remove the baby.

Moving carefully Lawrence tugged at the child. The rigor mortis of the mother's arm around it formed a powerful hold, and for a terrible moment he thought he may have to break the bone.

Then the baby slid unexpectedly free from the dead mother and Lawrence found himself with the warm little body in his arms.

He stared at the tiny features. The child could not be more than a few weeks old.

'There is no need for that noise now,' he said, clucking and rocking the child. 'We will take you and find you some food.'

Lawrence mind searched for possibilities. He could think of no way to acquire milk. But he was sure the answer would come to him.

'I always wanted a child of my own,' he told the baby, as he carried it through into the hallway. 'But my wife and I were separated before we had the chance. I will see you are well cared for,' he added.

The baby wriggled in his arms. It had stopped wailing and was making sucking noises with its mouth. A request for food, Lawrence deduced. He put his knuckle in the child's mouth and was rewarded with an enthusiastic suckling. This delighted him.

'Perhaps first I will find if there are clean clothes in the house for you,' he muttered to himself, thinking the baby must be soiled beneath the long christening robe it wore.

He turned aside the garment to see beneath.

His hand went rigid.

The tokens were all over the child's body.

Something in his movement must have alarmed the baby, because it started up crying again. He realised now these were muted sounds, as though it was running low on strength.

Lawrence sat heavily on the dusty wooden floorboards, the child in his arms.

Within an hour the cries had stilled to ragged dying breaths. And after two, the warm body had begun to grow cold.

Standing with difficulty Lawrence carried the tiny body back into the room he had found it in and tucked it carefully back in the dead arms of its mother. Then he covered it back up with its christening robes.

Two fat tears rolled from Lawrence's face onto the baby's head and he wiped them off.

'You will be better with your mother,' he whispered. 'The angels will have joy of you both.'

Then he walked back through the hallway, trying to calm the shaking which had started in his legs.

He closed the door, sat on the steps, put his head in his hands, and sobbed.

It must have been a long moment later when a searcher tapped his arm.

'There has been another letter,' said the searcher, looking urgently into Lawrence's face. 'Mister Blackstone writes of his progress outside the city. He managed to find a messenger to deliver the missive.'

Lawrence looked up and held his hand out for the paper.

The searcher pushed a single page into his hand, and he glanced at it through tear-filled eyes.

Blackstone had made some unexpected headway on the witch-murders.

Lawrence sat up a little.

Whilst keeping track of King Charles, Blackstone had unexpectedly stumbled upon the symbol to a long disbanded group of men who called themselves the Sealed Knot.

Lawrence stopped reading for a moment, wondering whether he had the energy to care about such trivial matters.

Almost all of London's officials had fled, and the plague had chewed through his thousand strong staff of searchers, five times over.

They had dug enormous pits in Stepney and Shoreditch which now overflowed. And food deliveries had dried up.

He let his eyes flick over the last few lines of the report, hardly caring what they said. But the words were enough to surprise him.

The Sealed Knot, Blackstone wrote, consisted of many powerful and important men. Most had died or vanished after the Civil War. But one name very high on the list still worked in the city.

Amesbury had been a member of the Sealed Knot.

Chapter Sixty-Eight

Charlie awoke to a mouth full of dust. He rolled upright trying to work out where he was. The blinding sunlight and the empty dirt track told him nothing. Rubbing his face he tried to remember how he'd got there. Then it came to him.

The wagon.

And Maria. Maria was gone.

Pained from the impact he struggled up and limped along in the direction of the wagon for a few moments before accepting pursuit was useless. Malvern's vehicle had disappeared far ahead.

Charlie took a moment to assess his situation before deciding it was worse than hopeless. The wagon couldn't have taken him more than a few miles out of Wapping. And the fastest route to London was the most dangerous. It would take him days to track round to the north and enter that way.

Malvern's plans were due to be enacted. But far worse was what he might do with Maria.

Charlie stamped his foot helplessly into the dusty road. Then for want of a better plan he set off walking.

The Thames was still nearby, and he veered towards it.

Something like white wings flapped in the distance beyond the roadside foliage.

Ship sails. Some boats were on the river.

Probably these were the private boats of Londoners who had travelled up river to avoid plague. He remembered Marc-Anthony telling him, as they locked up the sedan-chair, that this was a strategy he would adopt if the plague in London reached a height.

Charlie let his eye roll over the sails, imagining his friend on one of the boats. And then the realisation hit.

Marc-Anthony was likely on one of those boats.

As a possibility clarified Charlie broke into a run.

Travelling by river he might yet be able to outrun Malvern. Water was slower than wagon. But the route was more direct. The river cut straight into London with no impediment.

Charlie made a rough calculation.

If he could find Marc-Anthony and persuade him to the cause he had a chance, a small chance, of saving Maria from whatever Malvern had planned for her.

Chapter Sixty-Nine

Charlie stared out onto the Thames. The river was wide near Wapping, and the breadth of water had attracted a large cluster of ships, taking shelter from the plague. They bobbed on the water like a disparate citadel, at a wary distance from one another.

Charlie could make out makeshift munitions and rudimentary defences. Some ships had watchmen pointing rifles out to sea. Others defended more accessible parts of the hull by painting it in thick tar and pressing in broken bottle ends.

There were at least forty ships, and though Marc-Anthony talked of his smuggling vessel with pride, Charlie had never seen it in reality.

He squinted out into the collection of boats, trying to deduce which might be his friend's. Certainly, he could rule out all the small skiffs. They weren't large enough to carry the volume of cargo a smuggler required.

The two very large ships also, he decided, would draw too much attention at customs. That left around twenty tall ships, all of which, so far as he could see, would be adequate for smuggling.

Charlie plumbed his knowledge of seafaring. Like most river-side-dwelling Londoners he took regular ferry boats. But he wasn't familiar with seafaring.

He tried to think what he knew of Marc-Anthony's trade.

Marc-Anthony only sails to France. He says the colonies are too great a risk.

Charlie looked back out onto the water and ruled out a couple more ships whose weather-beaten hulls attested to transatlantic journeys.

What else would single out Marc-Anthony's craft?

His eyes roved the ships anew. They all looked very similar to him. The sails hung limply in the breeze, against slack cobwebs of rigging.

Charlie tried to relax his mind against the throbbing panic of Maria's kidnap and let his talent for observation get to work.

There!

His gaze seized upon a strangeness in one ship. The two anchor ropes were secured with a slip-knot, halfway down. Charlie thought on this.

A slip-knot meant a quick getaway. In an emergency the ship could simply abandon its anchors rather than pull them in.

He noticed something else about the ship, obvious now he was looking for it. The prow of this particular ship faced into the current, when all others looked downstream.

Charlie knew enough about currents to know this to be a bad practice. Facing the current meant the swell of water hit the blunt back of the boat, jolting the craft uncomfortably.

But he would bet money the slip-knot anchors and current-facing were for the same reason.

Old habits die hard.

Marc-Anthony had not masterminded a smuggling business for fifteen years without a supernatural talent for caution. The smuggler hadn't been able to help himself from positioning his ship for a fast escape.

That is Marc-Anthony's ship. I am sure of it.

And without further hesitation, Charlie dove into the water.

Marc-Anthony's ship was not one of those staffed by armed guards. But as Charlie neared the vessel, crew members leapt into action, shouting and threatening.

'Get Marc-Anthony!' called Charlie, reaching the first anchor rope. 'He's a friend.'

But instead of calling the captain, the sailor nearest to Charlie stuck a knife between his teeth and began shaking the rope.

'Call for Marc-Anthony!' shouted Charlie desperately. 'He knows me well! I help carry his sedan-chair.' He fought to keep his slippery hold on the rope as it swung, forcing him to clutch it with both arms.

Having failed to dislodge the intruder, the sailor dropped himself down towards the rope like a monkey, the knife clenched between his bared teeth.

'I mean no harm!' shouted Charlie, as the filthy Thames water splashed his face. 'Only to get to the City.'

'Let go!' The sailor had removed the knife from his mouth to issue the warning. It was a practised gesture and his lithe feet held him simian-style and single-handed. 'Get off the anchor!'

'Please! If Marc-Anthony is aboard call for him.'

The sailor replaced the blade between his calloused lips and began to move down the rope.

'Wait!' called Charlie. 'Hold!' But it looked as though his choice was to abandon ship or lose his fingers.

He tried for one last plea. 'I know he must be on this ship! He told me this is where he would wait out the plague!'

The expression on his assailant's face said it all. He wanted Charlie off the hull at any cost.

'Wait!' a familiar voice sounded from the deck above, and the sailor turned his head up in confusion.

'Let him aboard!' said the voice. 'I know him. He is a friend.'

The sailor's eyes narrowed. He seemed unwilling to take the new instructions with an interloper still hanging on the anchor.

A curly mop of hair appeared over the side of the ship.

To his great joy Charlie saw the familiar face of Marc-Anthony.

'Hello Charlie!' shouted Marc-Anthony. 'He will let you up presently. Let him up Davie! All is well.' And to Charlie's great relief the sailor began to retreat back up the rope.

When Charlie had finished explaining the events leading to Maria's capture Marc-Anthony looked at him solemnly. 'There are no officials who stay still in London,' he said. 'Even if you find this villain out you cannot enact his arrest. Parts are deserted entirely.'

'But I was in the City less than a week ago,' said Charlie, 'and there was plenty of life in the west. Sure that cannot have changed so sudden in that short time.'

'We may only dock in the east Charlie. The King deserted the city. And when he did all law was forgotten. Only a few brave grave-diggers and aldermen remain.'

'I must find her Marcus. I must get back into London.' Charlie looked at his friend. 'If you can persuade your crew to sail back towards the City I might outrun him still. It is a small chance but it is possible.'

'What mean you to do in the City?'

'I will go to the Alders Gate. That is where wagons would come in from the east. I will ask there after Malvern. If I have got back to the City faster than he then I have some hope of following where he goes and finding Maria.'

Marc-Anthony was shaking his head. 'There will be no one on the gatehouse,' he said patiently. 'I tell you I have seen it, and there is nothing left in the East. In that part of the City all are dead or fled. All.'

'I must find her! Do you not see? He has her. He has taken her for God knows what reason. I do not have time to wait and discover what he wants with her. If I can get to the gatehouse maybe there will be some tracks. Or . . . or something else . . . some other way to find him.'

'You love this girl don't you?'

'I . . . I need to get back to London, that is all.'

'You value her enough to risk your life in any case.' Marc-Anthony rolled his eyes to Heaven. 'I always said it, that the most foolish acts in the world are done for love. But where should we be without them Charlie?'

'Please Marcus. I am begging you. Can you get me into the City?'

'We can get you as west as the Tower,' said Marc-Anthony. 'I could not risk the men onboard to go further than that. But the tide is slow. We are not likely to outrun him. And what is your plan if he has already arrived? You have no idea where this Malvern is headed.'

It was true, Charlie realised, with a sinking heart. If the tides were too slow to outrun the wagon then he had no chance. Malvern would disappear into the city with Maria and might never be found.

The thought brought a fresh wave of despair.

'Charlie Tuesday!' said a sudden voice behind him, 'I owe you my life.'

Charlie swung around to see a vaguely familiar face. Recognition set in. It was the old fisherman he'd sold a certificate to, in the Bucket of Blood.

'Your certificate got me and my daughter both safe to the docks,' continued the man. 'I am in your debt.'

Charlie smiled vaguely, knowing the fisherman's promise was worthless to him now.

'I am glad you left London, but I must go back there,' replied Charlie distractedly.

'You must not!' replied the man, aghast. 'All is death.'

'I seek a man,' explained Charlie. 'Malvern. He has made a kidnap on . . . On a person I hold dear.'

Something strange flickered in the fisherman's features. It was gone in a flash, but Charlie's thief taker experience seized on it instantly. He could spot recognition, in even the best poker-face.

'You have heard the name?' he asked, 'Malvern?'

The fisherman's face had blanched. He shook his head slowly.

Charlie grabbed his shoulders.

'This is life or death,' he urged, 'if you know something, please. You must tell me.'

The man seemed to be fighting some internal battle.

'I gave you my word,' he said finally, 'that I'd repay your kindness and now, by God's grace, my time has come. I only pray I don't do wrong.'

Charlie blinked at him, wondering what on earth the man had in mind. Certainly a fisherman from Billingsgate had no obvious powers to find Maria.

'My daughter,' continued the man. 'My daughter was near caught by your Malvern. But she got free and hid on this boat. I've told none since that she hides here. But I tell you true Charlie Tuesday. Because I gave you my word.'

Marc-Anthony looked as though he might have something to say about the bad luck of a woman aboard during plague times. But he caught Charlie's face and thought better of it.

'Take us to her then,' he said.

The man's daughter was blonde, and pretty. Despite having been stowed beneath a hessian sack for the last few days. In contrast to her accent the clothes she wore were expensive, suggesting she sold her body, at least some of the time.

'Go on Jenny,' said her father. 'Tell them what you know of Malvern.'

Jenny looked at Charlie uncertainly.

'He is an evil man,' she said, with a terrified stare. Clearly her status as stowaway was making her reluctant.

Her father nodded encouragingly. 'Go on.'

'I . . . I know not much else about him,' Jenny admitted. 'Only he looked familiar, like someone I have seen before.'

'But you do not know who?' urged Charlie.

She looked to her father. He nodded she should continue, and she shook her head sadly.

'Tell the Thief Taker everything you know,' pressed her father. 'We both owe him a debt. For it was his certificate which got us safe to the docks.'

'I know Malvern gambles,' said Jenny uncertainly, looking from Charlie to her father.

'Know you where?' asked Charlie, trying to drill down to a possible location as fast as he could.

Jenny nodded. 'In Smith and Widdles. On Botolph Lane. I saw him sign his name in the gambling books. He placed a very large bet,' she added, 'that plague would spread to the west of the City. Where the rich people are.'

'Plague has not yet passed badly that way,' said Marc-Anthony uncertainly. 'So he looks to lose if that is what he gambles on.'

Charlie let this fact settle uncomfortably in his mind. Perhaps Malvern was planning on winning a great deal of money to finance an uprising. But if that was the case he would have to somehow control the spread of plague. Such a thing couldn't be done.

He turned the possibility over and over, but couldn't make it fit with what he knew of Malvern's plans.

'Did he sign an address in the betting book?' asked Charlie hopefully. 'Some place I might track him?'

But Jenny shook her head. 'If he did, I did not see it.'

'Did you go to his home?' pressed Charlie. 'Perhaps you remember the street?'

'He took me to a church,' said Jenny, her face stricken. 'Full of mouldering food.'

She shuddered and went on. 'I only made my escape by hiding in a priest hole. But he had a brute load of bloodied tools. God forbid what he might have done to me.'

Charlie tried to quell the agonised thought that Maria could be encountering those same tools.

'Where was the church?' he said, fighting to keep his tone even.

'I do not know,' admitted Jenny. 'Only that we wandered for a while through backstreets. Girls such as I are not welcome in churches,' she added apologetically.

Charlie felt a terrible paralysing feeling sweep over him. That he would not find her. He thought back to Malvern's map, but it was no help to him. No churches had been marked, and there was no pattern to the crosses to suggest a headquarters.

'What size was the church?' he tried. 'Was there anything to mark it out?'

Jenny shook her head slowly. 'I think you would call it large,' she said slowly, 'Or so it seemed to me. And it stank inside,' she added wrinkling her nose.

Charlie let out a breath.

'Did it have a graveyard?' he tried, panning through ways to narrow things down.

Jenny nodded. 'I think so. Yes. It did. We walked through it. I remember, I tried to make a joke about walking over graves.'

Charlie let his mental map of London range around Botolph Lane. There were seven churches within walking distance. Only three had a graveyard.

Fen Church, St Clements and All Hallows.

What could distinguish those churches?

'You said it had a priest hole?' Charlie said, taking Jenny's arm urgently. 'You hid inside?'

Jenny nodded. 'Hid inside, shaking for my very life,' she affirmed.

'That could only be St Clements or Fen Church,' decided Charlie. 'All Hallows never hid priests.'

He toyed with the facts for a moment. But they brought him no closer. Time was too short. He would have to take a guess.

Of the two, Fen Church was nearest to the river. It was nothing better than an educated guess, but if Malvern planned an uprising, proximity to the Thames might be tactical.

'Can you take me to the Tower of London docks?' Charlie asked, turning urgently to Marc-Anthony.

'We can sail you to St Katherine's docks,' said Marc-Anthony. 'But that part of London is deadly dangerous Charlie. Plague has made it a no man's land. You should be prepared for the worst.'

'What worst is that?'

'I think you may be horrified Charlie. To see what has become of your City.'

'Yet I must go, and quickly,' said Charlie.

Marc-Anthony signalled to his men, who loosed the anchors and set about manoeuvring the sails.

The ship heaved off into the swelling current, and Charlie felt relief to be taking action.

Marc-Anthony disappeared momentarily and returned with a long rifle.

'You should take this,' he said, handing the gun to Charlie. 'It is only a rabbit gun, but it is the sturdiest weapon on board.'

Charlie took the gun. 'Are you sure you can spare it?'

Marc-Anthony waved the comment aside. 'It shoots out a spray of shot which could slow a man down perhaps,' he said. 'If the angle were right.' He considered for a moment. 'If you got a good shot right in the face it may do some greater damage.'

'Thank you Marcus.'

'I am sorry I cannot arm you properly,' said Marc-Anthony sadly. 'But you know how it is Charlie. All the good pistols belong to rich folk. This is the best we have, but better than nothing eh? When terrible men abound.'

Chapter Seventy

Maria felt the hard stone floor beneath her and a tomb propping her upright. Her wrists were still bound tightly with rope, and a gag of rough cloth cut into her cheeks. She was in a church. But the building had been repurposed.

A terrible smell hung in the air. Like the butchers at Smithfield on a hot day. As though meat had been piled up to rot.

Maria twisted her head for a better look at her surroundings.

The church had been filled with piles and piles of weapons. There were stacks of swords and pikestaffs lining hundreds back against the wall. From the look of the cache they had all been purchased second-hand. Most bore the chips and scratches of battle with regimental marks from the Civil War. The occasional bulk was newer, presumably bought up from some rich householder who held a larger private supply. Malvern must have been buying up stocks for some time.

In a neat stack in the corner was what looked to be the contents of a fine domestic house.

Perhaps Malvern, like other better-off householders, had removed his possessions to secure storage against plague looters. There were chairs and tables. Rolled rugs and tapestries and chests.

A familiar symbol caught her eye. The crown with its array of looping knots.

It was wrought in metal and attached to an unusual looking trunk. The design was Dutch and the largest she had ever seen. A sea-chest, she decided, looking at the make of it. The kind of strong box you would need to store all your worldly valuables on a voyage, protected from the elements.

She thought of Charlie's key. Too small for a door. Too large for a chest. But this chest. This outsized chest might fit.

There was a fluttering sound. Pigeons. She had seen a cage of them in the wagon. He used them to send messages, and she had seen him set the cage in the cemetery outside the church. No doubt they were part of his wider plot.

But the knowledge was useless to her in her current situation.

Maria twisted hard in her bindings. The ropes had been secured tightly enough to cut into her skin, and every movement hurt. Steeling herself against the pain, she bucked and writhed, managing to point her bound hands towards her hip, where her purse hung.

Was there a needle as she hoped? Her fingers fumbled, catching the edge of her purse, and she stifled a cry of pain as the ropes bit deeper.

Finally the edge of her little finger caught the top of the purse. She manoeuvred it awkwardly, delving inside. Her fingertips first seized on the wax cosmetic, and she cursed. Groping further inside, she explored the edges for a hidden needle.

But there was nothing but a few coins. A great surge of hopelessness swelled up, and she drove down the urge to cry.

The heavy sound of a door closing echoed across the church, and she froze.

Footsteps rang across the flagstones.

For a moment she caught a flash of heavy canvas cloak. And then, standing in front of her with his ghastly iron mask, was the plague doctor.

She felt her lungs contract. The beak tilted to one side and then back again. Then the great mask dropped down so as to hold its glittering crystal goggles level with her face. Two black unblinking holes stared out. Maria dropped her gaze, trying to steady her breathing.

The monster spoke and her heart pounded anew.

'You remind me of my wife.' The voice was low and distorted by the mask.

Maria stared back into the glass eyes.

'Shall I tell you what happened to her?'

The plague doctor settled himself a little nearer and Maria pressed herself back against the tomb.

'She had been sent to a nunnery for her own protection,' he said. 'For Civil War was rife and you have likely heard what Protestant soldiers did to the wives of rich Catholics.'

Malvern peered at her face for a moment. 'You are too young to remember,' he decided. 'What terrible deeds were committed then. You may think now is a dread time to be Catholic in London.' He gave a low humourless laugh. 'Men never did worse things than to their own countrymen in the name of God.'

'I was but a boy when I saw soldiers murder my parents. They let me live. But I sometimes wonder if that was a mercy.' He brought the gloved fingers to where his mouth might have been. 'You do not think in the same way,' he said. 'Some things you see and they change the way you think. You do not feel for your fellow man as you once did.'

'By the time the Civil War was over, I had lost all,' Malvern continued. 'But I still had my wife. She at least was safe from the horrors.'

He looked thoughtful at this, as though the image of his wife had fortified him through horrors.

'And then they told me,' he said, the emotion drained from his voice. 'At first I would not believe it for myself. When I found her . . . .'

There was a long pause.

'When I found her they were keeping her locked in the barn. She was roaming around on all fours. No better than the animals penned in there with her.'

The gloved hands began to rub together. 'I never found out what they did to her.'

He stopped as if unable to verbalise the memory. 'Those of us who fought for the King thought we would be rewarded. And now his son has returned and betrayed us.'

He took a little roll of paper from inside his cloak.

'This is his downfall. This little roll of paper. When it arrives, London will fall and then England. The King will arrive back to find his country is ruined.'

A sound which could have been a laugh issued from behind the metal mask.

'They think I spread plague, those country fools who try to slow my journey,' he said. 'But I spread something far more powerful in the City. The contamination I bring will force the traitor King to his knees. And it is the greed of his own people who bring his downfall, for they take my infection to every place in the city.'

Malvern moved closer to Maria suddenly.

'It has always interested me, the difference between Catholics and Protestants. On what can be borne in silence.'

The low voice had a different texture to it now.

Maria noticed the bag. It must have been inside Malvern's cloak, but he had brought it out as he talked. Well-worn leather, like a workman's satchel.

Inside she could make out the glint of iron tools. Brands and pincers. Torturer's tools. The implements made by the Thames Street blacksmith flashed through her mind.

'My wife is not with us now,' said Malvern. 'But she is owed a final spell. A water spell.'

371

He considered for a moment.

'I know not how she might perform it, so I must improvise,' he said, moving closer. Malvern's hand glided reverently over the iron tools. His eyes glittered.

Maria's body had set to cold hard ice.

'How do you think your faith will fare,' asked Malvern. 'When unspeakable things are done to you?'

Chapter Seventy-One

It took over four hours to sail up the river and Charlie felt the fear build every second.

Then the edge of St Katherine's dock finally hove into view.

A gust of wind blew along the ship and men called for the sails to turn.

'Wait but a little and we will dock you safe to shore,' said Marc-Anthony. 'You had best not swim the waters in plague time.'

The wait was agonising and the view more terrible as the docks inched closed.

St Katherine's docks housed the squat shape of Customs House, and the area was usually teeming with sailors and export officials, traders and retailers all eager to deal in imported merchandise. Today there was no one.

Charlie looked to Marc-Anthony and his friend's face said it all. He plainly thought a journey into the heart of London to be a suicide mission.

The ship drew level with the dock and Charlie made a heartfelt thanks before hopping to dry land. Behind him the sailors leapt into action, swinging the sails with loud shouts in their urgency to get back out onto the wider river.

Charlie took in the deserted docks. The only import sat on the once heaving wharves was a single barrel which buzzed with flies. It was a shipment of cod and peas, which had been broken open and spoiled.

Turning from the sad scene Charlie made his way west, following the river towards London Bridge.

Along the shore the huge warehouses had been looted. When he passed London Bridge he gasped aloud in horror.

London Bridge was formed of thick arches which slowed the river to a crawl during summer and caused it to freeze over entirely in winter. The narrow apertures had been stopped up with hundreds of bloated-blue corpses. A handful lolled at the shore, but the current had swept the rest to a thick cluster which bottle-necked against the stricture of the brick bridge. There were so many that they formed a ghoulish dam to the natural tide.

The people floated naked, or dressed in thin vestiges of decayed clothing. Partial dress revealed the skin from their limbs peeling away in black ulcerations. Their stomachs bulged at the surface, distended and huge, whilst their legs and arms hung limply underwater.

Charlie looked for any evidence that anyone was trying to clear the waterway of its unholy cargo. There was none. No one had even tried.

Swallowing hard, Charlie turned back inland. Time was running out.

He made his route to Alders Gate through what were once the most populated places. But the sights swelled the unease in his stomach to horror. Leadenhall showed stand after empty stand, and a litter of filth had blown into the unkempt marketplace on the breeze.

He passed a church where the mass graves were over-filled and rotting Londoners burst above ground.

At first he didn't recognise Fen Church Street at all. Grass and thistles had knotted up amongst the pavements.

The plague must have run unchecked here for months, he realised, with no authority realising how bad the spread. Nature was halfway to reclaiming the district. Another month, he thought, and the ground level would be entirely swallowed up.

Charlie had expected the plague would have him mourn people. But he had never thought it would be his own City he grieved for.

Chapter Seventy-Two

Breathe in. Breathe out. Breathe in. Breathe out.

It took all of Mayor Lawrence's attention. The restriction on his breathing had come so suddenly. He had heard of plague cases where a victim complained of a headache and was dead within the hour. But he had not even felt the headache. Only the sudden weight of breathing as his lungs began to stop working.

It has come so fast.

Lawrence tried to remember when breathing had first become hard, trying to calculate how long he had left. An hour? Two?

He saw Blackstone close on the doorway.

'Keep away,' he managed.

It occurred to Lawrence he should be embarrassed to be found crawling like a dog on his own office floor. As it was he was only glad Blackstone had returned.

'Would you have me call a holy man?'

Lawrence smiled through the pain. Blackstone always knew the right thing to do. 'There are none . . . there are none of my faith in the City.' Talking was exhausting.

'Some food then? Or water?'

Lawrence shook his head.

'I have good news,' said Blackstone. He did not wait for Lawrence to reply. 'It is the King. He returns.'

'The King . . . thinks . . . plague has died down?'

Blackstone answered carefully. 'He knows of the good we do in keeping the streets cleared of bodies,' he said. 'And the numbers have fallen a little. It could be a good sign.'

Lawrence tried to focus.

'Blackstone?'

'Yes Sir?'

'I have . . . There is provision. For you.'

Blackstone was silent.

'I have made it . . . . Alderman. Appointed.'

'Thank you Sir.' Blackstone looked at the ground. He and Lawrence had been colleagues but they hadn't been close. Certainly he had never expected to rise to any higher role on Mayor Lawrence's recommendation.

'There is something . . .' said Lawrence.

'What?'

'In the City. Priests. Could you . . . send for one?'

Blackstone shook his head sadly. 'All the Protestant priests have fled. Those you hear preaching now are Catholics. They have come to attend to their own people.'

'Please,' said Lawrence. 'Any priest you can . . . find.'

Blackstone nodded, dumbfounded.

'Do not tell anyone,' said Lawrence. Tears began to roll down his cheeks.

'You must not fear for the City sir,' said Blackstone.

'There are papers in my office,' Lawrence managed. 'Amesbury. You must discover his connection to the Sealed Knot. I think he means to betray the King.'

'I would help you to a bed,' started Blackstone, but Lawrence shook his head.

Blackstone headed back into Lawrence's room.

Scattered on the desk were a number of different papers. They numbered the figures of the dying which had steadily risen from February. The last balance sheet showed a hundred thousand dead.

'A quarter of the City,' he murmured. 'And all the rest fled.'

Sifting through the documents he came across those which numbered the dead of the city officials. Lords, members of parliament, searchers and nurses. Death did not discriminate. Although the poor, as usual, were more vulnerable at the onset. Then he noticed something about the figures. Or more precisely, about the occupation of those who had died.

The rat catchers, he noticed, seemed to have a greater tendency to plague than any other profession.

He sat down for a moment to think about the discovery. And then he heard a loud voice from outside.

Blackstone looked out the diamond-paned window. What he saw outside brought his first real smile in months. Perhaps years. It was a Catholic priest. He had taken to a public pulpit and was preaching openly in the centre of London. Such a thing had never happened in Blackstone's lifetime.

Sitting back at the desk he let the feeling of wonder wash over him. Then his eyes fell back down to the dead count. For the briefest of moments the gaze rested on a paper with Amesbury's name on it. And a familiar symbol.

Slowly, Blackstone stood. He bundled the documents and pushed them into a drawer. Then he shut it carefully.

There was important business to attend to.

Chapter Seventy-Three

As Charlie approached Fen Church a low kind of groaning went up.

He remembered Wapping. That the dead crawled to die in the sight of a church.

As the doorway of the church came into view Charlie caught sight of a thick swathe of infected Londoners. Some were clawing ineffectually, trying to get inside, but many others were sat blankly on their haunches, staring at the building as if willing it to open up.

A handful could be mistaken for ordinary citizens, but most had more evident tokens. Blue fingers, or swollen necks or creeping purple veins inching over their cheeks. Between them they made a horrific hum of pain and despair.

Keeping back from the entrance Charlie slipped around the side of the church. To his relief no plague sufferers had migrated towards the graveyard and the fence was low.

He scaled it into the graveyard with relative ease. Inside the fence it was overgrown with grass and the ancient graves of long dead Londoners. Night had fallen properly now, and in the pitch-black the white of the tombstones stuck out like giant teeth.

Heading towards the back of the ancient graveyard Charlie drew a breath. Tombstones had been flung aside. He scanned the church for a route in.

Then he saw a huge pit, freshly dug, lay open in the middle of the cemetery.

He drew nearer. Deep in the bottom of the pit lay corpse after corpse thrown headlong over one another and wrapped winding sheets.

Plague pits are not filled with bodies wrapped in winding sheets. They are for pauper's corpses.

There was a cooing sound. As if a flock of pigeons were nearby.

This was probably what Malvern transported, Charlie realised. Flung into this grave and disguised as bodies.

He looked up at the church. Knowing Malvern's plans could give him an advantage for freeing Maria, if he was fast.

For a moment Charlie's courage failed him. In the darkness it was impossible to tell whether the pit of dead was real or of Malvern's construction.

Steeling himself he crouched and then leapt downwards. His feet collided with hard metal and the impact threw him painfully to his knees. The rabbit gun which Marc-Anthony had given him fell clumsily away, but to his relief it didn't discharge.

Wasting no time, Charlie stuck his knife into the fabric and ripped into it. The hidden contents of the winding sheet now sparkled into the moonlight.

It held silver coins. Thousands of them.

He slashed into another, and the same glittering innards spilled forth.

'Shillings.' He said it aloud as the tiny silver coins winked out into the grave. So this was Malvern's cargo. *Shillings.*

His first thought was that someone was financing Malvern to build an army.

But it didn't make any sense.

Why would they send such small coins? Larger currency would be far easier to transport and smuggle in. Jewels, gold bars, there were so many better ways to provide illegal finance.

Unless . . . .

He reached into his coat and removed the map he had found in the confession booth. Then picked up one of the coins and studied it for a moment. In the darkness a slow understanding spread across Charlie's face.

Counterfeits. They were counterfeit coins.

The crosses on the map didn't mark the most populated places. They showed areas of high commerce. Markets, shops and taverns. Malvern chose locations where money entered the economy quickly and without trace. Outlets which distributed coins widely within London.

So this was the scheme. This was the contamination Malvern had planned.

The money was not to finance an uprising. It was to undermine the English economy.

Charlie let out a slow breath. So Malvern *was* spreading an infection in London. But it was not some contagious disease. He was masterminding the spread of false coins.

Charlie considered this. A few forged coins could be easily absorbed.

But release enough of a fake currency at once, and it would undermine the treasury. Prices would skyrocket as coins became lower in value. And then the bloated economy would collapse.

Suddenly the plot became obvious. Malvern meant to cripple the King where it mattered most – his treasury.

Presumably whatever weapons he was amassing would be put to use afterwards. After the monarchy had fallen.

But to successfully undermine the treasury, Malvern would need to release thousands of coins, and all at the same time. How could he spend them all at once?

Then Charlie remembered Malvern's bets at the gambling house. And it all made sense.

He doesn't bet to win. He bets to lose those coins.

Malvern was betting to lose. And when he did the gaming houses would release his forged coins in a flood amongst the rich aristocrats of the west.

Using winding sheets to conceal the imports and burying the loot in a graveyard was another inspired touch. No citizen would come within a mile of a plague pit, far less open up the wrappings of a corpse.

Charlie realised he had underestimated Malvern. He had believed him a crazed man of spells and enchantments.

This strategy showed him to be far colder and more ruthless. Malvern was willing to see his entire country fall to take his revenge on the King.

Charlie stared up at the dark walls of the church. He knew he needed to stop Malvern's plans. But first he must rescue Maria.

Praying Maria was inside the church, he sized up the dark walls, his mind racing with his discovery. Several trees grew alongside the belfry. If he could climb up and clamber onto the roof then he might be able to get inside.

Before climbing back out of the grave pit Charlie took a long last look at the rabbit gun. He couldn't bring it, he decided. The long muzzle would only slow him down, and he had already nearly discharged it accidentally. Besides, it wasn't powerful enough to kill a man. He decided to leave it lying with Malvern's loot.

A shriek pierced the air, then a chorus of cries broke out in accompaniment.

As Charlie wrapped his arms around the trunk of the tallest tree and started to climb he made out a huddle of dark heads around the entrance to the church.

More of them were on their feet now and close against the locked door, petitioning to be let inside.

Charlie climbed along the thickest branch and over towards the top of the church.

Hauling himself onto the slate roof Charlie sat for a moment to get his breath back. Up ahead was the steeple and suddenly, as if timing his arrival, a light winked on inside the church.

Chapter Seventy-Four

Tip-toeing along the side of the roof Charlie made it to the bottom of the belfry. A little door was set into the side of tower.

It must have been built to allow people up to repair the roof, Charlie decided. And holding his breath he turned the handle. It opened, revealing a tiny set of dark stone steps.

Squeezing into the confines he paused to listen. The sounds of the plague victims outside seemed to be echoing into the nave of the church below. But as far as he could tell there were no noises from inside.

As quietly as possible he eased himself down the steps, hoping the cacophony outside would drown out any sounds he was making.

At the bottom of the steps he saw someone had hung a lantern in the centre of the church. It had been placed there so recently that it still swung back and forth, in and out of view of the window.

Charlie froze, scanning for any evidence of whoever had left the lantern. Then his eyes grew wide as he took in the contents of the large nave.

Food was everywhere. But all was rotten and bad. The smell was appalling.

Then his eyes settled on the cache of weapons. Rifles and swords were piled up. Enough for an army.

So this is where Malvern keeps his armoury.

There was a knocking sound. A slow steady tapping.

He waited for a moment, trying to match the sound with the source. And then he realised. It was the plague people outside, petitioning for entry to the church.

Turning away from the sound and into the light of the lantern Charlie saw it.

The crown and loop of knots.

It had been fashioned from shining nail-heads hammered into the side of a huge sea-chest. Hewn of a dense teak, it sat squat and impenetrable. Thick bands of black steel encased an intricate-looking locking system.

Charlie's eyes travelled up to where elaborate metalwork hinged the mighty trunk. It was a Dutch design.

A Dutch chest.

Slowly Charlie's hand went to the symbol at his neck. The keyhole of the strong-box stared back at him like a single challenging eye.

It had been loaded in amongst a pile of domestic-looking possessions and Charlie took a moment to consider the context. He recognised a rolled up rug and then an elaborate table-leg. The objects were so familiar he thought for a moment he must be dreaming. They were the furnishings from the great house of his childhood.

Malvern must have packed away his household safe from plague robbers. And here was this chest in with them.

Was it possible the trunk had lain sealed all these years, with Charlie carrying the only key?

Holding his breath he walked closer. From around his neck he silently drew off the key.

Malvern is coming.

Something whispered at the edge of his hearing, and he stopped, thinking for a moment that someone had spoken. Then he moved forward again. The chance to discover what his mother had wanted him to find was suddenly in front of him, and he felt his legs propel him towards it.

At the chest, he took out his key, knelt, and twisted it slowly in the lock. The tumblers turned. The great mechanism of interconnecting bolts rolled away. And Charlie lifted the lid. It was designed to be self-locking with an ingenious system he had never seen before. A spring-loaded device inside worked to seal the lock automatically once it was closed. He had heard of similar inventions in jewellery cases, but never in a trunk of this size. This chest had been designed to transport a great deal of money by sea.

Inside was a pile of papers. He caught a glimpse of a royal seal and some Dutch writing. His eyes scanned it, knowing he could not risk taking the time necessary to translate the text. He frowned, trying to work out the connection.

The Royal Crest. And Holland.

His mother had hidden these papers. What reason could she have had?

There was another page written in English. Shivering in the chill of Cripplegate he lifted it out.

Charlie looked over to the enormous oak door where a slow splinter crack was forming. He turned his attention back to the single paper in his hand.

There was so much tiny writing on the page, it made his head hurt. Charlie's reading was adequate but slow. The paper seemed to swirl in a maelstrom of words.

He frowned, scanning down the document for immediate clues.

There was a royal seal at the bottom. And a signature Charlie recognised. Thomas Blackstone's looping scrawl. With Teresa Blackstone's name signed underneath it.

Charlie's gaze tracked to the top of the paper. Two large words formed a title, and he ran a finger under them.

Marriage Licence.

So this was Thomas Blackstone's wedding certificate.

Charlie let the paper hang limply in his hand, pondering, trying to ignore the heightening thudding of the plague sufferers at the church door.

Why would Sally Oakley hide Thomas's marriage licence?

Charlie squinted back at the crabbed script, trying to make out further particulars. No church name seemed to be listed. So the document was for a Fleet wedding – the kind made by disreputable priests who touted for business. A rather vulgar choice, for a wealthy man.

Charlie concentrated on finding the name of the person who had sanctified the marriage, but the sea of text was impenetrable for fast reading.

He needed time to study it carefully. But time was something Charlie didn't have.

Blackstone had Maria.

A great banging echoed around the church suddenly as one of the plague people attacked the door with particular gusto. Charlie's hand jerked in alarm, letting the lid of the chest fall back down and dropping the paper as he pulled his hand quickly away. The heavy sound boomed ominously through the church. Then there was a click as the chest sealed itself again.

Charlie was about to reopen the chest and draw out the papers. And then he heard it again, more clearly this time.

'Malvern is coming!'

It was Maria's voice.

Spinning around in the deserted nave he could see nothing.

'Maria?'

He could investigate later, he decided. First he would find Maria.

Outside the church the infected people had worked themselves to a fever pitch. They pounded anew, fists hammering desperately.

Charlie looked over to the enormous oak door. It surely couldn't hold for long.

'Charlie?'

It was Maria's voice.

Spinning around in the deserted nave he could see nothing.

'Maria?'

'Charlie!' The voice was muffled. 'Do not come close!'

He raced towards the voice and found her lying bound behind a tomb. She had been gagged, but had managed to work half of it away. Enough to croak out a warning.

Charlie tugged it off and began working to loosen her bindings.

'Do not Charlie,' she begged. 'You must go. It is not safe. He will hear the people knocking and know someone has come inside.'

The pounding sounded louder than ever.

Charlie turned his head a quick left and right, but seeing nothing carried on untying the ropes.

'He will come,' she insisted. 'He will be here any minute. You must go and raise the alarm.'

'I will not leave you here Maria,' said Charlie.

The knocking was mixed with a cracking of wood giving way. It sounded bodily against the door as though the people outside were hurling themselves against it.

'You must go Charlie,' Maria's hands broke free and she pushed him away from her. He fell back onto the stone floor. As he righted himself again in bemusement she held up a warning hand.

'Did he hurt you?' he said, thinking she might be trying to hide some injury from him. Maria shook her head.

'He meant to,' she said. 'And then he saw the marks.'

She drew up her skirt to reveal white legs.

At first he thought she had revealed a little birth mark. A wine-coloured thumbprint partway up her inner thigh. And then he saw another. And another.

'You cannot save me Charlie,' she said, her eyes staring into his. 'I am already dead.'

The tokens peppered her legs, fanning out into a mash of blood-coloured bruises and raised veins as they stretched upwards.

'I cannot come with you,' she said.

Charlie fell back on his haunches, his mouth open.

'Maria, I . . . .'

'You must go. There is a chance you can stop Malvern's plans. He means to send a message. Did you see the cage of pigeons outside?'

Charlie shook his head. Then he remembered the sound of the wood pigeons cooing just before he leapt into the pit.

'I heard them I think. In the graveyard.'

'It was a cage of messenger pigeons you heard,' she said. 'I saw him use them. The birds are to be used to signal the infection to begin. But he has not done it yet. He wanted first to acquire better plague protection, so he might be safe. From me.'

Charlie moved towards her but she pushed him back roughly.

'If you can get to the birds you may prevent the message being sent. All you need do is open the cage and free them.'

But Charlie wasn't listening. 'We can find a doctor. There is some potion or tincture.' He leaned forward and grabbed at her hand. 'Come. Get up. We will get you to a warm bed and you may sweat it all out.'

'His plans might still be stopped,' repeated Maria. 'But you must go *now*.'

'There is Venice Treacle,' stammered Charlie in desperation. 'That has worked for some.'

'Who?' asked Maria. 'Who has it worked for Charlie? None survive the plague. Stop Malvern's plans. That is all you can do for me.'

He shook his head.

'I will not leave you.'

'Then Malvern will have won. And I will die for nothing and . . . .'

She was interrupted by the sound of a door. Her eyes widened in fright.

'He is here,' she whispered. 'Get out now.'

Chapter Seventy-Five

'I know someone is in here,' Malvern's voice rumbled through the nave. At the low sound of it the thudding at the door seemed to grow more urgent, echoing around the church. 'I heard you both talking.'

The voice stopped and for a moment only the knocking could he heard. 'And he is in here still,' said Malvern.

Still crouched on the floor Charlie felt a blow from Maria's foot and moved away from her back towards the front of the church. He was still concealed by the tomb, but it wouldn't take Malvern long to find him.

He had been right about Malvern's identity, he realised. The familiar voice had confirmed it.

Heavy footsteps and the rustle of a canvas cloak sounded.

Charlie's gaze fell on the heavy oak door. It was still vibrating under the assault from outside. The middle was splintering, and before he knew what this meant, it happened.

The door smashed away and a torrent of people lurched into the church. Shattered veins at their necks and faces gave them an undead colouring as if they had crawled up from the nearby graves.

They limped on gangrenous feet with writhing black fingers. But there was hope on their faces. They had come for a holy man to bring them comfort, and they staggered forward in vain search of him.

In the confusion Charlie rose to his feet, covered his mouth and ran for the entrance. He brushed against stiff buboils and ulcerated limbs as he ran, but the crowd hardly seemed to notice him in their desperation to find sanctuary in the church.

Charlie turned to see Malvern in his plague-doctor outfit, wheeling around in shock as the diseased ran towards him. And then he vanished behind the tumult. Maria was nowhere to be seen.

Bursting out into the moonlit graveyard Charlie made for the open grave. He heard the pigeons before he saw them. Maria must have ducked back down behind the tomb, he decided, and he could only hope she would stay safe long enough for him to somehow get the better of Malvern. Then he would take her for treatment. There must be something. They would comb the city for it and find a cure.

The cooing birds guided him to the cage. His fingers closed on the door, seeking out the catch.

A voice came from behind.

'You look a great deal like your mother.'

Charlie turned.

'I have hunted for years for what she stole from me,' continued Malvern. 'And now I have finally found you out. For I know she must have hid my secret with one of her sons.'

He had brought out the struggling Maria and threw her to the ground as he spoke.

Charlie moved towards her but Malvern drew his sword in warning.

The mask cocked to the side. 'She concealed you both so cleverly that I never found you or your brother. Though I searched the London slums daily.'

Malvern's eyes settled on the key around Charlie's neck.

A low laugh came from under his mask.

'So that is where she hides it. In my own chest. Very clever. But all is done now. Give me the key.'

Charlie's hand closed on the key.

'Give it to me. And I shall tell you where your mother is.'

'My mother is dead.' It was a wrench to say the words.

'Know you that for certain? Would you not know for sure? I will not lie to you boy. I will tell you exactly where she is.'

A deep yearning surged through Charlie.

'You must have wanted to know all your life,' said Malvern. 'You must always have wondered. Now is your chance to find out the truth, once and for all.'

'She is dead,' said Charlie. 'If my mother were living she would have come back for us.'

'Your faith is very touching boy. What if you are wrong? What if this is your last and only chance to discover her?'

'I . . . I do not believe it that she still lives.'

'Yet you sound so uncertain. Do not lose this opportunity Charlie Oakley. If your mother lives and you may yet find her it would be very sad not to seek out the right facts.'

'I will not stand by whilst you ruin the country,' said Charlie.

'Has this King done so much for you? Your foolish monarch had me in London's employ, sending false reports of his mistresses to the Mayor under his very nose.'

Blackstone paused to judge the effect of his words.

'It is only the key I want,' he continued, his tone shifting. 'I will allow you to live.' He looked down at Maria. 'Both of you. You will know at last for certain,' Malvern's voice had dropped to a whisper. 'Where your mother is.'

'No!' He heard Maria's shout from where she had been thrown to the floor, but he could not bring himself to look at her.

'You have my word boy. I will tell you all.' Malvern was tensed. 'You cannot win.'

Charlie's eyes flicked to Maria and back again. His hand moved to rest on the key.

'Give it to me.' Malvern's gloved claw writhed impatiently.

'He will never give it over!' Maria's faith in him was unexpected. Charlie turned to look at her.

'You would not let him win,' she said.

Charlie looked from her face back to Malvern. His hand retreated away from the key.

'I will not give it to you,' he said. 'I would rather die than betray my mother's memory.'

A low growl came from behind Malvern's mask. With lightning speed he darted forward, grabbing Maria's blonde hair. He moved the sharp blade of his sword beneath her throat.

'Very well then boy. Since you are without sentiment for your own mother, perhaps this girl is worth something more to you.'

Maria was shaking her head. 'Do not give it Charlie. I am dead in any case. You will gain nothing by playing to his plans.'

'Well then,' said Malvern. 'If you would see her blood spilled, so be it.' With practised calm he began to draw the sword.

'No!' said Charlie.

Maria gasped.

'Hold! Please! I will give it to you.'

Malvern looked up from his task. The blade held still. 'Well then?'

Charlie fumbled for the key.

'Charlie! No!'

Ignoring her he tossed it to the floor near Malvern's feet.

Malvern let Maria fall to the ground and snatched it up. Charlie stepped towards her but Malvern held out his sword in warning.

'Come no closer.' Malvern's eyes glittered and his voice lost all of its previous persuasiveness.

'Your mother stole from me and I strangled her. It was not until later, of course, that I realised she hid my secrets. I thought her sons would have the answer but could never find you out.'

'She put us safe,' said Charlie. 'At the Foundling Hospital.'

'Such is maternal love,' said Malvern.

Charlie stared into the crystal goggles and Malvern's mask tilted back, assessing the man before him.

'See we are not so different you and I,' he said. 'If I told you what the soldiers did to my mother it would sicken you to your stomach. In comparison Sally Oakley had a merciful end. So we are the same, Charlie Oakley, in our malice at least.'

Their eyes locked.

'Perhaps in our malice we are,' said Charlie. He felt cold everywhere.

Part of him had always known that his mother must be dead. But something inside of him had broken and in its place an empty leaden despair rushed in. He wanted to crawl away and turn the hurt around in his mind. The anger which swam in the background of his life now had a firm direction. Thomas Malvern. Its intensity frightened him.

The only possibility for revenge stood close. The birdcage. He could set free the messengers and wreck Malvern's plans.

He inched closer towards the caged birds, mentally calculating the fastest way to free them.

Malvern took a step towards him. 'Do not imagine I am so foolish that I do not see what you do,' he said. 'I will sever your arm from your body before I allow you to release those birds.'

A sudden noise caused them both to turn. It was Maria. She had staggered to her feet and was walking towards Malvern.

As she moved into a shaft of moonlight the rash of veins on her neck and face came into stark relief. Her breathing was ragged and laboured.

Despite the protection of his plague-doctor costume Malvern stepped back uncertainly. His gloved hands fumbled to aim the pistol, but Maria was on him before he could fire. Reaching up with her bound hands she pulled away his mask. Malvern's disguise fell away, revealing the blue eyes, the black hair.

The mouth gaped in shock as Maria spat in his eye.

Beneath the hood was the Mayor's aide. Thomas Blackstone.

Chapter Seventy-Six

Blackstone fell down, clawing to wipe his face, and Maria turned to Charlie.

'Now!' she shouted. 'Set free the birds.'

Faltering in the unexpectedness of the moment Charlie paused for a second, and then he dived towards the cage and unhooked the catch.

A gunshot followed a moment later, causing the birds inside to tunnel out in alarm.

They swarmed up in a great mass of feathers and up into the sky.

'No!' Blackstone ran at the escaping birds, but they were too quick for him. Like a great grey cloud they winged away in one mass, far into the night.

Charlie looked back to where Maria had been.

She was no longer standing, but had fallen back. A plume of red was spreading out across her white shift. He ran to where she was.

'It was a mercy Charlie,' she said, as he tumbled to the ground beside her. 'I would rather go this way than the other.'

Behind him he heard Blackstone race to the open cage and pull frantically at it, searching for any remaining occupants.

He let out a sudden howl of elation and Charlie turned with a sinking heart. A flutter of wings confirmed his fears. One single pigeon was huddled in the back of the cage, too terrified to take flight. Blackstone slammed the little door closed, securing the bird.

Maria's hand slid from Charlie's. He saw the blood pumping from her chest slow and then stop.

'No.'

He turned her head up to face him, but the deeper he stared into her eyes the further she went. As Maria slipped away from him memories of her clustered thickly in his mind. But then there were images of his orphaned childhood in the Foundling Home. Watching his brother grow thinner by the day and of dead children in the bed.

'Please Maria.'

He thought he saw something. A final glimmer. Then her eyes closed and she was gone. Only his black anger remained.

He stood to face Blackstone and the words came choking out.

'You murdered my mother.'

The swell of his fury was so immense his words came out in gasps.

Charlie strode towards Blackstone.

Recognising the expression from the battlefield Blackstone's face set itself. He drew his sword. 'Do not think that a thousand such have not run at me in war,' he said. But something of his earlier confidence had waned just a little.

'Eight years, my brother and I starved as orphans,' said Charlie.

Without breaking his stride he picked up a branch from the ground and hefted it.

Blackstone swung his sword easily to use the handle for a club.

They neared each other, the barefooted stick-wielder and the armed Cavalier. Then Charlie struck out in a wave of fury.

The stick came down and Blackstone staggered back. Then he heaved the full weight of the sword hilt.

Charlie moved only just in time. The sword missed his skull but connected with full force into his shoulder.

He felt his shoulder wrench free from the socket and his body lift from the ground. The blow threw him several feet and he landed heavily in the open plague grave.

Blackstone's smile flickered for a moment. With the calculation of an experienced soldier he looked down to check his opponent was no longer a threat and then he walked to where his pigeons were held.

He removed the last cooing occupant and, stroking her head tenderly, attached a message to the leg.

'This goes to the Palace,' he said, 'and announces from the Mayor where plague spreads to in the City. Once that is done every wealthy gaming house in London will spread my counterfeit coins.'

Blackstone threw his hands apart and watched the pigeon wing up unsteadily into the air.

Charlie watched it with a sinking heart.

Returning to the open grave Blackstone leaned over. 'You see now the thing is done,' he explained. 'The message is sent and the King will soon realise the price of his betrayal.'

Charlie became aware of a new sensation. Something was digging into his back. It was the rabbit gun.

He had forgotten that he had left it in the grave, earlier.

Painstakingly Charlie worked his hand underneath until his fingers closed around the weapon. He could not kill Blackstone, he knew. But he could hurt him. Injure him. The thought brought a bitter sort of strength.

Blackstone blinked suddenly, realising he was looking into the barrel of the gun. He suppressed a smile. Perhaps the boy carried the weapon as a boast. But he knew nothing about arms. He held a rabbit gun. Likely it would not even fire in the damp air.

Above them the white belly of the pigeon winged away into the sky. And Malvern knew his plans were unassailable.

'Then kill me,' he said, playing to the boy's ignorance. 'Have your revenge. We are the same you and I. Both of us were betrayed and made orphans. Both of us seek revenge on those who have wronged us.'

Charlie couldn't see Maria's body, but an image of her face came to him. Instead of the white fright of her dying, the features were calm. Some of his anger abated.

Blackstone caught the emotion. It was too ridiculous. The boy was afraid to pull the trigger. Given the chance to avenge himself on the man who had killed his mother he was now uncertain. This was why the uprising would succeed. Because men like himself would not falter.

'Your mother would have not liked to see her son so weak,' he said, making to walk from the grave. He caught a glimpse of Charlie's expression hardening and paused for a moment. Perhaps the boy really would chance his immortal soul by attempting to commit murder. And it would be worth watching his face when the gun didn't work as he hoped.

From the depths of the grave Charlie felt the monster inside him stir.

'You may think me weak, but I am stronger than you,' he said.

Blackstone gave a cold smile. 'You do not know what strength is. You Protestants think yourselves strong in number, but that is nothing to a man prepared to defend his religion with his life.'

'It is not to do with numbers or force,' said Charlie. 'I am stronger than you because I do not need revenge.'

And he pulled the trigger.

Chapter Seventy-Seven

The gun exploded, blinding Charlie in a cloud of gunpowder and pressing him down into the pit.

At the edge of the grave he saw Blackstone start at the gunshot and step back. And then to Charlie's great relief the last messenger pigeon fell to the ground. He had not known how high the gun might fire. But the glimpse of white wing overhead had convinced him the spray of shot might hit its mark. A comforting plume of feathers floated down towards him.

Charlie had no idea what had caused Malvern to move away. He closed his eyes, awaiting the violent retribution.

It never came. Instead a figure appeared, white like an angel.

He blinked in disbelief as it hovered at the edge of the pit, ghostly pale in the moonlight. The gunshot had set a ringing in his ears.

Charlie stared up, squinting his eyes to better see the celestial shape.

'You had best get up and out of that grave,' it said in a surprisingly familiar voice.

'Maria?' His voice was half choked with shock.

'Who else would it be?'

Easing himself up Charlie clambered from the pit. He grabbed her shoulders and then wrapped both arms around her. She was warm and solid. Charlie drew back to look in her face.

'I cannot believe it is you.'

'Why Charlie?'

'You were shot,' he said. 'And infected with plague.'

Maria smiled. 'It was just a little bee's wax and berry juice. A cosmetic I carry.'

She raised her hand and rubbed at one of the marks on her neck. Then she held out her reddened hand to show him.

'I have it to make my lips look pretty. And it was more useful than a knife after all,' she added, more to herself.

Maria tilted her head to look up at him. 'Were it daylight that feint would never have worked. But by candle and moonlight they looked real enough. It was enough to fool Blackstone,' she added, 'and frighten him away from hurting me.'

'Why not tell me then?' he demanded. 'I thought you had plague Maria. I thought . . .'

He stopped himself from relaying the tumult of fright she had caused.

'I knew you would waste time untying me,' Maria said simply. 'I thought your labours better spent stopping the pigeons.'

'Blackstone shot you,' Charlie accused, 'I saw you die.'

Maria shook her head and tapped on her chest. 'It did not hit me full force, for I was turned away from it. And the shot did not penetrate far where it struck.'

She knocked on her thick reed bodice. 'And you say such fashions are foolish.'

'Besides,' she added. 'The injury bled only a little before it stopped. I was surprised you did not realise Charlie. A person must bleed for more than a few seconds to die of a musket shot. I even tried to signal you with my eyes, before I shut them, that it was an act I made.'

'I . . . I cannot say it strong enough, how glad I am that you live.'

They clung together for a long moment, a warm glow in the cool dark graveyard.

Maria drew away suddenly. 'Where is Blackstone?' she said. 'I do not see him.'

Charlie made a quick look around. Feathers were everywhere.

'I found a piece of gravestone and struck him hard on the head whilst you were in the pit,' added Maria. She looked around in confusion. 'He fell, but I know not where he is now.'

Keeping a tight hold of her hand Charlie moved past one of the larger headstones. A pitiful sight came into view.

Blackstone sat panting, his vast bulk pressing against the grave. He had fallen heavily onto his seat, and though his eyes were open they were glassy and fixed on nothing.

'Did you break his skull with the stone?' whispered Charlie.

'I do not think so,' said Maria. 'It did not feel as though his head broke when I hit him. Only that he went down.'

They stood for a moment looking at the figure. Then slowly Charlie raised his hand to point. Set into the white flesh of Blackstone's neck was the unmistakable red circle of a plague token.

'He has it.'

Maria nodded but said nothing.

'He must have had it for a long time,' added Charlie.

'I do not think so,' said Maria. 'There are a few cases where the plague strikes very sudden. He must have taken this kind.'

Then Blackstone spoke.

'Please,' he mumbled. 'You must bring me a priest to take my confession. Please do not let my soul depart without absolution.'

His eyes flickered, rolled upwards and then slowly shut. His great chest continued to heave in juddering gasps.

Charlie and Maria looked at each other.

'There is nothing we can do,' said Maria.

Charlie stared at the pain-wracked figure, gross with the tragedy of his life. A wave of pity swept through him.

'We might still bring him a priest,' he whispered, 'at least, we might try.'

'He does not deserve one. Beside, would you not wish to go now and open the chest your mother left to you?'

Charlie gave her a half smile. 'Some people poison their lives with revenge, and I should not want to make such a path for ourselves.'

She didn't reply, but he felt her hand tighten in his.

'Come then,' he said, 'we will see if there is one who might help him in the City. The chest will be here when we return.'

They rose and picked their way through the soft ground of the church.

Though the first streaks of dawn were on the horizon the air stayed chill. The heat of the summer had eased. Something like a colder breeze was sweeping through London. Autumn was coming.

Chapter Seventy-Eight

Blackstone leaned his huge weight against a gravestone behind him. The hunger swarmed into every part of him, and when his hand went to his neck it was thick, as though in swelling.

A wave of white heat drove up all along his nerves and he cried out in agony, kicking his legs wildly.

His eyes were clouding over as the night thickened around him. All his plans had been rent.

He shrieked, arching his back. It felt as though his head would burst.

'A priest,' he pleaded into the empty night. No one came. Then all was dark and he floated in the torture of his own dying body.

Blackstone blinked awake to see that the world before him had twisted into distortion. A low white light came through, but he could make out only writhing forms. *This must be purgatory*, he thought, sitting upright in his new environment. Every part of his body hurt.

A dark shape was edging closer towards him and he stared at it wonderingly.

Then the hood was lifted from his head and he realised his situation. In the throes of his illness he must have somehow put the mask back on. His shimmering vision had been through the gauze of the crystal goggles. Blackstone was still in Fen Church graveyard, but the sun was shining.

In front of him was the face of a searcher, his features drawn into confusion.

'Mr Blackstone,' said the searcher. 'Did you fall asleep on your duties?'

Blackstone swallowed thickly. His throat burned.

'I took a fever,' he croaked. 'But I am on my way to being righted now.' He tried to sit further upright. 'Give me a little drink,' he added, pointing to the searcher's flask.

'Do not be frighted,' he said, taking a long swig as the drink was passed to him. 'I have not lost my mind. I will live through this yet.'

'Inside the church,' the searcher said, 'There are some possessions from your house. We must clear out the church now. The minister returns.'

Blackstone fought for the memory. He had put some of his household goods away for safety. Could they go back now? He tried to remember what had been put inside and found that he couldn't.

Now that he thought of it, he could remember nothing of how he came to be in this graveyard. His last memory was taking his wagon to Wapping.

'There are some rugs and furniture in there,' the searcher was saying. 'And a large chest. Is any of it important?'

Blackstone struggled to locate the jumble of goods in his mind. 'There is nothing of value,' he managed. 'The rugs are not expensive. But the furniture was my father's.'

He thought for a moment.

'The chest is an old empty sea-chest, that is all. The key was lost long ago and we keep it for sentimental reasons.'

'Then shall I clear it away sir?' asked the searcher. 'There is some food in there also which is beginning to rot.'

'Yes,' said Blackstone. 'Clear it away.'

Three months later

The Bucket of Blood was crammed with afternoon drinkers as the landlord took to the nearest tabletop.

'Peace good people!' he shouted, one hand holding his long wig in place as he balanced on the shifting podium. 'We are to have an extra entertainment for you all, on account of God bestowing his mercy on us and choosing to vanquish this late and terrible plague.'

There were shouts of agreement from the jostling crowd.

'Our King has returned to us,' continued the landlord, 'and our fine City has been spared.'

He paused amidst the cheers, with his fist on his heart in a patriotic salute.

'Notice I do not say *fair* City,' he added. 'For she has a few smuts and stains does she not? But she is *our* City. Which makes her fine enough. And God in His wisdom has delivered her back to us from the clutches of the devil himself. And so . . . .'

He waved his hand to drive down the noise of the drinkers.

'And so we have today . . . .' He paused for effect. 'Not one . . . but *two* bare-knuckle fights, as will happen here. In this very room!'

The landlord raised both hands, gathering up the tumult of applause and then hopped down from the table to take the mounting flurry of drink orders.

From the other side of the tavern Charlie smiled up at Maria and they raised their tankards in a joint toast.

Since the cooler weather, London had made a miraculous recovery from plague, and her returning and surviving citizens had taken the opportunity for weeklong celebrations. Since the last case had been reported in September the City had transformed from an outpost to its former thriving glory in under a week.

Ships began to dock again and traders and shoppers set upon the glut of new imports with gusto. Theatres were reopened, taverns found themselves packed to the rafters, and Leadenhall Market enjoyed the only thorough scrub down in its three-hundred-year history before being packed out once more with fresh produce.

For the first time ever locals had taken their duty to maintain the streets outside their houses seriously. And whilst legislation had never been able to persuade them to clear rubbish or fix cobbles, the sight of their overgrown streets had them out in droves weeding and repairing.

The plague seemed to have drawn out a yen in its survivors to play the good citizen. And even the floods of returning aristocrats clubbed together for a new riverside location for the washerwomen, now that Moor Fields had become a burial site.

To make up for his abandonment King Charles doubled his visits to the general populace and the sight of the Royal party on the City streets was a colourful addition to the troops of brightly-dressed ladies capitalising on the lost opportunities for fashion.

Lynette had returned to London in all her finery and her stage performances were as popular as ever. But Charlie didn't feel the same tug of heartache when he saw his estranged wife arm in arm with one of her patrons. In fact he felt sorry for her. It must be hard work, he thought, being her.

Charlie and Maria looked out at the laughing company in the Bucket of Blood. A familiar ragged form stepped up behind then.

'You found anything else out about this Blackstone then?'

Charlie smiled. Since the night in Fen Church, Bitey had become fascinated with the mystery of Blackstone's disappearance.

The old man shook his head in wonderment.

'He must have been some fiend or witch,' he said. 'For how else could this man have had plague, yet cleared out all evidence of his treasonous ways before you could bring the constable?'

Charlie shrugged. 'Perhaps he had help. Certainly he was clever in what he took. All his household possessions gone, but the grave filled with shillings. The money must have been too difficult for him to remove in time.'

'And he took away that chest,' said Bitey, his eyes glowing at the puzzle of it, 'Something locked inside might tell you of your mother.' He pointed to the key which still hung at Charlie's neck.

'The Sealed Knot,' muttered Bitey, repeating the words which had been linked with the crown and the knots in Malvern's trunk. 'I feel in my bones I have heard those words before. Long ago. During the Civil War. But I cannot say where or how.' He shook his head as if trying to jolt free the memory and then frowned, defeated.

'If it were not for the foolishness of the constable we might know more,' said Maria. 'He would not accept that the coins were part of a plot. He thought it was simply the work of a clever forger who had likely died of plague and no darker purpose was at work.'

Bitey took a philosophical sip of his beer.

'Perhaps better to let sleeping dogs lie then,' he said, 'for the time being at least.' He looked up at Charlie. 'You been to St Paul's today?'

'Earlier today,' said Charlie, raising his tankard to Bitey.

'We shall drink to her then. Her and the City.'

Charlie mourned his mother at St Paul's, joined by countless Londoners who had also lost relatives to unknown burial plots. Understanding the people needed somewhere to grieve their missing dead, King Charles had granted them the Cathedral. Within the high holy walls one death became everyone's and strangers held hands and cried in one another's arms.

Charlie raised his tankard in reply. Then something occurred to him. There was someone who had now returned to the City who he owed a visit.

'Put down a bet on the second fighter,' he said, sliding a coin towards Bitey. 'There is someone I must see.'

Charlie knew that one tough-minded female would not have stood for anything so inconvenient as illness. And as he travelled the comforting leafy streets of Mayfair to Mother Mitchell's sumptuous townhouse he was unsurprised to find her safe and well.

During the plague she had taken the precaution of an ornamental silver tobacco pipe which she now smoked constantly. The use of it had given her throaty laugh an extra gravelly texture. Fumes wreathed her silken bulk.

'Plenty of work for us cheering the folk in country houses, with all so sad and dour,' explained Mother Mitchell.

She coughed and adjusted her enormous dress as Charlie explained the events of the past few days.

'Many royal plots and companies were formed during the war,' she said, 'perhaps some evil sect lingers still.'

'Blackstone's wife said my key holds the sign of the Sealed Knot,' said Charlie.

'It sounds familiar to me. And yet I do not know how. Do you know of it?' he added, knowing that if ancient Bitey knew nothing of the phrase then Mother Mitchell was unlikely to either.

But to his surprise Mother Mitchell stayed stock-still for a long moment, before nodding her head slowly.

'Aye, I have heard something of that,' she said. 'From long ago.' She lifted her eyes to meet Charlie's. 'The Sealed Knot was a secret group of noblemen,' she said. 'They formed during the Civil War. I know not their purpose. Only a little chatter from those high-born men who have passed through my arms and are too free with the secrets of their fellows. The Sealed Knot will have either won or lost with the late King's execution and whatever their cause laid to rest with it. But the men who were part of it were dangerous Charlie. Rich, powerful and war-hungry all.'

A secret company of noblemen, formed during the Civil War. Charlie considered the information as he pushed through the teeming square of Covent Garden and back into the Bucket of Blood.

One of the fighters was late to the tavern, and Maria and Bitey were watching the landlord try to calm the riled-up crowd as Charlie returned to his seat.

'Smell that?' said Bitey, turning slightly to clap him on the back in welcome. 'That's winter on the air. All's well that ends well, eh?'

'Why say you so?' asked Maria.

'Plague don't live through winter girl, everyone knows that.'

'And what about next year?' insisted Maria. 'It is 1666. Dark things are predicted by the astrologers. Fiery comets, low tides. 'It is the year of the devil's number.'

Bitey laughed, waving an expansive hand to the wider city. 'This whole sorry pile of timber might burn down next summer for all we know. Best to take one day at a time in this uncertain life and be grateful for those days that treat you well.'

'And is this a day that is treating you well Bitey?' asked Charlie, his mind still racing with thoughts of the Sealed Knot.

'Oh I should say so Charlie.' Bitey opened his cloak to reveal the soft snout of a tiny piglet.

Maria gave a gasp of delight and put out a hand to stroke the animal. It pushed its face into her palm and grunted.

'Found this little fellow snuffling about near Holbourne with nowhere to go,' said Bitey. 'Reckon if he grows fast 'twill be only a month afore chops and ribs a'plenty.' He licked his lips. 'I should say Charlie, this is shaping up to be a very good day indeed. I have heard you are very busy with murder as well as thievery these days,' he added.

It was true. Since word got out that he took on cases more diverse than theft Charlie had been besieged with Londoners wanting all kinds of crimes solved. It seemed that incompetence in the City's Watch didn't stop at stealing. His services were so popular in the west that he could afford to keep his lodging in the Covent Garden butcher's shop. He was even considering renting a place where he and Maria could both live together.

Charlie looked hard into his tankard of ale, thinking of the Sealed Knot, the secrets in Blackstone's missing chest and what they might still mean for England.

'There are crimes enough,' he said to Bitey. 'To keep me very busy indeed.'

Hungry for more Thief Taker intrigue?

Go to www.thethieftaker.com/secretscene to read a special **secret scene**, along with images and clues from *The Thief Taker* to help you unravel the truth of Charlie Oakley's real identity.

Acknowledgments

Books are a funny business. When I first started writing for publication, female authors of historical thrillers were a hard sell. Agents and publishers agreed my stories had something, but they thought I should be more like Philippa Gregory. Then a miracle happened. My brilliant twin sister (and bestselling author), Susanna Quinn, introduced me to the world of self-publishing. And in a fit of optimistic experimentation, I penned a romance novel which went on to sell 150,000 copies.

Suddenly it wasn't quite so important to be published. But fate is a fickle thing. And just at that moment I met the most amazing agent and friend in Piers Blofeld, who thought my historical thrillers deserved an audience. Piers found lots of publishers who wanted *The Thief-Taker*. And its strength, they felt, was it wasn't like Philippa Gregory at all.

So this book is dedicated to the many people who helped me on the long road to publication. Thanks to Kevin Harris, for giving great feedback on far too many early drafts, Laura Langthorne (on whom Maria is based), for perfect improvements and Don Quinn for suggesting Maria shouldn't die, and that a few more brothels wouldn't go amiss. And where would I be without my soulmate

Simon Avery, whose contrasting shouts of 'this is brilliant!' and 'this is boring!' have made the book what it is? Emilie Marneur at Amazon Publishing, you are not only gracious enough to treat me as a fellow professional, but you introduced me to the eagle-eyed Katie Green, who did amazing editorial work on the book. If Carlsberg made publishers they would look something like yours. I've also been fantastically lucky with the incredibly generous Peter James, Simon Toyne and Louise Voss. I am forever indebted to your kind testimonials. You are all proof positive that hugely successful authors are kind beyond belief. Finally, my enormous gratitude goes to the Amazon self-publishing platform, which has made it possible for me, and many others, to achieve paid employment as a writer.

Oh, and not forgetting my sincere thanks to Philippa Gregory ;)

About the Author

Richard Bolls

C.S. Quinn is a travel and lifestyle journalist for *The Times*, *The Guardian* and *The Mirror*, alongside many magazines. Prior to this, Quinn's background in historic research won prestigious postgraduate funding from the British Art Council. Quinn pooled these resources, combining historical research with first-hand experiences in far-flung places to create *The Thief Taker's* London.